BETTER T

"The purpose relocation of the plished," grow ____ on the council.

Yesugen willed her hands not to clench. They were all staring at her now. "That is true, Ghazan, and I take full responsibility for it. Our people fought bravely, and well. The error was mine in underestimating the force we faced."

"Sheep herders and fishermen, and a small, inexperienced army," said Ghazan disdainfully. "You could have destroyed them all from space."

"And risked total annihilation," said Yesugen, her voice rising. "The force has a name, Ghazan, and it is Kati. A young woman, yes, and seemingly gentle as a person, but when threatened, she has the power to destroy a world, or even a star! What she did to us is a tiny fraction of what she is capable. She have traveled through the gong-shi-jie in an instant and reduced our planet to a cinder!"

"It's a reality we must accept," said Kabul quickly. The conquest of Shanji is no longer a consideration. How, then, are the resources of that planet of use to us?"

"Kati believes my sincerity in making trade with her, and has agreed to a meeting with me to discuss details. I plan to do so in the near future."

"Accompanied by our Empress, I presume," said Ghazan. "Any plan that's approved will of course be hers."

Yesugen's fingernails dug into the palms of her hands. "We will meet alone, Ghazan, and my mother has agreed to it. What comes in future years will be decided by me, not my mother." She stiffened her back as she spoke, sitting a little taller on her chair.

"I will be Empress here, Ghazan. Remember that!"

BAEN BOOKS IN THIS SERIES

Shanji
Empress of Light

EMPRESS
OF
LIGHT

THE SECOND SAGA OF THE
SHANJI INTERSTELLAR EMPIRE

JAMES C. GLASS

Copyright © 2001 by James C. Glass

A Baen Books Original

Baen Publishing Enterprises
P.O. Box 1403
Riverdale, NY 10471
www.baen.com

ISBN: 0-671-31983-3

Cover art by Richard Martin

First printing, April 2001

Distributed by Simon & Schuster
1230 Avenue of the Americas
New York, NY 10020

Production by Windhaven Press, Auburn, NH
Printed in the United States of America

This one is for Gail

ACKNOWLEDGEMENTS

Special thanks go again to John Dalmas and Mary Jane Engh for their useful comments on the first drafts of this book. Thanks also to my Chinese friends for suggestions regarding Mandarin titles and familiars, and for their amusement at the liberties I've taken with the language.

AUTHOR'S NOTE

This account of the Mei-lai-gong's early life is a sequel to *Shanji*, and contains references to that story. The two books are best read in sequence.

CHAPTER ONE
BIRTH

Mei-lai-gong came to Shanji in the form of an infant, and the world welcomed her with early morning light of Tengri-Khan reflected from the glassy surface of the Three Peaks she had created only weeks before her birth. One peak glowed pink, the other two laced with swirls of red and green, rising like jewels beyond the high cliffs across the valley from Wang Mengnu's great domed city.

Kati had felt increasing discomfort the day before; the position of her baby had suddenly shifted, and although the pain in her back had subsided, there was new pressure in her groin that brought her near exhaustion by evening. She used her hands, drawing from the light of Tengri-Khan to relax her muscles and bring new energy to her child, although there seemed little need for that. Yesui had been extremely active all day, constantly turning, shifting position, and always there was that tiny

1

hand exploring and the wonderful energies coming from it, spreading everywhere.

Still, Kati was weary by the end of a day of continuous meetings, first with the nobles, then a group of factory managers from the east who listened sullenly to her lecture on their responsibilities to the workers under her new regime. Later in the day, she wrote orders for three of them to be replaced; having probed their minds, she'd found them to be immovable from the old ways, yet they'd not been honest enough to openly disagree with her. She would let them know that nothing could be hidden from the Empress of Shanji. The meeting with the Council of Ministers went well enough, but all were men, and everytime Yesui performed some new aerobatic that brought a gasp from her mother, they looked as if anxious to flee before their Empress could drop her child before their very eyes.

She retired to her quarters earlier than usual, and lay down on the canopied bed brought from the rooms she'd occupied as a ward of the Emperor, the bed on which Yesui had been conceived the night before a short but terrible war bringing Kati to the throne of Shanji. Energy drained, Kati watched Tengri-Khan's red disk settle down towards the summits of Three Peaks, then dozed. She was awakened by her husband's return, but kept her eyes closed at first as he padded quietly around the room so as not to disturb her. When she opened her eyes, she saw him standing by the little wooden crib brought to them by the Tumatsin, rocking it back and forth with his foot, his back to her.

"I think it will be filled soon," she said, and he turned around, startled.

"Did I wake you?" Huomeng said, coming over

to sit on the edge of the bed, and taking her hand in his.

"I was just dozing," she said, squeezing his hand, "and Yesui has been very active today. I think she is eager to leave her little place, and be with us in the light."

Huomeng stroked her forehead, leaned over and kissed her lightly as his hand moved to her swollen belly.

"She's quiet, now. Do you feel her?" asked Kati.

"No movement," said Huomeng, looking concerned.

"I meant with your mind, not your hand. Do you feel her presence as I do?"

"I feel something—yes. A kind of watchfulness, but no images. Did you really see her with you in the gong-shi-jie on the day of the explosion over Three Peaks?"

"Yes," Kati said patiently. "I felt her there, and the little green tendril of flame that followed me everywhere could only have been her. I've never seen such a thing before." They had discussed this several times before now.

"But how could she? She's not even born yet. How could she be so aware?" Huomeng rubbed her skin softly. "There is such warmth beneath my hand when I touch you here."

"It feels wonderful," said Kati, raising her hips slightly to meet his touch, and he grinned.

"Soon you will not be so fragile," he said.

"Soon," she said, and reached out to playfully tousle his hair.

He kissed her again, longer this time, then stood up. "Do you want something to eat? I'm starved."

"Not tonight. I just want to rest. Tanchun will fix something for you, and you can bring me honeycakes and tea for later."

"I will be quiet when I return," Houmeng said, making her giggle when he tip-toed comically from the room. His mask was put aside, as it usually was for her, and she felt his nearly childish excitement over the coming birth of their child.

Kati sighed contentedly and watched Tengri-Khan disappear below the peaks, the sky there now deep red. She listened for a mental sign from her daughter, but there was nothing. *Do you sleep, Yesui? Are you ready to be born yet? I feel so strange. I think the time is near.*

She wondered if Mandughai was watching her, then dismissed the thought. First Mother would be busy now with the return of her troops to Tengri-Nayon. Perhaps they'd already arrived there. Nearing sleep, mostly through the habit of years, Kati felt the urge to go to the gong-shi-jie, the place of creation, to wander among the auras of planets and stars, to feel the swirling energies of the purple light there which moved at her command. She suppressed the urge, for if she went now to the gong-shi-jie, Yesui might follow her, and the last time had seemed traumatic for the child. Kati was still haunted by the events of their return: the black, snake-like energy field writhing behind the green flame that was surely Yesui, the terrible explosion above Three Peaks turning rock into colorful glass, then Yesui kicking furiously in terror within her mother's body.

Now was not the time; she would hold Yesui in her arms before again taking her to the gong-shi-jie. The thought was her last of the evening. Her eyes closed, the matrix of twinkling, purple lights was there for a moment, and then she fell peacefully asleep.

But it seemed only moments later she was awake again, and Houmeng was warmly beside her. Her hands were clenched into fists, and there was a strong squeezing sensation in her lower body. She sat up with a gasp, and the squeezing intensified. The sheet beneath her legs was saturated with wetness. Fright turned to excitement with recognition of the signs. She prodded Huomeng's shoulder with her hand. "Wake up, dear, and get Tanchun to call my physician. Our child has decided it's time for her birth."

Huomeng was instantly awake. "*Now?*" he gasped.

"It's just beginning," she said calmly.

Huomeng leaped naked from the bed, and immediately crashed into something in the darkness.

"You do not have to rush so. We have time enough," she said.

"Yes, yes," he said. He found a light and hobbled to a chair draped with his clothes, then dressed. "You still insist on it being here? It would be much safer for both of you if you were in hospital."

"Our child will be born in this bed. I'll have it no other way," she said firmly.

Huomeng smiled as he struggled quickly into his shirt. "Empress or not, you will always be a Tumatsin, but I love you anyway."

"The mother of your child is pleased to hear that," she said serenely, but clenched her hands as muscles within her were suddenly as hard as stone. She opened her mouth, and breathed deeply as Huomeng fled from the room.

In moments he was back, with Tanchun pushing past him at the door. Well into her forties, the servant of Kati's foster mother Weimeng now served Kati as well, and was still slender and lovely. She ordered Kati out of bed, and had Huomeng walk her around the room while the bedsheets were changed. Other servants arrived with towels and basins, and a polymer tub, empty, on a cart. Unlit candles were placed around the room, Kati's shrine brought out from a cabinet and placed before the open door to her balcony. Beyond it lay the sparkling of stars above the western horizon.

Kati knelt with effort before the shrine, and arranged the elements there: the three candles; greenstone bowls with incense and sweetgrass. Huomeng helped her rise again as the physician arrived, a Moshuguang named Zhan Zheng, who had impressed Kati with his loving care of young mothers among Shanji's rural people in the east. He was well acquainted with home-birthing traditions, and respected them, even for his Empress.

Kati lay down on the bed for Zhan Zheng's inspection, and he was pleased with his findings. "She is well-positioned," he said. "I do not think your labor will be long. You may walk a little and meditate while you can. The contractions will soon become quite forceful."

Two nurses arrived, one of them a young woman newly trained in the great eastern city of Wanchou, and obviously thrilled by the honor of attending her Empress at such a time. Kati felt the fleeting desire for the presence of a Tumatsin mid-wife, but it had not been possible to arrange, and she reminded herself that the vast majority of Shanji's peoples were represented in the room. The lights of the room were dimmed as Huomeng walked her around again, and she lit each candle with a wave of her hand. With only the candles providing light, she knelt again at her shrine and passed her hand over it, igniting candles, incense and sweetgrass, breathing in their scents and going deep within herself. The purple matrix of stars was instantly there, and she moved towards it, felt Yesui stir inside her as a contraction came. There was no sensation of pain, only effort. She did not go to the gong-shi-jie, just hovered before it, focusing only on a single, purple star, a single entrance to the place of creation.

The light comes to me, and goes forth from me, and I am one with it. I bring it forth to give energy to myself and to my child for the task at hand. Come to me.

And the light came forth, waving filaments of purple from each twinkling star, rushing towards her until she felt warmth, first in her head, then spreading downwards to shoulders, arms and chest. Yesui suddenly turned within her, as if startled, then was quiet again as the warmth reached Kati's legs, permeating the hard muscles there until they seemed liquid. In one rush, her body was both relaxed and energized, and she sat erect to straighten her spine, a low growl escaping from her throat with a slow exhale of breath.

It was very quiet in the room. Kati opened her eyes, saw her hands cupping each other in her lap, an oblong shape of blue plasma floating just above them. "Ahhh," she breathed, and the plasma flowed into her palms and was gone.

"I am ready," she said. Huomeng helped her up and took her back to their bed, where Zhan Zheng and his entourage awaited her. They laid her down gently, her arms relaxed at her sides, eyes closing, breathing deep, and before her was only swirling, purple light from a place without time. Time *did* pass, she was told later, nearly three hours of it, but there was no pain, no sense of effort, only the swirling light that came to her in pulses of increasing frequency until finally she heard a voice from far off.

"Here she is. Quietly, now. Kati, wake up! She's here!"

Pressure on her chest. She opened her eyes, for one instant illuminating her chest in green to see a form lying there, rising up and down with her breathing, the physician bending near to examine it. "She's perfect," he whispered, "and still asleep. I think she slept through the whole thing. Bring the tub, now."

She is not asleep, thought Kati. *I feel you, my daughter, both your presence and a new awareness I've never felt before. You sense a new touch, a new part of my body, a breath of night air from Shanji, but mostly the warmth of the pretty light that surrounds us both. Do not open your eyes yet, for there is more to feel, and the light will keep you warm.*

Zhan Zheng lifted Yesui slowly, carefully from Kati's chest, cut and tied the cord, and floated her in a tub filled with warm water. Sounds of flowing water, and a sudden squeak of complaint, then stillness. Huomeng appeared at Kati's bedside in candlelit gloom, taking her hand in his, eyes glistening. "She is beautiful," he whispered, "like her mother."

The child was soon dried, wrapped tightly, and placed in her mother's arms. "Come closer," said Kati, and Huomeng sat on the edge of the bed. Together, they looked down on Yesui's face: the bow of her mouth, the button nose, the crown of her perfect head with wisps of dark hair. Her brows were knitted, as if she awaited a new sensation: a touch, or a sound.

"Yesui," said Kati. The baby's eyebrows raised, her lips parted. Her eyelids seemed to glow.

When she opened her eyes, she was looking straight up at her father, and his face was suddenly illuminated in emerald green.

There was a collective gasp from the people standing at the foot of the bed.

"Ohhh," murmured Huomeng. He reached out a

finger to touch Yesui's tiny hand, and she grasped it, her glowing eyes clearly focused on his face.

"You are surprised," said Kati.

"She is a newborn child. How can she—?"

"I draw from the light, and the light comes to me, and the glow of my eyes only signifies my connection to the place of creation. I bring it forth so—"

The three of them were suddenly illuminated in the light from Kati's eyes. Still grasping Huomeng's finger, Yesui turned her head and looked up at her mother's face. Her eyes widened, their glow brightening. The bow of her mouth quivered, then curled upwards at its edges.

Yesui smiled.

Kati!

She recognizes me, dear, from our brief time in the gong-shi-jie. The smile is real, not something from a gas bubble, and her eyes are truly focused. Her connection with the place of creation is already made, as you can see. You do not yet recognize your own daughter, Huomeng.

"What do you mean?" whispered Huomeng.

"You do not recognize the being the Moshuguang has worked for a thousand years to create, the being who will bring matter as well as light through, and from, the gong-shi-jie."

"The Three Peaks," whispered Huomeng, and she knew the truth had come to him.

"Hot gas and dust from our own sun, and not by my effort. I will build a shrine there to commemorate her first miracle. All of you, now, come closer, and look down on the face of the Mei-lai-gong."

The others drew near, gazing with quiet reverence at the child's glowing eyes. Yesui's smile disappeared as she looked at each individual. When her gaze came to the young nurse from Wanchou, the woman bowed deeply before her, eyes glistening.

Yesui looked again at her father, then her mother. The smile returned, and she kicked her legs hard within the tight wrapping, making a little cooing sound, and turning her head towards Kati's warmth. She squirmed suddenly, and whimpered.

"She's hungry," said Huomeng, shaking Yesui's hand gently, the little claw still clamped firmly on his finger.

"I will fix enough to last until your milk comes in," said Zhan Zheng, and he hurried from the room with the young nurse right behind him.

Yesui fussed only a moment while he was gone, and then her eyes closed in sleep. When they awakened her for a liquid meal, the glow in her eyes had vanished, and for the moment she was simply their child, sucking eagerly, mother and father taking turns in holding the polymer bottle that fed her. And when the first light of Tengri-Khan was on the Three Peaks, Huomeng took her outside on the balcony for her first glimpse of the world of Shanji. He held her up, turning her, watching her eyes move, eyes narrowed against the light, but targeting all she saw and dwelling for a long moment on the distant summits of Three Peaks.

She fell asleep in his arms, and Huomeng carried her back inside to Kati. They spent the morning studying her face, examining every part of her, and both would fondly remember that quiet, peaceful time.

Later, they would wish for such peaceful times, and the quiet joys known to parents of normal children. But Yesui was the Empress of Light. She was the Mei-lai-gong.

CHAPTER TWO
REFLECTIONS

Abagai, Empress of the worlds of Tengri-Nayon and First Mother to the people of Shanji, was pleased with the way her daughter was reacting to the defeat of their armies, and eventually told her so.

They shared tea in Abagai's private suite, lounging on thick cushions with the low serving table between them, and the young lieutenant who'd served them had just left the room. For the first time in nearly a year they were alone, and could talk privately. The windows were shuttered, the room glowing orange in the light of three oil lamps, for all power had been shut down during the storm that still raged outside. Even through thick plas-steel and concrete walls, they could hear the sound of sand scraping at their dwelling with terrible force.

Abagai sipped her tea, and said, "You're very quiet, Yesugen. Do you still think about Shanji?"

Yesugen leaned on one elbow, and shook her head.

"Not about the war, if that's what you mean. I think about the blue sky there, and how easy it would be to live without constant storms. Here we are again, Mother, living like burrowing animals."

"It will pass, dear. The storms are more infrequent each year; your children will see blue skies, and play under them."

Yesugen lowered her eyes, for the subject of children was a sensitive one with her. No man had yet dared to approach the Field Commander of Abagai's armies, even though her figure was striking when not clothed in armor. "Perhaps," she said, then sipped her tea and scowled. "Kati complains about the difficulty of her peoples' lives. She does not know what difficulty is."

"She has known hardship," said Abagai. "Is it Kati you think of? Do you hate her, Yesugen?"

Yesugen thought for a moment, and sighed. "No, that is not what I feel."

"Do you feel humiliated by her?"

"No. There is no humiliation in defeat by a superior adversary. Her powers are far beyond what I was expecting. Even my hardened troops so willing to die with honor were relieved when she showed mercy in those final moments. She could have destroyed all of us."

"Then what's bothering you?" said Abagai softly, for she knew what was there in her daughter's mind. The knowledge of it apparently showed in her eyes, for Yesugen quickly answered.

"You see my jealousy there." Yesugen's eyes glistened, but only for an instant.

"*I* have done that to you, not Kati, and I'm sorry for it. I did not seek to hurt you, Yesugen." Abagai felt an ache in her throat.

"But you have done so. You treat Kati like a

favorite daughter, and I have spent my adult life serving your empire. Am I nothing to you but someone to command your armies?"

Abagai sipped tea to wet her dry, aching throat. "I love you with all my heart, Yesugen, and I love your brothers, but there is a harshness in all of you that comes from your father."

Yesugen's eyes turned red in an instant. "He taught us to be strong! He gave us discipline!"

"With a closed fist," said Abagai. "He was a harsh, cruel man without compassion, and if he were alive to hear me say it he would strike me to the ground out of habit. When you were a child, you saw him do it more than once. Tell me, Yesugen, is that the kind of person you would trust to use the unlimited power of the gong-shi-jie? The power to *destroy*?"

Yesugen seemed stunned. "You see father in me, and so you do not train me in the gong-shi-jie? Instead, you train another, not even of our world, so she can destroy our armies. Do you *see* the powers you've given her?"

"I gave her nothing," said Abagai. "Her training only brought forth the powers that were already there. She was undoubtedly exceptional at birth, though I didn't sense her existence until she was four. For years I thought she might be the Mei-lai-gong we've sought to produce for centuries. I was excited, and struck by Kati's deep love and compassion for *all* people, even those who oppose her. I do not regret my decision to train her."

"You can tell that to the relatives of our soldiers she incinerated by Shanji's sea. She did not hesitate, Mother."

"That was war, Yesugen, and the war is over. When we left Kati, I felt no malice in her, only the desire that we can work together, even when it is *you* who rules here. I made it clear to Kati that you are to be my successor."

Yesugen lowered her eyes again, and picked at the fabric of her cushion. A sudden gust of wind rattled the heavy, steel shutters over the windows.

"You will not train me in the gong-shi-jie, but you trust me to rule in your place," she said sullenly.

"I *want* to trust you," said Abagai, "and to rule is your rightful inheritance. But I will be blunt with you, Yesugen. Your father is gone, and I am glad of it. Now it is you and I, without his influence or threat. You have my blood in you, and I want to see evidence of it. I want to see compassion in you, a concern for the welfare of our people."

"I suppose that includes the plague of migrants I have to deal with. They come here uninvited, and we have no place for them, and so they complain and riot, and you show sympathy for them. I would put them all on the next ship back to Lan-Sui, and let their incompetent governor deal with them," said Yesugen angrily. Her eyes were now ruby-red, and she sat up on her cushion, hands knotted into fists. "We live like moles under an angry sun, Mother. There are barely enough resources for our own people on the surface."

"Soften your heart, daughter! Lan-Sui is a dying world. The people come here because they want to live in sunlight, and breathe air that doesn't smell of oil and ozone, and have a life on the surface of a real planet. You have just spent a year in space. Would you prefer to live that way for a *lifetime*?"

"Of course not," said Yesugen, "but it's not *our* problem! We're just beginning to build on the surface here, and it will take all we have to provide for our own. We don't have the resources for new people!"

"Then we must find them. We'll work together to find a solution to the problem."

Yesugen sighed in exasperation. "Can't you at least stop the flow of migrants? The camps are overflowing, and there were two riots while we were gone."

"Were there killings?"

"No, but several were injured. Kabul was in charge, and I think he was softer than he should have been with them."

"I hear your father again. That is what I want to see change in you. Brutality does not win the hearts of the people, it only creates new problems."

"But the migrants keep *coming*! You risk a break in relations with Lan-Sui over this. They will cut off our fuel shipments, and then how do we run our reactors? We need those gases, Mother!"

"I've spoken with Governor Wizera about this," said Abagai. "Unauthorized travelers from Lan-Sui will not be allowed off-ship here any longer, but Wizera must control the smuggling traffic on his own world. Small ships land in our deserts every month, and we cannot police that. People are dying horribly out there, only because they want a better life. Can't you feel compassion for them?"

"I'm *sick* of that word! I want to build our world, not destroy it. I want a better life for *our* people!"

Yesugen's emotion was deep, and Abagai was startled by it. "Well," she said, "it's a start in the right direction. And I agree with you. Can we begin there? Will you work with me towards that goal?"

"I always have," said Yesugen, eyes lowered again.

Abagai stood up, stepped around the table and put her hands on Yesugen's broad shoulders. "Stand with me, daughter," she said.

Yesugen looked up at her curiously, then stood up,

facing her. Abagai grasped the hard muscles of Yesugen's arms, and pulled her closer. "You are my only daughter, and the heiress to my throne. Do you believe that I love you?"

Yesugen could not look her in the eye. "Yes," she croaked.

Abagai pulled her into a long hug, but Yesugen remained rigid, her arms stiffly at her sides.

Abagai sighed, "You are loved, daughter, but life will flow more easily for you if you allow yourself to be loved."

The terrible hardness was still there when Abagai released her.

By evening the storm had subsided; Yesugen put on her greatcoat and masked helmet to ward off blowing sand and went back to her own quarters in the dugout next to Abagai's.

In the gloom of her private suite, a sense of solitude and loneliness descended on Abagai only a moment after her daughter was gone, and her thoughts were suddenly about Kati and her unborn child. No, not unborn. It had now been over a year, yet she'd sensed nothing, but during most of that year she'd not ventured into the gong-shi-jie or made any effort to contact the new Empress of Shanji. Was the child now born alive, and well? As much as she loved Kati, her thoughts were mostly about the child, Yesui, and what she'd done while still in the womb of her mother.

It had only been a few weeks into the trip back from Shanji, and she'd been meditating in a cubicle smelling of oil, horseflesh and dung. Her mind and soul strolled the place of creation near the edge of the galactic wheel where the aural vortices of stars suddenly disappeared, and there was only shimmering violet light. Far beyond was another disk of deep reds and green that was another galaxy she had visited once, and now considered again, but then Kati's shriek of joy and pride had broken her reverie, and she'd returned without time-lapse to the aura of Shanji's sun.

Kati's cry had been powerful. *Oh, Mandughai! My little girl is with me in the gong-shi-jie, taking her first steps here! Come quick!*

Kati had called her, and so she came, but she could not bring herself to reveal her presence because the moment seemed so private, and amazing, and so she'd only watched. Kati's manifestation was the usual one: her own, beautiful face with the highly arched nose and long neck, the tall, slender figure clothed in a robe of royal gold. Hands folded on her stomach, face serene, she drifted towards the green vortex that was the aural signature of Tengri-Khan. *Come with Mother, dear*, she said without words in this place of creation.

Behind her, a tendril of green fluttered like a tiny flame, following tentatively at first, then quickening its pace. Abagai was instantly aware of a new, powerful presence, a presence that penetrated to the core of her being, a mental touch that penetrated her invisibility. Kati was gone in a flash, her manifestation seeming sucked into the vortex of Tengri-Khan, but the tendril remained behind for an instant, wavering before Abagai, as if studying her. Abagai felt warmth, a kind of euphoria mixed with excitement, and then the tendril descended slowly, slowly into the signature of Shanji's sun.

Kati was back in a flash, but the tendril of green seemed reluctant to return from real space, emerging slowly from the vortex and remaining attached there. Kati smiled when she saw it.

Did you come with me? Did you see the star, or

*stay here? This is enough for a first time, and
Mandughai still hasn't come to see you. Let's go back,
now. Stay close.*

Kati drifted away towards the dim, purple vortex
leading to herself, and the green tendril followed her,
but behind the tendril came a writhing, dark shape
streaming from the place of Tengri-Khan, a color so
deep red it seemed black in the swirling violet and
purple background of the gong-shi-jie. The swirls near
it were suddenly distorted, as if a great energy density
was disturbing them. And then an invitation came, so
strong that Abagai nearly lost control of her invisibility.

Come? Yesui.

The mental force was so powerful she followed
without thinking, and it was the green tendril she
followed, not Kati. There was the flash of transition,
and she was overwhelmed by emotions and visions:
fear from Kati, excitement from another, the sight of
a roiling mass of dust and glowing gas ascending from
a mountain on Shanji, then little hands waving, legs
kicking in a tiny place illuminated in emerald green.

Come Yesui. Hot. No.

The dark shape following the child had frightened
her, and she had disposed of it at a place she'd seen
through her mother. The strong presence, the child's
slow transition to real space, her return with energy at
incredible density, it all came together for Abagai at that
instant. The mental connection was still strong, and it
was not with Kati, who was still fearful, and oblivious
to her presence. So she went to the child, and showed
her a vision of watchful, emerald-green eyes. Within
herself she felt euphoria, and reverence for the being
so long awaited by the Moshuguang of her blood-line.
And the message she gave the child was similar to one
she'd given to the mother years before.

Yesui. Yesui—my child. I am Mandughai. I was with your mother, and your grandmother, and now I will be with you. Sleep, now, and build your strength. You have much to learn from your mother and me, and there is something I would have you do for me when you're a woman.

But the mental connection had weakened, then broken at that moment. Yesui had fallen asleep. So Abagai had returned to the gong-shi-jie without revealing herself to Kati, who now basked in the warmth of her husband's loving concern for her fright. Abagai returned to herself in the smelly cubicle on the ship, and discovered her own eyes were filled with tears.

Now it was a year later. The child was born, and Abagai had not kept her promise yet. She'd forgotten the dilation of time in moving at near light velocity, become absorbed by the logistics of moving and unloading an army, and now her attempts to grow closer to her own daughter.

For a moment, she was tempted to enter the gong-shi-jie, and make contact with Kati to hear news of the child. But Kati had not contacted her, and could do so at anytime. Surely the child had been born healthy, for in times of grief, Kati had always sought comfort from the woman she called Mandughai. No, Kati was herself busy with the duties of a new Empress, and the child would be recently born. Kati would see the magic of her first-born. Let them bond together, mother and daughter, and then it would be time for Abagai to become involved with them.

The urge to contact Kati persisted. Abagai yearned for a touch of that mind, the warm feelings there, the warmth she wished could be present in her own daughter. She busied herself with paperwork as a distraction, then opened the window shutters when the roar of the wind outside had subsided to a low groan. Sand was still blowing, and the sky above was a dirty brown where the light of Tengri-Nayon fought to be seen. A flyer had landed before her dugout after braving the wind, and a column of armored men was descending a metal ramp leading from the maw of the craft. Their face plates were up, and she could see faces. It was Yesugen's military advisory council, Colonel Kabul in the lead. They marched in cadence towards the dugout next to Abagai's.

Yesugen had wasted no time in calling her council. And the faces of all the men marching to meet their commander were grim indeed.

Yesugen had dreaded this moment for months, and now it had come. She would not make excuses, for there were none to make, but not one of the men on the council had been there to face Kati's awful powers. Any criticism would come from ignorance, and she would need patience in facing it. She had only moments to compose herself, sitting at the head of a table nearly filling the small room. The brown stucco walls were barren of decoration, dimly lit by the single oil lamp in the center of the table. She closed her eyes, and breathed deeply until the orderly opened the door and said, "They are here, Commander."

"Send them in," she said sharply, then folded her hands together on the table, and took a final, deep breath.

Six men entered the room. Only Kabul looked her in the face as he came to take his place at her right hand. The rest stood rigidly behind their chairs, eyes on the walls.

"Sit," she said, and they did. Still they did not look

directly at her, but at each other from either side of the table. She waited a long moment, but there was only a horrible silence, and the masks of their minds were like stone. Finally, she spoke.

"You've had time to read my report, and I'm here to answer your questions. Please do not be conciliatory with your comments. We don't have time for it, and it will accomplish nothing." Her voice was calm, but forceful.

Silence. No heads turned. Yesugen unfolded her hands, and tapped a fingernail on the table. "I'm waiting, gentlemen," she said softly.

Kabul looked at the others, then her, and cleared his throat. "We all share great disappointment in the outcome, Commander. Shanji was very important to our plans."

"Yes, it was," she said, "and it remains so. Shanji will be quite instrumental in our surface development if we proceed wisely."

"Perhaps you could elaborate on that for us, ma'am," said Kabul respectfully. "The report does not detail your discussions with Shanji's new Empress. It only says that they occurred."

Heads now turned, and they were finally looking at her. "The discussions were brief, and we spoke only in generalities, but it was enough for me to know that our relations with Shanji can be quickly normalized to the point that it can be a considerable resource for our growth."

"What we need is someone to take these vermin off our hands," growled Ghazan, the most senior on the council. He had served as a field officer under Yesugen's father, and bore the scar of a sword slash on one cheek. It had been given to him as a reprimand by his superior. "The purpose of your mission was to secure Shanji for relocation of these people, and that has not been accomplished."

Yesugen willed her hands not to clench. They were all staring at her, now. "That is true, Ghazan, and I take full responsibility for it. Our people fought bravely, and well. The error was mine in underestimating the force we faced."

"Sheep herders and fishermen, and a small, inexperienced army," said Ghazan disdainfully. "You could have destroyed them all from space."

"And risked total annihilation," said Yesugen, her voice rising. "The force has a name, Ghazan, and it is Kati. A young woman, yes, and seemingly gentle as a person, but when threatened, she has the power to destroy a world, or even a star! What she did to us is a tiny fraction of what she is capable of. She could have ionized all of us, and our ships, with a wave of her hand. If I had fired from space at anything except her flyers, she would have done so, and then, Ghazan, you, in your safe place here, might also have felt her power. She could have traveled through the gong-shi-jie in an instant, and reduced our planet to a cinder! Do not disgrace the names of our men who died by her terrible fire *or* her sword. Her powers are real, and overwhelming!"

"We've read of the destruction in your report," said Kabul quickly, "and it's a reality we must accept. The conquest of Shanji is no longer a consideration. How, then, are the resources of that planet of use to us?"

"We need metals, and synthetics, in considerable quantity, and there are excesses of such things on Shanji. Their agriculture is advanced, and tailored to surface farming. Ours is purely hydroponic. We need new plant varieties to match our erratic growing seasons and acid soils. Shanji has the expertise to develop them for us. We need trees that can stand dryness and hot wind, and chemicals to neutralize our soils. All these things can come from Shanji."

"And what is their return?" asked Toghril, who'd been given the task of constructing the holding camps for migrants and the command of security forces there. He was near Yesugen's age, and a captain, but had never known battle, and was not held in high regard by the others. "If the Empress of Shanji has such great powers, what do we have to offer her?"

"Space-faring capability, which her world abandoned a thousand years ago. I left two shuttles behind as a token of what we can provide. Also, she needs us as a market, to expand her economy and provide jobs for her people."

"You *gave* her two of our shuttles?" asked Toghril.

"No matter," said Ghazan. "We brought back far fewer troops than we sent. The dead have no need for transportation."

Nobody laughed.

Yesugen's fingernails dug into the palms of her hands. "Kati was very appreciative of the shuttles, and said so. She believes my sincerity in making trade with her, and has agreed to a meeting with me to discuss details. I plan to do so in the near future." Yesugen stiffened her back as she said it, sitting a little taller on her chair.

"You're leaving so soon?" asked Kabul. "Shanji is already a light-year from us."

"I will meet her in the gong-shi-jie," she said casually.

"Accompanied by our Empress, I presume," said Ghazan. "Any plan that's approved will of course be hers."

"We will meet alone, Ghazan, and my mother has agreed to it. What comes in future years will be decided by Kati and me, not my mother. I will be Empress here, Ghazan. Remember that."

Her voice was low, but the warning clear, and she'd had enough of him for the moment. Ghazan nodded respectfully, and looked down at his hands clenched on the table.

"We now begin surface construction in earnest, gentlemen, and I wish to move quickly. I need from each of you an overview of necessary materials and labor force for your individual areas, with timelines for each stage of construction. The figures may be approximate for now. I need only estimates for a first meeting with Shanji's Empress, but I need them within a month. Give your reports to Colonel Kabul, and he will collate them for me. Can you do this?"

Heads quickly nodded, and Yesugen suspected that such estimates had already been made during her absence. "That's all I have for now. Some of you have remained silent, so I presume my report was sufficient for you. I sense your disappointment about our action on Shanji, but I do not regard it as a setback. I think, in fact, that we have made an important ally. Let us proceed with that in mind."

Yesugen stood up, and the men stood with her. "You may return to your duties, gentlemen. Kabul, please stay for a moment."

Kabul smiled faintly, and stood by her side while the rest of the council left the room, closing the door behind them.

"Sit," she said, and they sat down together. Kabul seemed relaxed, and looked straight at her. In the four years he'd served her as Executive, she'd never sensed fear or hostility in the man, only a quiet strength and intelligence she admired. Her mother had chosen him for the job at the same time she'd declared Yesugen

Chair and Field Commander, and so far the arrangement had worked well, even though he was her senior
in age by ten years.

"When I criticized your handling of the camp riots,
I was rushed, and didn't ask for an explanation of your
actions. I would like to hear it now," she said softly,
then steepled her hands in front of her face.

"Yes, ma'am," he said, eyes steady. "They were not
really riots, but more like a demonstration. No property
was damaged, no fires, no weapons we could see, only
a mass of shouting people, and there were many small
children among them. But when people began climbing the fences, we moved in to support the small unit
of guards Toghril had stationed there. About twenty
young adults got over the fences, then ran from us.
I could see no threat from a few unarmed, half-starved
people, and ordered weapons shouldered. Women and
children were screaming in fear when we arrived,
Commander. Our troops are horrors to them, and
rightfully so. Upon physical contact, our troops beat
twenty young men into bloody heaps before I could stop
them. Several remain in hospital in serious condition,
but there were fortunately no deaths. Such harshness
was unnecessary, and I disciplined four troopers for
actions taken after I'd ordered the beatings to cease.
It was a matter of discipline, ma'am."

"The prisoners were escaping, and you would have
been justified in shooting them," said Yesugen.

Kabul shook his head slowly. "I don't think you'd
say that if you saw their living conditions. They're
stacked like cut wood in the barracks, and many spend
their nights huddled in the crawl spaces beneath the
buildings just to get away from the wind and blowing
sand. The camps aren't being built fast enough to
accomodate these people."

"I would put them on the first ship to Lan-Sui, and be rid of them, but our Empress won't allow it. How many arrived while I was gone?" Kabul was frowning at her, now, and she softened the sharpness in her voice.

"A thousand—two thousand. Now they come in private ships, landing far out on the sand plains. They straggle in here on foot, nearly starved, whole families of them, tiny children, pregnant women. Four children were born in the camp last week, and we provide what food we can. It's not *enough!*"

Kabul's voice shook with emotion, and the sound of it seemed to soften her heart. "We provide what we can, but I still think deportation is the solution," she said. "I should personally see if conditions are as bad as you say, and my mother should accompany me. If things are really so bad, perhaps she will agree to send these people where they belong. Can you arrange a visitation for us?"

"Right away," said Kabul, not looking disappointed, but relieved. "I'm grateful for your request," he added.

Yesugen nodded, and allowed herself a slight smile. "I appreciate your frank appraisal of what happened at the camp. You were correct in disciplining troops for not obeying your verbal orders. Their bioengineered instincts are vital in war, but must be kept under our control at all times. You may join the others, now." She waved a hand in dismissal.

Kabul stood, bowed, and went to the door, then turned back towards her and softly said, "I'm sorry that I couldn't bring you better news, Commander, but I'm very pleased to see that you've returned safely from Shanji. Welcome back, ma'am."

He closed the door behind him, and Yesugen was still sitting there, mouth open in surprise, and feeling strangely warm all over.

CHAPTER THREE
LITTLE VISITOR

"A loved one goes away, and my heart wanders to another."

Kati thought of this old Tumatsin saying when Yesugen called to her from the gong-shi-jie and said that Mandughai was also there.

It was late evening, and Huomeng had not returned from his work on the shuttles. In only a week, he planned to pilot one of them in making the first rendezvous with Shanji's great, orbiting mother ship in over a thousand years. The idea of his flight terrified her. Dispite his skill and confidence, there were so many things that could go wrong, and she would only be with him as a phantom presence.

Mengmoshu had joined them for a light meal in her suite, bringing along a large, stuffed *Shizi* toy for his granddaughter's second birthday. Yesui loved the toy, attacking them both with its cloth fangs and growling fiercely, then running off again. She had gone straight from crawling to running, falling often, but never with so much as a whimper. Mengmoshu called her "little darting one" in conversations with others, but now Yesui was in his lap, drowsy from the day, and he held her as gently as if she were a fragile porcelain treasure.

Kati watched them from her desk, but still managed to get some work done, reading new bills submitted to the People's Congress and writing her opinions of them.

Yesui nose, said Mengmoshu without words, and he touched her there. Yesui smiled, and her eyes glowed green. She reached up with a tiny finger, and returned the touch. *Gong-Gong nose.*

Yesui chin—head—hand—tickle! Mengmoshu tickled her under the chin, and Yesui squealed out loud with delight.

Don't get her excited, Father. She's nicely sleepy now.

Mengmoshu hugged the child tightly, and she was quiet again. *It's my privilege*, he said, and wrinkled his nose at Kati. *Besides, I'm inexperienced with little ones. My own daughter was seven before I found her. I'm making up for those lost years with you.*

Kati smiled serenely at him. *You've done that many times over.*

Mengmoshu smiled back, a thing that had recently become easier for him and seemed to soften his rugged face. Among the Moshuguang, the scowl of the Chancellor was still a sight to be feared, but he could not scowl at the little treasure in his arms. He was *Gong-Gong* or *Jofu* to her, and only he and Kati knew the legitimacy of his title as a grandfather. Yesui closed her eyes, and was now dozing again.

We should put her to bed soon, thought Kati.

In a little while, Kati. You have work to—

The matrix of purple stars was suddenly there, and one glowed brighter than the others.

Kati, Empress of Shanji, I feel your presence here, but I cannot find you. It is Yesugen, and my mother has left me here to talk privately with you. She says you will see the signature of my presence, and when we are finished she also wants to speak with you at another place. Kati, are you there? I don't see your aura!

Kati was startled, eyes widening, and Yesui stirred in Mengmoshu's lap. *You must go quickly, before she wakes the child. I'll wait with you,* said Mengmoshu.

Kati nodded to her father, put her hands flat on the desk, and closed her eyes. There was the sight of a rugged face hovering near, and a stuffed animal growling at it, and then she was rushing towards the brightest of the purple stars and down into it, coming out into the infinite expanse of swirling purple clouds dotted with the vortices of billions of stars and their worlds making a presence known in the gong-shi-jie.

I am here. She could feel a presence, but saw no manifestation of it.

Behind you. I could not find your aural signature, but now I see it. I didn't realize it was so faint, but it's much brighter now that you're here.

Kati turned and saw Yesugen's mental image of herself floating towards her. At their first meeting, Yesugen had shown her the image of a warrior slouched in an arrogant pose on a throne. Now she stood erect, clothed in a golden robe like Kati's, and a long mane of black hair covered her shoulders.

It is a lovely image. I remember you with armor, sitting on horseback with a sword in your hand.

Yesugen actually smiled at that, showing her short, white tusks. *I gave that sword to you, and the image is my mother's idea. She says we should come together as equals in this place. You are as I remember you, and now you have a child.*

You know about Yesui?

*My mother speaks of her. Perhaps she will speak to
you about her future at a place she says you remember,
a place at the rim of our galaxy you have visited before.
You must find it again when we're finished here. We
must talk, now. I have needs you can help me with, and
I bring knowledge that will help you achieve your goals
on Shanji. I hope you still feel there can be relations
between our worlds. We have not heard from you.*

Kati felt Yesugen's concern about making this
contact with her without invitation. *I apologize for
that, Yesugen. I've become so involved with my child
and the affairs of Shanji I've neglected everything else.
What is it that you want from me?*

Relative to real space, time did not pass in the gong-
shi-jie, for there was no space, or mass, or time there,
only the swirling energies that had created those things
at the beginning by pushing hot light through ten-
dimensional anomalies small beyond imagination. But
because time is perceived as a span of consciousness,
it *did* pass for Kati as Yesugen gave her a long litany
on the materials needed for surface construction on the
inner planet orbiting Tengri-Nayon. Finally, she was
finished, and Kati's mind whirled with numbers.

*Your needs seem immediate, and our warehouses are
indeed filled from overproduction. Much of the steel you
require is available, but it will take years for delivery.
My husband plans a first shuttle flight to our mother
ship in a week. We're just taking our first step into
space, and have only the fuel you left us. We have no
delivery capability for even small loads, let alone the
tonnages you require.*

We have foreseen that problem, said Yesugen. *We
have taken the liberty of sending five freighters to
Shanji. They left us a year ago, and should arrive in*

a few months. One freighter and several shuttles come to you as payment, and will be left behind. The shuttles will ferry materials to the freighters, and we're also bringing you the science and detailed plans for the cryo-generators you need to manufacture fuels. The rest will have to come from your own manufacturing.

Your payment is quite generous, said Kati. *I would say it's excessive. We should establish a currency between us, a rate of exchange, and put a price on everything, even your science and our investment in that science. I want an equal balance of trade between our worlds, to avoid any exploitation of each other in the long-term.*

Yesugen seemed pleased by that, even relieved. *You deal with us in good faith, even though we warred against you. I'm encouraged by that.*

The war is over, said Kati, *and I don't want a repeat of it. We're neighbors, Yesugen; let's help each other grow from this beginning.*

Agreed, said Yesugen. *And now my mother is waiting for you.* She lifted her arm, and pointed over Kati's shoulder.

My mind is a blur with all the figures you've given me. I'm not sure I can remember them all. Kati watched Yesugen drift closer, and turned, thinking they would go together to where Mandughai was waiting.

Now that we've met, our freighters will send a message to the Moshuguang, with all details, including minor ones I haven't given you. You should have it in a few weeks. I will not go with you to meet my mother, Empress of Shanji. I do not know the way to her, and will wait here until you return together. She has just begun to train me in the gong-shi-jie, and I need to remain here to memorize the aural signatures of this region. Mother simply left me here, and you

*were not present for me to target as in our first
meeting. Without your presence I was totally lost, but
I'm learning quickly.*

Kati sensed excitement, even joy in Yesugen, not
the hardness and hostility of their first encounter.
Perhaps it was because Mandughai now shared
Kati's training with her own daughter. *It is such a
beautiful place, here. Perhaps, when our duties allow
it, we can travel leisurely together, and see things
only your mother has seen so far.*

Yes, said Yesugen, now openly excited, *but now you
must go. She gave me one bearing, that deep, red
vortex straight ahead. Her place is in that general
direction, clear out to where the vortices end, and the
light becomes violet. She is there.*

So Kati left Yesugen behind, and drifted past the
deep red vortex that Mandughai had once warned her
about attempting to enter, for the real space there had
been pinched into a singularity, and re-entrance to the
gong-shi-jie was impossible. She searched her memory
for familiar signs from a trip years in the past, and
began to see them: a cluster of three, green vortices,
close together, a pattern of closely-spaced spirals of
vortices fanning out before her in whirling clouds of
blue, then purple, and beyond that a quiescent background of violet. When she saw the distant disk of
colors in the violet fog, she moved faster, for it was
the place Mandughai had once visited and so often
loved to look at from afar. They had talked about going
there together someday.

Now she hurried, and ahead of her was only a
sheen of violet, until suddenly a single spot glowed
brightly in emerald green, and they came together with
a thought.

Kati, dear. At last you've arrived.

The spot became a fan, then an image: the serene, motherly face, the highly arched nose, the glowing eyes and smile. They came together, arms outstretched, their images melding together.

It is not the same. I cannot touch you here, but it's so good to see you again.

I've missed you terribly, Abagai, but my life has been such a whirl I've been negligent in communicating with you. Please forgive me.

Abagai smiled slyly. *I will, if you forgive an old woman for her tricks, and for already knowing the news you're bursting to give me.*

You know about Yesui?

Yes. I knew her before she was born, Kati. I watched her magic in this place, and talked to her, but she will not remember me. I could not intrude on that precious moment you had with her here, and I was also amazed beyond belief. Surely you know that she is The One.

There have been signs, Abagai. She is beyond me in her movement of mass, and the slowness of her transition, but I don't know if she remembers doing it. The visions she gives me are of the people and objects around her. I will wait until she can speak more than a few words before I bring her here again.

Abagai nodded, then pointed out towards the twinkling colors of a distant, galactic aura. *Travel with me aways, dear, so we can look back at this place.*

They drifted in a mist of violet. When they stopped, Kati turned and saw the great wheel that was their own galaxy: four spiral arms separated by swirls of violet and purple, and dotted with the colorful auras of countless stars. *The violet you see is a special kind of energy I've yet to understand*, said Abagai. *Here it is light; in real space it is mass, and invisible. The energy is constantly moving back and forth between the two forms at incredible speed. Perhaps Yesui can learn how to harness it. I cannot.*

I see it, now, a kind of flickering in and out, but very rapid, said Kati. *But it was dust and gas from Tengri-Khan that Yesui moved through the gong-shi-jie. It could not have been my doing.*

Perhaps, said Abagai. *I will be interested in seeing what you can do together. You're thinking very strongly about her, now. I feel her presence through you.*

She's always in my thoughts. I left her asleep in Mengmoshu's lap.

Abagai looked wistfully towards the distant galaxy that was only an instant away from them in the gong-shi-jie. She pointed at it, and said, *I will take you there soon. You and I are two generations, Kati, and now there is Yesui, who will exceed both of us. Each goes beyond the other, and sometimes I wonder if there's an end to it. I wonder if there are others out there who are like us, or beyond us, beings who move the energies to make worlds and living things. Sometimes I think I hear them calling me, from way out there.*

Kati felt uneasy, sensing a sadness in the woman she'd once thought of as a kind of goddess. *Do you want to go further?*

No, not this time, dear, but someday there's a place I'll show you there, a place where twelve stars have melded their vortices into one colored the red of blood, so bright it can be seen from the galactic edge. Forgive my reverie, Kati. I watch you, and Yesugen, and now Yesui, and I think about the diminishing time remaining to me. The three of you are the future of our worlds.

Yesugen seems changed, said Kati. *There was no*

*hostility in our conversation, and we've taken a first
step in trade between us.*

*You are useful to her, and have powers she has
tested. She will be polite. Her jealousy of you has
softened, now that I'm training her in the gong-shi-
jie, but her father's hardness is deeply ingrained in her
and she still sees force as the solution to all problems.
I've placed a man second to her in command, a man
of moderation in thought and actions. Yesugen seems
to respect him, and so far his influence on her has
been positive.*

Abagai again looked wistfully at the rainbow colors
of the distant galaxy. *Sometimes I think Yesugen's
methods are more correct than mine. We are indeed
overwhelmed by the flow of migrants from Lan-Sui,
yet I've allowed them to come until recently. Now I
have been forced to deny them entrance, and still they
come, smuggled in by private ships, giving up all they
own for passage to a planet that doesn't want them.
They starve to death in our deserts, or suffocate in
the sand storms there. The few who find their way
to our surface settlements are placed in holding camps.
We do the best we can, but the living conditions are
terrible in those camps: overcrowding, inadequate food,
aimless hours with nothing to do, and the constant
storms. We simply don't have adequate resources to
care for them properly.*

Then why do they come? asked Kati. *Conditions
must be better for them on Lan-Sui.*

*They are, but only for the near future. Lan-Sui is
a dying world, a gaseous giant that has suddenly
grown cold. When I was a child, we called it "Ruby,"
for it glowed deep red, and the people there lived in
palatial cities floating in the eyes of ancient storms
in the upper atmosphere, basking in red light at a*

temperature only slightly less than what you enjoy on Shanji. Our civilization began there, Kati. The grandmother of the first Mandughai only fled from there to escape a purge by a political family more powerful than hers. She was royalty, forced to flee to an inner planet used for the mining and smelting of metals, a planet of underground cities, a barren surface scoured by terrible solar winds, a population of rough miners, metal workers, and the criminals who preyed on their earnings. My planet had a hard beginning, Kati, and its people are hard. Yesugen is like them, and I am not, but still I am Mandughai.

Abagai turned to look at Kati. *You think about Yesui again, dear. Do you feel she is somehow with us now?*

I'm feeling something, yes. A kind of anxiety.

I'm also feeling some distress from Yesugen. Perhaps we should go back to her. But the next time we meet here, we will journey far—out there. Abagai pointed to the distant galaxy, and smiled.

They drifted back to the rim of their own island universe and entered it, moving leisurely. Kati thought for a moment, then said, *If Lan-Sui has grown so cold, can the people survive there? Do you worry about an invasion by them?*

Oh no, it's not like that. The floating cities are still there, but their transparent domes are gone, replaced by shuttered metals. The liquid water on the moons has frozen, and the cities there have moved underground. Expansion has ground to a halt, but the population continues to grow. The people know we are expanding to the surface, beginning a new life in the light of a warm sun. It's the light they seek, an atmosphere that isn't artificial, and space in which to raise their families. They seek a new beginning. It is the common people who come to us, Kati. Those with wealth and comfortable quarters in the floating cities are quite content to remain where they are. But they resent the loss of their work force. Their governor has threatened me with economic sanctions if I don't stop the flow of migrants from Lan-Sui. It's a serious threat, since he provides the gases and liquid fuels we need for our reactors and conventional power systems. He thinks I encourage migration to build a work force for our surface construction, and I cannot convince him otherwise.

Kati tried to mask a sudden thought, but Abagai saw it anyway. *No, dear, the governor's threat came after our return. If we had known it beforehand, Yesugen and her supporters would not have pressed so hard for Shanji as a place to send our migrant population. But the war was still necessary to place you on the throne. Remember that. I can only hope the leadership of Lan-Sui will be satisfied with my closing of migration through normal channels, and that they'll cooperate with me in shutting down the smuggling traffic. But I will continue to oppose sending back the migrants already with us. I think they have the right to choose a new beginning for their lives, but I simply can't handle more of them now. With the materials you're providing for us, our construction will move faster and there will be more than enough work for everyone, including our guests. They will remain with us. Lan-Sui will continue to cool, and has no future. Our future is hard, but it's there.*

You are very convincing, said Kati, *and I will help where I'm able to. In many ways, the solutions to your problems are the solutions to mine. Your material requirements will put many people to work on Shanji, and soon we'll be able to have regular trade because of the technology you're sharing with us. Can we move*

*faster, now? The anxiety I was feeling is getting stron-
ger. I should return to Yesui; perhaps she's having a
bad dream.*

*I feel it also, dear, but I do not think it's a dream.
And Yesugen is becoming rather frantic. Do you
remember the way?*

I think so.

*Then I will follow you. Consider it a continuation
of your training.*

Kati willed calmness to avoid rushing blindly
ahead, for some aural markers she used were subtle,
many of them patterns rather than individual vortices. Anxiety boiled within her and she felt drawn
to the vortex of herself, intending to enter it as soon
as she reached Yesugen. Something was wrong with
Yesui, yet Kati had left her daughter dozing peacefully in a grandfather's lap. Kati looked around to
see Abagai following her, hands crossed over her
chest, a faint smile on her serene face as if she were
amused by a private thought.

Ma!

The call startled her, and now she was rushing past
the signatures of stars and planets, their colors blurring together, and ahead was the manifestation of
Yesugen, a misty cloud of emerald green. Yesugen
hurried forward to meet them, her eyes wide.

Ma come! Yesui want Ma!

Kati went right past Yesugen, heading straight
towards the deep purple vortex leading to herself.
*I must go to Yesui. Wait for me, and I'll return
soon.*

*In a moment, Kati. Please, wait just a moment.
Yesugen, what is wrong? You look frightened,* said
Abagai.

Kati stopped just short of her own vortex, and

looked back. Abagai hovered near Yesugen, arms stretched out as if to hold her.

There is a strong presence here. For an instant, I thought I saw something, a flash of green, but then it was gone, and I was suddenly afraid. It began shortly after Kati left, and has been building since then. Don't you feel it? Fear and anxiety. I feel threatened, Mother, but there's nothing here!

Abagai smiled at Kati. *Nothing we see, but she is here, hiding. Call her, Kati. Yesugen and I are strangers, but she will come to her mother. Call our little visitor out from her hiding place.*

Yesui? Here? She was asleep when I left her.

A part of her still sleeps. The Mei-lai-gong does not. Call her, Kati.

Kati concentrated hard to crush her own anxiety, her own fear spilling over her like great waves. She suddenly realized that what she felt was coming from Yesui, not herself, but from where?

Come to Mother, dear. These people are friends.

Nothing happened for a long moment.

Ma come Yesui. The cry was soft, and plaintive.

I can't see you, Yesui. I can't find you unless you show yourself to us. You belong here with us, dear. The woman in the black robe is like your grandmother, and the other woman is her daughter. Come out from your hiding place, Yesui. Please! These people want to meet you.

A tendril of green emerged like a flame from the vortex of Tengri-Khan, and wavered there uncertainly near where Abagai and Yesugen hovered.

There you are. Now come to me, Yesui. It is dangerous where you are now. There is a big ball of hot gas there.

The flame withdrew slowly from the vortex, and hovered there. *Pretty. Yesui touch.*

Kati was shocked, and looked at Abagai.

She has re-entered real space, and touched her star. Are you surprised, Kati?

As Abagai spoke, the green flame darted past her in a flash, and went straight through Kati's manifestation before turning to hover close to it. *Ma! Ma go! Leave Yesui! Ma no go!*

You were asleep, dear. I didn't think to bring you with me. We should go back to your grandfather, now. He will miss us.

Abagai and Yesugen drifted closer, and the little flame melded itself with Kati's manifestation. Abagai smiled sweetly, and said, *I am Mandughai, Yesui. I talked to you before you were born. Do you remember me?*

The flame buried itself deep within the image of Kati's robed form. *No. Yesui go, see Gong-Gong. Ma!*

This is my daughter, Yesugen, Abagai said patiently. *We will visit with you often in this pretty place, and become your friends if you want us. Can you show us what you look like, Yesui? Just think it, and we will see.*

No! See Gong-Gong!

She's upset, said Kati. *We must go, now. Do you mind if I bring Yesui with me when we meet again?*

Yesugen looked amazed, but Abagai only smiled serenely. *She is already one of us, dear. We will learn from her as she learns from us. Even the Mei-lai-gong must be trained, Kati. We must begin immediately, and I hope you will allow me to participate in it.*

Of course, said Kati. *Your knowledge and experience far exceed my own.*

Abagai nodded in satisfaction. *Then we will see you both again. I will call on you personally in a few weeks to see if our freighters have arrived safely. Goodbye, Yesui.*

I will also be here, said Yesugen firmly. *We have much to do, and quickly.*

Always business, thought Kati. The emotion of the moment seemed to be beyond Yesugen's perception. *I look forward to our times together. Stay close, Yesui. Now we go back to Gong-Gong.* Kati drifted to the vortex of herself, and dropped into it with a flash.

Silence, except for a faint creaking sound. Kati opened her eyes, and saw Mengmoshu scowling at her from his rocking chair, Yesui nestled asleep in his lap. The child murmured something, turning to press her little cheek against his chest.

"I felt her go," whispered Mengmoshu. "One minute she was dreaming, and then she was gone. I dared not move until your return, and then I felt her come back with you. I was frightened, Kati."

"So was I," said Kati. She told him what had just happened in the gong-shi-jie.

Mengmoshu rocked gently, and stroked the black hair of his granddaughter. "I think there will be unusual problems in the upbringing of this child," he said.

During the weeks following Yesui's visit to the gong-shi-jie, Kati awoke each morning with a vague nausea that made concentration difficult during early meetings. Finally, she'd had enough of it, and consulted with her physician. He examined her thoroughly, and made some tests. And when he called the next day, he told her that his Empress was not only in good health, but was, in fact, quite pregnant with her second child.

CHAPTER FOUR
SMUGGLERS

The wing of twelve flyers skimmed over the surface of Meng-shi-jie at an altitude of less than thirty meters as the first red glow appeared on the eastern horizon.

Yesugen sat in the rear of the lead fighter, pressed tightly between the fuselage and Kabul's hard shoulder, her rifle upright between her knees. Manek was in charge of the attack and kept looking back at her, obviously nervous about having his Commander so near if he made a mistake in the operation. Youthful insecurity, and he would have to deal with it, but Yesugen had insisted on being present when the smuggler's ship was intercepted. Their boldness in coming down so close to the settlement was an insult to her.

The ground flashed by, but there was little sound,

only a muffled whine from the baffled turbines of a craft designed for stealth operations. Sand hills covered with scrub and brown grass dormant before the short, severe rainy season rolled in all directions and there were occasional groves of *Tysk* and native Clawlimb whose lucky seeds had found a place where springs bubbled from shallow aquifers. Yesugen thought of Shanji, with its vast forests in the mountains, fields of green in valleys and plains under the light of a quiet sun. But Tengri-Nayon was near to rising, and there were no storms, and for the moment she could see the beginnings of life on her own world. For the moment, she could imagine forests and green fields on the planet of her birth.

Kabul broke her reverie. "It's only a few minutes. The ship has been forced down, but the crew is threatening to kill the passengers if we don't let them go."

Yesugen's first thought was to destroy the ship and all its inhabitants where it sat. "What does Manek have in mind?"

"A lightning assault, get inside quickly before the crew can carry out the threat, ma'am. He wants some crew members taken alive, so we can identify who the smugglers are and pass the word along to Governor Wizera."

Yesugen nodded in partial agreement, for at least it was not a timid plan. Ahead of her, a column of black smoke rose from behind a hill. Her craft suddenly bounced as fighters screamed past, breaking formation and fanning out into great circles converging on a point ahead. They came over a hill, and she saw the light cruiser hovering over a grounded ship belching smoke, the fighters coming in low from three directions while Manek, sitting just in front of her, spoke rapidly into his throat-mike. Sudden deceleration thrust her

forward, her own head narrowly missing Manek's as
Kabul thrust out an arm to push her back. They
hovered at the brow of a hill as the fighters went in
at ground level, disgorged troops running like ants, then
flashes of fire and they had penetrated the target, one
engine still belching smoke and flame from action by
the hovering cruiser.

Yesugen gripped her rifle hard in frustration. There
was fighting, and by tradition she could only watch. The
new Empress of Shanji did not have such a tradition
to contend with, and Yesugen still envied her for it.
She could lead them all, but on Meng-shi-jie it was
the men who did the fighting, and they kept her in
a safe place.

In minutes, it was over. Manek turned and grinned
at her. "We've taken the ship, and only a few have
been killed. We can move in, now."

The flyer shuddered and moved forward, landing
several meters from an open, scorched hatch in the
grounded, delta-winged vessel. The cruiser still hovered
above them, a threatening presence. Several troopers
emerged, and formed two lines radiating from the
hatch, their rifles held casually, but at the ready.
Yesugen walked towards them, aware of Kabul insinu-
ating himself slightly in front of her as a shield in case
there was trouble. But they waited only a moment
before people began spilling out of the ship in a panic.

The children came first: all ages, faces blackened
and streaked with tears. Many were crying, the older
ones looking stunned, but stoic. Women came right
behind them, some with babes in their arms, pushed
roughly from the hatch into the waiting grasps of
troopers. Manek listened hard to his head-set, then
turned and waved his arms. "Everyone back! They've
set bombs in the ship. It's going to blow!"

Everyone was running. Men in civilian clothes and armored troopers had begun emerging from the hatch when Kabul grabbed Yesugen's arm and hustled her away. When she stumbled, his arm went around her, and he lifted her from her feet with surprising strength, but in the excitement of the moment she didn't think about being angry at his boldness in touching her.

They ran back to the flyer, and there were screams behind them: children calling for their parents, women screaming the names of their men, and then a muffled thud that made the ground shudder. Smoke and fire belched from the hatch, along with the blackened body of a trooper. To her right, troopers were now streaming out from two other hatches, dragging screaming people with them. For one moment, Kabul twisted her around to face the flyer, his arms around her as the ground shuddered three more times in rapid succession. The third explosion knocked them down, and Kabul landed on top of her, burying his face into her back as people screamed all around them.

Kabul rolled off of Yesugen and helped her up, looking very embarassed. "Sorry, ma'am," he whispered. "I was only trying to protect you." For the first time in her memory, he did not look at her directly when he spoke.

Yesugen brushed clods of dirt from her hair and clothing. The third explosion had ripped open the belly of the ship, and thick, black smoke was erupting from the jagged opening there. People were getting up on their feet, others just sitting on the ground to watch the smoke. A shout, then another, a man and a woman running towards each other and coming together in an embrace. Other cries followed, women finding children, men finding both, whole families coming together again.

But not all were so lucky. Within the hour, there were those who walked in a daze, sole survivors of whole families, or those who clung together and cried over the loss of a child, a mother, or a father.

Yesugen walked among them, felt an ache in her heart, but could not bring herself to reach out in comfort. Kabul stopped often to put a hand on a shoulder, or give a comforting word. It bothered her to see a man doing that, while she could not. These people had not been invited here, and were not wanted here, but why couldn't she feel compassion for their loss of a loved one? She bit her lip in sudden anger at herself. What was *wrong* with her?

A group of dispirited-looking men sat on the ground, surrounded by a ring of troopers. Yesugen went to them, Kabul and a trooper right behind her. A young lieutenant snapped to attention as she approached.

"Who are these people?" she asked.

"Crew members, ma'am. All we could find. The rest barricaded themselves in the control area, and apparently blew themselves up with the rest of the ship's interior."

Yesugen shook her head. "That makes no sense to me. Why would they do that?"

"Suicide over execution, ma'am. They'd begun murdering their passengers when we got to the cargo bay."

"Have you questioned them?" Yesugen stood with hands on hips, glaring down at the captured men.

"No, ma'am. We're waiting for Captain Manek."

"No need to wait," she said. All the prisoners looked up sullenly at her, but one smiled faintly, a kind of smirk, and she pointed at him. "You! Stand up, and come here."

His response was a chuckle, then a growl as two troopers hauled him roughly to his feet, and pushed him in front of her.

"Your name?"

No answer. The man looked down at his feet.

"Where are you based, and who do you work for?"

Now the man glared at her. "I'll answer no questions. You'll kill us anyway."

"You seem quite certain of that," she said. "If you're smugglers, and skilled in space, we might have uses for you. What could you do for us?"

"There is nothing we'd do for you. Do what you intend to do! We should have died on the ship!"

"A fanatic," said Yesugen, smiling, "but for what cause? Money? Political favors? Who are you people?"

"They're moon-based members of the Governor's police!" shouted someone behind her. Yesugen turned and saw a crowd of civilians pressing forward, several troopers backing up in front of them.

"Who spoke?" she asked, and a man raised his hand.

"Let him pass," she ordered.

The man was tall and distinguished-looking, a mass of white hair spilling down over his forehead. His shirt and pants looked as if he'd spent weeks wallowing in filth, and his odor nearly brought tears to her eyes. "Identify yourself," she said.

"I am Altan Bator. Up until two months ago, I was Chief Steward of the Freightworkers Union on Gutien. I was arrested and ordered deported, along with my family. We are deportees, Madam, not smuggled migrants, and the people who brought us here are the Governor's police, acting on his orders. We are all union activists, and now he's rid of us. It was not our desire to come here, Madam, but we are here, and I ask you to grant us political asylum. We can be quite useful to you."

Yesugen was shocked. "Gutien is the source of our heavy water. Has production ceased?"

"No," said Bator, then paused. "Wizera has replaced all of us with his own people, and production continues under his dictates."

The man had left something out, and Yesugen wished that her mother were present to see the entire truth in his mind. Yesugen could only feel his emotion, a mixture of fear and anger boiling there. She turned to the prisoner.

"Is this true? Are you members of Lan-Sui's police force?"

"I have nothing to say," said the man, but he drew himself up into a brace as he said it, eyes cold.

"Then I will assume it's true," she said. "Wizera has sent you here to rid himself of political enemies, and add to our problems. Such an act is grounds for a declaration of war, sir. I am Yesugen, daughter of Mandughai and commander of her forces. I am prepared to declare war against Lan-Sui if you do not loosen your tongue and enlighten me!"

The prisoner only glared at her, and set his mouth in a hard line.

"He will say nothing," said Bator. "His family enjoys great privileges because of his loyalty, and he's prepared to die for it. All the crew were prepared to die, taking the rest of us with them, and it was only your quick action that saved most of us. We're most grateful, Madam."

"Save your gratitude for our Captain Manek. You're not wanted here. I intend to put you all on the next ship back to Lan-Sui."

"No! We'll all be killed! Please, Madam, grant us

political asylum! We're not like the others who've come here!" The civilians behind him surged forward, crying out, but troopers pressed them back with their rifles. One woman pointed towards the prisoners and began screaming hysterically.

"He's the one! He's the one!"

Kabul whispered into her ear. "Mandughai must be consulted about this, ma'am. This has become a political matter and we have chemical means of getting the truth from our prisoners back at the settlement."

"I hear you," she said, then, "how are you so different, Bator? Because you don't arrive in smugglers' ships? Are political dissenters and troublemakers more useful to us than the rest of the migrants we hold in our camps? I think not. You are less desirable than the others."

"We are *all* deportees," said Bator, "and all have been sent here on police vessels. There are no smugglers, Madam, only Wizera getting rid of people he finds undesirable. At first it was the unemployed, then people whose skills were no longer needed, and now those who actively oppose him. We're all the same. Please, Madam, if any of us are returned to Lan-Sui, we will die on the ships that bear us, and our bodies will be ejected into space to join others executed in similar fashion. It has been going on for *years*!"

Yesugen looked at Kabul, and he shook his head sadly. "Mandughai must hear all of this," he said softly. "It's no longer a military matter."

She agreed with him, but a declaration of war against Lan-Sui was clearly justified, and her mother would have to support it when she heard what this man Altan Bator had to say. The subjugation of Lan-Sui would be swift and simple, a long-overdue reunification with the old world, and there would no longer be problems in assuring the supply of fuels needed on Meng-shi-jie. And hadn't her mother talked often about unifying the worlds of Tengri-Nayon? Suddenly, the opportunity was there.

Her momentary excitement was broken by the renewed screaming of a woman behind her. It had turned into a shriek and the woman was clawing at a trooper, trying to get past him and pointing towards the prisoners. "Murderer! I want your blood on my hands! You killed my child!"

"Bring her over here," ordered Yesugen, "but restrain her until she can be calm."

The woman's eyes widened, and she was immediately calm, but a trooper held her by one arm as he brought her forward. The rest of the civilians were suddenly very quiet, craning their necks to see past the troopers holding them back.

The woman came forward, dishevelled and dirty, hair tangled, tears making muddy rivulets on her face. Her eyes were like glowing embers as she pointed past Yesugen, and growled, "He killed my Rani, and my husband! He killed my *baby*! I want him DEAD!"

Now the prisoners looked frightened, leaning away from where the woman pointed, leaving one man sitting there, his lips curled in an angry grimace. "*That* one!" screamed the woman, struggling to escape the grasp of the trooper holding her.

"Bring him here," said Yesugen. Now she glared at the prisoner she'd been unsuccessfully interrogating. "So, you were killing the people you brought here?"

His tongue was suddenly loosened. "No! We were sent to move them to an interior room when you attacked. We didn't even know about the bombs. It was Jagen who started shooting when your people were breaking in. The rest of us did *nothing*!" He did not turn his head to see the malevolent glare from the man who was brought to stand beside him, a look of such hatred that Yesugen's hand moved to finger the webbing of her slung rifle. The woman shrieked again, lunging forward and spitting at the man, but the trooper held her fast.

"He was only two years old!" she screamed.

Yesugen stepped up to the new man, and he came to a brace, cold eyes boring into hers.

"You are accused of murder," she said softly.

"I follow the orders of my Governor," he said gruffly.

"Indeed. Your loyalty is commendable under such difficult circumstances. You are undoubtedly an officer, a leader. I can see it in your bearing."

The man's brace became even more rigid. "I am a Captain, Madam."

"Carrying out orders regarding enemies of the state," she said. Yesugen suddenly felt cold inside, filled with an emotion she could not identify, an emotion triggered by the onset of sobbing by the woman behind her.

"That is correct," said the man, his stare unwavering.

"Then you admit killing this woman's child, and others?"

"I do, and I'm prepared for the consequences," he growled.

Yesugen put her face close to his. "Admirable. Now you are a brave man, and worthy of some consideration in your last moment."

"Commander!" said Kabul, but she waved him off, then turned to a trooper and said, "Give me your rifle."

The trooper was confused, looking at her own, slung rifle, but handed his weapon over to her. She took the prisoner by the arm, and said, "Come with me."

Kabul tried to block her, but she pushed past him. "Stay here, Kabul. Do not interfere with this."

"Please, ma'am, don't do this. It's impulsive. Yesugen! It's not wise!"

She ignored him, even when he spoke her name. She guided her prisoner to a spot several meters from the crowd, then turned him to face her. She carefully slung the rifle on his right shoulder, and stepped back two paces from him, watching his eyes.

He smiled.

"There is no honor in the execution of a warrior," she said softly. "And there is even less honor in the execution of a small child."

The man's left hand darted towards the sling of his weapon.

Yesugen's rifle was a blur as she whipped it from her shoulder, and shot him four times in the chest before he could bring his weapon into action.

He flopped down on his back, and was still.

Yesugen retrieved his rifle and returned to the others, who looked at her in horror. She went straight to the accusing woman, and looked at her sternly. "You have your vengeance," she said, "but I cannot return your husband and child."

The woman burst into tears.

Kabul was silent while arrangements were made to transport civilians and prisoners back to the settlement, and a crew arranged to search the charred interior of the ship. He was still silent as they returned to the flyer and pressed in together, waiting for a third trooper to occupy the remaining space on the seat. The trooper did not arrive, and they lifted off, but Kabul did not move over, and Yesugen did not ask him to do so. When they were only moments from the settlement, he finally spoke.

"You could have been killed. You had no way of knowing how fast he might be. How could you risk yourself like that?"

"You underestimate me," she said.

"No, I fear for you. And I don't understand you. I don't understand you at all." He looked at her, and his face was very close, his hands clenched in his lap. And what she saw in his eyes made her chest ache. She put a hand over his clenched fists, and left it there.

"I don't understand myself," she said, then inclined her head, resting it on his shoulder all the way back to the settlement.

She expected the man would lie through his teeth, and was surprised at the directness of his response. Yesugen had helped her mother compose the long message to Wizera, outlining their findings, their charges, and asking for reasons why a declaration of war should not be considered. The message was formal, and diplomatic, yet firm, and Yesugen learned from the writing of it.

When the answer came, it was early evening, and the shutters were open, for the weather had been clear all day. They sat together before Abagai's workstation as the plump face of Governor Wizera appeared on the screen. He read his prepared statement without apparent anxiety of any kind, and often looked at the camera, as if to emphasize his good intentions.

"I offer my deepest apologies to the leadership of Meng-shi-jie for the recent incident involving an official vessel of our police force. I was completely unaware of such actions taking place, but as Governor I assume full responsibility for it. I do deny, however, the charge that orders to kill passengers on this vessel, or any other vessel, have come from my office. They have not, and I'm now taking steps to identify the perpetrators of a strategic deportation operation that has apparently been taking place for some time. It was my feeling that citizens of Lan-Sui, particularly those on the moons Gutien and Nan, were looking at Meng-shi-jie as a place for a new life, and were leaving voluntarily. Now I see otherwise. I recall my own charges that you were encouraging migration from Lan-Sui, and am profoundly sorry for saying such things, based on my own ignorance."

A long, sorrowful look into the camera. Yesugen grunted, but Abagai watched the screen silently, hands steepled before her face.

"Dear Mandughai, as a planetary leader whose lineage goes back to a noble family on Lan-Sui, you know the difficulties of leadership. Your problems are numerous in developing a new world, where once there were only buried cities. But I must say I envy your problems, for Meng-shi-jie is beginning, while my world, home to my people and your ancestors for thousands of years, seems now to be coming to an end. Life has become difficult here; I can lead the people to the best of my abilities, but I cannot dictate to the powers of nature.

"There is unrest here, and forces that seek independence of our moons from Lan-Sui. I fear that this movement will disrupt the production of goods you have depended on for many years. A face-to-face meeting between you and me is long overdue. We must discuss our mutual problems in a detailed, conversational way, and seek avenues of support for each other. I request such a meeting as soon as possible, at a location of your choice. I think it's imperative that we move quickly on this before there can be any further escalation of difficulties between us. I say this with great sincerity, Mandughai, and I await your reply. We are an aging, weakening world here, while yours is vital and new. Let there always be peace between us."

There were actually tears in the man's eyes when the screen went blank. Yesugen made a rude sound, and said, "He's glib, and denies everything, but it wasn't what I expected. His normal, arrogant posturing was totally absent. He fears a war with us."

Abagai still stared at the screen, hands steepled. "Yes, he does, but if you listened carefully, you heard him ask for our support."

"I *did* hear that."

"I mean *military* support," said Abagai. "The man is in trouble. The moons are his only economic link to us, and an independence movement is underway. We could find ourselves dealing with a rebel government in the near future, and I smell political treachery in police being involved with deporting people without government knowledge or approval."

"If Wizera is telling the truth, yes. So we deal with the rebels, as long as we receive our fuels."

Abagai smiled. "Rebels have their own agendas, as you've recently seen on Shanji. Without Kati, we'd have no relations with that world, and you know it. No, I see a bad situation developing here. I will give Wizera his meeting, but with both you and me. From what he's said, and what Altan Bator told us, I suspect treason within Lan-Sui's police force. We might be called upon for a military intervention, Yesugen. Especially now, we cannot tolerate any interruption in fuel supplies from Lan-Sui."

"Will you answer him right away?" asked Yesugen. "We haven't finished interrogating the prisoners."

"We've heard enough for my answer. Lan-Sui

police are involved, and the ships originate from the moons."

Yesugen nodded. "Yes."

"Let us assume Wizera is innocent, as he claims. If you were Mandughai, right now, what would you do?"

"I would give him a meeting, on one of our ships, arriving at Lan-Sui with several cruisers in a show of force. If there was a hostile response to my visit, I would put the entire system under military control. His force is far too weak to oppose it."

Abagai smiled. "Close, dear, but not specific enough. You will hear my compromise to your position, but I basically agree with you, even though I've received news you haven't heard yet. It came in shortly before you arrived. You will see why I came close to a declaration of war myself in the last hour." She handed a disk to Yesugen, then a hand-held reader, and turned back to her workstation.

Yesugen read the disk as her mother began the message which would travel for nearly two hours to reach Lan-Sui. Her face became flushed, and there was a ringing in her ears, but now Abagai was speaking.

"We appreciate your prompt reply, and agree that a meeting is most necessary, but recent events force us to use extreme caution. Dear Governor, you need to know that four other police vessels from Lan-Sui have been intercepted and chased by our ships. When our ships drew near, these vessels disgorged their human cargo heartlessly into space, killing them all horribly: men, women and children. Acting on their own volition, my Captains have destroyed those ships and their crews for this criminal act.

"There are forces on Lan-Sui that are inhumane and evil, dear Governor. I trust that you are not involved with them. For that reason, we regard your safety as imperative. We will meet on the command vessel of a fleet I will embark on within the week. My daughter Yesugen, Commander of my ground forces, will accompany me with a full battalion of troops in several cruisers. If we meet hostility, or see any threat to your life, we intend to take military control until order is restored to your system. Our first targets will be your moons, and we will show no mercy to those responsible for the murders of helpless people.

"My hope is our meeting can take place without incident. Let us root out evil where it exists, and work together to solve our mutual problems. We are connected by a long history of peace and we wish for that to continue. You can expect us to reach you within a few days. I will have a ship sent for you with a military guard to insure your safety. Please be assured of our good intentions, even in the face of our force. We come as your friends."

Abagai's hand played over the keyboard, and the message was on its way. She turned back to Yesugen, and raised an eyebrow. "That has to be the strongest language I've ever used in a diplomatic exchange. But I won't know if I'm right about him until we're face-to-face. I cannot connect with him from the gong-shi-jie, so my message wasn't just to him, but to the ones responsible for these deaths. Are you all right, Yesugen?"

Yesugen had become pale, and felt numb. Her voice shook. "I've known war, seen men killed by the sword and Kati's purple light, but I've never heard of such atrocities against unarmed people helpless to fight back."

"Does it bother you, Yesugen?"

"Yes, it does."

"Good. Your father *did* give you a sense of honor. Harsh as he was, he would never have committed an evil thing like that. And he would have killed the evildoer as you did today, daughter. There was a sense of justice in him."

Yesugen's eyes were suddenly filled with tears, and she stifled a sob. Abagai reached over and took her hand, patting it softly.

"I know you loved him. In a bizarre way, I loved him too. It's you and I, now. Get some rest. Tomorrow will be filled with logistics."

Abagai embraced her when they stood up, and for the first time in her life Yesugen felt compelled to return it; they stood that way for a long moment, saying nothing, then Yesugen quickly left the room.

She marched straight to her nearby quarters, head down in contemplation. When she looked up, she saw Kabul waiting for her at the doorway, a file in his hand. "Nobody answered," he said.

"My orderly has retired," she said. "Come inside."

Kabul hesitated. "More bad news, I'm afraid."

"Please," she said softly, and unlocked her door, closing it behind them.

He handed over the file, looking into her eyes. "Four more ships have been intercepted and destroyed."

"I know about it. Mother showed me the report." Her voice cracked, and she cleared her throat. "I've seen death in space: the eyes red from ruptured capillaries, the open mouths, the blood . . ."

Yesugen struggled for control. "Now, I see women and children like that, floating alone in vacuum—and I want to *kill*!"

Her vision was blurred, and her hands shook. Kabul reached out his hands, then quickly drew them back, taking a deep breath, and letting it out slowly. Now tears were running down her cheeks, and she didn't care. Yesugen took one step, pressing her cheek against Kabul's chest, and putting her arms around him. His hands moved over her back, and then he was holding her tightly, his cheek on the crown of her head.

"Yesugen," he said softly, and squeezed her gently.

"That is my name," she said, and then she put her arms around his neck, and kissed him softly, yet deeply, without urgency, for a long, long time.

CHAPTER FIVE
MENGJAI

Mengjai was an ordinary child at birth and so his mother worried over him. Kati felt no mental presence while he was in her womb, and his birth was not unusual, only a perfectly formed newborn, crying when uncomfortable and demanding to be fed.

Huomeng was thrilled to have a son and fussed over him constantly, the bond between them immediate, and strong from the very beginning.

The bond between mother and son came much later, for Kati was constantly distracted by Yesui, who showed jealousy and disdain for her brother before he was even born. *He does not talk to me. There's something wrong with him,* complained Yesui, before Mengjai's birth.

"He's not like you," said Kati, "but he's your brother, dear. He will be your playmate, and as an older sister you will have things to teach him."

But these were things not destined to happen soon.

Yesui ignored her brother, and from his first day on Shanji was constantly after her mother for attention.

For four years, the palace of the Empress of Shanji was in an uproar. Kati could not escape Yesui, even in meetings with the nobles, or sessions of the People's Congress.

I want to see Da. He's been gone three days.

Not now. I'm busy, Yesui.

Then I'll go alone. I want to see what he's doing.

You will not. You wait for me!

I won't. And she was gone, at that instant. Kati would rush back to her apartments to find Yesui sprawled unconscious on her own bed, Weimeng in tears, wringing her hands in dispair, and then she would have to sit down and go after her daughter through the gong-shi-jie to the mother ship where Huomeng was supervising the loading of building materials on still another freighter bound for Tengri-Nayon.

She's here again, darling. I was just talking to her.

That's all good and well, but you know she shows no aural presence in real space, and now she's silent.

Yesui, you go back with your mother! If you don't, right now, I won't talk to you again when you come here.

Da! No!

Do it!

Something would always happen: the cables of a loading crane thrumming as if plucked by a giant hand, a massive packing cylinder suddenly assuming a higher orbit in the blink of an eye as Yesui vented her displeasure. Kati would make two transitions in an instant, head spinning as she opened her eyes to find Yesui crying on the bed, and Weimeng trying to comfort her.

The tantrums lessened somewhat when Huomeng explained to her how she was endangering the lives of people with her outbursts, and he talked Kati into allowing Yesui definite times to make the short hop to the mother ship when he was there. "Let her play alone a little in the gong-shi-jie," he explained. "As long as she stays close, it will be good for her."

Kati agreed reluctantly, and rightly so, for Yesui's "playtime" only led to further problems. A bronze vase in the childrens' room was found melted into slag. Yesui didn't like it there, and said her brother had laughed at the pretty colors of the light she'd used. Kati became fearful of her daughter burning down the entire palace in a snit. Things disappeared: unwanted clothing, old toys, a picture reader for children's stories that had ceased to function. When Kati questioned Yesui, the child only said she'd thrown them away, yet the reader by itself massed forty kilograms.

It was little better in the gong-shi-jie, even when Abagai was there. When she and Kati drifted together in quiet conversation, Yesui was always darting off somewhere, making them go after her. She was easy to find when she wanted to be found, her manifestation now a great, featureless fan of emerald green. But she could turn it off and on at will and often hid from them, giggling until they threatened to leave her.

Their meetings were infrequent, only two or three times a year, but the bond between Abagai and Yesui was immediate and trusting, the child focusing on every word the woman said. Her mind was like a sponge, absorbing everything with total recall at will. The ability to see the aural signatures of stars and planets had been with her at birth, and it was obvious that her "playtime" activities took her far from Shanji. The aural patterns were already fixed in Yesui's mind, well beyond the gaseous giants of Shanji's system, when they began to train her.

They took her to Tengri-Nayon and beyond, clear to the rim of the galactic wheel, and Yesui saw the violet light there.

This is different. It comes and goes, and I can see it faintly on the other side, said Yesui, after making the transition to and from real space there. Abagai and Kati were mystified by this, for beyond the galactic edge they could see only empty space.

Yesui played with the violet light, creating flickering, dark spaces in the gong-shi-jie, then complaining, *It won't move right. It's sticky.* So they returned to their own systems, Abagai warning Yesui about the terribly twisted space within the deep-red vortex of a star whose density was beyond imagination, and showing her more patterns she needed for her travel alone in the place of creation.

Those early days together in the gong-shi-jie would always be fond memories for Kati. They traveled leisurely, and talked, Yesui played, and all of it was without focused purpose or mission. And after their returns, Yesui would be well-behaved for days, playing quietly in her room without torturing her brother with tricks. There was only one incident to mar this record, but it was a terrible one, and it occured when Yesui was six.

It was evening, and Kati was working at her desk. Huomeng had gone to bed early and was snoring peacefully across the room from her, just back from another thirty days in space. They had made love earlier, to celebrate his return, and Kati still basked in the warm afterglow of it. To give them privacy, Weimeng had volunteered to put the children to bed.

Suddenly, there was a commotion in the childrens'

apartment next door to hers. Kati pushed back her chair, and started to get up as Weimeng burst into the room, crying out, "I'm sorry. You have to come. Mengjai is hysterical, and I can do nothing with him. Yesui has done something."

Kati rushed from the room, Huomeng shouting behind her, "What's going on?"

Mengjai sat on the floor in the middle of the room, crying his little heart out with racking sobs and kneading his hands in a pile of blackened debris looking like dirt and fabric shards mixed together. Yesui was huddled in a corner like a frightened, trapped animal, and she burst into tears when she saw her mother.

Kati picked up Mengjai, tried to comfort him, but he shrieked, and struggled.

"They were fighting over a toy, the big, stuffed mythical animal Mengjai got for his birthday," said Weimeng. "You know how he loved that animal, even slept with it."

"Yes."

"Well, Yesui took it away from him; he pounced on her and took it back, and then it just disappeared, poof, as if it was smoke. I couldn't believe my eyes."

"Yesui?" said Kati sternly. "What did you do with it?"

Her sobs were like hiccups. "I—I took it—away—where—he couldn't—get it."

"Yesui!" said Kati angrily. Huomeng came up behind her, took Mengjai from her, and the boy clung to him, arms around his neck, crying mournfully.

"What has she done now?" he growled.

Yesui looked like she'd just been struck. "Da! I brought it back! I—brought it—back." She looked at the pile of debris on the floor, and tears rolled down her cheeks.

"And that's what's left of it," said Kati, pointing.

"How could you be so cruel to your brother?" screamed Huomeng. "You are becoming a *bad* person!" He turned, and carried his son out of the room, mumbling to himself.

"DA!" screamed Yesui, and then she leaned her head against the wall; her eyes rolled upwards, eyelids fluttering.

And she was gone, her body limp.

"Aiyee!" screamed Weimeng.

Kati sat down on the floor, breathed deeply twice, and closed her eyes. A flash of purple stars, then the swirl of colors and a flash of green.

Yesui!

No answer. Kati began her search, remembering that no time would pass in the room she'd just left, and so she tried hard to be patient. But for her consciousness, time *did* pass, and it seemed forever. Yesui could be anywhere, perhaps already lost, beyond the range of her experience. Still, something held her in place: a presence, an overpowering feeling of both fear and sorrow. She'd sensed such a presence before, the first time Yesui had followed her to the gong-shi-jie. The child was nearby.

She drifted slowly. *Yesui, come back to me. You've done a bad thing, but we still love you. Your father's anger will pass, and Mengjai will forgive you if you're not cruel to him anymore.*

The presence was stronger, now. She neared the first signposts of the route to Abagai's special place, the huge, red vortex to her right. *Yesui, please. We want you back with us. We'll get a new monster for Mengjai, and he'll be happy again. But he will miss his sister!*

Ma! Ma—I can't!

Yesui, where are you?

Here! I—I can't get out!

Show yourself to me!

A flash of green. Kati's focus wavered, nearly driving her back to her own body when she saw Yesui's manifestation half-buried in the monstrous, red vortex that twisted real space into a singularity. She rushed to it, but dared not approach too closely, for she could already feel it pulling at her.

Ma! It's—it's pulling me in!

It's the great mass there!

I tried using the purple light, but it made it worse. The threads come so close together here. I'm stuck in a tiny hole, it's too tight! The green fan shook like a flame in high wind. *Ma, I'm sinking more!*

Get rid of the mass! Think it to here. Do what you did with the things in your room. Move the mass to the gong-shi-jie. Think it, Yesui, quickly! I don't want to lose you!

Yesui's manifestation jerked crazily. *If I—can— stretch—the threads*, then, *Ma! Get back! It's COMING!*

Kati reacted without thought, jumping to one side as a horrible, black thing erupted from the center of the vortex, writhing like a snake and breaking into branches, some reaching towards her. She fled, and watched from afar as the branches streamed to neighboring vortices, wavering there, smaller branches forming, then tiny filaments like twigs. The great, red vortex seemed to shrink, turning to orange, then yellow, as Yesui popped free and rushed towards her. *I'm out! I'm out! Oh, Ma!*

They melded together, and watched in awe as the black things that seemed alive broke into finer and finer pieces. And suddenly, where blackness had been, there was soft, violet light, flickering, and the place of creation was quiet again.

Quiet, yet different, changed by the action of a child. Where there was violet light, there now was structure in the gong-shi-jie, a quiescent smoothing between the vortices of stars, as if they were now influenced by each other. Still melded together, Kati and Yesui drifted closer. *I feel a pull, here, like a shallow vortex. There's much energy here*, said Kati.

I want to go, Ma.

Of course. But someday, I want to hear about how you make the mass move, and what these "threads" are you talk about. I've never seen them.

I will, Ma.

For the moment, it doesn't matter. You're here, and safe. Please, Yesui, do not be cruel to your little brother anymore. You are not that kind of person. You must be kind to all people. You are the Mei-lai-gong, the Empress of Light, and your powers must be used to help people, not hurt them.

Yes, Ma, I promise.

They drifted to Kati's vortex, and paused there. *Remember that we love you*, said Kati, a bit apprehensive about their return.

I will, and the fan of emerald green descended into the vortex before Kati.

She opened her eyes, as Weimeng said, "Kati went after her a moment ago. Yesui fled there, right after you scolded her."

"They're back," said Huomeng. He touched Kati on the shoulder, and went straight to Yesui, who held out her arms to him. "Da! I'm sorry, Da!"

Huomeng picked her up, and cuddled her. "I'm sorry, too."

Mengjai waddled past Kati, and held up his little

arms to be picked up. Huomeng scooped him up, and squeezed both children close. "I want my babies to be nice to each other," he said.

Yesui tried to put an arm around Mengjai, but he shrugged her off, and clung to his father. Yesui was suddenly very serious. "I will replace your monster, Mengjai. Da will buy you a new one, and I will work to pay for it. I will work, Da!"

Huomeng laughed. "I will hold you to that. To bed with you, now, and no more fighting."

They put them to bed, Mengjai sadly without his monster, and he looked up sullenly at Kati as she kissed him goodnight. Kati felt something, then, a terrible, disquieting feeling about her son, as if he had suddenly detached from her. She said nothing to Huomeng, but the feeling bothered her the rest of the evening, and she only let it go when her husband was again making love to her with great enthuthiasm.

And in the days to come, there was no more cruelty by Yesui against her brother. Mostly, she ignored him, and he ignored her also. Something inside of him had changed.

She was Empress of all the people, but still she was a Tumatsin, and it was the first Festival since she'd come to power. The ritual charge of Mandughai was now a thing of the past, replaced with a ceremony to commemorate the coming together of Tumatsin and Hansui to rid Shanji of invading forces from Tengri-Nayon.

Kati was thrilled to take part in Festival, but her schedule was tight and so they took flyers across the high plateau to the narrow, deep canyon with its waterfall and pool, and the burning coal-vein in the cavern of Tengri's eye. It was the childrens' first ride in a flyer and they had no fear, only excitement. Yesui enjoyed the sights, while Mengjai seemed more interested in what the pilot was doing to make them fly.

Yesui was amazed when Kati showed her the glassy spires of Three Peaks and told her how Yesui'd made them that way by bringing mass through the gong-shi-jie before her birth. "You can't move mass, Ma? I will show you how."

Kati laughed. "It is a special talent, dear. I can bring forth the light, as you can, but I only move mass in real space, not the place of creation. You may show me, but I doubt that I can do it."

For Kati, it was the recall of childhood memories as she pointed out the overgrown site of her home in the mountains, the routes she'd ridden on her beloved Sushua, the long trail to Festival, riding with her Tumatsin father on black Kaidu.

"You had *two* fathers?" asked Yesui, and Kati thought quickly.

"Mengmoshu is like a father by blood to me, but Temujin was my adopted father, and took care of me when I was a little girl. I will explain more when you're old enough to understand it."

Nothing could be hidden from Yesui. "But *Gong-Gong* is your *real* father. He just says I shouldn't tell anyone that, and so I won't. I will keep the secret."

How much did she know?

They landed at the mouth of the canyon: the royal family, several troopers and ten nobles hand-picked by Kati from the People's Congress. Horses awaited them, and Goldani was there on a magnificent chestnut, The Change upon her. They embraced warmly; Kati introduced Goldani to the children, who looked fearfully at the sharp incisors protruding from her mouth. "She is

Tumatsin, as I am. You will soon see me as she is," said Kati.

The children protested when Kati remained behind with the women leaders of the *ordus*. Huomeng mounted them on his horse, Mengjai in front of him, Yesui clasping him from behind, and they went off with the troopers and nobles down into the canyon.

She knew all the women; they were the ones she had met before the war, only now they smiled at her. "Will you wear a Tumatsin robe?" asked Goldani. "We still think of you as one of us."

"I'm honored to," she said, and shrugged out of her own, golden robe of office. The one they gave her was lighter, quilted with patches of red, brown and yellow, and felt cool. "I've brought something," she said, unwrapping a cloth bundle, and holding up a scabbarded sword. "It is the sword I used on that day, given to me by swordmaster Yung. It is not so pristine, now." She partially withdrew the sword to show the scratches and nicks on the curved blade, where once there had been the blood of warriors bioengineered for war.

The women all smiled approvingly. "It is most appropriate," said Goldani. "Now we will celebrate that day when we all came together. And we celebrate our Empress, who has made good her promises to us and brought down the barriers between two peoples. We have a mountain horse for your entrance."

It was a young mare, grey, with black spots, and colorful ribbons woven into black mane and tail. When she mounted her, Kati thought of Sushua, and there was a brief ache in her chest. She withdrew her sword, placed its pommel on her knee and The Change came upon her without thought, the gums in her mouth aching, face muscles tightening, and the emerald light from her eyes reflected from the metal of her blade.

The Change had not come upon her since that horrible day when she had killed so many, her heart filled with rage. Now it was there again, yet she felt serene and happy. It was a part of her, but she wondered what her children would think of it.

The women formed a line, and they went down into the canyon, Kati and Goldani in the lead. With the familiar, red sandstone walls closing in on them, the pungent odor of glistening coal seams, the sound of crowd noise and falling water ahead of them, Kati felt like she was coming home.

They came out onto the sandy beach by the pool, and the crowd was huge, suddenly quiet, packed shoulder to shoulder and shuffling back to make a lane for them. Many swords were thrust upwards as she passed by, and then the women were trilling, a sound she'd missed terribly. She looked for her family and didn't see them, but there were many familiar faces in the crowd.

They stopped before the pool. Goldani gave a short welcome, then gestured to Kati. In the emotion of the moment, she gave them a sign, bringing forth the light to form a visible, blue aura around her as she raised her arms.

"I see your swords raised, and I remember the day we came together as one people on Shanji. I'm blessed to be with you. Now, let us celebrate life, and each other thing we have to be thankful for, our loved ones, and our planet. Let us celebrate the new freedom of Shanji's people!"

"To the fields!" shouted Goldani.

The crowd cheered and trilled, drowning out the sound of the waterfall. The water had been allowed to continue falling during the opening of Festival, and there were no instructions regarding prayers before the Eye of Tengri. Festival had indeed changed.

Kati and Goldani led the women up the narrow, hanging canyon away from the beach, and finally she saw Huomeng and the children pausing by the Eye of Tengri. As she came up to them, Yesui turned in the saddle to look at her.

You look fierce, but your eyes are pretty. Why did you make that glow around you?

To give the people a sign of my power, dear. It makes them feel secure. The people need signs, Yesui. Otherwise, they don't have faith in what you do for them. The fire you see was a sign to them for many years.

It's only black rock burning in a cave.

Yesui turned back, unimpressed, as Huomeng urged his horse forward. And as they reached the plateau, there was another question.

Will I look like you, Ma? Will my face change like yours?

I don't know, dear. We'll have to wait and see, when you're older.

She truly didn't know, and the concepts of genetics still mystified her with their complex statistics. Yesui's powers were already far beyond hers, yet Mengjai was ordinary. Boys matured more slowly than girls; Huomeng had not shown his vast intelligence or the talents of a Searcher until the age of seven. Would Mengjai be like his father, or had the mixing of their bloods produced a son who would be forever normal? It had been a constant worry for her since his birth. But in the meantime, she was compelled to focus on Yesui's talents and develop them, and besides, Mengjai seemed closest to his father.

She thought this as they came to the plateau, covered with colorful *gert*, the playing field bordered by ribboned rope, the odors of cooking meat and ayrog in the air. Suddenly, she was excited, like the child in her memory.

They went straight to a large *ger* designated for the royal family, and dismounted. "You will sleep here," said Goldani. "The crowd is so great, there's not enough room on the beach, and all the *gert* here will be filled tonight. But the people are anticipating your heating of the pool for their bathing. They still think of it as a miracle."

"I will be happy to do that," said Kati, and Yesui again looked at her.

Another sign, dear.

The people streamed onto the plateau, and young boys rode straight to the playing field to show off their riding skills. The children went to the roped border to watch, and Kati was pleased when Yesui took Mengjai's hand to keep him close to her. He even allowed it, without complaint, and stayed by his sister the rest of the day. They seemed interested in all that they saw, but were excited by none of it, watching everything with stoic expressions while other children their age shrieked and clapped their hands at the antics on the field. Kati was disappointed by her children's reactions. They did not see the fun in Festival.

They ate lamb, breads, and potatoes mixed with squashes, the meal topped off with honeycakes. Huomeng was careful with the ayrog, but had enough of it to surreptitiously fondle his wife and Empress several times during the day. The nobles ate with them, but Kati forbade any talk of business and ordered them all to relax, enjoy themselves, and witness the Tumatsin culture.

Kati again felt disappointment that evening, when the little Tumatsin children went onto the field to receive their first horses. Goldani had talked about it for Yesui and Mengjai, offering Tumatsin gifts of mountain horses for them, but the children had shown no interest in riding and always stayed away from the animals, complaining that they smelled bad. Kati was diplomatic. Her children had no time for riding. She would buy two animals for each Festival, to be presented in her children's names to young ones whose families had no horses and could not afford to buy them.

Yesui and Mengjai watched the children receive their horses, heard the squeals of joy, the announcements of gifts in their names, all without reaction. Although interested, they saw no joy in the occasion, and Kati felt badly about it.

"They are like stone," she complained to Huomeng. "They feel nothing about what they see here."

Huomeng slid an arm around her shoulders. "You are Tumatsin, and they are not. You were born to this, and they are city children. Their life is in the palace, Kati, and they're happy there. This is an education for them."

"I know," she said, but wished it were otherwise.

It was no better that night, when Kati went down to the pool and made a great show of heating it, raising her arms and bringing forth a blue aura above the water. Within the glow, streamers of purple light from the gong-shi-jie heated the pool to steaming in an instant, and the people were properly awed, cheering and trilling. Yesui was not impressed, but took a short bath with her mother. Mengjai cried when his feet touched the hot water, so Huomeng held him in his lap at the edge of the pool.

That night, Yesui awakened screaming, twice, complaining of a dream. "I was in the vortex again, being sucked in. I couldn't *breathe*!" she cried. Kati soothed her both times, while Mengjai watched quietly, wide awake, and she had to tuck them both in again. By morning, both she and Huomeng felt like they'd had no sleep at all that night, and there was a whole day and night of Festival left for them.

The second day was the same. The men did their trick riding and shot their arrows, and her children just watched, not mingling with others, no efforts made to make friends with other children. Kati missed her brother, Baber, who again was away at sea with his nets, and Edi, the friend from her first Festival. The crowd was greater than usual, but many were missing, pursuing other things in their lives. She was almost glad when Festival came to a close, and it was time for the ritual charge of Mandughai, but even that was changed. Now it was Kati's charge, commemorating that day when her forces had swept down into the valley like a great wave to drown Mandughai's troops, the day she had ionized hundreds of fang-toothed monsters with light from the gong-shi-jie.

The ceremony was of her making, and something new. She assembled the men on horseback at the end of the playing field, The Change again upon her. "Remember the day!" she shouted, and raised her arms. Many meters overhead, a great ball of blue plasma flashed, sizzling, before their eyes. Heated air rose, forming a cloud that blocked out the light of Tengri-Khan, and a light mist fell only on the playing field. And then she raised her sword, and screamed "SHANJI!", leading them twice in a wild charge across the field.

It seemed that everyone but Kati had had a good time. The people filed by her in the hundreds to wish her well, smiling, mouthing their support for what she was doing for Shanji. But when the last of the ayrog was gone, the people began packing their things, and Festival was over.

Yesui again had nightmares that night, and all of them except Mengjai awoke exhausted. Mengjai seemed rested, and for once was in a happy mood. All of them were anxious to return home. They rode back to the flyers, and squeezed into them with the nobles and the troopers. Kati said her goodbyes to Goldani and the *ordu* leaders, who were all thrilled she'd joined them at Festival. None of them seemed to sense her dark mood. And when they lifted off, the children seemed to come back to life again, Mengjai sitting in the pilot's lap, pretending to steer the craft, Yesui chattering merrily about all the sights spread out below them. Kati leaned against her husband, and sighed.

I felt so at home there, but to the children it was another world. They are foreign to it.

Huomeng squeezed her gently. *I remember a frightened, little girl who was a foreigner in a strange place, and now she's Empress over all of it. Your world grew, and so will theirs. Home is where we are together, Kati, even in the heart.*

Kati snuggled against him. *You, and your words, but I love you anyway.*

Yesui looked back at them, and smiled.

Mengjai sat on his bed and cuddled Shizou while Yesui did all the work in cleaning up their room. It was her penance for taking his monster to the gong-shi-jie and being silly enough to think she could bring it back intact, even after her bad experiences with the other things she'd experimented with. Now he had a new monster and she had to do all the cleaning for six months, and Mengjai felt pleased with his efforts to make a mess for her.

Yesui did not react the way Mengjai wished. She seemed genuinely pleased to do the work, and was truly contrite about what she'd done to his first cuddly-toy. "I'm so sorry I hurt you," she'd said, "but I learned an important lesson. When I move mass, it breaks up into the tiniest pieces, and I must consciously reassemble it again. So far, I can't do it. I must begin with simple things."

Always bragging about her special abilities, but now she had to do real, physical work, and Mengjai was happy about it.

"There—all clean," she announced, then came over and sat on the edge of his bed, looking seriously at him.

"Have you forgiven me yet? You hardly say a word to me."

"I talk to Shizou," he said, squeezing the toy to him.

"He's a stuffed animal, not a person. What did you do today?"

"*Gong-Gong* took me to the pond for wading. I met a lady there."

"Show me," she said.

"She was a very nice lady. She said I was beautiful, and hugged me. *Gong-Gong* said it was all right to let her do it. He said Ma knows her very well."

"Why don't you show me? Ma and Da let me see all the time, but you never let me in."

Mengjai hugged Shizou harder. "Her name is Yang Xifeng. She was very sad, and cried when she hugged me. Her hands were soft."

"I know of her," said Yesui. "Ma had to do something to her mind to make her stop sleeping all the time. She was the Emperor's second wife, and her son died in the war. She has lost all her family, Mengjai. That's why she's so sad."

"She liked me," he said. "She wants to see me again."

"That's nice," said Yesui. "Are you ready to sleep, now?"

"Yes."

"Then I will be the mother." As he nestled into bed with Shizou, she pulled the covers up and tucked them under his chin. All the while, she was probing him, but as usual her efforts were feeble. "Goodnight, brother," she said.

"Goodnight." Mengjai closed his eyes as his sister turned out the lights to undress in darkness and get into her bed. He felt the coolness of sheets on her skin, so she'd gone to bed in her underclothes again. A vision of Yang Xifeng was in her mind, and himself wading in the pool, then nothingness as she quickly fell asleep. He lay there for awhile, deciding whether or not to give her another dream about the horrible vortex she'd hidden in, only to be foolishly trapped by it. He decided not to, for she was being nice to him, now. But he lay awake for a long time, thinking about the beautiful, swirling clouds in the gong-shi-jie, the vortices that were stars on the other side, the exhilaration of floating in emptiness above them. He wished he could really go there, and not just in the mind of his sister. He wished he could stretch the threads connecting the bright, purple points of their intersections, and move mass like his sister did; then maybe Ma would pay more attention to him. She would think he was special, like Yesui.

Mengjai decided he would continue his secret watching, and learn what he could, but if it turned out he was only a normal boy, there was another thing he could do to satisfy his yearnings to be where Yesui could go.

He would fly into space with his father.

CHAPTER SIX
LAN SUI

Standing on his balcony, far above the gates, Antun Wizera could still hear the angry shouts of the people. The swarm of humanity extended a hundred meters from either side of the gates, along the fences surrounding the compound, and seemed to grow larger and noisier with each passing hour.

He'd spoken to them earlier by loudspeaker, explaining again that the shutters must remain closed to maintain heat balance in the city, that he was doing everything possible to provide them with artificial lighting giving a sense of day and night. It was not enough for them. It was not the same, even when a day was the appearance and reappearance of Lan-Sui filling the sky over two minute intervals.

The planet whose atmosphere they floated in was now too cold to balance their heat losses, and he remained firm on his orders to keep the shutters closed.

Beyond the gates stood the spires of the city and ribbons of streets brightly lit in a myriad of colors to simulate those of Lan-Sui, but above them was only blackness, without stars or the turbulent bands of clouds to show them where they were. They were now a city-ship, in close orbit about a cold but lovely planet, and the people were not allowed to see it.

Antun Wizera sighed and went back into the room, closing the glass doors behind him. It was a formal dining room with a table seating twenty, now covered with embroidered linen. Large mirrors gave depth to the room, and the walls between them were papered with designs of entwined flowers. The ceiling was painted gold. Three chandeliers of delicate crystal hung from the ceiling, glowing dimly to give the room a peaceful mood.

The dining table had been cleared, Wizera's family retired for the evening, but Dorvod Tolui still sat there, sipping tea. Wizera sat down beside him and poured another cup for himself.

"What they want is such a simple thing, but I can't give it to them," he said.

"Most of the people understand that, sir. What you're hearing out there is a very vocal minority stirred up by absentee activists. You tell them the truth, but they believe the propaganda beamed at them from Gutien and Nan. It will continue until we can find those transmitters and shut them down."

Wizera sighed again. "No progress at all?"

"Sorry, sir," said his Chief of Staff. "They've gone deep, and on the moons the desire for independence is absolute. The workers are openly hostile towards Lan-Sui City, with words, but they'll do their jobs as long as Mandughai's military vessels remain here. They still think they can win her over to their side, even though she refuses communication with them."

Wizera chuckled. "Better they try it with Mandughai, and not her daughter. If Yesugen went after Kuril, his lifetime would be measured in minutes. And if this conflict drags on for many more years, it's Yesugen we'll be dealing with."

"We'll continue the search, sir. It's Kuril and the officers who fled with him who keep things stirred up."

Wizera banged his fist on the table, rattling cups on saucers. "To fit their own agendas! It continues to baffle me how such traitors could advance to the highest ranks in our police force, Dorvod. There must have been others behind them, even members of my own Council, and they're right *here*!"

"They all swear loyalty, sir. Our Sensitives found nothing, even with the use of drugs. The independence movement for Gutien and Nan has come from our intellectuals, sir, and they are not wealthy people. They see Gutien and Nan together as an independent, socialist state of workers, and you've given them the freedom to voice their opinions."

"So I have, and I don't regret it," said Wizera, "but what's happening now is something new, and it doesn't come from our intellectuals. My own police have become involved with the selective deportation of people from both Gutien and Nan. I had to first hear of this from Mandughai. Do you realize how humiliating that was for me?"

"Yes, sir. I'm sorry," said Tolui, lowering his eyes.

"Now she thinks I'm a complete fool, and perhaps I am. You wanted a secret service established, and I turned you down. I've been too trusting, Dorvod. Now you can have your secret police."

"Not police, sir, but an investigative bureau focused on the independence movement. We simply don't know who's behind it. I think Kuril has masters, sir. He's gotten rid of people for them, and now they hide him on the moons. He and his people are their only military force, but it gives them something to build on."

Wizera looked sharply at Tolui. "There's something you're not saying, Dorvod. Now is not the time to hold anything back from me."

Tolui swallowed hard. "Yes, sir. I think the independence movement is being used as a cover for something larger. I think there are people right here in Lan-Sui City who seek to overthrow your government."

Wizera's face flushed. "A coup? How long have you thought this way, Dorvod?"

"Since the city was shuttered closed, and within a week there was a call for independence of the moons. Too coincidental, sir. The people aren't happy being closed in. It's a perfect time to nurture opposition to your government, and things are going well in that direction. I think bringing Mandughai's military here was a wise decision, sir, but the people will resent it. We have to quickly find the real leaders behind the independence movement, and neutralize them. I want to begin my investigation right here in the city."

Wizera picked up his cup, but his hand shook and he spilled tea on the fine, linen table dressing. At that instant, they were interrupted by a soft voice from the doorway.

"Father? May I have a moment? I came to say goodnight."

Wizera willed his hand to be calm, and breathed

slowly, deeply, so as not to disturb his son. "Come in, Nokai. We were just finishing up, here."

Nokai seemed to glide rather than walk towards them. Slender at the shoulders, and tall for his age, he was dressed in a white sleeping robe, his coal-black hair in two pigtails hanging halfway down his back.

Wizera held out his hands, and the boy took them in his own, a gentle smile on his aquiline face, eyes dark and brooding.

"Good evening, Mister Tolui. I apologize for disturbing your conversation."

"Nice to see you again, Nokai. You've grown another inch or two, I see."

The boy smiled beautifully, and Wizera was suddenly at peace as the presence of his son washed over him. Nokai squeezed his hands warmly, and looked into his eyes.

"I heard the people shouting," he said softly. "They have no animosity towards you, Father. They only want things to be the way they were, and only a God can do that. You are not a God, you know."

"I know," said Wizera, putting his arms around the boy's waist, and hugging him, "but I thank the Gods, whoever they are, for giving my son to me."

Nokai placed a hand on his father's forehead, and smiled. "Ah, that's better. Your heart is quiet again, and now I can sleep well." He disengaged himself and bowed slightly to them.

"Good night, Mister Tolui—Father." He turned, and glided from the room, closing the door softly behind him.

Wizera leaned back in his chair, totally at peace with himself.

"An incredible boy," said Tolui. "He has the maturity of an adult, but he's only what, ten?"

"He will be eleven in four months. He is the joy in my life."

"An outstanding lad," said Tolui. "He will surely distinguish himself among the Sensitives when he's older. I feel his presence even now."

"He is never far from me, or his mother," said Wizera. "His touch is everywhere."

The maw of the freighter yawned wide, extending its narrow loading ramp for the crawlers. Seven machines worked second shift, hauling the frozen slabs of heavy water and canisters of pressurized gases for assembly and packaging in high orbit. The "day" on Gutien was only six hours, Lan-Sui now filling the sky, but moving rapidly west as Oghul Ghaimish worked his machine. Nearing the end of a twelve hour shift, his arms ached from jerking the heavy control bars, and his back was numb from the constant chattering of steel treads on rough terrain leading from the warehouse exit port to the freighter. The odor inside his environmental suit was now foul, and he itched in a thousand places, but there was no stopping to scratch himself once loading had begun.

The work was mechanical and repetitive: sweltering in the heat of warehouse lights while the cranes thumped icy slabs on the bed of his machine, the slow crawl to the freighter, the dangerous ascent of the steep ramp, then more hot lights. Back and forth, twelve hours of it, the horizon near and curving, heat, then cold, then heat again, all for a wage that had once been only pocket money for him.

When he finished his shift, Ghaimish turned over the machine to a man half his age who could barely comprehend the workings of a push-cart. He stripped out of his slimy suit and hung it to dry, then showered with the other drivers and laughed at their crude jokes. They ate together in the company messhall, and he endured still more of their blather, his reactions automatic, his mind somewhere else. He went back to his cubicle and locked himself in, enjoying a brief moment of quiet thought before there was a knock on his door.

"Yes?"

"It's Temur," came a voice.

Ghaimish opened the door to admit two men, both smaller than he, dark and swarthy, with broad shoulders. "You're early," he growled.

"They doubled up on my shift. I have to go out again in an hour," said Temur.

"Sacrifices for the cause," said Ghaimish, and he let them come in.

The space was barely large enough to accomodate them: a bunk, chair, small table, a sink in the wall next to a steel toilet. The walls were bare, the ceiling inches above their heads, a light panel glowing dimly there. On Gutien, a man's cubicle was his home, but he only slept there.

The men sat on the bunk, and Oghul Ghaimish pulled up the chair, sitting close to them to speak softly. He'd screened the cubicle for bugs, and kept an eye on the dark bulb of a receiver for the motion detector hidden in the outer door. If the bulb flashed, the topic of conversation would quickly change to something expected for men who worked cold freight for low wages.

"Any answer yet?" asked Ghaimish.

Temur nodded. "What we expected. She refuses to discuss anything with us, but guarantees our safety if we give ourselves up to her people."

Ghaimish laughed. "She's a fool to suggest it. Even

if we were willing to give up everything, the best case scenario would be deportation to Meng-shi-jie, and the many people there aching to get their hands on us. No, Temur, we must remain committed to this. We have our supporters, and the military presence of Meng-shi-jie cannot last forever. It's costly, and their expansion is slowed by it. There will be pressure from their own people to withdraw, if we only wait. Our friends in Lan-Sui City are patient people; they think in the long term. We must not make a move until those military vessels are gone."

"We will be patient with you, Tokta," said Temur.

"Be careful never to call me that outside this room," said the former Gutien Division Chief of the Lan-Sui police force.

"Yes, sir," said his number two, formerly a Captain, and now a hauler and stacker in Gutien's eastern warehouse. His real name was Baktu Kets, and he was like his superior in that he was a bachelor who had no family ties left in Lan-Sui City.

The third man looked up expectantly as Tokta Kuril turned to him and asked, "Is patience a virtue you share with us, Jumdshan? Your risk is even greater than ours, with your family here. You wouldn't want them to be a target for Meng-shi-jie weapons, would you?"

The man who was now Chief Steward of the Freightworkers Union bowed his head slightly. "I follow where you lead us, Tokta. I believe firmly in the cause of the workers, and owe you a debt for arranging my position. You give me the orders, and it will be done."

Tokta smiled. "When our day comes, you can be sure that all the workers will know about your contributions in making their lives better. Have you made any progress with that pilot you mentioned, the one who was transferred to Debris Control?"

"He agrees philosophically with our cause, but now enjoys the larger salary he receives in his new position. I've pointed out that most of it is hazard pay for patrolling the debris rings, and he has no disability insurance with the job because of it. He sees the unfairness of it, and will remain in our camp. But he's only a second pilot, and it will be some time before he's in a position to make command decisions. I helped him get his new job, with a flattering recommendation. He will listen to me. That's all I have to report, now, and I've left my station to do it. I must leave right away."

Tokta reached over, and patted the man's knee. "Then go quickly, friend, and work patiently with us. Our day is coming. We will have our new state, and the exploitation of the workers will be a thing of the past. The state will be theirs to command."

They shook hands, and Jumdshan left them. Tokta held up a hand in warning, watching the motion detector receiver for any sign of movement beyond the door, then sitting down again. "He's gone," he said.

"Inspiring," said Temur, "but what was that business about the pilot?"

Tokta pushed his chair closer, and spoke even softer than before. "It's nothing now, but it could mean something later. We need to have sympathizers among the freighter pilots, and the crews that patrol the debris rings. The freighters control shipping, and the armored patrol vessels control the safety of the system. They are busy people out there; there are constant collisions of ice and rock within the rings, hurling terrible things into the freighter lanes, even into low orbit near the city. Think how terrible it would be,

Temur, if a mountain-sized chunk of rock were suddenly to come crashing down on Lan-Sui City and all its helpless inhabitants, just because our debris control vessels were unable to intercept it."

"I see," said Temur.

Yesui was ten when she first saw Lan-Sui and its tiny moons. It was not a trip of pleasure, but training, and both her mother and Abagai were with her. She had learned much from them in finding her way around in the gong-shi-jie and defining the masses of stars by the colors of their vortices there, but those had been simple tasks compared to the locating of planets. The largest planets, all of them gaseous, showed up as tiny, blue dimples in the vortex of the host star. The smallest, like pebbles of metal and rock, did not show up at all. She learned to home in on a giant, then move deeper into the vortex through repeated transitions at random to search for the little ones.

How do you come to us so easily? she asked Abagai.

Ah, that's different, said her teacher. *First, there were the Moshuguang, like your grandfather, and then your mother. Their minds are like beacons to guide me, and yours is the strongest of all. I go to the mind, not the place. Your presence is so strong there are times I think you're two people.*

I cannot rely on a mind to guide me. There are too few of us, said Yesui.

True, but let me give you a demonstration. Yesugen, can you spare me a moment?

They were drifting near the vortex of Tengri-Khan, but the reply was instantaneous.

Yes, Mother. What do you want?

Just hold me in your mind a moment. I want to

show Yesui how close we can come to you. Kati is also with us, if you'd like to speak with her.

Yes, I would. She needs to understand our situation here.

Just hold the thought, dear. Do not make the transition before we arrive.

I understand.

Even Yesui could feel Yesugen's sudden presence pulling at her, but she followed her own mother and Abagai in a blur of swirling colors to the signature of Tengri-Nayon, diving into it without apparent target.

A huge planet banded in yellow, red and blue nearly filled her field of view, surrounded by several rings of debris so fine they seemed transparent. A dark moon floated nearby, its surface seemingly smooth, yet scarred with cracks and rills, and pin-points of light were there at several places. Just below them, only a few hundred meters away, was a monstrous ship of war, wedge-shaped, its surface bristling with antennae, shuttle cradles, and weapons manifolds.

It's beautiful, said Yesui, for she had never seen such a lovely planet.

Yes, it is, but alas, it is dying, growing colder by the year, and life has become hard for the people who live here. Yesugen, we're right above you. You did well.

Thank you. I'd like to meet Kati, now. Will she join me in the gong-shi-jie?

Certainly, said Yesui's mother, and she was gone.

Yesui again felt that flutter of fear when her mother was absent from her, but then Abagai said, *I'm still here, dear. Now let me show you another marvel. Down there, in the upper atmosphere of the planet we call Lan-Sui, is a floating city with many people. We are in good position, now. You see that large, blue spot near the equator, that oblong feature like a whirlpool?*

Yes.

The city is there. Target that feature with me. Put yourself there, in the very center of the whirlpool. Just let yourself go there, and I will follow you. We're in no hurry, dear. Relax.

It was not difficult at all, and Yesui even felt excitement in the doing of it. She felt a kind of pulling sensation, like when she slid along a vortex in random transitions to locate the small masses, feeling her way along the decreasing spaces between the threads of the interface between real space and the gong-shi-jie. This time, there was something more; she was not conscious of the threads, but of some other, unseen force, guiding her.

For Abagai, transition was a flash, but Yesui was conscious of her own return to the gong-shi-jie, coming out in the upper wall of Nayon's vortex, a short slide, then re-entrance, coming out again with bright light everywhere.

A thing like a crystal ball filled all space beneath her when she looked down. Its surface gleamed, so close it seemed she was nearly standing on it, but inside that surface was another ball of shining metal with several seams converging to a single point. It was huge, perhaps twenty or thirty kilometers across, and she'd nearly gone into it.

Do you see the city? It is round, like a moon.

I think I'm nearly touching it! said Yesui.

Really? Hmmm. Think of me, dear.

Yesui did that.

Now I have your viewpoint. Your accuracy was most extraordinary. My re-entrance point was hundreds of kilometers from here. How did you come so close?

I don't know, said Yesui. *It just happened that way.*

Well, here we are. Another time, we'll go inside it, but you see the clear shield that used to be the sky for the city when Lan-Sui was radiant and warm. Now the planet is cold, and the city is closed within a ball of metal and insulating material to retain heat and conserve power for other uses. The people live inside it, and cannot see this beautiful view. They are like travelers in a space-ship, traveling forever.

Why don't they go where it's warm? asked Yesui.

They want to, but nearby there is only my own planet, Meng-shi-jie, and we cannot accomodate them. There has been trouble because of this. That's why Yesugen is here with her warships. I'm sorry to say that the people who live here must remain here, forever.

Yesui had a sudden thought that seemed to bubble up from her unconscious mind without invitation.

If the planet is cold, why don't the people heat it up again? It's only a big ball of gas.

I can't imagine heating up something so large, dear, said Abagai, amused by the suggestion.

Why? You and mother both tell me there's infinite power in the gong-shi-jie. Use the purple light!

This time, there was hesitation before Abagai answered. *My understanding is that the problem is inadequate mass. When a mass of gas is compressed, it gives off heat, and if the mass is large enough, certain gases turn into liquid, and give off even more heat. This was true for Lan-Sui for millions of years, but now the compression has slowed so much that the planet is rapidly cooling. Lan-Sui doesn't have enough mass to speed up the compression, dear. You might ask your father to explain it to you better than I can. Now, let me show you the little, frozen moons, where*

*many more people are living. Follow me, this time.
I don't want to lose you again as I just did.*

So Yesui followed her, and saw the moons Gutien
and Nan, where working-class people lived underground in crowded towns owned by people in Lan-
Sui city. They lived in company housing and purchased
their goods in company stores, explained Abagai.
Tengri-Nayon was just a brilliant star in their sky, and
the gravity was quite low. Their children were all pale
and fragile. It was no wonder the people were not
satisfied, now that the heat was gone from the planet
that had warmed them.

A persistent thought now kept popping up in Yesui's
mind. If Lan-Sui needed more mass to become warm
again, then why not give it that mass? Dust and gas
were being continuously blown away by the fierce
winds of Tengri-Nayon, and much of it now resided
in a thick, spherical shell just beyond Lan-Sui. Also,
there was Tengri-Nayon itself. Obviously it had much
more than enough mass to sustain itself, for it was very
hot. Why not transfer mass to the interior of Lan-Sui,
and give the planet what it needed to be warm again?

It seemed like such a simple idea, and when they
returned to the gong-shi-jie she waited until Yesugen
had left before making her suggestion. Abagai and her
mother were discussing the conversation with Yesugen
when she boldly interrupted them to say, *I can make
Lan-Sui warm again.*

The women stopped in mid-sentence, and looked
at her with some annoyance for the interruption.

*Abagai says Lan-Sui needs more mass to be
warm. I can bring mass through the gong-shi-jie and
put it into Lan-Sui until it's as hot as the people
want it to be.*

There was a long silence, the women staring at her,

but Yesui knew that what she'd just said was being considered. Finally, her mother spoke.

You have confidence I never had when I was your age, darling, and your abilities are indeed beyond my own. But you've only begun to practice the moving of mass in the place of creation. Moving dust and gas from a star to empty space is one thing, but moving it to the interior of a planet is another. I think your idea is a good one, in principle, and should be considered. It's something that never occured to us, she said, looking at Abagai, who smiled and nodded in agreement.

I could begin right now, said Yesui, suddenly enthused.

Not so quickly, dear, said Abagai. *First, we must consider all the details of your idea, and consult with others. The balance of forces within a planet is a delicate thing, and you can't simply dump energy or mass into it. The planet could be terribly disturbed, and there's a city of many people floating in the atmosphere of Lan-Sui. You wouldn't want to hurt them, would you?*

No, but if I transfered just a tiny mass, it shouldn't hurt anything, and we could see what happens, she said impatiently.

This is not playtime, said her mother sternly. *We do not play with people's lives, Yesui. There are many details to consider: how much mass is needed, where to put it, even its composition.*

The composition of Tengri-Nayon and Lan-Sui is the same. That part is simple, said Yesui, and she was shocked by her own remark. Why had she said that, when she knew nothing about the compositions of stars or planets?

Have you been helping your brother with his lessons? asked her mother.

I have done some reading, she said quickly.

Well, you must do more of it, and consult with your father. He knows much about these things, and there are Moshuguang scientists who know even more. We must proceed slowly, Yesui, if what you propose is to happen. You must learn to measure the mass you move. You must learn to target the interior of a planet and navigate there, and these are things Abagai and I have never done. We will have to learn it with you.

They wanted to talk, consult, theorize, and wait, while Yesui felt compelled to experiment, starting at that moment. She felt some frustration, but her enthusiasm remained, for it was clear her idea was being taken seriously, and that pleased her.

Could we go inside Lan-Sui right now? See what it's like in there?

Not now, said her mother. *Abagai and I still have things to discuss, and I don't want you going alone.*

It made her angry. *Can I at least look at it again before we leave? It's so beautiful.*

Her mother raised an eyebrow. *Yes, you can look, but if you do anything else, I will know it. Promise me, Yesui. Come back when I call you.*

I promise.

Yesui went to the blue dimple in the vortex of Tengri-Nayon, and entered quickly there, coming out in real space at great distance from Lan-Sui, the planet now the size of a kick-ball held at arm's length. She was shocked by the distance, reminded of the delicacy of targeting even a large planet. This time she'd hurried, and Yesugen had not been there to guide her entrance, and so the error was large. This observation was sobering, and her confidence was shaken by it.

A plot had begun to take shape in her mind, but now she felt caution about pursuing it. Yesugen could not be there for her, but when Yesui had thought of the blue whirlpool that was a storm, she'd gone straight to the city without conscious focus, as if another mind had been there to guide her. If she could do it again, get close enough to see the storm, then the hop to the city, the tiniest slide would take her into the depths of Lan-Sui. But once she was there, could she bring the mass to her? Or would she have to drag it with her through all those steps in transition? The more she thought about it, the more her confidence seemed to weaken, but then her mother called to her.

Yesui, it's time to return. Come back, dear.

She returned instantly, followed her mother and Abagai back to the vortex of her home star, the wisp of spinning, purple mist that was the entrance to herself. The women were still talking when she left them.

She opened her eyes, lying on her bed. Mengjai was sitting before his learning machine, and turned to look at her.

"There's something here you should see," he said somberly.

He stood up so she could use his chair. She sat down, and peered at the screen of the machine. There she saw a theoretical model for the structure, composition and dynamics of all giant, gaseous planets that had been born with insuficient mass to become a star.

"I think it's a good model for Lan-Sui," said Mengjai, from behind her. "You must learn all of it before you try to move mass, and I will help you."

Yesui jerked around to look up at her brother standing there close to her shoulder. His eyes twinkled with amusement at her reaction.

"How do I know?" he asked.

"Yes," whispered Yesui.

Mengjai leaned close, and softly said, "Where you go, I go, sister, even in the gong-shi-jie. And you didn't even know I was there."

He was chuckling to himself as he left her room, and Yesui was still sitting there, unable to speak.

Yang-Xifeng was waiting for them at the edge of the pool in the hanging gardens just below the palace. She was robed in yellow and sat on a carpet of moss, eyes closed and face upturned to catch the warmth of Tengri-Khan. An open book lay in her lap.

Mengmoshu held Mengjai's hand as they went down the winding path of stone steps leading to the pool, and it seemed that the boy hesitated, pulling back on his grandfather. Mengmoshu found this strange, for Mengjai enjoyed his times with Yang-Xifeng: the quiet talks, gentle hugs, slender fingers smoothing the boy's hair, the little gestures of affection Mengmoshu wished his own daughter would show more often for her son.

They had met like this for three years, though Mengmoshu was always there to watch them, for he knew that beneath Yang-Xifeng's serene appearance was a lingering bitterness against Kati for the loss of Shan-lan, an only son. Her conversations with the boy did not reflect this, Mengjai could not see the darkness of her thoughts, and their times together seemed to momentarily soften her heart. Thus it was that Mengmoshu had allowed the visits to continue.

"Come sit with me, dear," said Yang-Xifeng sweetly, when she saw them.

Mengjai went to her, sat down, leaned against her as she hugged him, but his face was dark and brooding. Mengmoshu tried to penetrate his mind, but could not.

In the past year, Mengjai's mask had become a thing of stone, and he seemed to know when his grandfather was scanning him.

Yang-Xifeng's thoughts were clear enough. *Dear heart, you fill the void within me, a void left there by your mother's use of my son. In return, I will give you the love she holds back from you. I will treat you as if you were my own.*

They talked about little things: the carp in the pool, the book of poetry she'd been reading, then Mengjai's new studies with his learning machine. Mengjai's face softened, and he seemed to relax. Mengmoshu sat down nearby and pretended to watch the colorful fish, but he felt a tension that caused him to look often at his grandson, and he was looking at him when another dark thought came from Yang-Xifeng.

You are my little boy, now, not hers. I will love you and teach you, and as you grow older you will begin to see how evil she really is, how she uses people to—

Something passed through Mengmoshu's mind like white heat as he heard Yang-Xifeng gasp. She clutched at her chest, and Mengjai stood up, looking down at her. She looked back at him, mouth open, eyes wide with terror, and her body began to shake. The boy just stood there as she fell over on her side, legs kicking, chest heaving with uncontrolled spasms.

Mengmoshu jumped to his feet. "Mengjai!" he cried, but the boy didn't move, only looked down at the woman clawing at the moss beneath him. Mengmoshu ran to him, grabbed him by the shoulders and shook hard. The boy looked up at him, and there was no color in his eyes, only cold blackness there. Mengmoshu shook him again.

"Mengjai, release her. My grandson is not a murderer," he said softly.

A tiny tear issued forth from an eye as Mengjai whispered, "I do not want to see this woman again."

"Then it will be so," said Mengmoshu, "but now you must release her. She is ill, Mengjai. She's not responsible for her tortured thoughts."

Yang-Xifeng's spasms ceased in an instant, and now she lay prostrate, hands covering her face, sobbing uncontrollably. Mengjai walked away from her without looking back, and a guard appeared at the top of the steps, attracted there by the commotion at the pool.

"Take Yang-Xifeng back to her room, and call a physician immediately," instructed Mengmoshu. "I will be there to advise him within the hour."

The guard was helping the stricken woman to her feet as Mengmoshu hurried up the steps and along the curving stone path winding along the south wall of the palace, puffing heavily as he caught up to Mengjai and walked behind him.

They rode the elevator in silence to second level, and went straight to Mengjai's rooms. At the door, Mengmoshu grasped the boy's shoulders, turned him around, crouched down to look straight at his face. Mengjai's eyes were now brimming with tears.

"When you're ready to tell me, I will listen," said Mengmoshu softly. "What you have done, I have done to others. I will understand."

Mengjai's arms went around him, cheek against his in a fierce hug. "Thank you, Grandfather," murmured the boy, and then he released him and opened the door to enter his room.

During the brief instant the door was open, Mengmoshu saw Yesui inside the room, sitting at the learning machine, her mouth open with surprise, and then the door was closed again.

Oh, Mengjai. This is a complication we don't need now.

It was Yesui, but then her mask was in place again.

Mengmoshu sighed, and hurried away to advise Yang-Xifeng's physician.

CHAPTER SEVEN
REVELATIONS

After years of fighting, her children were suddenly close to each other and Kati felt relieved. They were constantly together now, usually in Mengjai's room where she often found them in animated discussion of something they'd called up on the learning machine.

She'd given them separate rooms when Yesui was ten, for the girl was becoming conscious of her own body and had expressed a desire for privacy. But it seemed she only slept there. The rest of the time, Yesui was with her brother and his learning machine.

Kati wished the children would get outside more; neither one had the strength she'd had at their age. They did not ride, or take lessons with the sword; long walks up and down the slopes of the city and around the terraced gardens seemed to be enough for them. Still, they did not seem frail, only slender, with skin white as porcelain.

For herself, there was little time for exercise. Once

a month, she made time for a lesson with Master Yung, and each time her body ached for days afterwards. Yung reminded her that in a few years she would be forty; she must practice regularly to maintain her flexibility and endurance, as he still did at the age of seventy-five. And he whacked his Empress soundly and often in *dongs* at sword's length, to emphasize his advice to her.

She also rode, but only occasionally, and always with her father. It was the only time they had any real privacy together and they would use the better part of a day for it, riding up into the mountains on the trail that had first brought her to the Emperor's city.

Kati had commissioned a pagoda to be placed at the summits of Three Peaks to commemorate Yesui's first miracle there, but publicly in memory of her dearest friend. It was a restful place, patterned after Stork's Tower where her beloved Shan-lan had painted and written his love poems to her. Four columns of *Tysk* supported the roof, and there were balconies looking out on the city to the north and the great sea glistening in the south. A full-sized figure of Shan-lan dominated the center of the floor, a casting in durable polymer that simulated wood, with a commemorative plate in bronze proclaiming, "In Loving Memory of Shan-lan: Artist, Poet, Warrior, Crown Prince and Dearest Friend. Wang Mengnu-shan-shi-jie, Year 2322."

It was the only artifact or document of her entire reign that would ever bear her full, formal name.

She and Mengmoshu had recently made the climb to the pagoda, and he'd said something there that disturbed her greatly, a revelation that had led to Kati's first real connection with her son. The conversation had begun pleasantly enough. They stood out on a balcony to look at the city sparkling in afternoon light.

"I hear that the young people have discovered this place," said her father. "It's said that lovers meet here." He raised an eyebrow, and pretended to scowl at her.

Kati laughed. "How lovely that is, when beneath this structure is the meadow where a man first touched me in a tender way. But I hear that writers and artists also come here. Shan-lan would be quite pleased with that."

Mengmoshu put an arm around her. "Memories," he said softly.

"Yes." She leaned her head on his shoulder. "Painful memories."

"But you are here, and there is peace, and Shanji is becoming a good place for all the people."

"Only because we work together. I could not begin to do it by myself, Father. Even the nobles have done far more than I expected."

"You pay them quite generously with land," he said, squeezing her.

"I pay them for good faith in the system. Their investments have been extreme: the reactors, mag-rails, cryogenics, hydrolysis plants, and now the new city in the northeast. They are rich in land and holdings, but the opulence of their private lives is not what it was under the Emperor. I hear that the wives complain about it."

Mengmoshu chuckled. "They live better than their Empress. You are most austere."

"My life is work, my husband and the children. What more can I want?" she said softly.

"More quiet times like this?" he asked, teasing her.

"That *would* be nice, though I must say that there's been much more peace in the palace since the truce was declared between Yesui and Mengjai. They seem to be inseparable, now, and yet Yesui would have little to do with her brother until I gave them separate rooms."

"Perhaps they were closer together than you thought."

"No, this is something new, and sudden. Now Yesui even praises her brother's intelligence, and calls him her teacher. Mengjai says nothing, and I cannot penetrate his mind. He has *always* closed himself off from me and it frightens me a little. Sometimes I fear I've lost him because of all the attention I've given to Yesui."

"Let's sit awhile," said Mengmoshu. He led her to a bench before the statue of Shan-lan, and they sat down to face it. "Surely you don't question Mengjai's intelligence, Kati."

"I did for awhile, Father, but not now. His progress with the learning machine is twice what mine was at his age. He is like his father."

"Then let me tell you what I think of my grandson," said Mengmoshu, taking her hand in his. "I think he's like *both* of you, and chooses not to let us see it. I think he hides a power that Yesui has recently become aware of, and that's why they're now so close to each other."

Kati looked at him in surprise. "What reason do you have for saying that? There is no Searcher with greater abilities than yours, Father. Have you been able to penetrate his mind?"

"Absolutely not," said Mengmoshu, shaking his head emphatically. "He remains as much a mystery to me as he does to you. I've *never* been able to read him, even when he was very small. Absolute control, that boy, yet his moods change with what I'm thinking: worry, peace, anger. I see it reflected in his behavior when we're together. It's as if he's constantly scanning me, yet I feel nothing."

"I've never felt his presence," said Kati sorrowfully, and Mengmoshu squeezed her hand.

"There is something you need to hear, Kati," said Mengmoshu softly. "It seems you have two exceptional children, not one."

"I love them both dearly, Father. You know that," she said defensively.

"I know, but there was an incident just weeks ago that tells me something powerful lurks behind that dark wall Mengjai puts up in front of us. It involved Yang-Xifeng, and I wasn't going to tell you about it, but now I think I should."

"Poor woman," said Kati. "I'm told she suffered a relapse, and is confined to bed again. I thought she was coming along nicely, and she's been so nice to Mengjai."

"So it seemed to me also, Kati, but she still blames you for the loss of her husband and son. There's a dark hatred inside her."

Kati sighed. "I'm aware of it. My hope is that she'll eventually let go of that, and be well again. There is good in her."

"Yes, you would say that," said her father. "I thought it so, when Mengjai was younger and Yang-Xifeng would cuddle him in her lap and cry with joy at his touch. Lately it has changed. Her thoughts have sinister overtones. She thinks of turning a son against his mother, and weeks ago she went too far with it."

"Did you say something?" asked Kati, suddenly concerned.

Mengmoshu paused, then said, "I didn't have to. Mengjai apparently heard her thoughts, and struck her dumb without moving a hand."

"What?" Kati recoiled from her father, putting a hand to her mouth.

Mengmoshu reached out to take her hand in his, and told her the entire story of the incident with Yang-Xifeng, then the return to Mengjai's room.

"Yesui knows about him, Kati, I'm certain of it. He is a Searcher; I can only guess at his level of development, but it's undoubtedly high."

"High enough to paralyze a human being," she said, deeply disturbed by what she'd just heard.

"Kati, promise me you will not admonish Mengjai for what he did. Yang-Xifeng was recovered physically within an hour, and she knows what happened to her. Mengjai has given her new reason to reconsider her hatred for you. What he did might even aid her eventual recovery."

"I will not criticize his action, Father, but I *will* tell him I know about the incident. I wish I'd known about it sooner."

"Sorry," said Mengmoshu, patting her hand. "After my talk with Mengjai, I thought he might reveal his abilities to you and give you a pleasant surprise. He is a complex boy."

"Then he *is* like his father," said Kati, feeling a strange mix of joy and concern. "Why would he keep his abilities hidden?"

"I don't know. Ask him. Acknowledge him. He knows you love him. For what other reason would he have done what he did to Yang-Xifeng?"

"I've neglected him," Kati said mournfully.

"Yes, you have, but it's easy enough to correct."

And she did. As soon as they'd returned to the palace, Kati went straight to Mengjai's room, and knocked softly on the door.

Come in, Mother, said Yesui, teasing.

They were both there at the learning machine, and Mengjai's eyes were wide with fear. Yesui only grinned at her. Kati pulled up a chair beside Mengjai, turning him by the shoulders so he was facing her. She pressed her lips together, and spoke without words.

Your grandfather has told me what happened with Yang-Xifeng. He says you are a Searcher, and have chosen to hide it from us. In doing so, you have closed yourself off from me and your father, and we cannot see into the heart of our son. I cannot share your joys, or sorrows, yet I love you with all my heart, and I believe you see that. I want to know you as you really are. I want to know my son! Please, Mengjai, talk to me. Come back to me! Tears suddenly flooded her eyes. She put her arms around him, and hugged him to her.

Her heart ached as she felt his arms go around her, one hand patting her back as if to comfort a little child. *I did not think it was important,* he said, *but I was going to tell you someday, Mother. I thought that someday I might be like Yesui, but I'm not.*

"Oh, my darling!" cried Kati, and she squeezed him so hard he grunted. "Do you think I love Yesui more because of her abilities? I love *both* of you, and not for your powers. You are my *children!*" She reached out a hand, and Yesui moved closer to embrace both of them.

She felt him, then, for the first time, a feeling that warmed her all over as he opened his heart to her. That first time would be forever in her memory, that first time when she felt a connection to her son.

Kati looked at Yesui. *Your sister's grin betrays her. She knew her brother was a Searcher, when the rest of the family did not.*

I only found out last year, said Yesui. *He was very sneaky about it.*

Kati released them, and laughed. "Now that I know, we must tell it to your father."

"Oh—I—I've talked to him without words," said Mengjai.

"What? He knows, and didn't tell me?" Now Kati felt angry, and betrayed. "He knows his son is a Searcher?"

"Not exactly," said Mengjai quickly, and Yesui looked alarmed. "I think he feels I'm very sensitive to him, that he senses my thoughts directly rather than me giving them to him. He hasn't thought it was anything special."

"Well, we'll talk about that later. Your father is very proud of you, Mengjai. Do not hide yourself from him. We both love you.

I know, Mother. I promise.

As Kati left the room, she caught one wisp of thought, and it was coming from Yesui.

I think Father is in trouble.

Kati masked herself fiercely. *Yes, he is.*

But when she confronted Huomeng that night, as they were preparing for bed, it was not as she expected.

"You haven't told me you speak to Mengjai without words, dear. Mengjai mentioned it to me just today," she said casually.

"Of course I do. Don't you?" he said, slipping into a robe for sleeping. "It's not like it is between you and me, but I hear him, and he hears me since the time he was little. I must admit that lately I've begun to wonder if there was something more. Mengjai is certainly sensitive to me, but my range is not what your father's is, and even Mengmoshu can only go out a hundred meters or so."

Kati masked herself hard, so he would not see that she had not attempted to communicate with Mengjai without words until that very day. "Mengjai has not seemed sensitive to me until now, and only because I confronted him."

Kati then told her husband about the conversation with Mengmoshu, including his opinions about his grandson, and described what had happened in Mengjai's room. Huomeng listened silently, and then they climbed into bed, her husband pulling her over to him, as usual, to cuddle her.

They lay quietly for a moment, then Kati said, "What is it that you wonder about our son?"

"As I said, it is my limited range. And lately, oh, within the last year or two, Mengjai has begun speaking to me when I'm on the mothership, or in transit to and from it. Very clear, and strong, always asking questions, some quite technical. He's learning very fast, Kati. Our son is brilliant. Yesui talked to me in space when she was very little, but now it's like she and Mengjai are there together. Maybe not. First one talks to me, then the other. I've never heard them speak to each other. If Mengjai is a Searcher, he has an unheard-of range, Kati. The mothership is out there some two thousand kilometers. I've begun to wonder if the children are somehow linked together."

Both of them fell asleep, still wondering about it.

"They're asleep," said Mengjai.

"Let's give them an hour before we go. Mother has her best connection to the gong-shi-jie right now, and that's when Abagai is most likely to be there. I'm glad they didn't fight. Mother was angry when she left us," whispered Yesui.

"Yes, but Father is getting dangerously close to the truth."

Yesui smiled. "In a way, he knew it before I did.

I didn't know you were with me when I talked to Father in space."

"You admit you were fooled, then?"

"I didn't say that," said Yesui. "I always felt something there, but I couldn't identify it. It was when I started saying things I had no knowledge about that I began to wonder."

"You were still surprised when I told you. We should tell Mother and Father everything. It's not fair to give them a partial truth."

"Not just yet," said Yesui. "There are some things I want to do first."

"Like now."

"Yes. What you've taught me in theory is fine, but I have to get in there to really see what I'm dealing with."

"It's a simple model, Yesui. You need to double the mass, and Tengri-Nayon has the best composition for it. The size of Lan-Sui's rocky core is irrelevant; you're dealing with a big ball of hydrogen and helium. Put the mass anywhere, and convection plus planetary rotation should distribute it. The helium rain should begin right away, and that alone should increase the surface temperature."

"It sounds easy, brother, but you're not doing it. I have to do the navigating *and* the mass transfer, and I can't do it in steps. Every time I leave mass in the gong-shi-jie for even an instant, it turns into that flickering, violet light that bends real space. I have to bring mass directly to Lan-Sui's interior, and you are my target."

"If I can stay there while you flit in and out," said Mengjai.

"Only experimentation will work; there's no theory for this," said his sister.

Mengjai nodded in agreement. "This game is dangerous. Take only a small piece of a flare, better still a prominence, where the densities are smaller. Too much mass could be like hurling a comet into the upper atmosphere."

"Yes, Mengjai. We've gone over this many times."

"Then let's do it! They must be fast asleep by now."

Yesui put a finger to her lips. "Wait a little, and call up that image of Tengri-Nayon again."

Mengjai's fingers jabbed at the keyboard, and an image of Tengri-Nayon appeared, a single prominence forming an arch above its surface. Yesui outlined a portion of it with her finger. "How much mass?" she asked.

Mengjai did the calculation carefully on his machine. "About a thousandth of Meng-shi-jie's mass. We want to see an effect, don't we? Try a larger portion, maybe out to here." He made a new outline with his finger on the screen. "That should be like a very large comet, and you'll be deep inside, but not too deep, I hope. We don't want to wait months or years to see an effect."

"I'll be happy just to get into the interior," said Yesui, and then she closed her eyes. Mengjai did it also, and they both listened.

"I think we can go, now," said Yesui. "Let's get comfortable."

They lay side by side on Mengjai's bed. If anyone came in the room, it would appear they had fallen asleep together, and only their parents or grandfather would know otherwise.

You're excited, said Mengjai.

Apprehensive. This is the first thing we've really done together, brother.

Lead on, said Mengjai. Their hands touched, and

joined, fingers entwined as Yesui let out a slow exhalation, and they were on their way.

Yesui seemed in no hurry at first, spreading the threads of the spiderweb-like interface of the gong-shi-jie, and closing it behind them.

Do you realize you're twisting real space when you do that? If you did that on a large scale, whole galaxies could be smashed together.

Really? Maybe I should give more attention to it.

The swirl of purple light, with the colorful signatures of stars stretched far in every direction, and they drifted without manifestation on their secretive mission to the vortex of Tengri-Nayon, already in view, yet nearly two light-years distant in real space.

You're still not relaxed, Yesui.

I'm thinking about what I have to do, brother. You only have to observe.

Yes, but what happens to you, happens to me, and we'll both do better if we relax.

Yes, yes. Yesui was still apprehensive, despite her solo time in the gong-shi-jie. There was a new presence in her consciousness, now, and it was different from her mother and Abagai being there. *Do not talk so much,* she said. *Let me concentrate.*

I am a mute, said Mengjai, and then he was silent for her.

They hovered above the vortex of Tengri-Nayon and the tiny blue dimple there that was Lan-Sui, dropping slowly towards it, correcting for drift, then dropping again. Yesui did not aim for the exact center of the dimple, but away from it, and was pleased with their first entrance when they came out into real space with Lan-Sui filling half their field of view.

We're nearly as deep as the moons! Abagai did little better than this, and Yesugen was here to guide us.

Yes, it's very good, but you went too fast. The threads went by me in a flash, and I wanted to see their patterns here.

You didn't say anything!

You told me to be quiet!

All right, you can talk, now. I feel better. Where is the storm that locates the city?

Real time passed as they searched for it. *Over to the left, right at the limb. It's just now coming around,* said Mengjai.

I think I can get closer. I'm going back.

Slowly, both ways. I want to study the thread patterns.

Yes, I heard! Don't nag me about it!

The slowness of her transition in both directions was designed to taunt him, but it was just what he wanted. He could see the pattern of threads that was the fabric of space, outlining a parabolic-shaped dimple with little shelf-like irregularities at two places. *There!* he said. *You can see the planet's edge, and that second irregularity must be the surface of the rocky core. You should navigate from here. Try it!*

I see it. But I want to try it my way first. I want to jump to the city, then to the interior.

Why? That's the hard way.

Because I want to! Then I'll try it your way. There's more than one way to do things, Mengjai!

All right, all right, I'm just an observer, and I promise not to pout.

Good, she said, and they were once again in Tengri-Nayon's vortex. This time, Yesui aimed closer to the center of the planetary dimple, and she also studied the thread pattern as they passed through it to real space.

Ohhh! she said, quite pleased with herself. Lan-Sui

filled their view, and the blue storm was right in front of them, the planet having rotated a quarter of a revolution while they were in the gong-shi-jie. *I'm getting very good at this.*

The hard way, said Mengjai. *Now what are you doing?*

Thinking of the city. Trying—trying—to get that feeling—yes, it's there, but weaker than the last time. Do you feel it? Like a force, pulling at me.

Mengjai concentrated. *More like a presence. Hello? Is someone there?*

They listened. No response, but the feeling was still there, as before. *So gentle*, said Yesui. *Yes, I think it's a person, but there's no awareness of us. I'm going to it, Mengjai, letting it take us to the city like it did before.*

That's why you wanted to do this, said Mengjai. He felt his sister letting go of her own will, to follow this gentle feeling washing over both of them—

And they were meters away from the clear shield surrounding Lan-Sui City, a great swirl of methane blue filling their field of view.

It worked again. We've targeted on someone here, but the feeling is the same, not stronger. It's not a Searcher's mind, said Mengjai.

But isn't it wonderful? said Yesui. *Such a peaceful feeling, like dreaming. It comes from the city.*

Her thoughts were open to him. *No, not now. We can look inside the city another time. Real time is flowing, Yesui, and we're in the upper atmosphere. Make your jump now.* She was momentarily distracted, mesmerized by the warm feeling that came from inside the city. She hesitated.

Please, Yesui. We have a purpose in being here. Let's get on with it!

Mmmm, she murmured, still mesmerized. *Just a moment, Mengjai. You are in too much of a hurry.*

There was nothing he could do, and so he waited impatiently, resisting the sense of peace that flooded over him. His mind wandered, then, and suddenly the city was gone, and all around them was white, swirling mist with streamers of blue.

We're inside, now, Yesui said casually.

We can't be very deep. That blue stuff is methane ice. We must be in the storm below the city. Can you make a translation at this depth?

His view flickered once, and the clouds around them were again white, but with swirls of yellow and red.

Is that better? she asked, and he felt her confidence growing huge.

Yes, but do you know where we are?

It doesn't matter, as long as we're not below the city. I do my job, now you do yours. Concentrate, and remain here while I go back to the gong-shi-jie for mass transfer. Tell me when you're ready, brother.

Mengjai looked for a swirl of color, a misty form, anything to concentrate on. He found a light blue cloud with the shape of an amoeba, focusing on it as the cloud began to change shape. *Go!* he said.

The cloud disappeared.

The vortex of Tengri-Nayon swirled below him.

MENGJAI! screamed Yesui.

I'm sorry. I guess I wasn't ready.

Now we have to do it all over again!

So use the thread patterns. It's easier, and now we've done it your way. You promised.

Oh, YOU! All right! We'll use the threads, but they won't tell me where the city is.

Now they will. The city is in daylight, if we hurry. Go to the nightside of the pattern. Hurry, Yesui!

They re-entered, crawling along threads like a spider in its web, the parabolic net of green threads glowing in total blackness. *Just below the surface—right here!* said Mengjai. *Remember it!* he shouted, as they made the transition.

Swirling clouds, with even more red and yellow than before. *The point is fixed in my mind, but it moves in real space. I want you* here, *Mengjai. Don't you make me do this again!*

I'll do my best. I hope we're not completely glued together.

It was something they hadn't considered before, and what he said seemed to calm his sister's anger.

If you think that, it will be true, she said. *I only need an instant in real time. Now CONCENTRATE!*

It was difficult, for everything was moving around them, and there were no permanent features to focus on. He thought of himself as a dust mote held in place by the eddies around him, spinning him, caressing him. *I am here,* he thought. *Hold me here.* His field of view blurred, as if he'd been suddenly absorbed by what was there, holding him in a kind of dreamworld.

He didn't even feel Yesui's departure.

And then his dreamworld exploded with a bright, horrible flash, and Yesui was screaming at him, *Come with me!*

They were back in the gong-shi-jie, and near the center of Tengri-Nayon's vortex a new mist of violet light flickered there before being sucked back into the depths.

Are you all right?

Yes, just a bit disoriented. It happened so fast. I'm afraid I panicked. Nothing could have hurt us in there, but I still panicked. I hope I haven't done something horrible, Mengjai. Oh, I'm afraid to look again.

Don't bother. It'll be at least days, maybe weeks before something shows up. The mass was small, wasn't it?

About what you calculated.

Then don't worry about it. You did it, Yesui! It'll be much easier, next time.

If there is a next time, said Yesui, still shaken. *Let's go back, right now. I've never felt so exhausted.*

I'm tired, myself, from the little I did, he said, and they hurried back to the single, purple vortex that was the entrance to both of them, re-entering it in a flash.

Mengjai's hand was numb from Yesui's squeezing of it, and there was no time for talk as they both opened their eyes, both sensing the same thing.

"Mother is awake," whispered Yesui. She leapt from the bed, and hurried out of his room, her mind totally masked from anyone else, though he could still sense her panic.

Mengjai turned out the lights, and quickly burrowed beneath the covers with his clothes still on. He breathed deeply, and held a vision of the great mothership in his mind. He let it grow, and brighten as the moments dragged by.

He heard a click as the door opened, and Mother was there, probing him. He showed her his vision.

There was a dark suspicion in her mind. *A nice dream—perhaps. But something did rouse me, dear. I hope you and Yesui aren't playing some new kind of game with me.*

The door closed, and she was gone, opening the door to Yesui's room, and in his sister's mind there were only the swirling colors of the gong-shi-jie.

❖   ❖   ❖

Nokai Wizera moaned in his sleep, and turned over on his side, pressing a cheek deep into his pillow. Perhaps it was a dream, but there was no vision of it, only a feeling, a wonderful feeling that made him want to laugh. It stayed with him, growing in strength until he was nearly awake, and then suddenly it was gone and he was left with a terrible sense of loss, of aloneness that brought an ache to his heart. *Please come back*, he thought. *Whoever you are, come back to me.*

He put an arm around his pillow, and cuddled it to his face.

CHAPTER EIGHT
RELATIONS

Civilized life spread steadily to the surface of Meng-shi-jie as soon as the stream of building materials from Shanji began to arrive regularly. And after a million years of violent activity, Tengri-Nayon had calmed to grumbling in only a decade. Now it burned steadily, an infant main sequence star looking forward to a lifetime of ten billion years.

With the stabilization of the solar constant, the atmosphere of Meng-shi-jie also calmed, with regular weather patterns varying weakly with the seasons, for Meng-shi-jie's rotation axis was nearly vertical to the ecliptic plane. The original mining settlements had been in the north at a latitude of fifty degrees, and it was there that civilization first appeared on the surface. It was there that the rains fell hard one month of each year, filling the great aquifers and underground lakes and nourishing the seedling trees brought from Shanji.

At first, there were only dugouts, structures of clay and stone half-buried in the ground, but then buildings of steel and concrete rose in their place, workers swarming like ants on scaffolds of white-bark. There was no shortage of labor, because the migrants had come; the work was something they could do, for many were unskilled. But Abagai refused to take advantage of them; she paid all an honest wage and guaranteed each worker a family apartment in the structure he helped to build. It was the migrants who built the first cities on the surface of Meng-shi-jie. They built the great aque-ducts that distributed the subterranean water; they planted the trees, and put down the concrete for the first streets while their children studied hard and learned skills their parents had never dreamed of. And in time, the children of those children would hold prominent places in the society of Meng-shi-jie, for with diversity in a culture comes strength.

Still, life was difficult in the early days on the surface. There was a long season of extreme heat, followed by a month of torrential rain, then heat again. The ozone layer was a feeble thing, and ultraviolet light a constant danger. People sweltered terribly in the heat, for only heavy clothing would protect their skin. With every breeze came clouds of sand and fine dust from the great deserts to the south. Respiratory ailments were commonplace, and even Abagai was not spared. She developed a deep, hacking cough, and began wearing a mask when she was outside. But the cough persisted, and sapped her strength, for she was now nearly eighty years old. More and more, she gave Yesugen the responsibility for man-aging everyday affairs, and kept to her rooms and office in the cool basement of the twenty-story building which housed the administrators, project managers and high-ranking military officers on Meng-shi-jie.

She'd been outside earlier in the day, and her chest ached. Even the mask did not filter out all the fine dust, and now those sharp, crystalline grains were scratching at her lungs again. Yesugen's apartment and offices were right above hers, connected by a helical staircase and an elevator. Lately, she used the elevator, for the stairs left her breathless. They had breakfasted together, and Yesugen had taken her to the greenhouse at the top of their building to see the new plant varieties and look over the city.

Hybrid *Tysk* lined streets radiating from the city's hub in morning light, and they were beautifully green. By mid-day, their leaves would roll up into tubes, conserving moisture in the heat, and so morning and early evening were the best times to see the greening of Meng-shi-jie.

Now she was back in the blessed coolness of her rooms, and it was time for a communication she had delayed until she could be sure her proposal was more than conjecture. Wizera would find it extraordinary, but hopefully believable, for he knew about the gong-shi-jie and Abagai's travels there. Her own genetic line went back to the Sensitives on Lan-Sui, and she'd searched for her own kind there long before she'd found Kati. No one there could do what Kati could do, and now there was Yesui. It was time for Wizera to know about them.

Her message to Lan-Sui was sent to Yesugen's flag-ship, and coded for "Governor's Eyes Only" before being relayed.

"Dear Antun," she said to her machine. "The time

has come for me to tell you about two extraordinary
people who have joined me in the gong-shi-jie. They
come from the extension of my genetic line through
the Moshuguang on the planet named Shanji. One of
them is now Empress of that planet, and the other
is her daughter, now seventeen. Both are far beyond
me in ability, and what they can do might bring life
back to Lan-Sui if you are willing to take risks that
might threaten your city."

She described Kati and Yesui in detail: personalities,
their movement of light and mass, including what Kati
had done in the war on Shanji, their clandestine visit
to Lan-Sui as mental apparitions, then Yesui's suggestion to transfer mass to Lan-Sui and heat it up
again.

"Yesui has become adept at moving mass in and
out of single stars, but she has not yet worked with
planets. We would have to proceed slowly and cautiously in many steps, but I'm convinced the girl can
bring Lan-Sui to its former self if you allow her to
do it. The approval for this project must come from
you, Antun, since it's your people who take the risks
involved. Yesui herself is confident and eager to
begin, but I'm not pressing you for a decision now.
I only want your comments on her idea as soon as
possible."

Message sent, she waited, and bathed in the huge
tub surrounded by potted plants in one room of her
living quarters. A meal was sent in and she meditated,
breathing in highly filtered air and feeling some
strength returning to her old body. Yesugen called once
to brief her on a meeting. The Advisory Council was
growing impatient about the continued watch over
Lan-Sui. The troops there could also be used for hard
labor in tearing down the old, subterranean villages

and converting them to cool pleasure centers by the lakes. She heard Kabul speaking to Yesugen in the background. She thought of the way her daughter now looked at the man, even when a mother was present, and she was gladdened by it. She was most curious about what they did with each other when the work-day was done, for now it seemed they were always together.

It was late evening when Wizera's reply finally arrived. Her machine beeped, and she urged her legs to move faster as she went to it. Only words on the screen, no image of his face, for the message was again coded for top secrecy. She wished to see his face, to read him in any way she could, but it was not possible this time.

"Dearest Mandughai," he said. "Your message is astonishing to me, yet I must believe what you say because you have never given me any reason to doubt your words. Still, I'm shocked to hear that such powers exist, and I am a person familiar with unusual abilities. My own son is a brilliant Sensitive, and I deal with him every day. My fear is that my people will not believe such news; they will think it a false promise I make to give them hope. The risks involved are extreme, as I see it, and a project like this must be a long-term thing to avoid disaster. It could take a life-time, or longer, to achieve, and there is only one person, this Yesui, who can do it. I have my doubts, Mandughai, though the restoration of Lan-Sui would be the answer to all the prayers I send to the forces that truly govern us.

"Yes, I wish to further discuss your proposal, but it must be done in secret. I do not wish to raise false hopes or concern with my people at this time. It is enough that Lan-Sui shows occasional spurts of life that could threaten us. Over the last few years, several new storms have appeared, but all to the north of us. Their roots were not deep, and they lasted only months, but if we'd been trapped in any of them the city would have been destroyed. Natural events, Mandughai, but the nerves of my people are already on edge because of them.

"Please send me a detailed plan as soon as possible. I would also like to meet this girl, Yesui, if it can be arranged, and also her mother. Let us move forward with this marvelous idea, but with careful thought."

Abagai saved the message to cube, and stored it in her desk. *Well, it's a beginning*, she thought.

The family was nearly finished with their meal when Antun returned to the room. He sat down silently across from his wife and son at the center of the long dining table, and picked absently at his food.

Nokai frowned at him. "You're troubled, Father," he said.

"Bad news, dear?" asked Hira, his wife of twenty years. She had worn a gown, instead of a robe, and it had slipped a bit, revealing a bare shoulder. Her face was long, with the delicate features she had passed on to their son.

Antun looked up, and smiled. "No. It was a message from Mandughai. Nothing bad." He picked at his food again, deep in thought, but felt their eyes on him, felt Nokai meld with his emotions to bring him peace. Finally, he put down his utensil, and looked hard at both of them.

"All right. I will share what I just heard, but it must not leave this room. No one else must hear about this. Do you understand?"

"Yes, Father," said Nokai.

"Of course, dear," said Hira sweetly.

If he did not tell them now, Hira would only coax it out of him in a dream, and Nokai had even more subtle ways of doing the same thing. But it was Nokai, as a novice Sensitive, who knew the histories of the Mandughai. Antun looked at his son when he spoke.

"You know about the gong-shi-jie, and the travels of the Mandughai there?" he asked.

"It is the source of creation, the place from which light came to form the universe. It is without form, or void, or time, having only energy, and the Mandughai travel there as apparitions of thought," said Nokai reverently. "They are one with The Mother. It is what I strive for, Father. I would be with The Mother, and do good works for Her Creation." It was a recitation, as taught in his classes.

"But few are chosen," said Antun softly, his heart full of love for the delicate young man sitting across from him.

"Yes, few. There have been thirty-three in our history, and now there are only two," said Nokai.

"There are four, my son," said Antun, and Nokai's eyes widened.

"We've not heard of any others besides the Empress of Meng-shi-jie and her daughter. Who are they?"

Antun explained, reciting what Abagai had just told him. Hira listened with interest, but remained silent, for she recognized that the true conversation was between her husband and son. Nokai seemed distracted at first, looking away from him, but when Antun described Yesui's idea for bringing new life to Lan-Sui, the boy looked at him with fierce attention.

"She's been *here*?" asked Nokai.

"Well, not really. She resides on Shanji, with her mother. Abagai says Yesui has been here. I suppose—"

"It is the spirit, the essence of a being that travels with the Mandughai. Only the body is absent, but the presence is all-seeing, all-knowing," said Nokai. His voice was soft, and reverent.

"You make her sound like a goddess," said Hira.

"She is. She can move mass in and out of the gong-shi-jie. She is The One we have awaited for thousands of years, and now she has come. She has come to Lan-Sui, and I—"

Nokai stopped himself, lips pressed tightly together, breathing quick. He put his hands to his face, and when he lowered them a serene smile was there. "She is the Mei-lai-gong, Father, the Empress of Light. The Mother has sent Her to us to give life to Lan-Sui. If She says it is to be done, it will be done. Blessed be The Mother. She has seen our plight, and sent The One to help us. Do not refuse Her offerings, Father. It *will* be done."

The boy leaned back in his chair, hands clasped over his chest in a prayerful attitude, while his parents stared at him in confusion.

"How many times has she come here?" whispered Nokai, eyes now closed.

"Yesui? I've only heard of the one time," said Antun.

Nokai laughed with delight, and clapped his hands. "Oh, there have been many other times. She is laughter, and sorrow. She is love, and anger. She is joy."

The boy stood up, still smiling at something beautiful in his mind. He leaned over the table to look closely at his father with moist, dark eyes, and said, "She is the Mei-lai-gong—and her name is Yesui."

And then he walked jauntily out of the room.

Antun looked at Hira with amazement. "What has gotten *into* that boy?"

Hira smiled, and reached out a hand to touch his. "He is sixteen, dear, and the body changes. Our son is in love with a dream."

Nokai paced his room, trying to still the pounding of his heart. He went out on his balcony to look out at the city lights, then up towards a black, steel sky. Tears came to his eyes, his hands clutching at the steel grating of the balcony like a trapped prisoner. He looked up at the blackness, and concentrated hard as if in desperate prayer, hoping that somehow he would be heard.

I have felt your presence so many times, but only now do I know who you are. Your presence here has brought me joy, and laughter, a feeling of connection to The Mother and a world I want to be a part of. Have you sensed the presence of this humble Sensitive? Do you know I even exist? I am not a telepath; I sense only feelings. How can I talk to you? How can I know you?

When you come again, I will be ready. I will do the best I can, but first I will call out your name. Yesui—Yesui. I am Nokai. Come back to me. Please come back to me.

He went back into his room, and got into bed. It was silent in the room, and his mind was quiet, with no visions, sounds, or foreign presences to disturb it. He quickly fell asleep, cheek pressed against a pillow that was soon moist.

"Yesui," he sighed, as sleep enveloped him.

✧   ✧   ✧

Everyone stood when she and Kabul entered the room. Yesugen carried the thick document they'd studied the previous night, and placed it before her as she sat down.

"Sit," she said.

Besides the conference table, and walls covered with architectural drawings, the room was sparsely furnished with a few chairs for relevant guests to these meetings. One chair was now occupied by a man who seemed out of place, a man whom Yesugen would soon call on to support her position on the matters contained in the document being considered.

He was dressed in military blues, stretched tight over a broad, thick chest, and he sat rigidly at attention in the chair, his feet barely touching the floor. His red eyes glared straight ahead, moving ever so slightly to scan the faces around the table, and two tusks protruded slightly from a tightly pressed mouth. Ribbons of field campaigns adorned his chest, including the one in gold leaf for the battle of Shanji, and there was a huge scar along his left cheek from a wound taken there.

What could not be seen were the purplish scar tissues along his right thigh, tissues that still cracked and bled whenever he became too cold. They came from a day when a young woman with blazing emerald eyes had raised her arms on a distant planet, and brought forth a purple light that had reduced most of his battalion to dust and hot gas. Now he sat and waited for the call of the woman he, and others like him, regarded as the true Empress of Meng-shi-jie.

Yesugen thumped her fingers on the document, and said, "We have read this, and considered it carefully.

Your figures seem to be accurate, and we cannot question the economic logic. We certainly agree that our continued presence at Lan-Sui is a drain on resources we can use for our own expansion. Where we disagree is on the political necessity of stabilizing the Lan-Sui system, and also on the kinds of resources needed for our expansion. If the revolt on Lan-Sui is allowed to occur, we risk losing future supplies of vital fuels, and I will not take that risk."

Ghazan scowled, and raised his hand to seek an audience.

"No," said Yesugen firmly. "Tonight you are here to listen, and nothing more." She glared at Ghazan, and saw Kabul also turn to frown at him. She probed their minds, saw nothing to indicate resentment against the man who now shared her power. It was Kabul they now sought out for private audiences, in hopes he could soften her stands during an intimate moment, and occasionally she allowed them success in doing it.

"I am, however, willing to make a compromise with you," she went on. "We have a better idea of what we're up against, now. The work of our migrant volunteers as moon laborers has been successful in isolating the location of the rebel leaders. They are on the moon Gutien, and Tokta Kuril is among them. I intend to take them all by force, if necessary, and until that is done we will not leave Lan-Sui. I anticipate a ground offensive to accomplish this, and the moon must not be destroyed in the process. Because of this, I'm willing to pull out all but two of our heavy ships, leaving only the flagship and a light cruiser. But the freighters and all ground forces will remain."

There were scowls all around the table, and muted grumbles.

"Listen to me!" she said, and it was quiet again.

"You cite the loss of expendable supplies in our watch over Lan-Sui. Most of these are involved with our heavy ship operations, and I'm giving them back to you. But when you suggest the use of our troops as hard laborers on Meng-shi-jie, our opinions diverge greatly. These men have but one purpose in life: the defense of Meng-shi-jie and all its allies. I need not recite the history of their deeds; you have learned it as children. And I will not speak further in their behalf. Instead, I have brought one of them to speak for all, a man whose proud line goes back to our first war of independence. He is Master Sergeant Yumzhagin Tsedenbol, a veteran of many campaigns, including Shanji, and twice decorated with our highest honor, the Order of Mandughai. Sergeant, if you would give us a few words, please."

Tsedenbol stood up, and walked to the far end of the table with a slight limp. He turned sharply and faced her, at a brace. Short, stocky arms rigidly at his sides, his eyes never left Yesugen's, and seemed to glow as he spoke.

"You are our Empress, our Commander, and our lives are yours to command. There are no families in our lives, no offspring, only the clones of our bodies who come after us. But when we are born, we have the memories of all who have gone before us, those who have fought bravely for the preservation of Meng-shi-jie."

At first, his voice had quivered with nervousness, but now, as he looked into Yesugen's eyes, it was a growl.

"I remember my death day in the first war of

independence. I remember my foster mother pinning the Order of Mandughai on my chest when I was in hospital after the second war. And I remember being a man with one leg after the third war which finally rid us of Lan-Sui. Each night, I live those lives over in my dreams. I have fought the pirates. I have fought the rebellion against Mandughai the First. Both times I died in battle. Now, in this life, I bear the scars of battle against The One who comes from The Mother, and now She is our ally. That memory will be there when I come again.

"I am bred for war. I am a soldier. It is my purpose, my reason for being. My life is The Corps. Thirty-one of my bodies rest with comrades in one of the caverns you would turn into pleasure parks. Will we still be there when you're finished? Will you throw us away?"

He paused, and there was a horrible silence in the room. Everyone except Yesugen was looking down at the table in front of them.

"If my Empress orders me to take the spade and dig in the dirt, then I will do it. I will follow her orders and move the dirt, but inside of me I will be dead. I will no longer be a soldier, but a digger of dirt. My purpose will be gone and the brave memories of my line will end with me. I will be dead forever."

He looked at Yesugen now with terrible intensity, and what she felt inside him brought her near tears.

"I speak for all my comrades, Ma'am. We will follow your every command, but please don't do this to us."

A pause, and Yesugen let it drag on.

"Thank you, Sergeant," she finally said. "You may leave, but please wait outside for a moment."

He left. Kabul smiled faintly at her. The rest were still looking down at the table.

"Our troops will remain where they are. You will have to find others to build your pleasure parks," said Yesugen. "This meeting is adjourned."

All of them left without saying a word, or looking at her.

"They will be after me tomorrow," said Kabul.

"And you will listen to them," she said.

They left the room, and found Tsedenbol standing there. Yesugen went to him, leaned over and put her arms around him, holding him close, and whispering into his ear, "Brave soldier of mine, your memories are safe. Now you have a ship to catch, and good hunting!"

He grinned at her. "Thank you, Ma'am. You can rely on us!"

They left him standing there, still grinning, as they went to Yesugen's living quarters to prepare for bed after the long day. They undressed each other, saying nothing, and slipped naked into bed, Yesugen nestling against him, Kabul's arms going around her, hands stroking shoulders, arms, the swelling in her stomach that was still hidden when she was dressed.

"We'll have to do something about this soon," he said, patting her stomach.

"Mother will announce our marriage next week," she said. "I've reminded her twice, and now she's written it down. She's not well, Kabul. I worry about her."

His hand moved down her arm, and over to a breast. "She should stay inside more. The constant dust isn't good for a person her age."

"Then *you* tell her. She won't listen to me." Yesugen tilted her chin, and kissed him softly. "I think she deliberately put you into my life, you know. She's very fond of you."

"I'm in her debt," he said, and kissed her back, his hand moving again. "And I love her daughter with all my heart."

"As I love you," Yesugen murmured, and then she gave herself up completely to him again.

CHAPTER NINE
MORTALITY

Yesui returned to her rooms in a downcast mood, for the happenings of the day had been her first experience with death. Juimoshu had died quietly in her sleep at the age of eighty-five, and the royal family had attended her funeral in the mountain vault that was the mausoleum for all past nobility and royalty of Shanji over its two thousand year history.

Yesui had only met Juimoshu a couple of times, but had touched her mentally and heard the stories of those days when her mother had first come to the Emperor's city. She'd not felt close to Juimoshu, though her mother considered the woman a dear friend, and thus they had attended the funeral.

The vault was deep in the mountain, beyond the Moshuguang laboratories and the caverns, now museums for the first wedge-shaped shuttles which had brought the people to Shanji. All the past Emperors were interred there, their granitic tombs marked with plates of bronze and receptacles for candles and incense. Panels of orange lights glowed dimly in a high ceiling of rough-hewn basalt, and Yesui had felt closed in, a squeezing sensation in her chest. Candles burned at many places along the walls. Her mother lit two new ones, and also incense, with a wave of her hand at the crypt of Shan-lan, and Yesui felt her sadness, her sense of loss. *You are gone forever, but my love remains, dear friend.*

Juimoshu's withered body was robed in Moshuguang black and lay in a concrete box lined with polished *Tysk*. There were no priests, no formal religions among the educated on Shanji, only an understanding that before the universe and the gong-shi-jie, there had been powers beyond comprehension, and those powers were still at work. The friends of Juimoshu spoke of her, exchanging fond memories, and they placed flowers in the casket. Their Empress placed a green pebble in the woman's stiff hands and then four workers lifted a slab of enameled copper to cover the casket, following that with a slab of concrete lifted by machine. Even as they walked away, another machine was lifting the closed casket to slide it into its final resting place within a recess in cold stone.

Yesui was already depressed, but then her mother pointed to other places along the walls, places with bronze plates without inscriptions, and she said, "Those are for us, when our times come."

By the time they got back to the tunnel and the mag-rail awaiting them, Yesui was nearly in tears, for her mother was open to her, and she was thinking of the ones she loved: her family, including *Gong-Gong*, and especially Abagai, who was now very old. She was thinking about losing them. For the first time, Yesui thought about losing her own mother, so much a part of her, and so the tears came. Her mother sensed it without looking, and took her hand as they seated themselves in the mag-rail car.

We are all mortal, dear. We live, and we die, and our atoms are scattered to become parts of new things. The atoms in your body have come from the deaths of stars, and they have been used for many things before you existed. Only the atoms are permanent, Yesui. All life is a transient thing.

But an atom is not aware of itself, thought Yesui, as her mother squeezed her hand. *It does not seem right for that to be so.*

They went back to the palace in silence, Mengjai staying behind with his father for a private inspection of the old shuttles there. At the door to Yesui's rooms, her mother took her by the shoulders and looked closely at her.

"I want to see Abagai, Yesui, and I want to see her alone. Will you feel badly if I ask you to remain here?"

"No, Mother. I understand. She is very old."

Her mother kissed her. "I knew you would see the reason. I will call when we are finished."

"Do you mind if I wait for you in the gong-shi-jie? I promise not to follow you, and there are some things I want to try with the violet light there. It might be useful for our project with Lan-Sui, Mother."

"Very well. I think that Abagai and I will be traveling quite far this time."

"I understand, Mother. She has made promises for years, and now you will hold her to them."

"Yes, dear." Her mother smiled, kissed her again, and left her.

So Yesui returned to her rooms in a downcast mood, her mother thinking of Abagai growing old and dying before they could make a promised trip to a distant galaxy where there was a special place to be seen. Yesui did not like her own bad mood, knew that only action would relieve it, and so she called to her brother.

Mengjai, I have a new idea for Lan-Sui, and I want to leave right away. Can you come with me?

We're on our way back now, came the reply. *Give me about fifteen minutes.*

Hurry!

As it turned out, his rush was not so necessary, for their mother had found several documents awaiting her review and signature, and was now working at her desk. Mengjai arrived with time to spare, but his excitement was not about traveling with his sister in the gong-shi-jie.

"I saw all the control systems, and sat in the pilot's seat! Father says that in two years my body will be ready for training in space, and he wants to start me out as a navigator! I can see myself now, piloting a freighter all the way to Tengri-Nayon, actually *being* there."

"You've already been there, many times."

"It's not the same, and you know it. It's not being their physically, walking on Meng-shi-jie, or seeing Lan-Sui city with real eyes. I don't *feel* anything when we're there. It's more like a dream. I want to *be* there!"

She felt the longing in his heart, and was strangely disappointed by it. "Will you go with me now?"

"Sure I will. Let's see what new idea you've come up with."

"As soon as Mother leaves. I think she and Abagai are going to that other galaxy they've talked about for years. Mother is afraid that Abagai will die before they make the trip."

"No wonder, after today. That was depressing," said Mengjai. "All that talk about death. I was glad to get out of there. I'm too young to think about death. My life is just beginning."

"You're still a mortal, and so am I, brother," she said, but Mengjai only shrugged and smiled at her.

And it was only a few minutes later when they felt their mother leave them, a part of her gone, although her body was still alive. A part of her was gone, as if in death, yet Yesui knew she would return. So it was not death. It was not permanent. Still, there was a similarity there that bothered her, and would continue to bother her for many years before she finally understood.

"Now, but carefully. I want to be certain about where she is," said Yesui.

There was no conscious effort on their part, no touch or ceremony required. They were simply together when they willed it. But their entrance to the place of creation was made cautiously, their emergence slow, without manifestation. *There*, said Yesui, without fear of detection, for the connection with her brother was something unobservable by any others, including her mother and Abagai. Together, as they were now, they were one mind, and she could mask for both of them.

Her mother never traveled without manifestation in the gong-shi-jie. Yesui suspected she could not do otherwise, but knew that Abagai had done it on more than one occasion, a shadowy presence that only Yesui herself could detect. The column of emerald green that was her mother drifted slowly to the vortex of Tengri-Nayon, within view, and waited there. Yesui heard her call, then the happy reply, and Abagai appeared in a flash, the two figures melding together in greeting. Yesui had never seen the two of them like this, thinking they were alone. Their affectionate feelings threatened Yesui's composure, and she made a conscious effort to retain her invisibility.

Her mother and Abagai chattered like children, exchanging news. Yesui caught the news of storms on Lan-Sui, and Yesugen's new love, before they drifted out of sight in the direction of Abagai's special place. *Now!* she said. *I've discovered some new things I can do, Mengjai, and I think they can be useful for Lan-Sui. I don't think what we've been doing there is going to work.*

That's because you're not using enough mass, or going deep enough.

Maybe, but you said yourself the ideal model would be to add low density mass everywhere, at the same instant, and it's not happening that way. Let me show you something.

They drifted to the vortex of Tengri-Nayon.

Mengjia asked: *Something's different here. Where did all the violet light come from?*

I've been bringing it in from the edge of our galaxy.

Why go so far? I've seen you make it by transferring mass from real space to here.

But only a little, and there is a great quantity of it around our galaxy. It's easier to just bring it here. Yesui seemed quite pleased with what she was telling him, and was leading him on. He obliged her with a question.

I thought you couldn't move this stuff. You said it was "sticky."

Were you with me when I said that, brother? That was a long time ago.

Then, and before then, said Mengjai smugly.

Aha, she said. *Well, anyway, yes, I couldn't move it with any speed. All other light here moves from A to B when I think it so. The violet light would not. It flickers all the time. It's here, and not here, over and over again, at very high frequency.*

I can see that. But light is light. What's the difference?

The violet light is not light, Mengjai. It is mass, she said dramatically.

Impossible! It's far too hot here, Yesui. We're surrounded by the light of creation. It had to pass through the interface to real space before it could cool enough to form mass.

Heavy particles first, then lighter ones, dying fast and making even lighter ones that make up our universe, said Yesui.

Yes, but that happened very fast. When it was done, it was done.

I agree, said Yesui, still leading him on, and nearly giggling with excitement, but still he indulged her patiently.

So, how can there be mass in the gong-shi-jie? he asked.

It's only here part of the time, where it seems like light. In real space it is a dark mass, but again only part of the time. The rest of the time it is HERE!

The transition was sudden, and they were not in real space. They were at the interface, and faint lines of green ran in every direction to infinity. Off to their right was the dense, parabolic-shaped pattern they'd used to target Lan-Sui in the vortex of Tengri-Nayon. *We are in it*, said Yesui.

In what? This is the interface, the fabric of space. Now he was becoming impatient with her.

The interface IS the mass, brother. It spends most of its time here. It was you who led me here, Mengjai, and now I've found it! I come HERE to move the violet light, not in the gong-shi-jie. It's "sticky," yes, because it is attached everywhere to real space. It IS the fabric of space. All those lines you see, I want you to be patient with me, pick one, and look closely. Relax. I'm trying to explain!

It was an effort, but he relaxed, and didn't focus so hard, and Yesui helped by moving in for a closer look at the threads. What he saw astounded him, for the threads were not constant, but flickering, and seemed to be broken at regular intervals into closely-spaced pieces.

I haven't figured out the green color, said Yesui casually. *I think it's illusion, an average between real space and the gong-shi-jie. Do you see the holes?*

The threads are broken in pieces, he said, *and they flicker.*

All right, they're oblong holes. That's where the mass passes back and forth. Where there's a thread, there's mass—for a while. Dark mass, if you want to call it that. I don't know what it is, but it makes the threads, and the normal mass comes to it. See over there, by Tengri-Nayon, how the threads get so dense?

The star's mass distorts space.

No. There was a distortion there before the star formed. Very small, but it was there, and the normal mass came to it.

You have it all backwards, said Mengjai.

You think you're so smart, she said. *Let me show you something you don't have in your learning machine. Watch those parallel threads right in front of us. I'm bringing the violet light there—now!*

She only thought it, and it was there, but it was not violet light he saw. The threads suddenly brightened, and were no longer parallel, coming closer together, and bending to form a small depression like a shallow hole, which began to move. *Now you see my new way of moving mass*, she said proudly.

The depression moved with increasing speed towards Tengri-Nayon, leaving behind the normal pattern of threads far apart and parallel. *You see how they attract each other?* she said. *Where one is, the other wants to be.*

When the disturbance in the threads reached the great depression that was Tengri-Nayon, it melded into it and was gone, and everything was quiet again.

I've put mass into a star, and uniformly, well, sort of. More went in towards the center, but some went in everywhere. I'm going to do that with Lan-Sui.

Dark mass in Lan-Sui? You don't even know what it IS! And do you have any idea how much mass you just moved? That "ripple" of yours was five times the size of what we see for Lan-Sui.

No, I don't. I'll have to work on that. But you get the idea.

Yesui! You frighten me to death with your hurry to do things! We don't know the composition, and the mass equivalent of that violet light is huge, from what I just saw. You could blow up a planet, or a star with that stuff!

I suppose so, she said, not impressed. *But what about the idea, Mengjai?*

I don't know, he said, oscillating between excitement and fright. *Let me think.* Something new was crawling in his mind, and Yesui waited patiently for him to dig at it.

You can certainly transfer lots of mass, and that will speed up Lan-Sui's compression. That's good. We don't know the composition of the mass, and that's bad. Compression is good, but heat takes a long time to get to the surface. We really need a helium rain to get the upper level heating started quickly. Dark mass by itself won't do. We need hydrogen, and especially helium along with it.

I've tried that, Mengjai, and all I do is make local storms. There's no distribution of mass like you predicted, she chided.

So use the dark mass to guide the hydrogen and helium. Use them together, from here! Bring in the violet light as you just did, then get mass from Tengri-Nayon and add to it. You can do it right now, Yesui. Try it!

All right, mister genius. Let's see if you can be right this time!

And so she tried his idea—three times—while Mengjai watched from the interface. The violet light moved easily for her, and it was obvious she'd had much practice with it. Each time it came, forming a well-defined depression in the fabric of space, a thing already moving as she fled to bring mass back from Tengri-Nayon. The first time she did not account for the motion, and missed the depression by a wide margin, the mass scattering over the interface as the depression disappeared into Tengri-Nayon. The second time she was closer, but the result was the same, and now she was angry.

I will start further out, she grumbled, then disappeared, back in a flash to form a new depression twice as far from Tengri-Nayon than before. It moved more slowly now, and before Mengjai could speak she was gone and back again, and with her came ripples in the threads which rushed into the depression, making it deeper as it rushed headlong into Tengri-Nayon and was absorbed there.

That's IT! he shouted. *Oh, I would give anything to have seen that in real space. It must have been spectacular!*

Yesui seemed exhausted by the effort. *It is very precise, brother. Very difficult.*

But it will work! And not just for Lan-Sui. Do you see what you've done, Yesui? You've taken mass without destroying it in the gong-shi-jie, and moved it at high speed just by bending the fabric of space. The dark mass does the accelerating. You can move anything this way. Oh, oh, the possibilities here. A spaceship, a planet, anything can be moved.

Yesui did not seem impressed. *Your imagination is soaring, brother,* she said, *and my mind is a blur. I don't think you realize how difficult that was for me. I've never had to concentrate so hard before. I want to stop, now.*

Yes, yes, of course. We can try other things another time; find a small asteroid, maybe, and move it, or something even smaller that—

Enough. I'm tired, and we've been here too long anyway. I promised Mother I'd meet her.

Very well, he said reluctantly, for he already had several new experiments in mind for her to try. *You've reached another stage, Yesui, and I didn't even see it coming. You've been practicing without me.*

You don't always have to be with me, Mengjai, and my practice is easier without your chattering.

I didn't feel you go.

You are not so observant as you think, brother, and your work with Father has been conveniently distracting.

I will fly in space with him, Yesui, and you will move our ship!

Perhaps, she said, as they came out into the gong-shi-jie, still totally immersed in themselves.

Two great columns of emerald green awaited them. It was their mother and Abagai, and the looks on the faces of the two women were expressions of both surprise, and pure horror.

They melded together in a warm embrace without touch.

Again, said Abagai, then frowning. *You are upset, Kati. A problem?*

No. I just wanted to see you again. I want to make that journey with you that we've talked about for years. I want to do it now, before . . . before it's too late. Kati opened her mind, and let Abagai see the events of her day.

Ahhh, said Abagai. *Another reminder of my mortality, but it is true. We should have gone before now, but much has distracted me.*

Abagai brought Kati up-to-date about the situation on Lan-Sui, including the mysterious storms there, and then she smiled.

There's also good news. Yesugen has found love with Kabul, and she bears his child. We had a grand wedding just weeks ago, and I cannot think of a time when I've been so happy, even with you. Her heart fairly bursts with love for the man, and my tears were bubbling during the entire ceremony. It's what I've always wanted for her, Kati. A love to soften her heart, and finally she has it.

They were drifting automatically towards Abagai's observing place, past a yellow vortex that had once been deep red, changed forever by a special child. *I'm happy for you, Abagai, and for Yesugen. Perhaps there's hope yet for my Yesui. She shows no interest whatsoever in boys.*

Abagai laughed, as they neared the edge of the galaxy with its quiescent clouds of violet light. *You're not nearly as old as I, Kati, and already you think of heirs. Well, so do I. We have our daughters, but wonder who will come after them.*

They did not stop this time, but drifted steadily outwards through violet mist that seemed to fade, then was gone, and they were in a featureless void. Far ahead was a colorful wheel of another universe only Abagai had seen before. Now they were finally going there, and Kati could not suppress her sorrow, somehow feeling it would be the first time and the last time for them to see this place together.

You think of my mortality, dear, and it is realistic. I'm not well, and I think there's little time left for me. But we're here, now, and this moment is ours. There is a wonderful place I want you to see. And I want you to enjoy it after I'm gone.

Oh, Abagai! cried Kati.

Now, now.

The galactic wheel was now large, yet they had drifted only a little while, and in real space light would have to travel for millions of years to reach it. But here they were, already coming in close, and Kati could see the clouds of violet light tucked in around the wheel like a great, misty disk with a bulge in its center. Patterns of vortices began to appear, great swirls of them, but towards the center of the wheel their colors were blurred together, as if smeared by the strokes of a great brush.

There are seven whorls of dust and gas where new stars are forming, Kati. We are going to the innermost

*of those, to the left of the hub. You see the line of
orange and yellow vortices?*

Yes.

*You pick the third one from the bottom of the
pattern, the one in orange. That is the first signpost.*

They were coming in nearly perpendicular to the
galaxy, the great wheel of it filling their view, and to
her right the number of vortices was huge, packed so
densely together she could barely distinguish them
individually, for the short spaces between them were
filled with violet mist.

Here we are, said Abagai. They came in to a vortex
in deep orange, nearly red, and again there were the
swirling clouds in blue and purple beyond purple, that
Kati was so familiar with. She felt a relief of tension,
for between this galaxy and her own there had only
been a black void with the tiniest trace of violet
shimmering there.

*Now we turn left. Look closely, a short ways, the
mottling of blue within the purple. The vortices there
have only recently formed. The three largest make a
triangle, and we come out in its center. It is that
simple.*

I see it, said Kati, and the transition occured as she
said so.

This is the place, said Abagai, but Kati was too
stunned to answer for a long moment.

In one direction, towards the galactic hub, the
field of view was packed solid with dim, red stars,
and their combined light was dazzling to behold. Up
and down from the plane of the wheel, few stars
were visible, many peeking out from behind dark
clouds of dust and gas. But it was the view away
from the hub that stunned her into silence. It was
as if she stood on level ground, looking up at a great

cliff made by pressing sharp spires tightly together, the top of it jagged and convoluted, as if boiling. This was not rock, but a billowing mass of dust and gas, a wall of it stretching as far as she could see in two directions, dully illuminated in red by the stars behind her. Protuberances issued everywhere from the wall, and along the top of it, and at the end of each was a stalk like a fine twig, and at the end of each stalk a tiny, dazzling light was shining forth from a point. All colors, a full spectrum from red to blue were there, as if a cosmic artisan had covered the wall with strings of lights for some great festival.

Ohhh, said Kati. *What a beautiful sight.*

A birthplace for stars, said Abagai softly. *Behind us are the old, and the dying. Before us are stars not yet born, all those tiny lights, struggling for birth. I've never seen another place like it.*

I can see why you love this place, said Kati, memorizing the sight before her.

There was a long pause, then Abagai said, *It is more than the view, dear. I'm afraid I haven't been honest with you. I've come here many times since I first promised to bring you along. I've wanted to be alone because of the feelings I have when I'm here. Now I have those feelings again, and I'm glad you're with me.*

Feelings? asked Kati. *Yes, I feel wonderment for this place. I could not imagine such a vision as this.*

Another pause. *You feel nothing special? No sense of a presence here?*

No, Abagai, I feel no presence but yours. The woman seemed disappointed in her answer.

It is more than one presence; it is many. I've only felt it here, and I feel it again, as if now both of us are watched.

Kati concentrated hard, but nothing was there. *I'm sorry, Abagai.* Now, she was worried.

It is not my imagination, dear. Each time I've come, the feeling is stronger, and now it is great, even with you here. It is like—a calling. I think of the first time you called out to me when you were a little girl. You called out, but didn't know who I was.

I remember, said Kati fondly. *I wanted you to make the thoughts of other people get out of my head. You showed me a vision of your emerald eyes.*

Abagai smiled. *Yes—so long ago. But I have no visions, only a feeling. I feel compelled to wait here, as if someone comes for me. Now it is very strong.*

Perhaps we should leave, said Kati, now terribly troubled by such talk.

You think I anticipate my death here. No, Kati, but the feelings come from beyond that wall of gas and dust and infant stars. I'm not imagining them.

It was all too much for her. *I'd like to leave now, Abagai. Yesui is waiting to meet us*, said Kati. *Can we go? There will be other times.*

Abagai looked at her sadly. *I think not, dear, but you've been here, now, and you know the way. I will leave because you're afraid for me, but there's no reason for fear. And we've had our moment here together. One last look if I may . . .*

Kati burned the sight into her mind, suffered guilt from her foolish fear and remained silent as they returned to the gong-shi-jie. Abagai sensed her mood, and said, *There is our universe, burning brightly. The voyage back is an easy one, and we'll hurry now to meet Yesui.*

She had to say something. *It's a beautiful place, Abagai. I'll go back there again and again. It's wonderful being there.*

I'm glad you liked it, said Abagai, smiling sweetly, but a part of her was where they had just been. *You might want to look back and see that first signpost again.*

Kati did it, but it was already firmly in her memory, receding from them quickly as they rushed ahead. They traveled in silence, but when their own galaxy filled half their view, Abagai suddenly spoke again, a whisper, as if in conversation with herself.

I do not think we are unique, nor are we alone in this vastness. I think there are others like us out there, and someday I will find them. I will.

It seemed a strange thing for an old woman to say, but Kati kept her silence. The mood of the conversation was too dark, and filled with thoughts of death.

The return to their own galaxy was swift indeed, and Kati had no difficulty in locating their entrance, for by now Abagai had taken her several times beyond the rim to study it. The rim was lined with dust, and a gap was there where a spiral arm of vortices came to an end. Violet light surrounded them as they neared the place, then broke into individual clouds as they passed the first vortices of young stars, following the curve of the spiral along its inner edge towards home.

A familiar feeling of excitement suddenly passed through Kati like a rush of wind. *Yesui does not wait patiently*, said Kati. *She's up to something.*

And near, said Abagai. *Tengri-Nayon is just ahead. I thought I saw a flash of light there.*

Light flashed again ahead of them, and its color was violet. They slowed as they came to the vortex of Tengri-Nayon, and saw streamers of violet and red emanating from it, then sucked in with sudden force.

Now what is she doing? asked Kati. For an instant she'd felt Yesui's presence again, but somehow it was different. They stopped before the vortex, and waited for Yesui's manifestation to reappear, but suddenly there was babbling.

I will fly in space with him, Yesui, and you will move our ship!

Perhaps.

A fan of emerald green erupted from the vortex of Tengri-Nayon, and froze there, right in front of them. Kati was shocked by the strength of its presence, but it was the realization of who was there in that manifestation that nearly drove her back to herself.

Oh, my, said Abagai softly. *This is a surprise.*

MENGJAI! said Kati. HOW DID YOU COME HERE?

Immediately, her sense of his presence disappeared.

Don't you DARE mask yourself from me! I KNOW you're here!

Yesui seemed delighted by the discovery. *He's always been here, Mother. He's been coming here with me for years. You're found out, brother. Say something.*

Say what? Yes, I'm here.

But HOW? asked Kati.

I don't know. When Yesui goes to the gong-shi-jie, I know it, and when I want to, I go with her. It has always been that way.

Oh, Kati, this is wonderful, said Abagai. *Two of them, together here.*

But you never told me! said Kati.

We were going to, Mother, said Yesui. *I think we just found a solution to the problem of mass transfer into Lan-Sui, and Mengjai has contributed much in finding it. If you'll calm down a little, I'll explain.*

Have you been experimenting, Yesui? asked Abagai.

Yes, but not with Lan-Sui. We just finished transfering some mass to Tengri-Nayon in a very clever way Mengjai suggested to me. It was difficult, but it worked, and I know I can do it with Lan-Sui so we can distribute mass uniformly, and not at one point.

Kati felt Mengjai's pleasure at being given credit by his sister.

Moving mass the usual way brings it in wherever Yesui is, at a point, and planetary rotation doesn't distribute it fast enough, said Mengjai sagely, *but perhaps too quickly.*

Mengjai! warned Yesui.

You've experimented with this? asked Abagai.

Yes, said Mengjai, ignoring his sister's apprehension.

You've put mass into Lan-Sui? asked Kati, horrified. *We gave you no permission to do that!*

Just little masses, Mother, said Yesui, *and we were careful to stay far from the city. We didn't hurt anything.*

But now we have a better way to do it, said Mengjai, *and it's less dangerous.*

Abagai was suddenly smiling. *Now I understand all those storms that have been appearing in the northern hemisphere of Lan-Sui. Governor Wizera will be relieved to know they are not natural, unexplained phenomena. I must say those storms have caused his people concern, and I wish you would have told us what you were doing.*

You would have told me I shouldn't do it! protested Yesui.

Theory is no good without experimentation, chimed in Mengjai, sounding like an academic. *Everything must be tested, and our first concern has always been the safety of Lan-Sui City.*

Abagai looked at Kati. *The two are one in this. It seems we are outnumbered. Let us listen to their new idea for transfering mass to Lan-Sui.*

Kati was still upset, and more than a little angry. *I will, if you both promise me you won't do anything more behind our backs.*

We promise, Mother, said Yesui.

Yes, said Mengjai.

Is there anything else about you two that I don't know about? asked Kati. *You especially, Mengjai. You've hidden a great deal from me.*

No, Mother, said Mengjai. *You know it all, now. I'm sorry, Mother.*

That satisfied her. *Very well. Let's hear your new idea.*

Kati understood little of it, especially about the threads, for she'd never been able to see them, and neither had Abagai. But the children were most enthused, and seemed confident enough. They recognized the dangers, and seemed to have proceeded cautiously with all their clandestine experiments.

I'm convinced, said Abagai, *but I have to get Wizera's permission before we begin. I think I can have it within a few days if you can give me some sort of timeline for what you want to do.*

Yesui and Mengjai gave it to her, a four-year plan for the restoration of warmth to Lan-Sui, but at the end of it, Yesui had an unexpected request.

It's important that I be able to target Lan-Sui City at all times, and I've been aided in it by a strong presence I've felt there in the past. It would be useful if that presence could be identified and enhanced, she said.

Perhaps you sense the many empaths there, said Abagai. *They are a kind of priesthood.*

If they knew when I was present, perhaps they could focus on me, even if it were only the calling out of my name.

I will suggest it to Wizera, dear, said Abagai.

Kati was mystified by the request, for she was sensing a strange feeling of longing within her daughter.

CHAPTER TEN
COMMUNION

They whined and complained and threatened riot, yet when he offered them a solution they did not believe him. The City Council members laughed at what they said was an attempt to cover up his collusion with Mandughai to bring Lan-Sui under the rule of Meng-shi-jie, and threatened to override his hereditary rule if he did not withdraw his wild promises for the restoration of Lan-Sui.

Television commentaries dismissed his announcement outright, saying it was only a frantic effort by a weak Governor to quiet his many critics and restore the peoples' faith in his ability to look after their welfare.

All of this was difficult for him, but somehow the worst of it was now, as he faced the Empath's Guild in their great hall beneath the city. Of all people, he'd expected the Empaths would certainly believe him, for they knew of Mandughai's powers in traveling

within the gong-shi-jie and revered her as an extension of their own genetic line, seeking to become like
her. But Shanji was a distant planet of another star,
and unknown to them. They saw themselves as unique
in their relation to Mandughai, and when he told them
about the Moshuguang and the bringing forth of first
Kati, then Yesui, with their powers to move light and
mass, they called him a heretic. Their angry shouts
drowned him out, and he had to wait for minutes until
the Bishop Robdan was able to silence them.

Antun Wizera grasped the edge of the podium so
hard his knuckles turned white, his rage barely suppressed. Tsewang Robdan apparently could see it in
his eyes, and now waved frantically to quiet the crowd
of yellow-robed Empaths who stood below the platform
on cold, polished stone. Their shouts echoed from the
domed ceiling far above them, and the six great columns
supporting it, all painted with stars and nebulae and
swirling clouds of color representative of the gong-
shi-jie. Here and there were the white robes of novices,
and one of them was his own son, leaning against a
column and looking up sorrowfully at him.

"You must stop this immediately, Robdan," he
growled.

"SILENCE!" screamed Bishop Robdan. "You
dishonor yourselves *and* your guild! This man is your
Governor; he believes what he says and you do not listen
to him. You do not *think*!"

Now there was silence.

"Not *once* have I heard a claim that either of these
people, Kati, or Yesui, are indeed The Mother. I hear
only that two special people are now among us, people
who share our blood with Mandughai. These people
have been given special powers by The Mother, and
now you scream heresy. You question an action by The

One who has created the universe, and all life within it. You do not *believe*! You strive to reach where Mandughai has gone, and would exceed her if you could. Do you think I don't feel your jealousy and frustration in learning that others from another world have been the first to do what you only dream of? Then *look!*"

Robdan touched a trickle of blood issuing from his nose, and held up his finger for all to see it.

"This is the blood of your wrath against The Mother. It is the blood of your jealousy and selfishness. Now *listen* to this man, and redeem yourselves by doing what he asks!"

Robdan turned, shaking all over, and nodded to his Governor. "They will listen to you, now," he whispered, and used a handkerchief to dab at an issue of new blood from his nose.

Wizera could only wonder what it was like to be an Empath, absorbing the wrath of a thousand like him, and so near. He looked down again at his son, but Nokai only leaned against a column, looking serious, and there was no blood on his face. Something the boy had once said came back to him as he leaned towards the microphone to speak again, but the words came hard, for he had no religious beliefs of any kind.

"The ways of The Mother are mysterious, and beyond my comprehension. I am only a servant of the people. But Kati, and now Yesui, have suddenly appeared with powers far beyond those of Mandughai. And it is Mandughai who has brought them here, as friends. She has known both of them since they were born, and trained them personally in the gong-shi-jie. You must first believe that Mandughai is our friend, and thinks only of our welfare. You've seen her ships; you know she could overwhelm us if

she wished, but she has not done so. She only guards
us against rebels who threaten our society and seek
power for themselves. And she protects her vital
interests in the products of our moons."

There were mumblings among the crowd when he
said that, and again he had to wait for their silence.

"Mandughai has seen the plight of a planet that
once gave us light and warmth, and has brought Kati
and Yesui here to restore that to us. All she asks from
you is a simple thing, and it is Yesui who has requested
it. She is strongly empathic, and has felt your presence
in her travels here. It has helped her in exactly
locating the position of the city and has kept us safe
during her first experiments in moving mass to the
interior of Lan-Sui. She has been here several times.
Perhaps some of you have felt her presence."

Again there were murmurings, people looking at
each other and shrugging as if ignorant of such an
event, but now Nokai was smiling, and his face seemed
to glow amongst the others around him.

"Her travels here have been recent, and there have
been signs of her work. The new storms in the northern
latitudes have been Yesui's doing, and they were far
from us only because she knew our exact location at
all times. Now it's even more vital she know our
position, for she has found a better way to enhance
Lan-Sui's mass, and it will involve the entire planet,
not just a small part of it. She asks that you think of
her when she's here, even if it is only the calling out
of her name. Your thoughts must be continuous, for
we can never be sure when she'll be here. But one
thing I can tell you with certainty; she will be here
before the next pass of Gutien overhead, and that is
less than a standard day. Mandughai informed me of
this shortly before I came to this meeting."

The silence was sudden, as if all sound had been sucked into the cold, stone floor. A thousand faces looked up at him, scowling.

"I'm not asking for prayers," Wizera said quickly. "Yesui is not a Goddess, but a young woman with special gifts from The Mother, and she is here to bring life back to Lan-Sui. Please, if you will, use part of your daily meditations to think about this, and call out her name. This is all I ask you to do. I ask it for our people in the city, and on our moons. I ask it for a planet that was once wonderfully warm for us, and can be so again."

The crowd still regarded Wizera silently and sullenly as Bishop Robdan stepped up to the microphone, putting a hand over it and whispering, "There is still disbelief in what you say, but there's enough belief for them to be frightened by it." He cleared his throat, took his hand away from the microphone and spoke with a strong voice.

"The request is a simple one, and requires little of you. There is no risk or harm in doing it, if only for a little while. If Yesui is truly here, and can do what it's said she can do, there will soon be signs of it. What is required of you now is an act of faith; I want you to return to your cells, and meditate on what you've just heard. I ask you to suspend your disbelief for just a moment, and consider the possibility of truth. Ask yourself why, after three thousand years of a genetic line that began with the ancestors of our own guild, two people should suddenly appear with the powers to warm Lan-Sui again at the very time it has grown cold. Coincidence? Perhaps.

"Or has The Mother brought these people to us in answer to our prayers? As Bishop, I ask you to first ponder these things in your hearts, then exercise your faith in The Mother by doing what has been requested of you. You will use powers The Mother has given you to hold a vision of our city in your minds, and call out the name *Yesui* as strongly as you can, and as often as you can."

Wizera looked down at Nokai, and saw that the boy had closed his eyes, his lips moving slightly with unspoken words. Others around him were doing likewise.

"You are one voice, for one planet. Let me feel the strength of it," said Robdan, also closing his eyes.

Wizera felt nothing. Below him was a sea of faces, all eyes now closed.

Robdan inhaled deeply, tilting his chin upwards and sighing, "Ahhh. Yes, that's it. Now, once again. To Yesui."

Again he sighed. For an instant, Wizera felt blank, as if his conscious mind had turned off to explore something deeper, but then the Empath Bishop was speaking again.

"One voice—one planet. Now go, and think, and do what we have just done together. And ask The Mother for strength. We are finished here."

The crowd dispersed, filing out several exits to long corridors leading to living quarters, libraries and meditative cells, the white-robed novices, including Nokai, forming a line to return to their classes after the others had left. Wizera turned to the Bishop and shook his hand.

"You've been very supportive. Thank you."

Robdan smiled weakly, but his handshake was limp and cold. "Do not thank me, Governor. My disbelief in what you say is as strong as those who have just left us. If The Mother had wished Lan-Sui to remain warm, She would have made it so. She makes our lives harder in order to strengthen our faith. But as you say, also in disbelief, perhaps she has sent these people to us for that very reason. We will honor your request, but only for a little while. The citizens of our city will hear of our support, and that will dilute the ravings that are sure to come from the rebel camps. We do not trust a rule by former members of your police force. We do *not* want to see them come to power here."

"I understand," said Wizera, "and I'll keep you informed about anything observable that happens in the near future. I've always held your Guild in high esteem, Bishop Robdan. Now I'm relying on it."

Robdan nodded. "Let us then hope for a positive outcome from our mutual efforts, Governor. This way, please."

Robdan led him from the platform and along a featureless corridor to the doors of the lift, where Dorvod Tolui awaited him. Robdan took the lift down without another word, and they waited for its return to take them up to the Governor's mansion.

"It seemed to go well enough," said Tolui. "At least the Bishop was supportive."

"He makes a show of it," said Wizera. "What he really fears is a takeover by the rebels. Kuril has no use for the Empath's Guild. He considers them worthless, and spent half his police career trying to dig up dirt about them. If he comes to power, the guild will be dissolved immediately. There are too many thinkers there to threaten him. Robdan supports my rule, but didn't believe a single thing I said."

"Will they do it?"

"Yes, for now. But we must have a sign of progress soon. When we go up, I suppose I'll find more rioting at my gates."

"No," said Tolui. "Not a single demonstrator is there. The people are strangely silent, despite all the television commentaries. I think they're waiting to see what will happen."

"So am I, Dorvod," said Wizera. "And it must happen soon."

Following the Bishop's orders, Nokai found an unoccupied isolation cell and went inside for meditation. The room was square, three meters on a side, with bare white walls and only a table with chair for furnishings. The door was solid, and there were no windows, soft light coming from a panel in the ceiling. As usual, it was hot and stuffy in the room.

Nokai sat down at the table and placed the palms of his hands over his face. He sighed.

Yesui. You are a gift from The Mother. We are here, awaiting your help. Yesui.

Nokai mouthed his thoughts silently, over and over again. Sweat broke out on his forehead, his breath hot and moist in his hands as the minutes passed by.

His reverie was soon broken by a soft knocking at his door.

"Yes?" he said loudly, irritated by the interruption.

The door opened, and Bishop Robdan was standing there, looking surprised. "Nokai!" he said.

Nokai stood up quickly and bowed. "Yes sir. I was in meditation, as you requested."

Robdan smiled, but remained at the doorway. "Indeed you were. I was passing by, and felt drawn to this door. You are a beacon, young novice."

"I try very hard, sir," said Nokai, bowing again.

Focus, and power, and something more. Do you search my mind, young man?

Nokai kept his gaze steady and forced himself not

to blink. "Is there something else you want me to do?" he asked politely.

"No, no, continue with what you were doing," said Robdan, stepping back and beginning to close the door. "You do it well, Nokai. There is a future for you in the Brotherhood."

"Thank you, sir," said Nokai as the door closed. Robdan was gone, but not his parting thoughts.

Possible, but not likely. It has been hundreds of years since a Watcher was in our midst. The lineage should be easy enough to check.

Nokai sat down hard on the chair. *A Watcher? Am I different from the others? What is a Watcher?*

Nokai's stomach churned from a rush of fear for himself, and his meditation was ruined for the rest of the afternoon.

They ate silently, after his father had shown no interest in carrying on a conversation. Nokai sensed a deep sadness there, and a feeling bordering on hopelessness that deeply disturbed him.

"This has been a difficult day for you, Father. I'm sorry for you," he finally said.

His father looked fondly at him, and smiled wanly. "Dare I think my son believes what I said today?"

"Of course I do. You know I've felt Yesui's presence several times. Surely many of the others have also felt it; they just didn't know what it was. Yesui is very real to me, Father, and I'm only a novice."

"I hope you're right. Mandughai says that Yesui's work now begins in earnest, and at least there will be one of you to call out to her. Has she ever answered you?"

"No," said Nokai. "There are only the wonderful feelings when she's here, and a terrible emptiness inside me when she's gone. My heart is already beating hard with the thought she'll be here again soon."

Nokai's face flushed when he said that, and his father smiled again. Mother was looking sidelong at him with a little smile of her own, and now he felt embarassed.

"Mandughai has told me some things about her," said Father. "She's near twenty, quite beautiful, but fragile in appearance. Her whole life has been exercises of the mind, not the body. She's unlike her mother in that respect. Her mother, Kati, was a warrior, and is now a powerful Empress on Shanji. She fought with sword among the foremost of her troops, and suffered a deep wound in her thigh. She used the light of the gong-shi-jie to destroy her enemies. Yesui's powers are even greater than her mother's, Nokai, and she comes from warrior stock. This young woman is not someone to be trifled with."

"This *older* woman," said Mother, still smiling at him, seeming to read his mind.

Yet she's so full of life, excitement, and joy. When I feel her in my heart, I'm in agony, he thought.

"She also has a brother," said Father. "Sometimes they work together in the gong-shi-jie, so he might be a part of the presence you feel. Otherwise, I know nothing about him, even his name, but he seems to be involved with our problem. You should focus yourself on Yesui, when she arrives."

It was as if the words were a signal, for at that instant, something passed through Nokai like a sweet scent, and his hands clutched at the table, his body suddenly rigid.

"Father," he gasped, "she is *here*!" He stood up so quickly his chair toppled over, and his parents were gaping at him as he rushed from the room and down the short hallway to his own quarters.

"Yesui," he whispered. *Yesui. YESUI! Don't leave me yet!*

His room was in darkness, but he left the lights off, hurrying to his bed, and sitting on the edge of it, hands clutched together in his lap. "Yesui," he said out loud, "I'm here to guide you, and I know why you've come. I want to help in any way I can. YESUI!"

The feeling was gone, a transient thing, so brief, and he was on the edge of panic, trying hard to bring it back. Nokai closed his eyes tightly, forming each word consciously in his mind before saying it.

"Come back! How can I talk to you? I'm only an Empath, not a telepath. I can only sit here, and speak to a dark room, while you're out there somewhere, traveling in a place I can only imagine. Yesui, I'm *here!*"

He felt a touch, then, a soft thing like a breeze blowing across his forehead. There was a dull buzz in his ears, as if they were clogged, and his skin was suddenly cold and clammy. When he heard her voice, it was inside his head, yet it seemed she sat right next to him.

Who are you? she asked. The words were drawn out, and seemed to echo back and forth inside his head. His heart was pounding so hard he could barely breathe. Should he think the words, or just say them? He took a deep breath, and whispered.

"I am Nokai, a novice Empath. My father is Antun Wizera, and he is Governor of Lan-Sui. I've waited a long time to feel your presence again."

Feel? Don't you see me?

She sounded disappointed. "No, not in my mind, and I'm sitting in darkness with my eyes closed," he said.

*Well, open them, then. I've taken the time to make
an apparition for you.*

Nokai opened his eyes, and recoiled from what he
saw, nearly falling backwards onto the bed, but catching
himself on his elbows. Floating before him, in the
center of the room, like a projected hologram, was
a pair of giant, blazing, emerald-green eyes.

"Oh," he said.

*Do you like it? It's my first try, though. Abagai says
I need to work on apparitions of myself when I deal
with people this way.*

"They—they're the eyes of a giant," he said. "The
whole room is glowing green with their brilliance."

*You're impressed, then. Good. Can you think of an
image of yourself? I want to see you, but my eyes are
two light years from here.*

Nokai sat up again and tried to relax, but now his
heart was full with feelings of excitement, childish joy,
and more than a hint of mischievousness. There was
an image from a mirror in the morning, a photograph
of himself with his parents, a reflection in his window
as he stood on the balcony—

*Don't jump around so much. It's confusing. Settle
on something, please.*

He picked the image on his balcony, and focused
on it, showing himself gazing up at the darkness of
shutters closed around the city.

You are very young, she said.

"I'm eighteen."

Liar. You're less than that.

"All right, seventeen, but I'll be eighteen soon."

Yesui laughed, and now his whole body was aching.
"You have such a joy of life in you," he murmured. "Will
you show me what you look like?"

I am a hag, with warts. You don't want to see me.

"I'm told you're twenty, and beautiful, and yes, I want to see you. I want to see the face of the Mei-lai-gong."

Oh, well, let me see— Oh, shut up, Mengjai! I'll take as long as I like with this. Go play with your threads, or something.

"Someone's with you. Your brother?"

You've heard about him? You have fame, brother. Say hello to Nokai.

Hello, Nokai. This is all very nice, but we have work to do.

Nokai felt no hostility, only impatience and indifference to him within the new presence, but then it was quickly gone.

Find something to do, Mengjai. I mean it, and I'll leave when I'm ready to. You're only delaying things.

Very well. Be careful with her, Nokai. She is devious, and selfish, as well as stubborn. I only put up with her because she's my sister. All other men avoid her. MENGJAI!

He was gone, and Nokai felt her hot anger within himself, fading quickly.

Do you have a brother?

"No."

Consider yourself lucky. Now, where were we? Oh yes, a vision of myself. This is good practice, Nokai. Abagai has been after me to do this for years.

"Abagai?"

You know her as Mandughai, I suppose. Everyone calls her that, except Mother and I. Here, see what you think of this.

The giant eyes floating before him disappeared in a blink. In their place, a fan of shimmering green appeared, starting at the floor, and reaching up towards the ceiling.

It is my manifestation in the gong-shi-jie, she said, now quite excited, but he also felt an anxiety that made his heartbeat quicken. *Here I am, Nokai, rising from the depths of my flame.*

A figure in green emerged from the shimmering fan, as if pushed up through it from the other side. The head appeared first, hair pulled up into a billowing mass at its crown, then a long, slender face with a small, delicate nose and mouth, eyes closed. Her neck was long, her body slender at the shoulders, but curving wonderfully beneath a robe tied at the waist. When she had fully emerged from the glowing fan, she opened her almond-shaped eyes, which blazed like green stars, and smiled.

Well?

Nokai could not speak. He could not breathe. His eyes stung, and his forehead felt cold from the perspiration that had suddenly formed there. All of it was wonderful, and then the apparition's lips moved, synchronous with the voice that was only in his mind, soft, and sensual. The light of her eyes penetrated to his soul.

You drown me with emotions, Nokai. I've never before felt such intense feelings from another human being. Now I know why I had to come back to find you.

Nokai discovered his voice again. "You—you are perfection. The Mother has created the Mei-lai-gong with perfection. I've never seen a person more beautiful than you. I—I cannot describe what I'm feeling right now. You came back to find *me?* Many Empaths now call out your name, by my father's orders."

I hear them, but they are mumblings compared to what I feel from you. You are a gifted person, Nokai, and so gentle. I don't detect a hard thing

*about you, and when I was here before, it was you
I sensed, not the others. Such wonderful feelings, and
I couldn't forget them. I had to know their origin,
and now I've found it.*

Now he was embarrassed, and apprehensive. "You
are the Mei-lai-gong. You see into my soul, and I
cannot hide anything from you. What I feel is not
right, or proper, and now that I've seen you it's even
worse. I'm sorry, Yesui. I dishonor you."

The apparition's smile grew broader, and the eyes
seemed to sparkle. *You do no such thing, Nokai. You
make me feel wonderful, and about myself, not just
the things I can do. You are more than my beacon
to the city. I want to know you. I want to know you
well. You say you're an Empath. I say you're much
more than that, or else this touching between us would
not be happening. I will often be here, now, and I'll
find you, awake or asleep, for there is only one like
you. If I call you, will you talk to me? Will you speak
everything that's in your heart?*

So she saw even that, yet he could not say it, not
now. "I'll try," he whispered, burning the apparition's
image into his mind. "And you are always in my
thoughts."

The apparition was fading before his eyes. *As you
are now in mine. But Mengjai is back again, nagging
at me. We do have work to do, and he was born
impatient. I think I'll leave him behind next time, if
he's going to be such a nag.*

I warned you, Nokai, said Mengjai. *She can be
difficult when she doesn't get her way.* The apparition
had faded to nothingness, and there was only a dark,
silent room.

Think of me. I will return soon, said Yesui, still there
for an instant, and then she was gone, and Nokai gasped

at the sting of tears flooding his eyes, a horrible, empty feeling engulfing him. He sat on the edge of the bed for many minutes, ignoring a soft rap on his door, knowing his father was there with a mind filled with questions. Somehow, he knew the questions, and he thought about answers he would give when morning came.

He went to bed early, slipping naked between the sheets, and relishing their coolness. And when he was near sleep, he pressed his face against his pillow, and murmured into it the thing he had not been able to say to her.

"Oh, Yesui—Yesui—I love you. I love you so much."

Nokai slept well, but towards morning he neared a waking state with a vision of swirling, colorful clouds surrounding him, and ahead, close, was a magnificent fan of green.

Kati sat up with a start, and rubbed her eyes. Before her, the desk was heaped with files and the screen of the computer was dark. All this work, and she had slipped away again, rushing to the gong-shi-jie to talk with her husband and son. Even with the work, she felt increasingly lonely, especially for Huomeng, for their times apart were growing longer and longer, and now Mengjai was with him. They were orbiting Ta-sui after a four month journey, and had dropped a probe into Tengri-Khan's largest gaseous giant to analyze its atmosphere. They'd been analyzing the data when Kati had contacted them, and her only comfort had been the excitement of her son.

It's all hydrogen and helium, Mother, an unlimited source of fuel to reach Tengri-Nayon.

I don't want to think about it. That trip will take years, and I miss both of you right now.

If we can get far out, Yesui will fold space for us, and the trip will be much faster. We can be there in less than a year.

That's still conjecture, Mengjai, and Yesui is busy with other things. Are you having a good time?

Oh, yes. This is what I want to do.

He's progressing well, dear, said Huomeng. *Working with his sister, he'll be a navigator beyond imagination when we begin jumping in space.*

You, too? The idea terrifies me, Huomeng. You know that.

Anything to shorten my absences from you, darling. I miss you, too. I suppose you're buried in work.

I am, but I wanted you with me. Are you on schedule?

Yes. We should be back in four months. No files on your desk the night of my return.

I will arrange that. Mengjai, are you still working with Yesui on Lan-Sui?

The last time was a month ago. It's routine now, Mother, a little mass at a time, and mostly she's alone, at her own request. She wanted some help in gauging the mass, but her estimates were quite close and we're seeing effects now. The helium rain alone has increased the temperature by sixty degrees so far, and the contraction effects should show up soon. She still comes by to chat on her way back from Lan-Sui, and gives me up-dates.

She seems all right, then? I hardly see her, and she's become moody, spending all her time in her rooms.

Mengjai laughed, his humor a tickle in her mind. *I will not tell her little secret, Mother. You'll have to dig that out of her.*

Mengjai! Are you trying to frighten me?

Not at all. I'm happy for her. For once, she's acting normal. If you want a reason, just ask her.

I most certainly will!

Now she thought of that, glaring at the mountain of files before her and knowing they would have to wait longer for her attention. She left her desk, and went to Yesui's suite of rooms which had once been her own when she'd first come to the Emperor's City. She knocked softly on the door, but did not feel her daughter's presence, surprised when there was an answer.

"Come in, Mother."

The door was unlocked. She entered, looked towards the right, and saw Yesui standing before the mirror in her bedroom, putting a comb in her hair. The sight of her daughter was striking, for she usually cared little about her appearance, lounging about in a simple, black robe of the Moshuguang, her hair a tousled mass constantly spilling down over her eyes. Now her black hair was carefully combed up onto the crown of her head, a long tail hanging to her shoulder-blades and secured with a band of gold. She wore a sleeveless, green dress that showed every curve in her slender figure, and her skin glowed like fine porcelain. When she drew near, Kati saw rouge on her daughter's lips, a blush on her cheekbones, an outline of green around her emerald eyes. She came up behind Yesui, and put her arms around her, looking at their reflected images in the mirror.

"Oh, Yesui, just look at you. You're lovely."

Yesui leaned back against her. "Do you really think so? It's not too much?"

"No. You're beautiful, darling. I wish your father could see this."

Yesui sighed. "Hmmm," then, "Mother—when you first met Father, did you love him immediately?"

Kati laughed, and nuzzled Yesui's long neck. "Absolutely not! I despised him. I thought he was an arrogant, self-centered boy. But we were very young, and I hadn't discovered boys yet."

"But you discovered them," Yesui said dreamily, her hands carressing Kati's.

"Oh yes. I had a lover when I was even younger than you, but it ended badly. He could not accept me as a Changeling, and thought what we did together was unclean. I was devastated, and it was your father who came to comfort me. When I think back on it, it was that moment when I began to have feelings of love for him. It was a gradual thing, dear, not love at first sight. That's possible, of course, but rare."

Yesui sighed again, and Kati squeezed her. "I will tell you a little secret, daughter of mine. Your father and I were not married when you were conceived. That happened the night before the war with Abagai's forces. Your father came to me, and we made love on the bed you now sleep in. How fierce it was, too, with both of us thinking the other might be dead the following day, and the fact I was a Changeling was irrelevant to his love for me."

The memory was sweet, and Yesui smiled. "He was there for you, and you could touch him, hold him. He accepted you as you are. I'm not a Changeling, Mother. I'm not like you."

"So it seems, Yesui, but it's not important. It's the least of our differences. You are the Mei-lai-gong, dear."

Yesui stiffened. "I'm a person, not a God."

"Of course, but you're very special, and I know that feeling of wondering why. You are what you are.

There doesn't have to be a reason for it. Your father helped me to understand that."

"But he didn't pray to you like you were a God," said Yesui.

Kati paused, squeezed her daughter gently, and kissed the nape of her neck. Their eyes locked together in the mirror.

"Oh, my sweet, you mask yourself so well, but I know the signs. You have found someone. You are in love."

Yesui's eyes filled with tears. "Yes," she sobbed.

"Then you must tell me all about him," said Kati.

They sat down on the bed to talk, and three hours had passed when Kati finally got back to her desk again, revived from her loneliness, and feeling wonderful.

CHAPTER ELEVEN
SIGNS

There were signs in the sky, but the people of Lan-Sui City could not observe them directly. The shutters remained closed, and so the people clustered around their television sets to see the weekly pictures of Lan-Sui that came in from the moons Gutien and Nan, and they listened to the commentaries and raging debates among experts enjoying sudden fame from exposure to the public eye.

In the vicinity of the city, the changes were subtle. The colors of the great storm, swirling only a thousand kilometers below, had lightened somewhat; instruments attributed this to a sudden increase in helium content and its precipitation with other gases such as neon. Local wind velocities increased from two hundred eighty to three hundred twenty kilometers per hour over a period of seven months, but with no observable effect on the city.

To the north and south, the changes in Lan-Sui

were not so subtle. The zones of high winds at thirty degrees north and south latitudes seemed to change daily, a complex whirl of colorful vortices coming and going, and occasional eruption of plumes the experts said were a mixture of hydrogen and ammonia ice. It was in these regions that a temperature increase was first noted, climbing steadily from one hundred fifty degrees to two hundred twenty absolute over a year's time, then steadying there. While the temperature was rising, there was tremendous excitement; the television networks were saturated with requests for advertising, and the evening news enjoyed its highest ratings in history. An enterprising young blue-collar worker, named Win, initiated a lottery, selling twenty-lan tickets to match future dates with temperature, and became a multi-millionaire in four months.

All of it seemed transient. After three weeks of constant planetary temperature, the lottery had faded away, and news networks were again hustling for advertising in the light of plunging ratings. Still, they had hope, for a huge audience remained for the weekly pictorial up-dates from Lan-Sui's moons.

It was different for the workers of Gutien and Nan, especially those who spent their shifts on the surface. They did not have black shutters to cover the sky, keeping in their heat, or keeping out whatever might threaten them from the changes on Lan-Sui. What they had was a marvelous view, working long, hard shifts at minimum wages under a naked sky to pay inflated prices at company stores and feed families living in cramped, cold quarters of dimly lit rock.

They were not happy people to begin with. And when Yesui worked her early changes of Lan-Sui, it was the moon-workers who felt the effects, not the people in Lan-Sui City.

The first relevant sign was the observation of an increase in radiation levels on the surface of Gutien. Radiation levels had always been monitored, for the moon lay near the inner edge of a torus of particles trapped by the strong magnetic field of Lan-Sui. Film badges routinely worn by surface workers were developed weekly to check their exposures. Suddenly, within weeks after the temperature had steadied on Lan-Sui, those films were turning up black in the developer.

Dosimeters were placed on the surface, then scintillators for spectral analysis. The radiation level was up by a factor of fifteen, and rising daily. Protons and unusually energetic electrons were the prime culprits, but the worst news was X-rays, broad spectrum, highly penetrating.

Company officials huddled together, calculating exposure rates and the cost of insurance for additional risks to the workers.

The hours of workers on the surface were promptly cut by fifty percent, without consulting the union, and single paragraph announcements were sent to each affected worker without warning.

The union called a general strike meeting for the following morning, and sent one paragraph invitations for attendance by company officials.

The attendance was one hundred percent. No room was large enough to hold them all, so they met in a warehouse, and the meeting was delayed through lunchtime for four hours while crawlers moved tons of shipping and storage containers around for a standing-room-only crowd of sullen, hungry men who had abandoned their shifts for the meeting. On the surface of Gutien, nothing moved. And all production had been shut down the night before.

Two thousand men stood packed together on a hard stone floor to bake under hot warehouse lights and hear why the company had decided not to pay them a livable wage. Another three hundred watched with them through closed-circuit television on Nan.

A kind of podium had been made by placing boards on four upturned packing modules, and Chief Steward Mamai Jumdshan ascended to it on a ladder, followed by two pale-faced representatives from the company. Every man on the floor was shouting to be heard by the guy next to him, and Jumdshan had to wave his arms for a long time before everyone finally quieted down.

"Okay, that's enough! We're all here, so let's get on with it. But let's get one thing straight at the start. This is a strike meeting. We're here to ask questions, and get the answers, but if we don't like what we hear, we're gonna take a vote! Agreed?"

The chorus of assenting howls echoed from the walls and high ceiling of rock.

"All right! This here is Isrow Den, and he's representing the company officers who oughta be here, but aren't. They were too busy with other things, I'm told."

Catcalls, from all over the room.

"Now Isrow, here, is just a liaison man, a kind of secretary, and he's been given a lousy job to do, so be polite to him. The real people responsible for this mess aren't even here. Be quiet, now, while Isrow reads you a prepared statement from his bosses, and then you ask your questions. Got it?"

Heads nodded, and it was quiet again.

Den was in his twenties, a kid just out of school, and looked terrified. At least he'd had sense enough not to wear a suit. Someone had given him a worker's canvas jumper to wear, and that was smart. Give the poor kid a chance, they thought. The guy with him was forgotten quickly, a kind of aide who'd set up some recording equipment and was now fiddling with it. Den started to read from a single sheet of paper, but his voice came out a squeak, and then he looked ready to faint. Somebody near the front of the crowd yelled out, "Relax, kid. It'll be weeks before we're ready to eat people," and everyone laughed. Den smiled faintly and tried again, and this time his voice came out loud and clear.

"Radiation levels on Gutien and Nan have become a threat to the health of all surface workers," he read. "It is for this reason alone that working hours have been greatly reduced. We expect this situation to be temporary, until safeguards against overexposure can be provided. New environmental suits are being fabricated at this moment, and shielded cabs will be installed on all crawlers within the next few months. Until then, your stewards are authorized to make job reassignments within the current budget and wage designations. We regret this complication in your lives, but we must react to this change in nature that threatens your safety. Please bear with us for the few months it will take us to get you outside at full schedule again. You are important to us, as members of the corporate family. We will protect you and your families, at all costs, from changes within Lan-Sui that are beyond our control, both now and in the future."

Den paused. "It is signed by Mondo Bator, Chief Executive Officer. And now your questions, please."

Steward Jumdshan waved his arms to silence the many who called out for attention. "Let me get mine in, first! Isrow, I've *seen* the budget. All hazard pay for the surface workers has been pulled out of it, and they even took the expendibles' money for the crawlers. How do they expect me to make job reassignments when I have nothing to reallocate? Where did the money go?"

"Well, there *are* expenses," said Den. "The new safeguards will be expensive, and product cannot be shipped until they're in place. There will be no income for the next few months, so—"

"So the expenses for safeguards come out of the hides of the workers. I can invent new jobs, and the surface workers do work they're not supposed to do with a forty percent cut. Have you even read our collective bargaining agreement, young man?"

"Of course I have," said Den, looking nervously at his sullen audience.

"Then you know that transfer from one job classification to another is not a part of it. We all have our assignments, and that is the thing we do."

"That decision is being left up to you, Steward," said Den, glowering at him. "You might consider making changes in the agreement, if it's a problem."

"Should we do that, boys? Throw out what we worked years for, and start over again?"

"NO!" The walls seemed to tremble with the sound, and then Jumdshan pointed down at a man who'd been waving for attention for minutes. "You, Ghaimish. You got something to say? Get up here."

Den looked curiously at the steward, for he'd picked that one man without even looking at the others. The man came up the ladder like an athlete, his bare arms muscled hard, and his face was square, eyes slits, a prominent cleft in his chin. Den drew back instinctively, feeling as if a predator had neared him, prepared to strike him down.

"Identify yourself," said Jumdshan gruffly.

"Oghul Ghaimish, crawler foreman, third shift. And the last time I looked, I still had my balls!"

"Hey, Oghul!" someone called out, and everyone laughed.

" 'Course I don't need 'em much. No wife or family, like a lot of you guys. Look, it's the families we gotta think of. Us singles can bunk together, and cut expenses. We can donate extra hours to the guys with wives and kids for a little while, only it ain't gonna be for a little while! We've all seen the reports. The radiation levels are still rising, and this is all just a stall by the company. These new safeguards we're hearing about will be no good by the time they come, and we'll have to do this shit over and over again. The real problem is what's goin' on with Lan-Sui, and it's gotta stop!"

"Yeah! Tell 'em, Oghul!"

"I don't believe some supernatural girl is doin' it. Do you?"

"NO!"

"It's all lies. The *Governor* is doin' it. His scientists have found a way to heat the planet, to make things comfy and warm in the city, and he doesn't give a damn about what happens to us!"

Screams turned to howls. The podium shuddered and Den felt paralyzed, unable to speak.

"I say we stop it *now*! Show our independence from folks who treat us like slaughter animals. There's only one customer for what we produce, and that's Meng-shi-jie. Their ships are still here, loaded with troops. I say we shut everything down, and stay shut down until Meng-shi-jie takes out the Governor and puts someone in there who cares about the people who make the fuels they need. And I say *stop* the changes on Lan-Sui before we *die* here!"

"STRIKE!" shouted someone in the back, and that was the trigger. Everyone was stomping their feet, and screaming, "VOTE, VOTE, VOTE . . ."

Den grabbed Jumdshan by the arm, but the man jerked it away from him. "Careful, son. It's a long way to the floor, here."

"You're the Chief Steward. Do something!"

"I have," said Jumdshan, "and now you can tell your bosses to go piss on themselves." He stepped up to Ghaimish, took his hand, and they raised their arms together. "All in favor of a strike, let me hear it!"

The response was like thunder.

"Opposed?"

Total silence, except for cheering coming from a video receiver off to one side of the crowd, and someone yelled, "The vote on Nan is *unanimous!*"

Chaos erupted, everyone screaming and stomping their feet. The man named Ghaimish turned and stepped up to Den, face so close he sprayed him with spittle when he spoke. "Now, you get the fuck out of here, and go warn your Governor that the time for him and his kind has come to an end."

At the back of the warehouse cavern, two men dressed in the orange jumpsuits of electromagnetic separation workers watched the celebration calmly, and smiled. One turned to the other, and said, "Oghul Ghaimish, a crawler operator of all things. Tough, hazardous work. I never would have guessed."

"Crawler *foreman*," the other corrected. "A leader of men. He looks lean, and fit, compared to the last time I saw him, but he still looks better in uniform."

"Same face, though. The thought of smashing that face was all that kept me alive during the dust storms."

"Well then, let's see to it," said his companion. The

two men left quietly, while the din of the strike celebration was still going on, and they took the stairs down two levels to where the transmitter linking them to Yesugen's flagship was hidden.

The seven debris rings of Lan-Sui were not ancient by any standard. Two hundred thousand years before civilization had arrived at the planet, there had been a catastrophe of sorts, the capture of two moderate-sized asteroids which settled into seemingly stable orbits around the gaseous giant. Unfortunately for the captives, they were not the hardiest of specimens, composed primarily of silicates and water ice, loosely compacted around iron cores, and the orbits they settled into were within the Roche limit of their captor. Within centuries of their capture, both asteroids had thus been torn to pieces by the strong tidal forces of Lan-Sui and scattered by collisions within the orbital plane. Over the next hundred thousand years, pieces of rock and ice ranging in size from centimeters to a hundred meters interacted with the gravitational forces of Lan-Sui, Gutien, and Nan, and came into resonance with them, forming seven beautiful rings about the planet.

No ring system is permanent. There are constant collisions within the rings which tend to disperse them, and the most stable are those blessed with "shepherd moons" which patrol their inner and outer boundaries. Their gravitational perturbations set up a new resonance with the protected ring, and provide a delicate check on its dispersal. But even this is not perfect, and the spaces between the rings are constantly populated by pebbles, even boulders, of rock and ice that have wandered from home. And for twelve centuries, it had been the task of the daring pilots of Debris Control ships to hunt down these wayward missiles, to remove them as hazards to shipping and Lan-Sui City itself.

The ships were the size of light cruisers, heavily armored and fusion powered, with hypergolic thrusters port and starboard for rapid maneuvering. They bristled with weaponry: twelve laser canons fore and aft, fourteen turrets with rail-guns protecting their flanks. But the weapons were mostly used for harvesting, rather than destruction, for over the centuries a secondary industry for Gutien and Nan had been built on the collection of debris between the rings and the refinement of metals, mostly iron, aluminum, and indium. Once a target was reduced to fine rubble, electromagnetic scoops swept it up into the open maws of the ships for transport back to the moons.

The pilots were all young and single, with egos the size of the ships they flew. With luck, they might live to see age forty, rewarded with huge pensions subsidized by Lan-Sui City, for the hazards of their work were historically extreme. Every young boy dreamed of being like them, and they were the fantasy of women, their adventures fictionally exaggerated and exploited in books and television.

They were based on Gutien and Nan, but had no permanent quarters there, living on their ships, and since they spent most of their time patrolling the alpha-ring nearest the planet, enjoyed most of their port time in Lan-Sui City itself. Their adventures in the bars and nightclubs there only added to the mythology about them.

But in fact, their lives were no longer so hazardous, for centuries of debris patrol had cleared away most of the wanderers between the rings, and many of their days were spent in fruitless search of new targets.

And then Yesui began her work with Lan-Sui, adding mass to it.

The effects were most extreme in the alpha-ring, its inner edge only twenty thousand kilometers above Lan-Sui City. There, the ring was shepherded by the iron cores of the system's ancestor asteroids, both of them solid chunks some twenty kilometers in diameter. Each chunk, each pebble in the ring, rotated at a distance and velocity defined by the mass of Lan-Sui, and suddenly that mass was increasing.

Now gravity is a central force, and does no work on an orbiting object. Orbital velocity remains constant, but its radius increases with increasing central mass, and larger objects respond less quickly to changes in forces.

So one day, as Yesui added new mass to Lan-Sui, the outer edge of the alpha-ring struck a glancing blow on its shepherding moon, and scattering began, pebbles and boulders flying off in every direction with the sudden disruption of a resonance established over tens of thousands of years.

In fact, given time, the entire ring system was now doomed.

Lingdan Zedenbal was only a day out from Lan-Sui City when radar showed a shower of debris coming right at his ship. The alarm was sounded, the captain was called, but efforts to revive him were futile. After three nights of partying in Lan-Sui City, he'd returned to the ship again with sufficient smuggled reserves to keep him drunk another day or two. This was not a new phenomenon, and for nearly a year the crew had seen Lingdan Zedenbal as Captain, not First Officer. He was always there, always alert, although he partied with them, and when he was not on station he was in the simulator, constantly working.

Everything he'd learned and practiced was suddenly necessary to their survival, and he was ready for it.

"All fore and aft stations, hands off! We're doing this by computer, so enjoy the ride! Turret gunners only, hands on! Watch our flanks for anything near a meter, and take it out!"

The computer gave him the necessary simulations: the cone of particles, its trajectory intersecting Lan-Sui City's orbit, the zone of collision. He set the forward laser canons for a six degree spread at full, continuous power, beginning at a range of two hundred kilometers.

"Into the breach, gentlemen, at full thrust, and hold onto your asses!"

Lights dimmed and stayed dimmed as the lasers fired, and ahead was a continuous lightshow as a thing like a living cloud hurtled towards them at awful speed.

"Eiiyaa!" he shouted as the thing swept past them. The hull of his ship screamed with the shriek of rock on metal and shuddered with bursts of rail-gun fire, lurching only once when something big hit them.

Then silence.

"All stations, damage reports!" He looked at the radar screen, holding his breath, then let out a sigh of relief. The cone of debris was now hollow, a huge shadow zone with the computer projecting Lan-Sui City to be at its center.

One turret had been evacuated upon decompression, and the storage chamber forward had lost all pressure from a breach in the armored hull. No injuries were reported, but he had a damaged ship.

He turned the ship around, and headed back to Lan-Sui City for repairs. Half-way back, his Captain was finally revived, but the man still did not look well under the lights of the television crews who fought their way through the mob of people there to greet them.

The whole thing had been seen on television, taken by cameras on board a sister ship, and the high resolution system keeping watch on the city's surface. The streets had been filled with people to hear the clattering of fine pebbles on the black, shuttered sky as the hollowed cone of debris safely passed by them to burn up in Lan-Sui's thick atmosphere.

Before the day was over, Lingdan Zedenbal had been interviewed a hundred times, his "I was only doing my job" attitude romancing the entire audience. His Captain was interviewed only once, by the Company, and summarily dismissed from his position.

There were parties and receptions for Lingdan and his crew, but then came the hard part, the audience with Governor Wizera and his presentation with the City's Order of Merit. Lingdan accepted the medal stoically and shook the man's hand, though he despised him.

In the middle of a lavish party at the Governor's mansion, a messenger sought him out in the middle of the dance floor and delivered his new orders. He was now a Captain, and the ship under repair was now his to command. Crew members pounded him on the back, and his dancing partner, a lovely brunette, rewarded him with a wet kiss.

In the wee hours of the morning, Lingdan Zedenbal returned to his hotel room numb but elated, humble yet euphoric. Most of all, he was deeply grateful. Sleep would not come, and so he placed a videophone call to Gutien to thank the man most responsible for putting him in the right place at the right time.

The face of Mamai Jumdshan appeared on the

screen, haggard-looking, but smiling when he saw who his caller was. "Lingdan, my lad, I've heard the news. How wonderful for you, and well deserved. Lan-Sui needs more heroes like you in these times."

Lingdan did not wonder about how Mamai had received news of his promotion so quickly. "I owe it all to you, Mamai. Without your recommendation, I'd still be piloting a freighter. I'm in your debt, sir."

"You did it yourself, Lingdan," said Mamai. "When the job needed to be done, you were ready for it, and I'm proud of you. It pleases me to have had a small part in what has happened for you. My days have not been pleasant lately, with the strike. I've made many new enemies in the Company."

"We have plenty of old ones. It will be that way until we gain our independence," said Lingdan.

"Then you still believe?"

"I do. And if things go badly, I'll support any call for a strike by Debris Control as well."

Mamai shook his head. "I have no intentions of risking lives, Lingdan. The common people aren't responsible for what Wizera and his scientists are doing to Lan-Sui. It's people like you and me who have to deal with the effects, and protect the helpless. I fear for you, Lingdan, and the crews of all Debris Control ships. Until we get rid of Wizera, and stop the changes in Lan-Sui, your lives will be increasingly dangerous."

"We can only do our best," said Lingdan. "In the meantime, remember my support for independence, and call on me if there's anything else I can do to help you."

Mamai seemed to choke back a sob, and there was a little tear in his right eye. "Thank you for that, lad. I'm sure there will be something. And thank you so much for your call."

The connection was broken, Mamai sobbing as he disappeared from the screen. So much for the man to bear, all because of a Governor who thought only of warmth for the city people, and not of the consequences for working people on the moons. Yesterday, Lingdan had saved the lives of people in the city. But what about tomorrow?

He could not think about it now. Having given thanks to his greatest benefactor, Lingdan's mind was empty. He went to bed, and quickly fell into a dreamless, peaceful sleep.

Abagai was sitting up in bed, reading, when Yesugen came to see her. It was early evening, and the blinds were up, allowing the light of Tengri-Nayon to warm her chest and relieve the suffocating feeling she'd had for most of the day.

Yesugen led Niki by the hand, but he let go and ran to the bedside to peek over the edge at his grandmother.

"I see you," said Abagai. "Now give me a hug."

The five-year-old scrambled up on the bed, threw his little arms around her neck, and hugged her fiercely. "Ohhh, you're getting so strong," she gasped, then sat him beside her, cuddling him.

"How are you feeling?" asked Yesugen, sitting down on the edge of the bed.

"Better. At least I can breathe when I sit up. When I lie down my lungs seem to fill up within minutes."

"I can bring in another physician if you like," said Yesugen, her brows knitted with concern. "Your medications don't seem to be helping."

"What can be done is being done, dear. My lungs are dried up like old leather. They've lost their resiliency, and it's not reversible. I must accept that and live life one breath at a time. Your mask is up, dear. Is there news that troubles you?"

"There have been unforeseen complications in Yesui's work, Mother. The additional mass has increased the size of the radiation belts and produced instabilities in the rings. Wizera is quite concerned about it, but he hasn't asked for a halt in the operation."

Abagai studied her daughter's face, and probed at her. "Is that all?"

"For now. We're watching closely to see if the rebels will use these new events to incite riot, and I ordered the return of two cruisers to Lan-Sui this morning."

"Then you're expecting trouble," said Abagai, grabbing at Niki's hands when he began tickling her for attention. "Oh, you are a squirmy worm," she said to him, and tickled him back.

"Yes," said Yesugen, smiling at the two of them, the serene smile of a woman newly pregnant with her second child.

"Have you talked to Yesui about these new problems?" asked Abagai.

"Just yesterday I did, Mother, but you know her attitude. She says the effects are transient and will cease once Lan-Sui has its proper mass. And if the moons remain in danger, she will move them to a safe place."

Yesugen raised her eyebrows as she said it. "Can she do that, Mother?"

Abagai laughed, and fought off a new attack by her grandson by wrapping her arms around him. "She only works for short times with Lan-Sui, dear. The rest of the time, she and her brother are constantly experimenting with new things, so I wouldn't be surprised at anything she does."

"Mengjai wasn't with her when we talked," said Yesugen, and then her face brightened. "She has a new manifestation in the gong-shi-jie, Mother, and wanted me to tell you about it. For the first time, I've seen her face. She really is quite beautiful, and shows her entire figure in that fan of green we've known for years."

"How wonderful. I must see her soon, and ask how she finally overcame her shyness."

"She said nothing, except that she knew you'd be pleased by it."

"And I am," said Abagai. Niki had ceased his attempts to tickle her, and now nestled in her arms, eyelids drooping. Abagai turned her head, and coughed softly, a deep, rattling sound, a bubbly feeling in her chest. Yesugen shifted herself, put a hand on her mother's where it rested on the grandson's little shoulder.

"There's more, daughter, but you choose not to tell me. You are Empress, now, not I. It won't be long before the people know. You are struggling with hard decisions, and I trust you to make them. You can mask your mind from me, but not your heart. I think you'll do well when I'm gone."

She reached over, and put her hand on Yesugen's stomach. "The finest thing you can do for me now, is to give us a granddaughter to continue our line, but even that is beyond our control. So many things are that way. Things happen, and we can only react to them as wisely as we can."

Yesugen stroked her mother's hand. Niki now dozed, his cheek against Abagai's chest.

"Mother, just how firm is your commitment to Wizera, and the rejuvenation of Lan-Sui?"

"It's absolute, dear."

Yesugen nodded, and smiled. "That's all I really needed to hear from you." She reached over, and picked up her son, his head lolling over on her shoulder. "Rest, now, and I will go do the things I must do."

Yesugen stood up, and walked out of the room, leaving Abagai with empty arms and an open book in her lap. *I must see Kati and Yesui at least one more time*, thought Abagai, and then she gasped for breath as her chest spasmed once again.

Niki was awakened by the food odors as he approached the table, and Yesugen sat him down next to his father. Kabul served his son, looked up at her. "Aren't you joining us?"

"In a few minutes, darling. I have one more thing to do." She leaned over and kissed him, and he took her chin in his hand.

"How is she?"

"Very bad. And there's nothing we can do about it."

Kabul nodded, and squeezed her chin. "Hurry back. I'll make up a plate for you."

Yesugen went to her office in the adjoining room, the only light coming from the console screen, the received messages still there: the strike; the new, periodic showers of debris threatening Lan-Sui City; the discovery of an enemy whose request for support was also there. Her fingers moved over the keyboard, composing a short message to her flagship.

```
DELTACOM:YES:GSJ40
NEW OPS:


1.   Zeta one and two to Nan, on
     station.
```

2. Alpha to Gutien, all troops in harness.
3. Beta to City, stand by to evac Governor and family.
4. Gamma, monitor all freighter and Debris Control activity, and report.
5. Gutien probes one and two, monitor activities, stand ready to terminate subjects with extreme prejudice on short notice.

YES:GSJ40:FLD:COM

A strike of her index finger, and the message was sent.

Yesugen turned off the monitor, leaving the computer on for a reply, and went back to the dining table to join her family.

CHAPTER TWELVE
RENEWAL

"When I was young, life was continually changing, and I was excited by it. Now it continues to change, and I feel only a sense of loss," said Kati.

She sat at the edge of the pool in the upper gardens, with flowers cascading down the rocks behind her and Mengmoshu at her side. She'd pulled up her robe to dangle her bare feet in the water, and watched the colorful carp there darting in and out to inspect her toes. "I've become lonely, Father," she said.

Mengmoshu took her hand in his. "Yes, I know. Lately, you've spent much time inside yourself. You'd like to have your family with you all the time, but now they pursue their own lives and you don't seem happy for them. I think it's selfish of you, Kati. You must release them and get on with your own life. Perhaps you need a holiday."

"Holiday? The last one I took was for Festival, and

I didn't even recognize it. There was no parade of *ordu* leaders, no ritual charge or ceremonial passing of The Eye, only a grand party for everyone. And the only family to accompany me was *you*."

Mengmoshu leaned against her. "Was that so bad?"

"Oh, Father, you know what I mean. I can excuse Huomeng and Mengjai for being a light-month away, but Yesui was *here*, and she wouldn't even consider going."

"Her work does not allow distractions."

"Her work is also *here*," said Kati. "Who do you think will replace me, when I'm gone? She spends all her time with other worlds, and has no interest in the affairs of Shanji."

"Her work with Lan-Sui will end soon enough, Kati, and she's only twenty-three. Do you think you'll be gone so soon? You're not even middle-aged." Mengmoshu put an arm around her and squeezed gently. "You have two talented children who do things you would not attempt, and Huomeng's dream of travel in space was known to you before you married him. Now he has realized his dream, and you resent it. Please, Kati, get out of your pity and look around you. See the things you've done. You've become a hermit in your own palace. You've lost your connection with the people you nearly gave your life for when you were young. Let me take you on a grand tour of Shanji, to see what changes your reign has brought about. You need to see the good you've done."

"A tour?"

"Yes, beginning in Wanchou, then northeast to Jensi City. You've spent twenty years signing orders for things to be done, and not once have you personally seen the results. The people have nearly forgotten they have an Empress."

"That is not so bad," said Kati.

"Kati! You made a promise to return in Wanchou, when all the people were suffering. You healed, and gave them hope with your presence and touch, and you were not even Empress then."

"They thought I was a God," said Kati sullenly.

"In a way, you were, and still are. You heard the cries of your people, and did something about it. If there are Gods, and I doubt it, they do nothing to ease the lives of the people. You have done it for the Gods. Let me take you on a tour to see what has been accomplished, Kati. It will make a fine holiday for you, and the people will know you still watch over them."

Kati wiggled her toes in the water, and a carp darted away from them. "Maybe Yesui could join us?"

Mengmoshu shook his head. "Just you, Kati. Let your daughter do her work. It's *you* the people need to see. Yesui's time will come, when she's ready, not now."

Her mood of self-pity was suddenly gone, her thoughts turning to the human misery she'd seen years before: the poor, stacked like cordwood in tiny rooms, the sick, without medicines or doctors, then a child she'd brought back from the edge of death in a village which accepted death as the will of First Mother. And who *was* First Mother for them? Was it Mandughai, to whom the Tumatsin had prayed for deliverance? Certainly not. She was Abagai, a human being, special, yes, but a person of flesh and blood, and Kati's dearest friend, now near her death.

Kati's heart ached with that thought. It was Abagai who had come to her, trained her, brought out her powers to do good for the people. Not a God. If there was a God, a thing beyond human powers and comprehension, it could only be the universe itself, with that beautiful complexity of physical and biological laws only partially understood by its inhabitants. It was those laws that had led to the powers of Abagai, herself, her children, even the Moshuguang. The powers of the universe were the powers of God. And it was people who used them for good, or for evil.

"Well?" said her father.

"Yes. I'll do it, but I can't spare more than a week. Can we cover everything that fast?"

Mengmoshu laughed. "You still remember our slow journey by horse and wagon, Kati. You have *no* idea what has happened in the last twenty-three years, yet all of it has been your doing. I find that incredible. I'll arrange the trip right away, but give me two weeks. People must be notified of your visit."

"I *do* know about our transportation system, Father. And no lavish receptions, please. It's the life of the common people I want to see again. I have more than enough contact with the rich and influential every day of my life."

"I will see to it," said Mengmoshu, squeezing her again, "and I'm happy to see you feeling better again."

She *was* feeling better, except for one thing. She thought about Abagai, the fading aural colors of the woman in the gong-shi-jie, the hesitancy in her speech, the continued references to that special place in a distant galaxy where something awaited her. Of all people, even her father, it was Abagai whose love she felt the most, a constant touch, even when they were not together in the place of creation. Life would be so terribly empty without her, and Kati could not suppress the strong feeling the time for that was coming soon.

They left early in a morning, taking the mag-rail through the tunnel in the mountain at a constant, gentle slope down towards the floor of the eastern plains. This was not new to Kati, for she'd dedicated the system on its opening day and ridden it all the way to Wanchou with dignitaries in the first year of her reign, coming out at a little station surrounded by the squalor of a shantytown thrown up to house jobless refugees from outlying regions and the city itself. She was twenty-two, then, her emotions still close to the surface, and the royalty who would benefit from commercial use of the tunnel had felt her rage in public, cringing at her pledge to with-hold further commercial development until the poor had been provided with adequate housing.

Again, she felt guilt. The shantytown had been torn down, and high-rises built for the poor, yet in the twenty-three intervening years she had only believed a report, and never personally checked to see if it was true.

Her entourage was small. Besides herself, there was Mengmoshu, a recorder, and four security guards from the Moshuguang elite. She did not wish to be conspicuous, and dressed in a white pants suit with high collar, her hair coiled up into side-buns, and she carried the little, silver fan so often used by women of the noble class. She hoped she would be seen as one of them, though the emerald green of her eyes might betray her.

She was not so lucky. When the door of her car opened, there was a crowd there to greet her, jostling for position. Reporters bowed respectfully, then thrust their microphones at her.

"How long is your visit? Will you travel to Jensi City, or remain in Wanchou? Is your daughter with you? Does the market remain open with Meng-shi-jie? Do you anticipate any overproduction that might cause layoffs in the near future?" And so on.

She gave them short answers, Mengmoshu taking her arm to guide her to a small man who smiled brightly, bowed, and held out a hand to her.

"I recognize you from somewhere," she said, shaking his hand.

"I am Jin-yao, Madam. Many years ago I drove a wagon for you. Now I have the honor of being Mayor of Wanchou. Welcome back."

"Thank you, Jin-yao. I've waited far too long in coming here again," she said to the former Comptroller.

"I will be your driver again, Madam, but the wagons are gone, and I promise there will be no major receptions to occupy the time you have with us."

"You anticipate my wishes," she said, glancing at her father.

The reporters followed them, held in check by her security people, but she felt heat from the lights of their cameras. "Do you now have television here?" she asked.

"No, Madam, only radio. The people with cameras are from Jensi City," said Jin-yao.

Radios in Wanchou. Even in her capital city, these were not common. Despite vast reforms all over Shanji, her own home remained traditional, and was known as a center for arts, with outdoor concerts and plays from ancient times, held in the many gardens and sheltered from all weather. The towers she'd erected, including the pagoda on Three Peaks, had become the daily refuge of writers, poets, and painters.

Twenty years ago, this station had been a concrete slab and an awning. Now it was a monstrous complex with a dozen tracks, and crowds rushing in every direction, men and women dressed in white, steering their little electric carts piled high with luggage.

Her party stood on a moving walkway which took them to the entrance, where eight men with side-arms came to flank them. Reporters were held back and she was guided outside to waiting, canopied vans, bullet shaped, and electrically powered. Of the hundreds of people they'd passed, only a few gave her a passing glance, but some smiled, nodding in recognition.

Kati sat next to Jin-yao. Her father with the recorder and one guard were in the back seat. The rest were loaded into a second van that followed them closely. "We will spend the rest of the day just driving around," said Jin-yao, "but there will be a small reception for you this evening."

And Kati saw what had been accomplished in Wanchou.

The housing for the poor was indeed reality, a cluster of forty-level high-rises near the station, white and clean-looking, with balconies where people kept their own gardens of little trees and potted plants. They went first to the old city, a short drive, streets still narrow, but now smooth, not the rough cobblestones she remembered. Kati sniffed the air, and Jin-yao smiled at her.

"No stink, Madam. The sewers were our first improvement, and they drain into treatment lakes to the east of the city."

"Everything looks so *clean*," she said, looking up at buildings erected before her time, but fresh-looking, painted in green and yellow hues. Again there were balconies everywhere, sprouting green, not the racks of drying clothing she remembered.

"We resurfaced everything, and added tinted resins that cured with the concrete, Madam. The colors are quite permanent, and the resins are impervious to water or sunlight. We've used them in the interiors as well."

Many people were on the narrow sidewalks, most of them dressed in white, only a few with the drab, canvas clothing she recalled, and there was little traffic, just a few vans like their own, and many one-person scooters that veered around and past them like darting flies. "It doesn't seem to be as busy as I expected," she said.

"The mag-rail is underground here, Madam. The lightning-bolt symbols on the signs you see designate the stations beneath various buildings. Few people actually live in the old city, now, and they leave their personal vehicles at home. The mag-rail takes them anywhere, and runs every ten minutes."

One building was familiar, as they neared the edge of the old city. "I remember that place. It was a hospital." *Dark, stinking of death, my hands moving over a dying woman.*

"Now it's the Agricultural Operations Office," said Jin-yao. "All these buildings are for commerce and banking, Madam. The hospitals and schools are in the new city, where the people live. It's just ahead of us."

It seemed the city had expanded only to the north. West and east, the land was suddenly empty and green, but only a kilometer ahead a cluster of tall buildings gleamed white, a single spire towering above the others. As Kati looked at them, the van suddenly slowed.

"There is an artifact you must see," said Jin-yao.

Coming up on their right, along the edge of the road, a stone cairn rose like a sea shell standing on edge. A cluster of young people stood around it, taking pictures with pocket cameras, several scooters parked nearby. "Tourists from Jensi City," said Jin-yao, bringing the van slowly to a stop. "We will wait a moment."

The young people took their pictures, then crowded close to the cairn, placing objects there and stepping back with hands clasped reverently at their faces, bowing several times, as if in prayer. When they began walking back to their scooters, Jin-yao got out of the van and opened the door for Kati, then her father, but as he led them to the cairn, a girl turned around and saw them. There was whispering in the group, and they turned to stare at Kati as she approached the cairn, Mengmoshu at her side.

There was an altar, with three candles burning under envelopes of glass, a stone bowl of green pebbles, a cylinder of foamy, soft polymer bristling with sticks of burning incense, and above it, encased in hard, clear plastic were the remnants of a robe once richly purple before being burned and buried. A few purple shards of cloth still showed; the garment was mostly charred black, but had retained its form.

"Oh my," said Mengmoshu softly. "I didn't bury it deep enough."

Kati was shocked. Wearing that robe had been the first time she'd felt like an Empress, but it had been saturated by the bloody mucus of a young patient, absorbing the mess that had nearly killed him, and so they had burned the thing rather than carry it all the way back on horseback.

"The shrine went up only months after your departure," said Jin-yao. "It disappeared overnight, when the Emperor began tearing down shrines, and reappeared the same way. Now the people come, and put their little stones in the bowl. They ask First Mother for wisdom, and for Her guidance in their everyday affairs. My wife comes here often. Once, I thought she was foolish, but then I personally witnessed the powers of First Mother. Now I believe in Her."

Jin-yao lowered his eyes, and bowed slightly to Kati. Around them, the young people had returned, and were edging in apprehensively for a closer look.

"I am not Her," said Kati, feeling uneasy.

"I know," said Jin-yao, "but She does Her work through you."

"She does it through all of us, Jin-yao. We care for ourselves, and our neighbors." As Kati said this, she looked at the faces of the young tourists who crowded in to hear her, and saw reverence there. Each of them, men and women, wore greenstone amulets on leather thongs about their necks, fingering them as they listened. The amulets were no simple pebbles, but intricately carved, and Kati was curious about them. Her security guards were right at her back, shouldering their way into the ranks of the young people to move them away. "No," she said, "let them stay here."

She stepped up to a girl, perhaps eighteen, who lowered her eyes reverently and clasped her amulet with both hands.

"You honor us, Mother," said the girl, voice quavering. The others bowed their heads, not looking at her.

"Why do you call me that? Don't you know who I am?" Kati took the girl's hands in hers, and moved them away from the amulet so she could see it. The girl was startled, and gasped at her touch.

"You—you are Empress of Shanji, and our emissary to First Mother. We came here to visit your shrine, Ma'am, and all the others in the countryside."

Kati fingered the amulet, an abstract carving of a woman holding an infant child. "You've come all the way from Jensi City to see a simple shrine?"

Waves of fear were now coming from the girl. "We are soon to be confirmed, Ma'am. The Church requires it of us."

Mengmoshu was suddenly in her head. *Don't ask about the church. I'll brief you later, and the amulet is a symbol of both you and Yesui. They'll assume you know what it means. Give them some advice, and let's go. I didn't anticipate this so soon.*

"Of course," said Kati. "Your amulet is lovely, but please remember that Yesui and I are people, not Gods. We are not beings to be worshipped."

"We are taught that, Ma'am, but you're our link to First Mother; we follow your actions, and words, and they are the pattern of our lives."

How much news do they get?

Plenty. There are even fairly accurate reports floating around about what Yesui is doing with Lan-Sui. Maybe they get it through radio traffic from the freighters. Rumors are always flying there. Let's GO!

The girl was shaking, and so awestruck that Kati had to do something. She brought heat to her fingertips, touched the child's chin and raised it so she had to look at her. "Life is simple, dear. Work hard, and use all the abilities given to you. Love yourself, and all others. If you do these things, you will be happy. I must go, now. Perhaps I will see you again in Jensi City."

The girl's eyes were brimming, and she only nodded, unable to speak. Her companions had not moved or spoken, just stood there with bowed heads.

Mengmoshu led her back to the van, and they drove away, but not before Kati had seen the girl collapse sobbing into the arms of her companions.

Kati sighed. *That was very uncomfortable for me, Father.*

I know, but there'll be more of it, I'm afraid.

The girl said she's taught that Yesui and I are people, but in her heart she sees us as Gods!

I see no harm in it.

But it's not the TRUTH!

Jin-yao caught her eye. "I shouldn't have stopped, Madam. I'm sorry."

"No, no," she said. "I found it quite interesting. Now tell me, what is that tall spire ahead of us, the one with the bulging top?"

"A radio tower, Madam, but also a museum, and the thing on top is a restaurant. The tower is mostly decoration, a thing to distinguish the skyline of the new city."

They drew near the cluster of new buildings, all tinted white. At the edge were the high-rises where the people lived, arranged in groups of four, surrounding a park with gardens and lakes, and a playground for children. "Each unit of four buildings is a cooperative," explained Jin-yao, "with underground shops and a mag-rail station. It is like a company, Madam, and the people own everything except the mag-rail connection. They control all small business in the city, but the large stores still belong to the nobles. It seems to work well, so far. Your people are quite industrious, Madam, especially when there are profits to be made. Small business is expanding quite rapidly here."

The streets were wide, and filled with traffic: vans, scooters, and many four-seat cars half-domed with plastic bubbles, the bubbles partially retracted to let in fresh air on a warm day. Most of the drivers were women, and Kati never saw more than two children in a car. She started to ask about this, but suddenly Yesui was in her mind.

Mother!

Yes, dear. I'm in the middle of something here.

I'm sorry, but I've just seen Abagai, and I'm concerned about her. She seemed so sad and confused, and her colors weren't right. She wanted to know where you were, and she always knows that. Something is very wrong with her!

Is she still there? Abagai?

No. She faded away a moment ago. She wants to see you. What should I do?

Wait where you are, dear, and give me your sign. It could be several hours before I come, but for you it's an instant. Be calm.

I'll try, Mother, but hurry!

She was gone. Jin-yao was talking again, and she hadn't heard a thing.

I'm afraid, Father.

We can have Jin-yao stop and find you a private place if you like.

No. He might think I'm getting bored. But soon, Father. An hour for me is an hour for Abagai, and I don't know how many more she has left!

"Our major hospital is over to your right, that complex at the far edge of the lake," said Jin-yao. "There are still a few Moshuguang physicians here, but all of them are retired from private practice, and serve as clinical professors of medicine. Most of our interns end up in small clinics scattered all the way

from here to Jensi City, but we still have a problem
with providing sufficient pharmaceuticals to the rural
regions. Their hygiene has changed little since you
were last here, and they still use human waste in their
fields, but they welcome our clinics, and use them.
They live longer lives, now, and have fewer children.
We encourage no more than two children per family,
but the farmers still ignore our advice. It's getting
better, though."

Kati's mind was light years away, but she nodded
at appropriate times and asked simple questions the
rest of the afternoon. Her mental autopilot served well,
for Jin-yao never seemed to sense her distraction and
was thrilled to show her everything there was to be
seen. But after hours of sightseeing, it all looked the
same to her, and she was desperate to find a private,
secluded place for herself.

"I think it would be good if we have time to
change clothes and rest before the reception," said
Mengmoshu.

"Of course," said Jin-yao. "We're only minutes
away from the place, that cooperative ahead, and left.
It's an informal affair, Madam. I hope you don't
mind, but no nobles have been invited. The ladies
of the cooperative have prepared a buffet of everyday
foods for you, and the guests were chosen by lottery.
Tonight you dine with common people, and then
there will be a tour of the underground shops."

"How wonderful," said Kati, suddenly back again.

Jin-yao smiled. "It was also a profitable fund-raiser
for the cooperative," he said. "Two thousand tickets
sold for one hundred winners, and sixty-five of them
are women. You will not be burdened with talk of
business and politics this evening, Madam. It should
be relaxing for you."

How thoughtful of them, Father.

And informative, said Mengmoshu.

There was no crowd to greet them, not even a single official. They stopped at the back entrance of a building, where there was a playground and a pond, with acres of green grass criss-crossed with beds of flowers and dotted with *Tysk.* Jin-yao led them inside and down some stairs to a basement, where there were cooking odors that reminded Kati she was hungry. A long hallway, bare walls painted white, had several numbered doors on both sides. "Guest rooms," explained Jin-yao. "We have three of them for your party, Madam. I will return in two hours to take you to the reception. It is in the Common Room, nearby. My nose tells me the ladies have already gone far with the cooking." He showed them to their rooms, bowed, and left.

Two beds, a dresser, table and two chairs, a small bathroom with tub and sink, an open closet with a rack for hanging clothes, the room was spartan and simple, yet accomodating. Kati's security people were moved into rooms flanking hers. There was no telephone, no radio, just soft light from ceiling panels. Quiet.

"I will bathe first," said Mengmoshu, "while you do what you've been thinking about all afternoon." He went into the bathroom, and closed the door.

Kati quickly unpacked a change of clothes, then lay down on the bed and closed her eyes. The purple matrix of stars was there, three of them pulsing together, and she went to them, coming out so accurately she nearly melded with her daughter's manifestation.

Good, you've arrived, said Yesui. *I didn't even move, waiting here.* She sounded impatient.

They went quickly to the vortex of Tengri-Nayon, and Kati called out, *Abagai, it's Kati. I'm here now, if you still want to see me. Yesui's here with me.*

No answer, no flash of green, or the familiar, smiling face.

Abagai, please. Yesui is worried about you, and so am I. Please come.

Nothing. *She just faded away when I was talking to her, and I was right in the middle of something,* said Yesui. *Her face disappeared first, and then her manifestation turned muddy, all brown and yellowish. It flickered a couple of times, then dimmed to nothing. And when I called again, she didn't answer.*

Abagai! You're frightening us! Please answer!

The answer came not from Abagai, but her daughter.

Kati? What's going on?

We've been trying to reach your mother, Yesugen, but she doesn't respond, and we're worried. Kati concentrated hard, trying to sense a familiar presence, but felt nothing there.

She was asleep when I looked in on her an hour ago, Kati. I'll go check her again—

She's asleep, and I can't rouse her. I'm calling her physician—

Oh, Kati, she's in a coma! She's dying! We're moving her to hospital—

The machines are helping her breathing. I saw her eyelids flutter once, but her heartbeat is so slow!

How much time has passed, Yesugen? I had an appointment in two hours when I came here.

It's nearly that, now.

I must leave. Yesui will stay here and relay any message from you. I'm sorry, Yesugen, very sorry.

I understand. I'm at her side, now.

Kati opened her eyes with a start, and burst into tears. Mengmoshu was sitting on the edge of the bed, face grim, and held out his arms to her. He cuddled her, stroked her hair until the sobbing began to subside. "There's nothing you can do except wait, Kati. You cannot prevent what is natural, and she has lived a long life."

"I know," sobbed Kati, "but she's like my own mother, and now I'm losing her."

"I will miss her, too, but Jin-yao waits for us in the hallway. He arrived several minutes ago. What you're wearing will be fine for the reception. The people wait for you, Kati."

She nodded, and sniffed, and wiped her eyes dry. "Once they waited for First Mother, and now she's dying. What do I tell them, when it happens?"

"You tell them nothing. If there is a First Mother, it is not Abagai, or you, or Yesui, but something else, a natural power beyond our comprehension. As long as there is a universe, there is a First Mother, Kati. Try to think of it that way, and it will be easier for you. First Mother has always been, and always will be. She is everything there is, and we are a part of Her."

Suddenly she felt comforted. A life, having been lived, ends, and the atoms of the body are dispersed to form new things. The atoms of her own body had once been parts of many stars, then clouds of dust and molecules, then planets, then ... Was this immortality?

Kati hugged Mengmoshu, and kissed his cheek. "As usual, you've found a way to make me feel better. I love you, Father."

"And I love you," he said, returning the hug. "Are you ready?"

"Yes, if I don't look like I've been crying."

Mengmoshu smiled, and touched her cheek. "Your eyes are wonderfully green again."

Kati sighed, followed him to the door and outside, where Jin-yao awaited them. The man led them down the hall to the common room, where she came together again with her people for a meal she would long remember, not just for the food, but for conversation.

The room was narrow and long, with tables pushed together to form an oval. Lanterns hanging from a high ceiling cast an orange glow on everything, and the walls were decorated with large, colorful butterflies made from sticks and paper. The meal was served in twelve courses, and Kati sat at a different place for each one, Mengmoshu beside her. Most of her dining companions were women, and they talked about everyday life: children, schools, the increasing costs of city apartments, the rising interest rates on loans for the shops they operated in the evening hours after their husbands had been fed, the complaints of the men in serving as evening mothers to the children.

One thing was quickly obvious. There was now wealth among the common people, and with it dreams and ambitions. Many talked about leaving apartment life in Wanchou, and moving to Jensi City where there were better jobs, more opportunities for business, and single-family dwellings with land for gardens and privacy. Jensi City was more progressive, they said. It had theaters and cultural parks, even television. Mostly, it was new, and not yet crowded like Wanchou.

The talk was uplifting, and for three hours Kati was totally distracted by it. Her people worked hard, saved diligently, and invested. They dreamed of still better lives, and felt empowered to realize those dreams. Kati's own ambition had been realized; the people themselves had become the driving force for progress on Shanji.

At the end of the meal she gave a short speech of thanks, bringing them greetings from First Mother, and promising to return more regularly in the future, with Yesui accompanying her. Several people had asked about her daughter, and the rumors of Yesui's powers, and Kati had frankly admitted to the truth of them. The people were most eager to meet the future Empress of Shanji, but for now they were satisfied with a promise.

Kati returned exhausted to the quiet of the guest room, and all distractions were gone, Mengmoshu falling quickly asleep in the bed next to hers. She lay awake in the darkness, but closed her eyes and again sought the place of creation, rushing towards the three strobing points of purple light that were the sign of her daughter's presence.

Yesui was there, her face frowning within the lovely manifestation of green she'd adopted for her new love on a distant planet, a young man she could not truly be with, or touch.

Anything new?

No. I just called Yesugen, and she said there's no change.

I see your worry, dear. We must continue to have hope for a recovery; there's nothing else we can do.

Yesui's frown deepened. *It's not just that, Mother. Do you feel anything new here? Are we alone at this moment?*

Kati looked around at the swirls of blue and purple

clouds, the spots of red to green within the vortices of stars in every direction. *I feel nothing special*, she said.

I do, said Yesui, *but maybe it's because I wish it. I remember how Abagai masked her presence from you, before I was even born, when you first brought me to the gong-shi-jie.*

She watched your first steps in this place, but gave us our privacy because it was such a precious moment. Yes, she told me.

But I saw her, mother, a tenuous, black mist, without form. Now I feel something here with us. I've looked and looked, but there's nothing.

She's in a coma, dear. She can't be with us, now.

Then why do I feel a presence other than ours? asked Yesui, looking all around her again. *It grows stronger by the minute, but there's no manifestation. Abagai, is it you? Please!*

Kati felt nothing except sudden apprehension, for Yesui's sight was indeed beyond hers. *When she awakes, she'll be with us again. We must wait, but I have to return now. Keep watch for me.*

I will, Mother.

But don't forget your own body, dear. You have to eat, and time passes quickly beyond this place.

Yes, Mother. I'm doing that. Mengjai has also reminded me.

Kati smiled at her daughter's irritation. *Call me*, she said, and Yesui nodded at the instant of the purple flash accompanying transition.

Darkness, and quiet, except for the soft snoring of her father. The body told her she was exhausted, ready for sleep, but the mind kept her awake for several minutes, replaying the time with Yesui. No, she decided, there had been nothing there with them, only the roiling clouds of purple beyond purple that had created the universe.

As sleep neared, she had an intriguing thought. If her father were correct, perhaps the clouds of purple light themselves were First Mother.

She fell asleep with a vision of Her in her mind.

CHAPTER THIRTEEN
GODS

Three days later, they boarded a shuttle for Jensi City, and for the first time in her life, Kati was happy to be flying. Four days of travel by mag-rail, van and then horsecart was enough for her. Most of what she'd seen was at least familiar, though changed by improvements, but the city would be a brand new experience for her.

The factory complex north of Wanchou was as she remembered, but the high-rises for workers were now well equipped with electrical appliances. They also included air-conditioning, and some workers now owned their own apartments. Employment was full, the foundries and mills operating three shifts per day to keep up with the demands of Meng-shi-jie and Jensi City for building materials.

But the town itself was still drab and unkempt looking, and there were none of the privately owned shops she'd seen in Wanchou. The people, both men and women, worked long, hard hours in the factories and seemed to have little energy left for anything else, but when she talked to some of them it gave her hope, for she heard their dreams. The people worked hard and spent little, putting most of their earnings into special accounts for the purchase of land and single-family dwellings in the rolling hills north and east of the company town, and a few had already accomplished their dreams. The hills were dotted with little stone houses topped by peaked roofs of polished wood, like little pagodas, and surrounded by gardens with stands of adolescent *Tysk*, and again there were the little bubble-canopied vehicles she'd seen in Wanchou.

The countryside had changed even less, and they left the mag-rail station in horsecarts sent by the village Kati had visited twenty-four years before, to meet the young man whose life she'd saved there. The fields were the same, waving green and stinking of human excrement, but there were no longer storage bins full of rotting produce, everything now quickly transported by mag-rail to Wanchou and the surrounding communities.

The people were unchanged. They met her quietly, politely and reverently, placing her on a saddle-throne among the elders within a circle of earthen huts to eat a simple meal of boiled grains with strips of beef and lamb, and home-brewed ayrog. They asked her to bless their shrine, which she did by igniting candles and incense with a gesture, and then they brought the boy to her. He was now a man, and his name was Wan-lin. He was tall and straight, bronzed by sunlight, a man of high esteem in the village, for it was said that the hands of First Mother had been placed upon him to save his life, and now She returned to see the results of Her work.

Kati was uncomfortable with all of it, but Meng-moshu would not allow her to protest.

These are simple people who require little of you. Let them have their faith in First Mother, and show that you care about their lives here, he said without words.

Wan-lin brought his family to her: a wife and two small children, a boy and a girl. He asked for her blessing on his family, and she brought heat to her hands when she touched them, her eyes glowing green. "The blessings of First Mother are upon you, and your lives will be fruitful," she whispered, and they believed her.

There was a short visit to the new clinic in the village, then they were back in carts for a bumpy ride to the mag-rail station and a blurring trip back to the shuttle-field just north of Wanchou. At last she was cushioned by soft fabric, and the air was cool. An attendant served them cold drinks as they lifted off in the wedge-shaped craft reserved only for her party.

Kati cupped her chin in one hand and looked out the window at the great valley lined with grassy hills passing below them. After some minutes, her father said, "You are very quiet, my dear."

"Just thinking," she said. "The village people still see me as First Mother, and I can't seem to convince them otherwise. I don't like living a lie, Father."

Mengmoshu chuckled. "You wouldn't have such a problem with that if you could believe we are all a part of First Mother, whoever or whatever She is. We are all a living presence of Her."

Kati looked at him sharply. "Do you really believe that?"

"Not really, not as it sounded. I've told you I don't believe in Gods. If there's something beyond us, it's the universe itself and all the natural laws that govern it. You think too much about such things."

Kati rejoined: "Your view of the universe, however, is quite narrow. You've not lived in the gong-shi-jie, or seen the birthplace of new stars in another galaxy like I have. And I think Yesui sees even more. She's always talking about a fabric of green threads that fills all space, yet I've never seen them there. There is much we don't see, Father."

"I have enough trouble dealing with what I *can* see," said Mengmoshu gruffly. "Everything else is speculation. It's only an hour to Jensi City. We should talk about your visit there, and you need to compose a short speech."

"More receptions," said Kati.

"Not many, although there will be at least one. We have a request for you to speak to the congregation of the Church of The Mother."

"What?" said Kati.

"No red eyes, please. I didn't promise you'd do it, but I think you should. It's something new in Jensi City, and most of the people there attend services. You're regarded as the intermediary between themselves and First Mother, Kati, just as you've said to the people all along."

"I said I was an emissary."

"Yes, they accept that. They accept all that you've said, even in Congress. It's all been recorded in a book they read from and discuss in services. They believe all you've said and done has been inspired by First Mother."

"Oh, Father!"

"Shhh. Not so loud. That secret has so far been kept. Kati, it's not a religion, exactly, more like a philosophy, a way of living. You are the center of it, like it or not, and you should speak to them. You must accept the fact that you're more than Empress to the people. You have special gifts which you seem to take for granted as you grow older. You forget the miracles you've wrought, but the people remember. They see you as more than human, and it's the truth. It's even more true with your children. When are *you* going to accept that?"

His voice was an angry whisper. "Your humility is generous, but misplaced. I want you to see yourself as you really are. I don't know where your powers, or your children's, have come from, and I don't care. They are real, and you've used them for good. Yesui follows your example. Acknowledge yourself."

"As a super-being?"

"Yes. That is what you are, as is Yesui, even Meng-jai, and very likely the children they will produce. You don't have to be brilliant to see that."

"Fine, but I'm not a God. I don't want people offering up prayers to me." Kati turned away from him, and looked out the window again. Below her was a solid green mat of forests covering hills of substantial height, with narrow river-cut valleys meandering between them.

"There are no prayers in services, no forms of worship, Kati. They believe First Mother knows all, and speaks directly to you. And if people offer up private prayers, it can't be prevented. You saw the young people by the shrine; you saw their faith, and felt it as I did. Let them have it. What's the harm?"

What can I say to them?

You will think of something. "I have your itinerary here. Let's go over it quickly before we begin our descent."

It did not seem so bad: a three-day stay for touring, two small receptions, one with city leaders, the other with a small business guild of shop owners, then her appearance at the Church of The Mother. Tours would include a reactor, lumber mill, shuttle fabrication plant, and a cultural park.

The turbine whine of the shuttle suddenly decreased in pitch, and Kati's stomach seemed to float. "You might start looking for the city," said her father.

Below her, the forests stretched to the horizon, but as they descended she began to see structures nestled among the trees: pagodas, and towers of polished wood, surrounded by walkways, colorful gardens, and roads spiraling away from them along the hillsides. Suddenly there were other structures, white, in clusters, and a myriad of roads heading east, and she craned her neck to look ahead. She saw a valley much like the one by her own city, but there were no open fields, only a mass of white buildings covering it as far as she could see. Mengmoshu leaned against her shoulder to look past her.

"There are no high-rises here. All those buildings are private homes, all owned by the people who work here. You can barely see the city center far ahead, those glistening buildings, not so high as in Wanchou. We will land to the east of it."

"How many people are here?" she asked.

"Around two hundred thousand so far, but they're coming in rapidly, now. The boom started only a few years ago, and thirteen years ago there was nothing here but forests and grass. It is a restricted city, Kati. You can only move here if you have a good job and sufficient funds to buy a home. There are no rentals allowed. Any property you buy here must be for your own, personal dwelling."

"A city for the elite," said Kati, not pleased with what he'd said.

"No, a city for the successful," said her father. "It is the peoples' dream to live here, and it drives them. Education and hard work is what it takes, and the opportunities are open to all of them. Jensi City is only the first, Kati. Other cities are just beginning south of here, all the way to the sea. What you see here is the future of Shanji."

They came lower, and she saw homes of all sizes, some small, like little blocks of stone, other clusters elaborate and sprawling, with parks at their centers. The streets crawled with vehicles, like sparkling bugs, all heading to and from the city center, also spread out, buildings no more than twenty stories, shining like golden glass in the morning light.

The eastern edge of the city was dominated by a heavily forested area, with green lawns bordered in swirls of color, and open spaces with pagoda-like structures and what looked like crowds of people, and then there were open fields and ribbons of concrete rising to meet them. In seconds, they had touched down and were rolling to a secluded hanger away from the main terminal, a sprawling building of red stone.

"We'll try to keep you away from the television people as much as possible," said Mengmoshu, "but your appearance at the church will be televised for all the people, and that day has been declared a holiday."

Kati sighed, her mind a whirl. "I'll need time to compose something."

"You'll have it," he said. "Now relax, and see the good things your reforms have led to."

It was easier to do that when she saw that only a few people were actually there to greet her, and none of them were reporters.

Ming-hau, mayor of Jensi City, presented her with a bouquet of flowers, introduced her to the six members of his council, all men, then the chair of the Small Business Guild, a woman. They bowed graciously and shook her hand when she offered it, but in a few minutes she'd forgotten their names. The last member of the greeting party was dressed in a white robe, an elaborately carved amulet hanging on a gold chain around his neck. Kati probed him, and liked what she first felt there. Before Ming-hau could introduce them, she stepped up to the man and held out her hand, his robe suddenly green in the glow of her eyes.

No fear, only a serene, reverent feeling was within the man. "I bring you greetings from First Mother, Elder Hanshou," she said, bringing warmth to his hand when he softly shook hers. "I look forward to speaking to your congregation while I'm here."

Hanshou bowed, and touched his amulet with his free hand while Kati held the other, still probing him.

"My soul rejoices in the feeling of your presence, Madam. We have long awaited your visitation. Welcome to our city."

"Thank you," she said, and released his hand. Suddenly, she was not so fearful of her speech at the Church of The Mother, for although Hanshou held her in deep reverence, he saw her first as the Empress of Shanji, and not someone supernatural.

Four vans awaited them, and Ming-hau was her driver. Kati sat beside him, her father, Hanshou, and the recorder in the back, an arrangement not pleasing to her security people. They left the hanger, went through a gate far from the terminal and drove bumper to bumper back towards the city center only minutes away.

Ming-hau pointed out the vast cultural park east of the city. "The day after tomorrow will be spent there so you may see our arts, and meet many of our people in a festive setting," he said solemnly.

"It sounds wonderful," she said, smiling.

"Tours of our technology centers are today and tomorrow, but we'll try to be brief and give you time for relaxation. We want your visit to be enjoyable, so you'll return again soon."

"Oh, I intend to," she said sweetly. "I've heard marvelous things about what you've done here."

"All credit goes to our people, Madam," said Ming-hau. "Those of us who govern the affairs of the city are only their servants."

Kati probed the man's mind, and instantly liked him.

The city center was small, some four square kilometers of buildings faced with clear polymer, and tinged golden to filter sunlight. The streets were jammed with rushing traffic: vans, scooters, and bubble-cars, broad sidewalks crowded with people, all hurrying somewhere. Store windows were filled with goods on display, including strange yet obviously fashionable clothing she'd never seen before. Restaurants were everywhere, with tables under awnings along the sidewalks, and at every intersection it seemed there was a little fountain surrounded by young *Tysk* and beds of flowers, and terrifying round abouts where cars darted from one lane to another to speed away in a new direction. Twice she saw the familiar mag-rail signs by stairs leading underground from the sidewalks, people coming and going there.

"There is a suite for you at one of our hotels, Madam," said Ming-hau. "We will deposit your luggage first, if you don't mind, and then get on with the tour."

"Very well," she said, feeling rested.

The hotel was like the other buildings, revolving doors at its entrance. Their meager luggage was unloaded by uniformed men in seconds, and was not even inside the building before they sped away again, Ming-hau honking his horn at a driver who cut closely in front of him. "Sorry, Madam. Driving is not yet an art, here. Cars are like toys to some of the people, and sometimes they play rudely."

"The pace of life seems quite rapid here," she said, trying to quiet her heart.

"It is, Madam. There is so much to be done here, you see." The van careened through a round about, changing lanes twice, and accelerated southward along a broad street until the passing scenery was a blur.

How do they keep from killing each other in these things? This is terrifying!

Her father chuckled audibly behind her. *Accidents are not common here. The people have quickly taken to their little cars, and actually drive rather well. There are no speed limits here. The people won't tolerate them.*

Mercifully, traffic thinned as they left the city center, and Kati could unclench her fists again. They drove at high speed for twenty minutes until Ming-hau pointed ahead to a complex of buildings surrounding a shining dome. "Our reactor, Madam. The rest of the complex is a factory for shuttles and all the vehicles you see on our streets. There is time to see only part of it, but it's our most important industry. Over thirty thousand people are employed here, and a new factory is being added just to the east."

The afternoon was a blur to her, and she was awed by the sights, the huge scale of everything. The fusion reactor was a ball the size of her palace, sprouting bundles of thick cables like a squash gone wild, workers the size of bugs from where she watched on a high viewing platform for visitors. The shuttle factory was even more huge, a single building a kilometer long with a ceiling hundreds of meters up, lines of shuttles in various stages of manufacture, swarming with workers. She watched an assembly line for vans, three of them being completed and driven outside in the few minutes she was there. Several workers waved, and she saw Hanshou wave back to them.

"Members of your congregation?" she asked.

"No, Madam. I work here as a welder. That is how I make my living. There are no paid servants of the Church."

Now Kati felt even better about him, *and* his church.

In the evening there was dinner with Ming-hau and his council in a wood-paneled room by an elegant-looking restaurant filled to capacity in her hotel. Their politeness was surreal: no requests or complaints, no demands for political favors, only responses to her simple questions, and cautious inquiries about the lives of her children. Again she felt the peoples' desire to meet Yesui, a virtual unknown to them, yet destined to be their future Empress.

Her suite was enormous: three rooms, two with beds large enough for a family, flowers everywhere, a refrigerator stocked with tea and ayrog and delicious fruits. Flowered wall-paper and a gilded ceiling surrounded her. Mengmoshu had his own bedroom, now. He winked evilly at her, and took four bottles of cold ayrog with him when he retired.

Kati was quickly into bed, and the lights off when she called to her daughter.

Anything new, dear?

*No. Abagai has stirred a few times, but that's all.
Yesugen continues to have hope. I'm still feeling that
presence, Mother, but now it comes and goes. Are you
having a good time?*

*Oh, yes. You must come with me next time. The
people are asking about you.*

All in good time, Mother. I have so much to do here.

*You'll be Empress someday, Yesui. It's time to start
thinking about that.*

Oh, Mother, you'll be Empress forever.

Of course, dear, she said, amused.

Only the young think they're immortal.

The visit to the lumber mill and brick factory was
hot and dusty, and made her sneeze convulsively until
she was given a mask to wear. She was glad to get
away from it, and was rewarded with an afternoon
at the cultural park. Her visit had been well pub-
licized, and the crowds were huge, though orderly,
an army of security guards making a path for her
wherever she went. In the sea of humanity around
her, about each neck there was a greenstone amulet,
many elaborately carved, many others only abstractly-
shaped pebbles, but always there, always fingered as
she passed by.

The people did not jostle rudely for position, nor
did they shout out to her or cheer, but the ones
nearest her held out their hands, and she touched as
many as she could, her eyes glowing. The feelings of
goodwill coming from the people brought her near
tears, but the tears only flowed when she came to the
Museum of the Miniatures.

A walkway formed a circle within a grove of *Tysk*,
and along its circumference were displays of Shanji's
historical centers in miniature to a scale of twenty

to one. The first thing she saw was old Wanchou, with
its slums and decaying buildings, then the new city
as she'd recently seen it. Next came her own city,
complete with bubble canopy and the golden dome
of her palace, and she admired it while her recorder
dutifully took pictures of everything. The next display
surprised her, for it was a reproduction of the Tumatsin *ordu* where her brother lived by the southern sea,
and near its edge, gilded in gold, was the burial place
of her parents.

Mengmoshu put a hand on her shoulder. *They know
all about you, from the very beginning. The next
display shows it more clearly, and you should not be
afraid to show your emotions over it.*

The first thing she saw was the life-sized bronze
statue of a young girl with braided hair falling across
shoulders and chest, dressed in riding leathers and
sitting on a small, mountain horse. She was gazing into
the distance over the heads of her visitors, her face
strong, resolute, and hanging from her neck was a
necklace of seashells. Behind her was the miniature of
an *ordu* in the mountains, partially burned, bodies
sprawled around it, a column of troops walking their
horses away along a trail, one soldier clutching a little
girl to him in his saddle. The figure of the girl had
been painted gold.

It is called "The Beginning of Our Lady," said
Mengmoshu. He put his arm around her as her tears
came. Her body shook, and she pressed her face
against his shoulder. The silence around them was
broken only by the sobs of a few people who dared
to cry openly with her. Ming-hau looked very nervous,
and clenched his hands together over his chest.

"It's beautiful," she quickly said to him, "but the
memory is very painful to me. Can we move on,

please?" She wiped her eyes, and managed a smile
for the many who now looked sorrowfully at her.

The last display was of Jensi City itself, and before
it another life-sized bronze of a robed woman with a
halo of blue porcelain fixed over her head, showing
the visable aura of the Empress of Shanji.

"I've never seen such fine work with bronze," she
said, calming herself slowly.

"You've encouraged the arts, Madam, and we select
only the best artists to live here," said Ming-hau. "There
are many retreats and studios for them in the quiet of
the forests west of the city."

She saw many of those artists that day, their work
displayed in kiosks around the entertainment pavilions:
paintings, small sculptures of animals, pagodas, gnarled
trees, and herself. By the end of the day, she'd purchased five pieces, insisting on full payment to honor
artists stunned speechless in her presence.

She was entertained by dancers, singers, and
acrobats on the stages of four pavilions, and there was
a parade which she watched like an ordinary tourist,
security people at her back, the crowd pressed in
behind them to watch her reactions. There were jug-
glers, and musicians, a parade of clowns on stilts, a
float with people dressed like Tumatsin, banging
cymbals and blowing horns, and the people cheered
with her as it passed by. She was delighted, and giddy.

Oh, this is wonderful, Father.

We're one people, Kati. That is the point of this.

Indeed, a platoon of armored troops came next,
armed and severe looking, their heads made up to
show them as Moshuguang elite, then a platoon of
men dressed as soldiers of the old empire, then one
of Tumatsin warriors on horseback, armed with curving
swords and bows.

The Moshuguang disguise needs work, grumbled Mengmoshu. *Our heads are really not so large as that.*

Kati laughed at him, but then a float was coming to end the parade. Drawn by twenty men and women, it was covered with flowers, a miniature of Kati's palace at the front, a throne behind it, on which sat a beautiful young girl in a golden robe. The girl smiled beautifully, waved serenely to the crowd, and her eyes were emerald green.

How does she do that? asked Kati.

Special colored lenses on her eyes, said her father. *You're not offended?*

Of course not. She's beautiful.

The girl saw her, then, and seemed stricken. She bowed deeply, and covered her face with her hands.

Sit up straight, child, and smile for me. Your appearance does me great honor. Kati stretched out her arms as she said it, and the girl responded, smiling again, and holding out her own arms, but now there were tears in her eyes, and then she was gone, the parade over.

Kati was still happy when they drove back to the city. She remained that way throughout a meal with the women representing the Small Business Guild, and then an hour of quiet time in her suite to compose a short speech for the Church of The Mother. She could remember few times she'd enjoyed herself so much in a single day, her worries forgotten.

Mengmoshu retired early, exhausted by all the walking they'd done. Now sixty-nine, he was not used to such extended exertion, and even Kati felt it in her own legs. She went over her speech, rehearsing it twice in her head, and then crawled deliciously into bed. Immediately, she sent out a call to her daughter.

Yesui? It's Mother, again. Do you have news for me? I've just had a wonderful day.

There was no answer. She waited a moment, and called again. Still nothing, and her eyelids were heavy, the sheets cool on her skin. She fell asleep without another thought, and languished in dreams about the day: the smiling faces, beautiful arts of the people, then the lovely girl who had portrayed her.

She is like the little one I remember, but now that one is a woman, and her daughter works new miracles in this place. Dear Kati, I love you so. I will miss you so much.

Kati stirred in sleep. *I still think of you, Abagai. Now you're in my dreams.*

No, Kati. I invade your dreams to tell you I'm here in our usual place, and I have little time. Please come to me quickly, so I can see your face again before it's too late for me.

She was not awake, but nearing it. The huge, emerald eyes she'd seen as a child were suddenly before her, then the matrix of purple stars, and she rushed blindly towards one of them without thought of becoming lost, entering the gong-shi-jie with a flash to find Abagai standing before her.

One last time, dear. If only we could touch each other in saying goodbye.

The familiar, smiling face was there, but Abagai's manifestation was a frightful thing: dim, and muddied, nearly devoid of color and closely hugging the body, like a faintly glowing sculpture.

I called Yesui. She should be here soon, said Abagai. *She was talking to the young man who occupies her heart these days.*

Oh, Abagai! said Kati. *I thought you were well again, but what I see—*

*Is a woman near death, dear, any instant, now, and
I wanted to be here when it happens. You might even
call it a compulsion. I should be here, it seems, with
you, and Yesui, while Yesugen tends to my body. Come
here, Kati. Meld with me. It's the closest we can be
to touching each other here.*

They came together, a mental twining in a place
without mass, or sound, or touch.

Yes, said Abagai, *I remember it, too, when we held
each other long ago. You were bloodied from battle,
your hands hard and calloused.*

Yours were soft, said Kati, fighting for control.
Abagai! You're back!

Yesui rushed in to meld with both of them, her
sudden presence a shock of both joy and apprehension.
You're well again!

Abagai disengaged herself from them. *You can see
that's not so, dear. I only came to say goodbye to both
of you. My time has come.*

NO! screamed Yesui, and her manifestation blazed
with streamers of red. *I won't let it be!*

Abagai smiled at her. *Sweet child, there are limits
to what you can do. I've lived a full life. All my hopes
for you, your mother and Yesugen have been realized,
and I have no regrets. I am not afraid. Now it's time
for something else.*

What do you mean? asked Kati, wondering at
Abagai's serenity.

Abagai hesitated, then said, *I feel called to go
elsewhere, but where is a mystery to me. Even now,
there is a presence, a force that tugs at me. It seems
impatient. Perhaps it's my own mind, wishing for
an end to my struggle to breathe. These last two
years have been like slow suffocation for me, Kati.
I welcome relief from it.*

Oh, Abagai, Kati said miserably.

I feel a presence, said Yesui softly, *and it's not you. I felt it when you weren't here.*

I was asleep, dear, but now I'm awake. My eyes are closed, and I feel Yesugen's hand in mine, and I see you here. I feel love from all of you, and it's a comfort, yet I'm compelled to leave all of it. There is something else for me. There, you feel it? Isn't it wonderful?

Kati felt herself slipping away. *I don't want to lose you. Your love has held me up so many times.*

It is wonderful, but what is it? asked Yesui. *I feel it very strongly, now.*

STOP IT! said Kati. *You cannot recover when you think only of death. Please, Abagai, focus yourself!*

Yes, I'm doing that, but not as you wish. Abagai's manifestation flickered. She raised her chin, and closed her eyes. *Oh—oh. Yes, I'm ready, now. Kati, Yesui, my love will always be with you. I hope with all my heart that we will see each other again.*

Abagai's face disappeared. Her manifestation began to dim.

ABAGAI! shrieked Kati, but she was drowned out by Yesugen's call.

Mother. MOTHER! Oh, Kati! She's GONE! I just felt her GO!

Yesui momentarily lost control, her manifestation disappearing and reappearing in a blink as she returned for one instant to her own body.

Abagai's manifestation dimmed, and lost form. It began to flicker, feeble sparks of red and yellow within muddy brown, and then there was a terrible flash, an implosion sucking in nearby purple mist of the light of creation, so intense that Kati and Yesui jerked backwards in their astonishment.

They could only stare at what was now there. Where Abagai had been there was now a brilliant ellipsoid of light, silver mixed with purple, opaque, like a solid thing, and immediately it began to move rapidly away from them, heading in the direction of Tengri-Nayon.

Yesugen! Come quickly! Something has happened here!

I can't. My mother has just passed away, Kati. How can you ask that?

Her manifestation is still here, but changed, and it's moving away from us. Please, Yesugen, come quickly!

Kati and Yesui rushed after an apparition that quickly threatened to outdistance them, and its route was instantly familiar to Kati. *Her special place, Yesugen. It's heading in that direction!*

The vortex of Tengri-Nayon was just ahead, and the ellipsoid passed it just as Yesugen's manifestation flashed green within the clouds of creation. Clouds and vortices were a blur as they rushed headlong after the thing.

What is it? shouted Yesugen.

I don't know, but it came out of your mother's manifestation, and I think I know where it's going. We must go faster!

Kati had never traveled so fast in the gong-shi-jie, yet Yesui was managing to stay ahead of her, Yesugen struggling to keep up, the ellipsoid pulling away from all of them.

Clouds of shimmering violet, and the edge of their galaxy was nearing. The ellipsoid crossed it and headed straight towards the distant galaxy Kati had visited before. *Faster!* she urged. *We have a long way to go yet!*

They plunged into violet mist, gaining speed, and

suddenly it was as if a massive vortex of galactic size had appeared in order to pull back on them. The ordinarily quiescent background of violet was now roiling about them, sending them tumbling out of control, and ahead of them a whirling thing, organized in its motion, reaching out like a snake to swallow the remnant of what had once been First Mother to Kati and her people.

Abagai! she shrieked once, and the ellipsoid they'd been chasing was swallowed up, the thing that had taken it collapsing with a splash like water receiving a falling stone, ripples of light passing them as they continued to tumble.

And then it was quiet again. Around them was only the quiescent presence of Yesui's favorite light. Immediately, their tumbling ceased, and they were alone, the great wheel of their galaxy clearly visible behind them.

GONE! screamed Yesugen, and she disappeared, her control lost.

Kati looked longingly at the distant galaxy where Abagai had shown her the birthplace of new stars, and Yesui knew her thoughts.

Will we go there, Mother? I have a strange feeling we should not go further, not now.

I feel it, too, said Kati, the first wave of sorrow hitting her as she said it. *It is over. She is gone.*

I didn't feel her, Mother. It was an energy field of some kind, very concentrated. It disturbed things here. Do you still feel that mysterious presence, Yesui? No, it's disappeared, too.

Then they have gone away together, said Kati.

They fled to their own bodies, as the tidal waves of their grief struck hard.

❖　　❖　　❖

She was exhausted, without sleep, and Mengmoshu had spent most of the night comforting her. Their faces were haggard, eyes bloodshot, and she explained to Elder Hanshou that she'd just received news of the passing of a beloved friend.

The Church of The Mother was a stone structure one block square, with a steepled roof of polished *Tysk* stained red. Twelve massive stone columns supported a plastered, domed ceiling, the walls also plastered white, without windows. Soft light came from panels in the dome to illuminate the rows of pews separated by a single aisle in their centers. The pews were filled two hours before she arrived, and there was a huge crowd outside to hear her message over loudspeakers placed there for the event. The people made way for her quietly, and with little bows as Hanshou led her into the church, but once inside she began to cry again.

"Do you wish to have a moment for quiet meditation?" asked Hanshou, his feelings soft and understanding about her grief.

"Oh, yes," she said, and gripped his arm.

He led her down a helix of stone steps to a wooden door, opened it, and peered inside. "Do you wish to be alone? There are a few people here. The Chapel of Light is open to all people, at any hour. They come here to reflect on their lives."

"Please let them stay," she said.

"I will wait for you here," he said.

The Chapel was small, nearly dark, light coming from swirls of luminous paint on a hemispherical ceiling: purples, reds, greens and yellow mixed together, and somehow familiar. Even her private descriptions of what she saw in the gong-shi-jie were known to the people, and in this room was their effort to simulate it.

There were several pews, a center aisle leading to a shrine on which two candles flickered, and there was an odor of smoldering sweet grass. As she walked down the aisle, several kneeling people stood up, as if to leave.

"Please stay with me," she said softly, and then they kneeled again. She went to the shrine, ignited four candles with a wave of her hand, then returned to a front pew and kneeled there, tears trickling down her cheeks. She clasped her hands before her face, going deep within herself, as if in prayer, her eyes still open.

I travel in the place of your creation, and when I call the light it comes to me and goes where I will it. My daughter moves mass as well as light, and changes one to the other, and from the time I was a child I wonder about the sources of such powers. Why me? Why Yesui? And now the woman who first brought me to the gong-shi-jie has been taken away, and I cannot help but think she is not gone, only changed, and I have witnessed a new force beyond my comprehension. What is that force? Is it First Mother? I want to understand. I want to understand everything, but in the meantime I can only follow my heart, and do what I feel compelled to do.

Beads of sweat broke out on her forehead, her emotion so intense that her eyes were glowing, and green mixed with the blue of a visible aura she'd not consciously sought to bring forth. *Is there someone or something out there to hear my thoughts, or is it my imagination? May I please understand? First Mother— please?*

There, it was out, her first prayer since she'd prayed as a child for release from other peoples' thoughts, but it was Abagai who had come to her rescue. It was Abagai who had been First Mother to her, a mortal woman now dead. Or had she only taken on a new form?

Abagai, I miss you so. I will always love you.

There was a release of sorts, though her chest still ached, and her eyes burned. She wiped them with a hand, stood and walked up the aisle, saw wide eyes glistening in candlelight and aural blue on both sides of her. "The blessings of First Mother are upon all of you," she said, and then found Elder Hanshou waiting for her just inside the exit door.

He led her upstairs and into the people's sanctuary, and a crowd of two thousand rose as she walked down the aisle. Many others stood crammed together at the back of the church, and two television cameras were also there. There was no altar in the church, only a riser and a lectern of elaborately carved wood. Hanshou left her, and sat with her father in a front pew as she stepped up to the lectern and put her two pages of notes there. The aura, the glow of her eyes, had not left, but now she was aware of her appearance, and allowed it to remain as a sign to the people before her: upturned faces reverent, amulets everywhere, in each pair of hands the book that recorded her words spoken over a twenty-four year reign. Television cameras were red eyes glowing in the distance, taking her to hundreds of thousands of people in their homes.

Follow your heart, dear. It was as if Abagai were speaking to her, and Kati swallowed hard, clearing her throat before she spoke. Her hands were cold, and her knees felt weak. She took a deep breath, and stretched out her arms.

"There is love here," she intoned. "Now feel with me the love of First Mother for her people." She focused hard to give them what she felt, and saw heads bow everywhere. "I bring you Her love, and blessings upon you for long and fruitful lives. She is most pleased with what you have done, and for your kindness to Her emissary."

She lowered her arms. "Please sit."

As they did so, and settled themselves, she looked at her notes, and suddenly the words were all wrong. She crumpled the papers into a ball, and looked into her heart to find what should be said.

"Love," she said. "What is it? A feeling, an emotion, a pounding of the pulse, or something more? Perhaps it's caring about another, a suspension of selfish desires, a sacrifice to provide for the lives and needs of others. The Mother has shown me the universe in our travels within the gong-shi-jie, and everywhere there has been love. I've seen great clouds of molecules and dust. They are born through the deaths of old stars, they live, then sacrifice their lives in giving birth to new stars, beginning a new cycle. They are part of First Mother.

"The stars themselves are a part of Her. They warm the planets that bear life, and then they die, changing form, dispersing themselves to form new stars, new planets, even life itself. The atoms of your bodies have come from the deaths of stars. That is a gift to you. In death, the stars have taken on new forms, and all are a part of First Mother.

"Death is change, and rebirth in new forms within The Mother, but as living beings we have unique opportunities to show Her love, opportunities not available to stars or planets or clouds of gas. We live, and First Mother is within each of us. Every Empress, noble, skilled worker or unskilled, those with jobs or without, every human being is a living manifestation of First Mother. We are One within Her, and must care for each other, for The Mother shares Her love equally among all of us.

"Your city is a marvel, and it has come from your special skills and efforts. But you are still part of a whole, and it is Shanji. Do not forget your neighbors, especially those less fortunate than you. With your success comes the power and responsibility to show the love of First Mother within you. Do not be caught up in the excesses of living once practiced by the nobles of the old empire. Where you see poverty, eliminate it by sharing what you have. Care for the sick, the elderly, all those who cannot work, or do not have the skills you've been blessed with. As long as one needy person remains on Shanji, the work of First Mother has not been completed here. Remember that in the cycles of life, you could have been one of them."

Kati paused, and suddenly, what she'd said seemed enough.

"This is the will of First Mother," she said solemnly, then smiled.

"I've had a wonderful visit here, and I hope to return regularly in the future. Thank you so much for your kind hospitality."

There was no applause, only a respectful silence as she walked down the aisle, Mengmoshu, then Hanshou behind her. She touched a few hands, and saw a sea of smiles on both sides of her.

Well?

Very good. You've anticipated a problem with the elitest attitudes that have been developing here. You can be sure your words will be in their little books by the end of the week.

Vans awaited them, the crowd outside parting for her, amulets waving. Hanshou stayed behind, and she pressed his hand warmly. "You are a good person, Elder Hanshou. Please keep what I said today in your heart, and practice it."

He was still bowing to her when the van pulled away. They drove straight to the shuttle field at terrifying speed, Ming-hau at the wheel, and again to the private hangar, boarding quickly after more thanks, compliments, and warm handshakes. As they rolled to a takeoff strip, Kati called to her daughter.

Yesui. I'm coming home now, dear. Are you feeling better?

Oh, Mother, please hurry! I'm in my room. I can't think! I can't work!

The rest was unsaid, but both Kati and her father heard it anyway.

Morbid thinking, said Mengmoshu.

No more than my own, Father, and she sees what I see. When death comes to me, I will be there to greet it in the gong-shi-jie.

CHAPTER FOURTEEN
REVOLUTION

He was nearly asleep when the tele-module beeped at his bedside. Hira stirred and turned over, her back to him as he tapped a key and saw the face of his secretary on the little screen.

"Yes?"

"A caller for you, sir. Red-line; I've routed it, and put it on hold." Priority one, governor's ears only, and no name given.

Antun Wizera clicked off, got up and put on a robe, pulled the covers up over his wife's naked shoulder and quietly left her sleeping there. He went to his private terminal in a room next to Nokai's, faraday-screened and soundproof, speaker and palm-scanner at the door. He placed his palm on the plate there, and said "Enter." The door slid open, and then closed behind him. The screen of his console was brightly lit and Yesugen's face was there. The icon for real time was pulsing below her.

He sat down, and Yesugen smiled faintly. "I'm sorry to disturb your sleep, Governor, but I just arrived."

"You're on your flagship, then," he said, feeling suddenly uneasy.

"Yes."

"Please accept my sympathy for the loss of your mother. She was a fine woman, and wise. She has shown patience and understanding regarding our problems here, and I hope you will continue to support us as Mandughai."

Yesugen's eyes were suddenly narrowed and hard. Wizera sensed a bitterness there, and a stoic, cold resolve that made his stomach crawl. "Calm yourself, Governor," she said tersely. "Before her death, my mother made it clear to me her commitment to Lan-Sui City was absolute, and I will honor that. My methods, however, are different from hers, and always have been. She had patience where I did not, and Lan-Sui is a good example of it. This business with the rebellion has gone on far too long. It must end. It must end *now*."

Wizera's face flushed. "Are you here to invade our moons?" he asked bluntly.

"I'm here to prepare for it, yes. In the end, I think an occupation will be necessary, at least until things are stabilized. I don't intend to have a permanent presence here, Governor. It's a drain on resources needed for Meng-shi-jie, and I've been under pressure for a long time to withdraw. Now that my mother is gone, that pressure will only increase, and it's not easy to argue against it.

"The only excuse for intervention is to assure our supplies of fuels. I could do that easily by simply taking over Gutien and Nan and declaring them protectorates of Meng-shi-jie, and it's only a promise I made to my mother that prevents me from doing it." Yesugen's voice was nearly a growl, and her eyes blazed red as she said it.

"There is little we could do to prevent it," Wizera said humbly, and lowered his eyes. "All our armored vessels are now fully occupied with the protection of our city from what Yesui has done to our alpha ring."

Yesugen made a rude sound. "You asked for new life to be brought to Lan-Sui, and now that it's happening you can only complain. Did you think it would be an easy thing?"

"The people fear what is happening. It inflames them, and the rebels have used it to strengthen their position. If Yesui could cease her efforts for just a little while I could—"

"She will continue what she does until her mission is completed; the people will have to live with their fears, and it's up to you to lead them. If you think you can't do that, then appoint someone else who can."

Wizera felt a surge of adrenaline that quickened his heartbeat, and brought him a rare anger. "That's exactly what the rebels want! Are you now sympathetic with their cause?"

"I'm sympathetic with none of you," said Yesugen, her eyes still red. "You've lived soft lives for generations, and now that things are not so easy you react like small children. I have no patience for that. You have problems. Now solve them. You have complaints. Now act on them. There are rebels, yes, and we know their leaders. We know where they are, and I can have them killed with a single command. Do you think that will solve all your problems?"

What she said confused him. "I don't condone assassination for any reason, of course, but without leaders the rebellion would surely falter. I don't see what—"

"Wizera! Open your eyes! Do you really think a former police chief and a few henchmen are behind all of this? Can you possibly believe that one man can work to put himself in your office without commited support from important people in your own city?"

"I'm aware of sympathies for the independence of Gutien and Nan. Many people have relatives there. We have a democracy here, Madam. I do not dictate how the people must think." He said it indignantly, then winced as Yesugen exploded back at him.

"I'm not talking about that, you fool!"

"Then please enlighten me," he muttered, shaking all over with rage.

Yesugen's face was a frightening thing, her tusks bared, hands clenched tight into fists, but then the hand of someone else appeared and grasped her shoulder. She turned to her left, and said, "Yes, YES! I'm *trying*!" When she looked back, she leaned forward, so close he could see her tongue moving.

"Listen to me, Wizera. For the past few months, several shipments of arms have been received on both Gutien and Nan, and another arrived just yesterday: laser rifles, battery packs, and now even heavy stuff for ships. You worry about asteroids. Are you aware that only *half* of the debris control ships are on patrol now? The other half are on the ground, being outfitted with additional tight-focus weaponry designed only for the penetration of armored hulls. *My* hulls, Governor, and the shutters of your own city. While you sit around and wait for a strike to be settled, the moons ready themselves for war against you and your city, and your real enemies are there with you, undoubtedly preparing to flee when the time comes."

"But *who*?" he asked.

Yesugen held up a thick folder. "I have all the

manifests, bills of lading, the dates, the ports of exit and entry, everything shipped as machine tools. I've even broken it down so you can see which tool is what kind of weapon. Everything here is on cube. I'm sending it to you as soon as we're finished here."

Now she smiled, and fluttered the file at him. "Would you like to know what shipping company is exclusively involved?"

He nodded.

"Inayo Industries, a subsidiary I believe you're acquainted with."

"But that's owned by Bator Corporation!" he said, astounded.

"Really. Well, they own most of Lan-Sui and its moons right now. It looks to me like they want all of it. Have you been having problems with them?" Her smile was now a smirk.

"Only the usual complaints about taxes and subsidies, especially since the start of the strike, but they've been private. In public, the company has always supported me."

"It seems you must have a private chat with them, Governor, but not before you've gone over what I'm sending you, and ferreted out the labyrinth of accounts undoubtedly used to pay for all those weapons. Your tax people can quickly do it for you. And while they do that, you might also let it be known that as of today I have placed a blockade around both Gutien and Nan. Any approaching ship will be ionized without warning, and that includes any vessel on debris patrol. And any vessel leaving the moons will be immediately destroyed."

"This is an act of war," he gasped.

"Your war, not mine. Like it or not, what I'm doing is in support of your office. The next steps are yours to take. Your little democracy isn't working, Wizera. You've allowed it to approach anarchy, and the next step is a dictatorship under a few people who only think of their own profits. Your powers are hereditary, going back thousands of years. It's time for you to use them, or else you are lost, and then your moons will be mine. Is that clear enough?"

"It's clear that the moons now have an excuse for revolution, and the people here will support it. They will see me as your puppet." Wizera's voice shook with emotion.

Yesugen *laughed* at him. "Oh, how soft and simple your life has been, and how unfortunate for you to be such a humanitarian. Mother always admired you for your good heart. I do not. You are Governor of Lan-Sui. Now use your political mind, for once. You have called in my forces to suppress a rebellion that threatens your city with destruction. We act on *your* orders. You have uncovered a sinister plot behind it, a plot by the very corporation that controls all moon operations.

"If you truly believe in democracy, and I think you do, then no single corporation can be allowed to have the power Bator has accumulated. You must nationalize it, or regulate its operations. You have caught them attempting to overthrow the government! And if the moons want independence, give them the semblance of it. Let them have mayors or councils, but as protectorates of Lan-Sui. Simple solutions, Governor, but your belief in pure democracy has made you blind to them."

Her voice was softer now, even conciliatory, as if speaking to an ignorant child. He wanted to be angry, but couldn't do it. His mind whirled with projections of how the people would react if he followed Yesugen's suggestions. How would he feel in their place? What did they want? A safe, comfortable place to live, food on the table, interesting work, a few luxuries, these were the basic things. And as Governor, he was expected to provide them the opportunities they required. It was not the political system that mattered, but the quality of peoples' lives, and that was now surely threatened.

"Very well," he said. "I will say you act on my orders, but if what you send me does not implicate Bator Corporation in backing the revolution, I will be finished here."

"Then you must move quickly," said Yesugen. "I will not wait for you. At the first sign of armed camps on the moons, I will occupy them and take military control. That could happen soon—today, or tomorrow."

"I understand," he said. "We've said enough. Please send that material right away."

Yesugen was nodding at him when her image disappeared from the screen.

The material she'd promised was already coming through when he awoke his Chief of Staff. "Dorvod, I'm sorry. Come to my office right away. We have an extreme emergency on our hands," he said, and hung up before the man could answer him.

Dorvod Tolui arrived minutes later; Wizera showed him what Yesugen had sent, and told him everything.

Dorvod did not seem surprised. "Our investigators drew blanks in finding the backers of moon independence, but we were beginning to see the true extent of Bator's holdings and influence. They now control nearly seventy percent of the commerce in Lan-Sui City, and essentially everything on the moons. This has been building for years, sir."

"Well, it's going to stop right here!" said Wizera, with a new rush of determination.

Two accountants were called in from Treasury, and they worked with extreme security at Wizera's private terminal. Passwords were of no consequence; the tax people had all of them, even for the elements of the conglomerate that was Bator Corporation. For hours, they followed a maze of shipping orders, purchase orders, work orders and payment vouchers from one Bator subsidiary to another, then back again, looking for convergence to a single order, letter, anything that had initiated all of it.

Wizera waited tensely in his office, stomach grumbling over a missed breakfast. He filled it with strong tea until he was shaking, and busied himself with minor things. When Dorvod arrived with a thin folder in his hand, Wizera looked up expectantly, and his heart was thumping hard. Dorvod was frowning, and he laid the folder down by Wizera's hands. "The news is not good, sir."

There was a sharp pain in his chest, but only because he'd forgotten to breathe. He opened the folder, read its contents quickly, and the pain went away. He smiled.

"No, Dorvod, the news is *good*. It is excellent, the best I've ever received."

Tolui looked at him strangely. "Sir?"

Wizera laughed, and slapped the folder closed with the palm of his hand. "I'm fine, Dorvod, but there's one more thing. I need copies of the letter, and all the signed checks. Get those, please."

"Yes, sir," said Tolui, and as the man turned to leave, Wizera was already punching numbers into his tele-module. He made three calls, but it was the third one he savored the most.

"Bator Associates," said a lovely young woman from the screen.

"Mondo Bator, please. This is Governor Antun Wizera calling."

"He's in a meeting, sir. Can I have him call you back?"

"No, you can get him right now. Tell him it involves the doubtful future of his company. Say it exactly that way, please."

She stared at him for one instant, then went away, and the beefy face of Mondo Bator was on the screen a minute later.

"What is this, Antun?" growled the man.

"Something unfortunate for you," said Wizera. "Treasury agents and police will be at your office within minutes. All your files have been downloaded, so you needn't bother to erase anything, or try to hide yourself. The charge is treason, Mondo, treason against Lan-Sui, but there's a secondary issue involving misappropriation of funds that the union on Gutien and Nan will find most interesting."

"You're insane," said Bator. "You've finally gone over the edge."

"I suppose I have," said Wizera cheerfully. "Oh, there is another thing. As of this morning, I've used the ships of Meng-shi-jie to set up a blockade around Gutien and Nan. Warn your people there, Mondo. Any ships that attempt flight will be destroyed on sight, and debris control ships attempting approach will be treated likewise. And you can expect ground forces to land on the moons at the first sign of armed men there. You must tell Tokta Kuril, or Oghul Ghaimish, whatever you call him, that he should keep your weapons safely in their crates."

"This is the end of you," said Bator, jowls flapping,

his forehead glistening with sweat. "The people will be swarming at your gates by noon."

"It will be a wonderful opportunity for me to explain everything, Mondo. I'll get right on it. And I look forward to seeing you in court."

The screen of the tele-module went blank with the snap of a finger striking a key. His energy had returned. He felt refreshed, renewed, but his stomach still grumbled, and it was time for lunch. He went down the hallway to the dining room in his living quarters, whistling a little tune to himself. Lunch had been served an hour before, but the remnants were still there: some bread, a few slabs of vegi-meat, a serving or two of cold noodles congealing in a tureen. Nokai was still there with his tea, reading a book.

Wizera served himself a plate of food, and ate greedily, oblivious to the slimy consistency of the noodles. He caught Nokai peeking at him from behind the book, frowning, yet smiling at the same time.

"You have a question, son?" he asked, tearing off a chunk of bread with his teeth and chewing vigorously.

"You're strangely happy at a time of great danger, Father. I've never seen you quite so pleased with yourself."

Wizera looked at his son, now a man, and beautiful, both in body and soul. "No question, then. You see everything, and not just from the expression on my face, or the color of my emotions. You know my every thought, including what has happened this morning. What else do you see there? Here, I'll think it strongly for you."

Nokai smiled, and put down his book. "I see how much you love me," he said softly.

"There, you see? On Shanji you would be called

Moshuguang." He scraped the remaining mess of noodles onto his plate, and twirled some on a fork.

"They're not empaths, Father, and so far there's only one person I talk to without words."

"Ah, yes, Yesui, the supernatural mystery woman who brings mass to Lan-Sui. Is that why she's interested in you, because you can talk to her?"

"It—it's more than that," said Nokai, nearly stammering.

Wizera stuffed the last of the noodles in his mouth, and swallowed them whole. "You love her," he said. "I see it in your eyes when her name is spoken."

"Yes," said Nokai, intertwining his fingers on the table. "I love her very much."

"Have you told her that?"

"She is the Mei-lai-gong, father. She sees everything in me."

Wizera wiped his mouth, and stood up. "She's also a woman, and if you love her you must say it! Ask your mother, if you doubt me. Do it today! Today is a day of action for our family!"

Antun Wizera marched out of the room to rejoin Tolui, leaving the agony of personal decision-making to his son, and without thought of consequences.

There was no coup, no internal takeover by Oghul Ghaimish and his followers, when word of the blockade arrived. Even those who'd still remained loyal to Lan-Sui were suddenly on his side, for all they could see was armed conquest of their world by the Empress of Meng-shi-jie, and a dictatorship to follow it. Despair had turned into grim resolve when they heard of the cache of arms Ghaimish had obtained for their defense, and they cheered as he cracked open the first crates to show them what was there. Now they had formed orderly lines, each man receiving laser rifle and power pack, and going to his designated platoon as assigned by Chief Steward Jumdshan. For the moment, weapons in hands, there was no fear, only resolve in defending their homes and families. They did not yet think about the force coming against them.

The news, however, was not good when Jumdshan returned from Communications, frowning.

"Well?" asked Ghaimish.

"I couldn't reach them on either frequency, and then I called my brother. Bator and the others have been arrested, and charged with treason and fraud. It was all on television. There was a huge protest at the palace gates, and Wizera used it as a forum to explain what has happened, and now the people are cheering him."

"He was not supposed to be alive," growled Ghaimish.

"The blockade was so sudden, without provocation or warning," said Jumdshan. "I doubt that the team to take out Wizera had even been set up yet. We weren't expecting this for *months!*"

"Are you aware of any television sets here, Jumdshan?" asked Ghaimish, watching the ranks of platoons growing around the walls of the great warehouse. The men were fiddling with their weapons like children, and laughing.

"No."

"Then the men have no need to know what has happened. To know that Yesugen's monsters come to invade their homes is enough."

Jumdshan grasped his arm hard. "But now our situation is untenable. Yesugen's surprise move has destroyed our timing, Oghul. Half our ships are still here, Wizera is alive, and Bator's arrested. The coup in Lan-Sui City has been snuffed before it could start. *Now* what do we do?"

"Proceed as planned," said Ghaimish, "and if you don't let go of my arm, I'll break your wrist right in front of the men."

Jumdshan released him. "How can we?"

"Threaten the city. Force a compromise. I have no illusions about resisting Yesugen's forces. The best we can do here is buy time. Her blockade can work for us, now that our debris control crews remaining on station have declared their strike to protest it. She will see soon enough that all her ships must be used to protect the city, but we must have time!"

"That could be days! The shutters around the city can withstand the impact of anything smaller than a meter, and most of the major debris has been cleared out again."

"Then we must arrange something larger," said Ghaimish. "There's still a pilot out there who owes you a favor."

"Zedenbal, yes. He initiated the strike vote by the pilots, and they respect him."

"I will go with you to call him. It's time for you to collect that favor," said Ghaimish.

He pointed at the men in their ranks. "Look at them. Most have never held a weapon in their hands. It was all intended to be posturing, a show of determination to win the sympathy of the city people when Bator was Governor. Damn Yesugen. Damn her and her unborn child! The pilots are our only hope now, Jumdshan. I want to talk to your man."

They left the cavern and went below to Communications, ordering the men there out of the room. They moved like loyal sheep, seeing Ghaimish as leader of their defense. Jumdshan worked the transmitter and soon had Captain Lingdan Zedenbal on the air, voice only, for visual transmissions would be open to interception by Yesugen's ships.

"Lingdan, it's Jumdshan again. Our situation is very bad here, and we need your help."

"Anything, sir. What is it?" came the immediate reply.

"Oghul Ghaimish is here with me, Lingdan. Your instructions will come from him. I've assured him of your loyalty to our cause, and he has trusted my judgement. Please do your best for him. We need your best if we're to survive."

"You've got it, sir!" said Zedenbal, then, "Good evening, Mister Ghaimish. A pleasure, sir."

"It's *my* pleasure, lad," said Ghaimish, "to be speaking to the man who saved Lan-Sui City. I can think of no other person brave enough to do what is required at this time, and I will not mince words with you. The conquest of Lan-Sui is now underway. Meng-shi-jie's blockade was sudden, and now we have word that Governor Wizera has become the puppet of Empress Yesugen. The government has fallen. We expect an invasion by ground forces at any moment and have armed ourselves. We can hold out for a day or two before being overwhelmed by Yesugen's monsters, and I don't have to tell you what they'll do to our women and children after the men are dead. We need time, lad, time to force a stalement and negotiate a compromise, and it can only be done from space. You and your fellows are the only people we have there, Captain, and our survival now rests solely on your shoulders."

A pause of two beats, then a quiet voice, "I understand, sir. Just tell me what must be done, and I'll do it."

Ghaimish allowed a quiver to infect his voice. "Oh,

if only there were more like you I could call to action now. We're all very proud of you, Captain. Our situation is so desperate, but there *is* one hope, and it relates to Empress Yesugen's greed. She seeks to conquer the moons and assure her world a supply of free fuels, but she also wants the city, with all its manufacturing facilities and workers who can be her slaves. She wants *all* of it. She *needs* all of it, Captain. What I plan is a real, physical threat to destroy what she needs and at the same time to create a diversion that will allow us to get our newly armed ships off the ground with weapons that can penetrate the hulls of her ships and give us a fighting chance."

"We *have* such weapons?" asked Lingdan.

"Yes, from friends in the city, dear friends now imprisoned by Yesugen and her puppet governor. The weapons are installed, and the ships ready to fly if we can somehow draw ships away from the blockade. The task of doing that must fall to you and your fellow pilots. There's no other choice for me, and I hesitate to ask it because there will be a terrible risk to your lives. Only someone like yourself would even consider it, Captain, and now you're our only hope." His voice cracked and faltered as he said it.

Ghaimish hesitated, waited several seconds until he heard that calm yet firm voice once again.

"What are your orders, sir?"

"Where are you now?" Ghaimish asked quickly.

"The inner edge of the alpha ring. We've been picking off the larger stuff as it comes out on trajectories that pass close to the city, and leaving the smaller things to remind the Governor we're officially on strike. We'd heard he ordered the blockade, sir. Now I see we were wrong."

"He carries out Yesugen's orders, Captain. He's

betrayed all of us. You once saved Lan-Sui City from destruction, and now I'm asking you to threaten its destruction to create the diversion we need."

"Sir?"

"I want you and your fellow pilots to seek out several bodies large enough to shatter the thick shutters protecting the city, and guide them there on a collision course. When you're certain of the trajectories, release your asteroids and return to a station we'll assign you at the edge of the blockade zone."

"You're asking me to destroy the city, sir. I can't kill innocent—"

"Do you think Yesugen will allow destruction of her city, Captain? She will respond quickly by pulling her small cruisers from the blockade to blast those asteroids, and it's the small cruisers that keep our ships on the ground. Once they've lifted off, our ships can attack her heavy cruisers *and* her flagship, destroy her infantry, and put her on the defensive. The city will be in no real peril, Captain. I've studied the woman's history. I know how she thinks. But you must move quickly. Begin right now. Your threat against the city must be obvious within the next two days, or we'll all be either dead, or slaves of Meng-shi-jie. You're our only *hope! Please!*"

A few seconds of silence was an eternity. Ghaimish held his breath.

"All right, sir, I'll do it. I can only speak for myself, but I'm pretty sure the other pilots will go along with it. They all have families on Gutien. I'll contact you on this frequency for any updates."

"Thank you so much, lad. I— I—" Ghaimish felt dizzy with relief, his voice gone.

Jumdshan leaned close to the transmitter, and said,

"He's filled with emotion, Lingdan, and so am I. The Mother has sent you to us for this day, and She will be with you. Good hunting, son."

"Sir!" said Lingdan Zedenbal, and he was gone.

Ghaimish sighed, and wiped his brow. "What a relief! That was close."

Jumdshan was frowning at him. "Why? He believed everything you told him. You lie very well, Ghaimish. Mondo Bator is even better at it. Did you know all that money he held back from my budget went into his pockets, and those of his major investors?"

"Of course not," he lied. "Another lie, Jumdshan? Or a coverup? You're in the best position to know if it's true or not. Our cash is kept in *your* vaults. Now let's get back to the men."

They left Communications and climbed the stairs again, Ghaimish thinking, *Twenty thousand new shares of company stock down the drain, but that cash would be useful if I can get away. But where? Nan? Not the city, or Meng-shi-jie. It must be Nan. It must be soon. Damn that Yesugen! Damn her to slow death and eternal pain! If only I could be the instrument of it!*

The words of Nokai's father burned in his mind as he returned to his room. Nokai tuned out everything, the muted babblings of his fellow Empaths, the excited conversation between his father and Tolui, and he opened the windows to look out at the city. There was a crawling sensation in his stomach, and he breathed deeply to calm it. *What am I feeling?* he wondered.

There was sympathy, for his father, a good man who loved him, a man of peace, but slow to make decisions until subconsciously pushed by his own son. Nokai felt guilt in the doing of it, though he'd always followed what his father wished to do. What he regretted was the necessity of pushing his father into action. *I do not want such control over people*, he thought.

But you have it, came a reply from within him. *It's not a bad thing, if you use it for good. You are a Searcher, and more. Yesui sees it in you. You are noticed.*

Nokai closed his eyes, exhaling slowly and seeing a matrix of purple dots twinkling in blackness, a vision that had often been there since his first contact with Yesui. Meeting her, then loving her had opened up something new within him, and lately there had even been visions of roiling, colorful clouds sprinkled with points of light from blue to red. He sighed, and the vision was suddenly there again, a point of light bursting forth at the end of a protuberance from a roiling mass of greenish brown mist.

You see far, Nokai. There are wonders within you yet to be explored, yet you hesitate to tell Yesui of your love for her, even when she sees it. She waits to hear such words from the one she loves, and grows impatient over it. Tell her what you feel.

The thought was like a soft whisper close to his ear. Nokai's face flushed, and he sank to his knees, bowing over, and covering his face with his hands. *Oh, Mother, I'm only your servant! Please give me the courage to follow your will, and guide me in your ways. I am obedient to you.*

All are within The Mother, Nokai, and are Her servants. I will watch over you, and also Yesui, for both of you are important to us. You will bring new life to Our Creation. Rest, now. Yesui will soon come to you again, and you must speak your heart. Know that I will be with you.

The vision of green mist flared brightly with a single pulse, then faded to blackness as Nokai's heart raced. A tingling sensation flowed down his arms to his fingertips, lingering there for a moment. His eyes stung, and he blinked several times, then stood up, breath rapid, and leaned on the railing of the balcony. Blackness above him, city lights far out and below his place, and he could hear the faint sounds of traffic in the streets, the clatter of dust and pebbles on the shutters overhead. Nokai held out his arms towards the lights, thinking of Yesui.

"We are within The Mother," he whispered solemnly.

CHAPTER FIFTEEN
COMFORT AND DISCOVERY

Yesui fled from her grief and found both comfort and love within a single week. For one week she'd remained in her room to stare at the walls, eating little, caring nothing about herself or her work and refusing to answer Mengjai when he called with a new idea or something he'd seen in his travels.

But then her mother had returned and the evening they'd spent crying together had seemed a relief for both of them. Feeling her mother's pain had somehow diminished her own, and then there was the talk about what they'd seen and what it might mean. Was Abagai truly dead, or had she been changed into another form and rushed away to begin a new existence elsewhere? The force they'd encountered, what was it? She had sensed an incredible energy density in that brightly glowing ellipsoid born of Abagai's manifestation. Light from the gong-shi-jie had been sucked into it, and then it had moved with direction and purpose, as if alive.

The thing that had swallowed Abagai's remnant had twisted the threads of the fabric of space into a vortex, then a singularity at the instant the ellipsoid had disappeared. Her mother hadn't seen it, could not see it. Yesui tried making a sketch of the thread pattern for her, but the drawing was crude, only a hint of what she'd seen. And when Mother said she would await her own death in the gong-shi-jie, it had only made Yesui cry hysterically again.

They talked out their grief, their hopes that Abagai still lived happily in a new and wonderful form, and then Mother went back to her desk to resume the duties Yesui would someday have to face, but not yet. Yesui went her own way, drowning her grief with the work that was her life, and again spent most of her time in the gong-shi-jie. Play or work, it was all the same to her, and, as usual, in her enthusiasm she went rapidly from one thing to another.

Mengjai nagged her about folding space to move their ship faster and said she should experiment more with the threads. Father even joined their conversation, amused by it and taking nothing they said seriously. His reaction only made her more eager to try it, and she did, but on a grand scale near the galactic edge, bringing in the violet light to form mass and making a little dimple in the pattern of threads there.

But the mass was fixed, and a dimple was not a folding, like holding a sheet of something and bending it to bring the two ends together. Yes, the fabric of space was distorted by mass, but only locally. To truly fold space, she must somehow work directly with the threads as if they were physical things, with real, elastic properties. But it seemed they were *not* physical things, only strange indicators of the presence of mass, or the lack of it.

How to manipulate them remained a mystery to her, and so she cleaned up her experiment by flashing the mass she'd created into light, and bringing it back to the gong-shi-jie where it was again violet and quiescent as before. Even that process she did not understand, for it was only necessary that she think it, and it would happen. The fabric of space, however, continued to disobey her mental projections of its folding, and so her interest waned and wandered.

It was then that she returned to Lan-Sui.

Mass transfer to the planet had become a regular routine over the past two years, but now it was more delicate, for Yesui was nearing the mass Mengjai had calculated for her. She could only estimate the mass she transfered each time, her accuracy little better than Shanji's mass, and in the end it would be the surface temperature that would tell her how close she'd come. Compression had most certainly begun, but heat transfer from the dense interior was a slow, convective process dependent on the distribution of mass she brought to it. She had argued with her brother for hours over it.

"So, give me a model for where the new mass is going."

"It goes everywhere. It follows the threads."

"Then most of it is very deep. It could be thousands of years before we see an effect."

"But the surface is covered with new storms, with the majority now appearing near the equator!"

"Helium condensation. That's more transient. I'm talking about compressional heat production."

"But the helium is a part of the mass. It must not

be so deep, if things are already happening at the equator!"

And so on.

It could be a week, a year, a thousand years before Lan-Sui's surface was truly warm again. It was now at one hundred eighty absolute, and steady, yet the surface was dramatically changed, huge hurricanes ten diameters of Shanji across forming each week, monstrous ovals in red, yellow and blue. Even the storm below the city had changed. Once blue, it was now red, the center of the vortex seeming to fill with new gases, a ring of boiling clouds billowing higher at its rim each time she saw it. Yesui had had a dream of those clouds reaching up towards the city, touching it, tumbling it, the city sinking deeper and deeper and Nokai calling out to her as the storm swallowed him up.

Yesui dipped into real space to see her handiwork, then to the interface of the gong-shi-jie to examine the threads. The violet light came to her, went to her focus and continued to come until the ripple in the threads was the size she wanted. She released it, then watched the ripples flow into the depression of the thread pattern that was Lan-Sui. Only then did she flash again into real space. There was no visible effect from what she'd just done, yet the mass was now very close, no more than one, perhaps two transfers left to do, and the planet was still too cold.

Two frustrations in one day, and so she went to Nokai.

Hello. I'm back again. What are you doing?

Reading a book and missing you, wondering if you're still sad.

It's better, especially when I stay busy. I'm trying some new things with the threads, and I'm just about finished with your planet. Mengjai says the mass is just about right for a thousand degree surface temperature at equilibrium. What are you reading?

A history written by an old priest around a thousand years ago. It's something for class. He talks about The Mother here. Did you know that in the beginning She created many universes, not just one?

Really?

Yes, many universes, all at the same time, all expanding but somehow separated.

I'm sure Mengjai has heard all about it. Do you really miss me?

Yes. I think about you all the time. Now that you've nearly finished with Lan-Sui, will you be going away? I've been thinking about that, too.

Well, I have many other things to do, but I can come back to visit if you want me to.

Yes, I want you to come back. I—I—

What? Your mind is stuck again, Nokai. You can't hide from me.

All right, I don't want to lose you. I don't want you to go away at all.

Why?

A ten beat pause. *There's a twinkle in the eyes of the image you show me. Am I amusing you?*

Yes. You have such a hard time saying what's in your heart, and I have to torture it out of you. Why don't you want to lose me?

You know why, and it's not fair. You see everything in me, while I can only sense your emotions, not your thoughts.

Yesui concentrated hard. *Here's something that's deep in my heart. Can you feel it?*

Oh, Yesui.

Do you feel it, Nokai? Do you know what it means?

Yes—I mean, I feel it. I want to believe I know what it is, but a part of me is saying it's not possible.

Then I will say it, but only if you tell me what's in your heart, Nokai. I want to hear the words that say what I also feel for you.

The floodgate was opened by the last thing she'd said, a sweet, mental flood washing over her. *Oh, Yesui, Yesui, by The Mother, I have no right, but I love you! I love you with all my heart and soul, but you are the Mei-lai-gong.*

And you are my love, Nokai. I love you very deeply. Believe me, it is real. She had never felt so wonderful.

You have such power, and I'm so ordinary, and we can never meet face-to-face. I—I want to touch you, hold you—kiss you. When I say it, it seems like blasphemy to me. You are like The Mother.

I'm a woman, my love. When you touch your face, like now, I feel it. I feel your cheek, your lips, so warm, your soft hands. They say I'm the Mei-lai-gong, Nokai, but she is also a woman who loves a man and desires him. I want your arms around me, your lips on mine. I want that very much.

I cannot touch you, he said mournfully.

I'm not so terribly far away. There's a constant stream of freighters between Meng-shi-jie and Shanji. As I recall, the current travel time, one way, is approaching nine years.

NINE YEARS?

Well, yes, that is a long time for us. The military ships do it in six, but that still won't do. I'm working on that, love. If I can get the threads to fold for me, travel distances can be considerably reduced, and I know I can do it.

Oh, Yesui, would you wait even six years for me,

*wait for an empath you've never really seen, when
there are probably suitors all around you?*

*I have no suitors, Nokai. I've been too busy for that,
and besides, it's you I want. Don't you believe me?*
Again she focused hard, to show him her deep love.

*Yes, but I think we're dreaming dreams. Meng-
shi-jie's military vessels are all readying for war
now. They've blockaded our moons. Things are very
bad here.*

*Yesugen has told me. She wants me to stay
around until things are settled. I think she sees me
as a secret weapon she can use. The purple light,
you know, very powerful. I've ionized small moons
with it during my experiments. I'm a strategic
weapon, it seems, but Mother has more practice
with that.*

*We could use some of your ionizing right now.
There's a constant rain of debris hitting the city
shields, and it sounds like a thousand hammers
pounding in unison all the time. Sleep is impossible,
and I had to close the windows just to be able to
think when you arrived.*

*I thought you had debris control ships to take care
of that.*

*We do, but their numbers have been cut in half by
the blockade, and the rest aren't working very hard.
We're all sitting around waiting for a really big rock
to come in and crack the city dome, but so far it's all
been small stuff.*

Would you excuse me for a moment?

She flashed into real space before he answered, but
targeted on him, coming out a thousand kilometers
from the city. Tengri-Nayon was shining brightly
behind her, and she saw a fan of dust swirling towards
the city, tapering to a point near the distant, yet

innermost ring of Lan-Sui. A simple task, something she could do while hovering in real space.

I call the light, and it comes to me, and—goes— right—there.

Space exploded in purple brilliance as far as she could see along the fan of dust; there were flashes of red and green, even gold within it, and then it was dark again, distant stars now steady spots of white and blue, no shimmering fan left to be seen.

She returned to the gong-shi-jie, then to Nokai. *Back again. The debris comes from the inner ring, and if—*

It stopped! The noise just stopped! What did you DO?

It's only temporary, Nokai. I ionized everything as far as I could see, but you were right. The source is the inner ring, and more debris will be coming. If it gets too bad, I'll just remove the ring. It's only a decorative thing, anyway. What's wrong? Nokai—don't you dare think of me that way!

I can't help it! Your powers aren't human!

STOP IT! I LOVE YOU!

Oh, Yesui, I love you too. What are we going to do?

Get you to Shanji as soon as possible. Trust me, Nokai. I'm getting to work on it right now. I just had an idea about the threads. Get some sleep while you can. That banging on the city's shields will probably start again in a few hours. Gotta go. Loveyouloveyouloveyou.

Me too.

Swirling purple and violet all around her, and the giddyness of love in her soul. The idea had come out of nowhere, while they were talking. To work the threads, she must truly understand them, understand their structure and dynamics, and she didn't. The idea had been a vision of those threads, recalling the time she had first really looked at them a long time ago.

Mengjai had been with her, and with his scientist's mind he'd noted details in the threads that she'd somehow forgotten in working with them. Now she remembered the threads were not continuous, but a series of points, closely spaced, glowing green. To see that, she had to be close to them, and for years that had not been necessary, had not even been desirable, for her work had required that she see the whole pattern of threads on a large scale and that meant working far from them.

Yesui went to the vortex of Tengri-Nayon in the gong-shi-jie and paused there to relax herself. *Playtime*, she thought. *This is when I have fun, and just let things happen. Slowly, now.*

She eased herself slowly through transition, the thing her mother and even Abagai had never been able to do. The web of green threads was instantly there, far off, spreading in every direction. For the first time, she noticed that the matrix of purple lights had not yet appeared. *There are two boundaries here*, she thought, *and they're not together.*

But when she thought of the purple matrix, it *was* there, flashing once, and she found herself back in real space, the huge disk of Tengri-Nayon glaring at her.

Oops. Mustn't think of the purple matrix. This is very delicate. Why was it so easy when my brother was with me?

She tried again and kept the purple matrix out of her mind. The threads were there again, but looked solid. She thought them larger, focusing on one of them, and it rushed towards her, or she towards it, she didn't know which. Glowing points of light, then fuzzy patches, then—

Flash—purple matrix—flash again, and Tengri-Nayon was again there.

Ooooo! If she had hands to throw something with, she would have thrown it. *With Mengjai, I did it the first time!*

He was a distraction for you. You're trying too hard, and must be patient with this. Don't think so much!

Thank you, mind, for that sage advice, and now I've started talking to myself.

You're welcome. Now try again.

She did that, and the threads were there again.

Easy, now. Focus on a point, and relax. You're drifting, drifting, slowly, slowly coming in. One point. Forget the rest. There it comes. See? Not one point, but a cluster of little ones, very close together. Stop here. Look at it.

It was like a globular cluster of green stars, and it was flickering.

Why is it flickering like that?

Energy comes to it in pulses from the Other Side, and sustains it.

The Other Side?

Another universe, next to yours. This is the boundary between them.

And where did I come up with that idea?

You didn't. I did.

Suddenly she was a little girl again, and felt like giggling at her invention of an imaginary playmate who could share her travel in the gong-shi-jie. Perhaps it was her missing of Abagai, or wanting again to be with Nokai, or wishing that Mengjai were here with his nagging insights on things.

Okay. What's your name?

I don't have one. You can call me Mind if you like.

Okay, Mind, what do I do now? Yesui was now amused at herself and having fun, letting herself totally go with what was happening.

Make the cluster of lights glow brighter by bringing more energy to them.

From the gong-shi-jie?

No, silly, from the Other Side! That's where the energy for the threads comes from. It's purple beyond purple, just like you're used to, but once on This Side, it's green. Call out the green light, and the rest will follow it.

Silly, indeed, but she was still having fun with this wild fantasy of hers, and she had *never* been so close to the threads before. Whatever she was doing, it was working for her.

All right. *I call the green light, from each point that I see, and it comes to me—right—here!*

The cluster of green blazed forth so brightly it was like a single star, growing in size large enough to nearly envelope her, and she was frightened by it, her call forgotten and instantly there was only a cluster of green points flickering dimly as before.

What was THAT?

That was very good. You can do it at any distance, if you just focus on one point. Two or more will not do. Let's back off a little, so you can see what happens.

Anything you say, Mind. This was *really* getting interesting, now. Yesui drifted away from her chosen thread, until she could barely see the fuzziness of each point within it.

Far enough. Now focus on one point, and call the light again.

Yesui did it without hesitation. A single point flashed brightly, but as it dimmed she noticed a circular wave of flickering lights moving out from it, across many threads, not just one responding to the initial disturbance she'd created. But the wave seemed to quickly dissipate.

All the points are connected, you see, and there is a leakage of energy back to the Other Side. The more energy you bring to a single point, the further the wave will travel, and it moves very fast. The wave you just created moved perhaps a light month in real space in only an instant of time.

Mengjai should be here to see how quickly I'm figuring things out, thought Yesui. *He'd be amazed at my genius.*

We give you the answers because it will soon be necessary for you to put them into practice.

Um? We? Well, she thought, if Mind wanted to be multiple Minds, why not?

I'm sorry, Mind. The credit of discovery goes to you.

That's better. Now let me show you the use of this. We need to find a small object in real space, a small asteroid, perhaps.

The rings of Lan-Sui are full of them, Yesui said, wondering, *What am I up to now?*

No. Something more isolated, said Mind.

Well, there are many icy moonlets in a great cloud far out from Tengri-Nayon, and some move quite independently of the others in eccentric orbits.

Let's try that, then.

So Yesui took herself to the icy cloud that was like a spherical shell some light minutes thick and half a light year in radius, surrounding the Tengri-Nayon system. Wandering a little, she finally found a little snowball some kilometers across, moving outwards from the cloud and alone, probably the recent victim of a collision.

That's a nice one, said Mind. *Can you target it for us?*

Of course. We're here, aren't we?

Yes, but it's vital that we remain here in space-time.

Excuse me?

We're going to the threads at the location of your little snowball, and you'll bring energy there to produce a wave. The snowball will move with it along a straight line defined by its motion at the instant the wave is produced.

I wish Mengjai were here to see my incredible insights, thought Yesui. *He would not be so cocky with me about his mental prowess.*

Please, said Mind. *Actually, the snowball will not move, relative to space. It's the space it occupies that will move. Now make your transition.*

She did it, but it took her four tries before she came close enough to the local thread. *You only need practice*, Mind assured her.

Yesui called the green light to her, and it obeyed. There was a flash, as before, dimming quickly.

She returned to real space.

The snowball was not there.

It's GONE! Where is it?

Out there somewhere, said Mind, *likely far enough to be difficult for you to find. You moved the space occupied by the snowball and they went away together. The coupling between them is complicated and involves the exchange of a very massive particle that formed at the birth of time, but you don't need to know about that now. The point is, you've moved mass without accelerating it in local space. I believe*

*that's what you were looking for, and now all you
need is considerable practice.*

She could move a moon, a ship, anything, and
without acceleration. Yesui was thrilled. *I must tell
Mengjai and Nokai right away. It's amazing how
suddenly this has come to me. My subconscious must
have been working on it for a long time.*

My gift to you, said Mind, *and you're ready for it.
There are other things we can teach you, but that will
be in the future.*

How many minds do I have? wondered Yesui.

Oh, there are many of us, said Mind. *Goodbye,
now. I have other assignments besides you. Use what
you've learned here. And Yesui, it's very important that
you come together with Nokai on Shanji. There is
another step in your lineage to be achieved. I'll be back
when you need me.*

For one instant, Yesui's mind seemed fuzzy, as if
a part of her had wandered away, and when clarity
returned it was with a sense of loss, of being alone
again in the blackness of space. *What an experience,*
she thought. *I've actually touched the creative part
of my mind. What insights could I achieve if I could
control its comings and goings?*

She was happy and excited. She rushed first to
Nokai, then to her brother, telling them about what
she'd done. Nokai listened quietly without understanding, but putting his faith in her and showering her
with wonderful feelings that held her lovingly for long
moments. Mengjai was truly excited, but busy, and
their conversation was short.

*You've probably been developing this for years,
Yesui, and now that it's ready, you're conscious of it.
I must give you credit for a marvelous achievement.
Now, when can we try it on my ship?*

I have to practice first. The range of the wave is energy dependent and I have to learn how to gauge and control that. Do you think a lifeform could be hurt by moving it this way?

I doubt it, not physically, anyway. There's no real acceleration involved. When you're ready, we'll start with a little jump, if Father will agree. I'll talk to him.

Mengjai was gone, and Yesui went back to play in the great cloud of icy debris surrounding Tengri-Nayon, but as she searched for a new toy there was once again a sense of loneliness. She had touched a part of herself she had never experienced before, and already she was missing it.

Nine wedge-shaped ships assembled in a vee formation spanning a hundred kilometers, and began moving towards Lan-Sui City only twenty hours after Lingdan Zedenbal had received his call. Each ship pushed a small mountain of rock, iron, and frozen gases twice its size, while on-board computers calculated and refined trajectories. After four hours of constant pushing, the ships moved back from their missiles, then went in several times to nudge them into corrected trajectories convergent on the city. Now they were backed off again, flying in formation with mountains.

Lingdan Zedenbal sat in the Captain's chair to eat a light lunch and keep his eyes on the forward observing screen, now filled with the roiling surface of Lan-Sui. Intercept time was less than forty hours away. "The planet looks ready to boil," he muttered. "There's the real threat to the city."

Ral Darpo, his co-pilot, chewed thoughtfully. "I can think of safer places to live, but the moons should be safe, don't you think?"

"Sure, once we stop Yesugen. Thinking of your wife again?"

"Yes—and the kids. You don't have a family, Captain?"

"Not yet," said Lingdan, "but I've got my eye on a little brunette in Lan-Sui City."

Darpo frowned at him. "Don't you worry about her? I mean, what we're doing here, you know, it could—"

"Yesugen's ships will take these big rocks out long before they reach the city, Ral. Don't worry about it."

A long pause, then, "The men are talking. Some say we're on a suicide mission."

"Hmm," said Lingdan. "I'd better talk to them again. Orders are to fly escort until Yesugen's ships move, and then we get out of there. I thought I made that clear. Do you believe in what we're doing, Ral?"

"Yes, sir! I don't want my family touched by those monsters!"

"Try not to think about it, and relax. About another thirty-six hours should do it, and then we'll get the—"

The entire observing screen was suddenly filled with incredibly bright, purple light that illuminated their compartment without shadows, and seared their eyes.

Lingdan's eyes watered, and he closed them tightly, bright spots of purple and blue floating in darkness. When he opened them again, all seemed normal: Lan-Sui's roiling surface there, the distant edge of the inner ring disappearing behind it, otherwise only black space.

"What in Mother's name was *that*!" said Darpo, rubbing his eyes.

"I don't know," said Lingdan, his fingers moving over his console. "Sensors okay. Something internal, maybe. A power surge."

Everything checked out, and Lingdan relaxed, but then the other pilots called in to say they'd seen the same thing on their screens, and it bothered him.

It bothered him a great deal for the rest of their mission.

CHAPTER SIXTEEN
ATTACK

"I don't think we should wait any longer," said Yesugen. "If we strike now, they won't have time to seal up surface level, and we can go right in."

"I agree," said Kabul, "but I think we should do everything possible to avoid casualties on both sides. We're moving against civilians, not professional military, and they believe we'll slaughter their families if they don't kill us first. Once inside, we have to convince them it isn't true."

They had taken breakfast in their tiny cubicle on board Yesugen's flagship after a cramped though intimate night sleeping together in her narrow bunk. Now they hunched over a small table, an architectural drawing of the Gutien facilities spread out between them. Yesugen tapped the drawing with her finger.

"The major ports are here, here, and here."

"Warehouses, and this one is maintainence for the crawlers," said Kabul, pointing. "All supplies go through the warehouses, and the locks are large enough to hold ten crawlers at a time. We'll have to go in at these places. The layout for Nan is smaller, but similar. Do you want to see it?"

"No. We're not moving against Nan."

"We're *not*? We have six thousand marines on the ships there!"

Yesugen ignored his comment. "What are these smaller ports here?"

"Emergency exits for personnel, and always sealed. The releases are activated from inside in case of fire or toxic gases. The people have to exit in single file along these narrow hallways and stairwells." Kabul's finger moved over the drawing in several places. "Their living quarters are down here, on fourth level."

"That's where the families are," said Yesugen.

"Yes, most of the time. There is a recreation area, up here on level three."

"Not likely to be occupied while they're under attack," said Yesugen, and Kabul shrugged his shoulders. Yesugen looked at him, and smiled.

"I'm confusing you, dear. You wonder what I'm up to."

"I always wonder what you're up to," said Kabul, smiling fondly back at her.

"Well, here's what I'm thinking," she said. "They will be expecting a massive frontal assault at one or more of these major ports, and we're going to give it to them. All we need is one cruiser, landing here," she tapped. "Two companies, with engineers, will hit these two ports. If our inside people can get them open for us, fine, but I'm not counting on it, and we'll probably have to cut our way in. I don't want our ship to blast those ports."

"They'll just sit and wait for us, Yesugen. It's going to be brutal."

"Possibly, yes, but while we're banging on their front door and they're preparing to slaughter us, we'll be going in here, and here, to cut off their living quarters and families from them."

"Hostages," said Kabul.

"So it will seem, until we make it clear we're there to protect their families from harm. Our inside people must open these smaller ports for us, Kabul. Are they electronic?"

"Yes, but there are manual releases at each port, connected to an alarm system. The locks are small, Yesugen. Twenty people at a time."

"Then thirty of our marines will fit in there. I think sixty will do, at each port. Two shuttles, landing here, simultaneous with the cruiser, unobtrusively. If our inside people can open these ports, we can be inside in a few minutes, down these halls and stairwells to occupy the living quarters, and set up defenses here, and here." Her finger was now tapping rapidly on the drawing. "The halls are narrow there. They can't fight backwards with any strength along those routes, but they must know we're there, that the families are in our hands, but not threatened by us. Hopefully, they'll give up at that point."

"Tokta Kuril has them scared to death of atrocities our marines will perform with their women and children. He'll fire them up for an all-out assault."

"Kuril will be dead, and Jumdshan with him. I want both of them terminated at the moment our cruiser comes in."

"If our people are caught doing it, those ports won't be unsealed," said Kabul quickly, and he frowned at her.

"Then we'll blast our way in. The living quarters have their own seals. I don't like assassination either, Kabul, but killing these two men can end this thing quickly, and save lives on both sides. If I can help it, not a single marine or worker will be killed, but Kuril and Jumdshan are now central leaders in this action, and I want them dead."

"I understand," said Kabul softly, and Yesugen reached over to hold his hand in hers.

"There was a time when your soft heart irritated me, darling, but in the end I fell in love with it. Now we're at war, and I must be harsh again."

Kabul nodded, and squeezed her hand. "I know," he whispered.

When the cruiser came in, they were as ready as they could be with untrained men. Packing crates had been piled high against the doors of the inner locks, and also served as barricades, behind which the men waited quietly to fondle their weapons like children with toys. They had been waiting like this for a day and a night, and Jumdshan had just come back from Communications with nothing new to report. Yesugen's ships were still in place, although one cruiser had left Nan and was now heading towards them apparently to reinforce the Gutien blockade. Shuttles had been seen leaving Yesugen's flagship earlier in the day, in transit to a nearby cruiser now below Gutien's horizon.

Jumdshan stood at the back of the warehouse and watched the men dozing behind their barricades. Oghul Ghaimish was trying to keep them awake, going from man to man with a slap on a shoulder, a little shake, a few soft, encouraging words.

Jumdshan still felt uneasy about the man after hearing his lies to Lingdan Zedenbal. They'd been so smooth, and with conviction, all for the cause, of course, but Jumdshan had had to bite his tongue while he listened to them. The veiled insinuation about his safekeeping of payroll cash had been an insult, for he'd trusted Ghaimish enough to let him be there on more than one occasion when he'd opened the vault. Anger had turned to suspicion, and he'd gone to the vault again to count everything in it, but found it was all there. Still, he felt a nagging distrust of the man, a feeling that there was more to his agenda than a quest for independence, and now the critical moment of that quest was at hand.

"There's a message for you, Steward!"

Jumdshan turned around, startled, saw a man in the orange jumpsuit of second level, beckoning to him. "I was passing by Communications, and they sent me to get you. It's something about ship movements in the blockade." The man turned, walked away towards Communications, and Jumdshan followed him quickly. *Now it begins*, he thought.

They went down a corridor and made a right turn towards Communications, along a narrow hallway brightly lit by ceiling panels. Halfway there, the man ahead of him slowed, and turned left, giving a little wave to indicate he was taking his leave of him, now that Communications was only a few doors ahead. Jumdshan waved back, and walked past him.

He only made it two steps before a hard arm snaked around his throat, pulling him back in a strangling grip, and choking off his cry. There was a horrible, sharp pain in his lower back, then numbness everywhere as he was released, crumpling to the floor.

"Now for Ghaimish," muttered his assailant, and the sound of shuffling feet faded away with Jumdshan's last breath.

"It's not the usual stuff, Ma'am. There're some pretty big pieces in this swarm, and we calculate impact with the city in just over four hours," said the voice in Yesugen's ear.

Yesugen pressed a hand to her other ear when Kabul shouted an order to someone behind him, and waved a hand at him for quiet.

"I can't spare any ships, now; we're moving in on Gutien!"

"Wouldn't help anyway, Ma'am. Under full thrust, you're still seven hours out from the city. It'd be too late for them. Should I warn the city?"

Yesugen thought furiously; the child she carried seemed distressed by her sudden mood, and shifted inside her. "No. There is something else I can do. Keep tracking the swarm, and let me know if there are any changes in trajectory."

"Yes, Ma'am."

Her face felt hot, and the baby shifted again, poking at her with a little fist, or foot. Kabul shook his head, and gripped her arm.

"Couldn't be worse timing. The shuttles are down, and the cruiser is coming in," he said.

"Take over for a moment, Kabul," she said. "I must call Yesui for this."

Kabul nodded, and Yesugen leaned back in her chair, folding her hands together, and closing her eyes.

Yesui! It's Yesugen, and I need your help. Come quickly!

No answer. Yesugen bit her lip in frustration, and

mumbled, "Oh, don't you *dare* to be off playing somewhere. You promised to be *here!*"

Yesui! Please!

The answer was like thunder in her mind.

I'm here. I'M HERE! Don't be so impatient, Yesugen. I just did the most marvelous thing with my brother's ship, and there was only a small problem with—

Yesui! Listen to me! An asteroid swarm is approaching Lan-Sui City, and some large pieces in it could destroy the city. I'm too far away to help, and we're beginning our attack against Gutien. Can you use the gong-shi-jie to take care of those asteroids, Yesui?

Of course. Where are they?

About a hundred thousand kilometers out from the city, and closing fast. Do you want coordinates?

No matter. I see them, now. Oooh, there are some big ones in there. I really need to eliminate the alpha ring to stop all of this. I'll get right on it, Yesugen. Bye!

And she was gone. Yesugen opened her eyes, and saw Kabul grinning at her. "She's a delight," he said, for although he'd not heard Yesui's words, he'd felt her presence.

Yesugen shook her head. "When I see her in the gong-shi-jie, she's a beautiful, grown woman. When I talk to her, she's a child."

She stood up, patting her stomach. "I want to get ready early, Kabul. Let's see if I can still squeeze into one of those environmental suits."

"I wish you wouldn't go down there," he said. "I can take care of everything."

"The fighting will be ended, dear, and I need to be there to assure the men and their families there will be no atrocities committed on Gutien. Now be a good father, and find me a suit that will allow our child room in which to move."

They hurried away to the shuttle bay.

The warehouse floor shuddered, as if something enormous had been dropped on it. Everyone's eyes went wide with surprise, and they hunkered down reflexively behind the barricades. Ghaimish snorted at their frightened reaction, and walked to the pile of crates before the inner door of the lock, rifle in hand. He pressed an ear to the steel wall there, and listened, then jerked back when there was a loud clang.

"They're outside!" he shouted. "Get ready!"

Ghaimish was halfway back to the surrounding barricades when a warning came from a loudspeaker.

"ENEMY CRUISER LANDED! PORT TWO, TEN METERS OUT!"

And then the alarms went off, loud and warbling.

Ghaimish's heart fluttered from the sound, for it was not the staccato scream warning of an opening lock, but that of a fire or toxic gas emergency. Somewhere, the seal of an emergency exit near their living quarters had been broken. His mind whirled. Operations were shut down, so how could there be fire? Panic in the face of attack; someone inside trying to flee, or—

"I need ten men!" he shouted, pointing at frightened faces. "You, you, and you! All of you, come with me! The rest of you wait until that door slides up, then *fire at will!*"

The men he'd pointed to stumbled forward to form a ragged line behind him, their breathing loud and hoarse with fear. "Keep those rifles at port arms!" he roared, fearing one of them might accidentally shoot him. "Fire only as commanded!"

He led them down a long corridor toward stairs above the living quarters, and past Communications, where he nearly shot a man who dared to peek outside. A man in an orange jumpsuit jerked back at an intersection and stared at them as they raced past. Ghaimish's eyes darted to the man's face, and something on the floor behind him, something wrapped in clear polymer and tied with rope.

The stairs neared, and to the right was a short hallway leading to one emergency lock, two others back towards the warehouse along another corridor. One seal broken, or all three? He tried to slow down, but the men were pushing in behind him and he was forced into the middle of the intersection when they reached it.

He looked right, leveling his rifle. A man dressed in orange stood by the lock door, waving an arm, and men were piling out of the lock, small men, in environmental suits, visors black, rifles swinging in his direction as they saw him. Ghaimish dropped to the floor, getting off one shot as he shrieked, *"Fire!"*

The corridor lit up with the blue flashes of laser fire. Men screamed. One fell on top of him. He hauled the man up in front of him as a shield, and left him as a smoking ruin, stumbling back down the hallway leading to the warehouse, men backing up behind him, firing blindly at walls and floor. "Cover the intersection!" he yelled, then fled down the hallway, two men running right behind him.

The man in orange he'd seen minutes before stepped out in front of him, and a blade flashed in his hand.

Ghaimish twisted his body as he crashed into the assailant, and the man just behind him cried out as they all went down in a heap. Fingers clawed at Ghaimish's eyes, and he smashed a knee into the assailant's groin, rolled him over, then slammed the butt of his rifle against the man's temple. Ghaimish scrambled to his knees, gasping for breath. One of his own men writhed on the floor next to him, the hilt of a knife protruding from his stomach. The other was standing, staring down at them, a rifle shaking in his hands. Ghaimish pointed at his assailant, and gasped, "Kill him."

The soldier-worker looked like he'd just been ordered to kill his own child, and didn't move.

Ghaimish stood up, and rolled his assailant over on his back. The man looked up at him, and smiled. "You're finished, Kuril," he growled.

Ghaimish shot him twice in the face, just above the bridge of the nose.

His companion stared in horror. Behind him, the hallway flashed with laser fire, and there was another scream.

"Get back to the warehouse, and bring at least twenty men back with you! I'll stay here to help hold the intersection. If they get past us, your families will all be dead in minutes!"

The man sprinted away from him. Ghaimish looked towards the intersection of halls near the exit port, saw the backs of three men huddled at the corner, other men blackened and sprawled on the floor. He turned back to the corridor his assailant had come from, and stepped into it, out of sight of the others. The polymer-wrapped bundle was still there. He looked down at it, and saw Jumdshan's staring eyes looking back at him through clear plastic.

"*Damn* her," he growled, and sprinted down the corridor, around a corner, then another, rifle leveled.

Anyone who saw him now would die. He had minutes, at least, with all the chaos of battle, but there were a myriad of hallways leading to the shuttle bays, and he had no intention of leaving empty-handed. He went down a flight of stairs to second level, and straight to the Steward's office.

Jumdshan's secretary was there, a young woman in her twenties, eyes wide with fear. The vault was open, and she was furiously stuffing wan notes into mail bags, two of them already bulging with cash. She seemed relieved when she saw him.

"Have you seen Jumdshan? He has to tell me where to hide these bags!"

"How nice of you to do all the work for me," said Ghaimish.

He shot her once in the chest, and she crumpled to the floor.

Ghaimish grabbed one filled bag, and ran back up the stairs, the cash bag light in one hand, the rifle heavy in the other. The route to the nearest shuttle bay passed near the warehouse, and where the hallway ended, he'd be in sight of it. Two sets of tracks were there at floor level, a wide expanse of concrete along which robotic cars transfered their cargos to and from the shuttles, and above it the metal trellis with catwalks servicing the heavy cranes that moved units too large for the cars. Once up onto the trellis, he would not easily be seen, and could move quickly to the shuttle bay with little chance of detection.

The open, helical stairwell going up to the catwalks was near when someone ran by, and Ghaimish flattened himself against a wall, waited, inched forward agonizing steps at a time, looked around a corner. No cars on the tracks, and one man, still moving away from him towards the shuttle bay. A clanging sound from the warehouse, men shouting, but no sound of laser fire as yet.

He leapt to the stairwell, and scrambled up stairs to the top, where a single catwalk stretched far, a straight line to where he wanted to go. He was tempted to run, but didn't, padding softly along, conscious of every squeak in the metal under his feet, and looking often towards the tracks ten meters beneath him. He came to the control cab for the cranes, rifle leveled, but it was not occupied. Another two hundred meters, and he was—

A clang, and then the distinctive sound of the warehouse lock door sliding open. Laser fire erupted in the warehouse.

The lights went out, and he froze where he was, standing in pitch blackness, and then there was the sound of the lock door shutting again, and a few flashes of reflected light from warehouse rifle fire. Men were now screaming in panic. Below him, some-one ran back from the shuttle bay, carrying a hand-torch, passing so close he could hear the man's ragged breathing, and then there was a terrible silence.

Ghaimish found the handrails of the catwalk, and kept moving in the darkness, grimacing at each little sound he made. Five meters—ten—

A loudspeaker broke the silence.

"CEASE FIRING, AND THROW DOWN YOUR WEAPONS! Your position is sealed off, and we have your families under protective custody. We have no desire to take your lives, but we'll do so if you don't surrender immediately, and we will protect your families from any foolish decision you make. Your outer lock is now open to space, and we have control over all locks. If you refuse to surrender, we'll open your inner lock and begin depressurization. You have ten minutes to decide your fate. If you're wise, you'll place your rifles at the center of the floor, and step back to your barricades, hands on heads. We have you under infrared surveillence. TEN MINUTES!"

Ghaimish kept going, cursing under his breath, forehead cold with his anticipation of sudden decompression. Another ten meters, then twenty, one shuffling step at a time, until suddenly a railing pushed hard against his stomach. His breath rushed from him and he grunted in surprise, nearly dropping his rifle. Below him, red lights glowed softly from the edges of two wedge-shapes, and there was a whine of electrical generators within their hulls.

He felt around with hands and feet, found the stairs leading downwards, and descended them.

Just as he reached the bottom of the stairs, the bay was suddenly flooded in bright light again.

Yesugen and Kabul entered the warehouse within a phalanx of guards, helmets cradled under their arms. Hundreds of men sat on the floor, hands on their heads, sullen and frightened when they saw her. *These are not bad people*, she thought, and so she tried to give them some words of assurance.

"I am Yesugen, Empress of Meng-shi-jie," she said in a loud, growling voice, "and my forces are here for the sole purpose of bringing order to Gutien. You and your families will not be harmed in any way, now that you've put down your weapons, but we'll remain here until Gutien is functioning again. That is our only interest in you.

"You seek independence from Lan-Sui, and that is a decision for your Governor to make. I do not control him. He has uncovered corruption in your own union, and in the company that pays your wages, and

he's taken the guilty parties into custody. Many of your
problems have been caused by this corruption. Your
Governor is a good man, but now you must talk to
him directly, not through others who've lied to you,
and I think you'll find that your lives here *will* be
better."

The men still looked at her sullenly, but their eyes
told her that fear had waned, and for the moment,
it was enough.

Colonel Manek came over to brief them, and
Yesugen smiled. "Nice to see you again, Colonel.
You've risen two ranks since I saw you last, and now
I see why."

"Thank you, Ma'am," said Manek, "but it was the
speed and determination of our men that determined
the outcome. We did have casualties: four dead, and
seven seriously wounded, otherwise a few flesh burns.
I'm sorry to say there are thirty-five civilians dead,
including Jumdshan and a young woman we found in
his office, and so far we haven't been able to find
Tokta Kuril. He was seen here when the fighting
started, and we're still searching for him. The families
are coming out one by one, and we suspect he's
hidden himself among them."

"All the surviving workers are here?" she asked,
pointing at their prisoners.

"Half of them, Ma'am. We didn't hit the second
warehouse, but the people there gave up without a shot
as soon as they heard what happened here. We also have
to get crews to come out of nine debris-control shuttles
that are docked here. They've surrendered, but locked
themselves in until their safety is assured. They sent an
emissary to us, that man over there in the blue jumpsuit,
standing. He's taking us to a shuttle bay in just a few
minutes to get two of the crews out. Those ships are

really something to see, Ma'am. We don't have anything
like them."

"I would like to see them with you," said Yesugen,
but then Kabul grasped her arm.

"Too dangerous. Let them get the crews out first,"
he said.

"Really?"

"I doubt it, Ma'am," said Manek. "It might even
be easier if you were there to assure them of their
safety. There *is* risk, of course," he added quickly, for
Kabul was glaring at him.

"I want to see those ships," said Yesugen, and that
was the end of it.

A few minutes later, surrounded by a phalanx of
guards, she began the walk along the high, wide bay
leading to where two of the newly armed and armored
shuttles were now docked.

"Five minutes to release, Captain, but the Meng-
shi-jie ships haven't even moved yet. They *must* have
seen us, by now," said Ral Darpo.

"I don't understand," said Lingdan. "All the facilities, the workforce in the city, why would she just let
it all go? It doesn't make sense, Ral. If she made a
move right now, would she get here in time?"

"I've already calculated it, sir. At best, she'd have
to fire at a range of sixty-five thousand kilometers, but
that was if she'd moved minutes ago. I don't think it's
possible, not with targets our size. We're going to
destroy the city, Captain."

Darpo looked at him somberly, and saw something
in his eyes. "We were supposed to be a diversion, and
it hasn't worked."

"Then the mission is over," said Lingdan softly.
"There's no further need for what we're doing."

"Yes, sir." It seemed the man was reading his mind.

"We're still quite a ways out. A short radial burn should put those asteroids into Lan-Sui's atmosphere. Do we have the fuel for it?"

Darpo checked. "That, and enough to get back to the alpha ring, but not enough to reach Gutien."

"Call the others," said Lingdan.

All pilots reported in within a minute.

"This is Zendenbal. Abort mission! Repeat: the mission is aborted! Engage your cargo, and initiate a five-minute radial burn immediately! Verify!"

All called in. "Why?" was the only question.

"Yesugen's ships have not responded to our diversion. Do any of you want to destroy the city without reason?"

Silence.

"Verify compliance, please."

All replies affirmed his command, and he steered his own ship into engagement with the mountain of rock, iron, and ice that flew near him.

They did a five minute burn under full thrust, and prepared to disengage. "That ought to do it," said Lingdan, feeling relieved, and he looked up at the forward observing screen as the nose of his ship turned towards the direction of Lan-Sui City.

Distant stars, the alpha ring curving over them and down beyond a boiling, planetary atmosphere, huge, convective plumes reaching upwards from it, and then, quite suddenly, all of it seemed to boil, even the ring, the images of the stars.

A shimmering, purple curtain appeared like mist to fill the blackness of space, growing brighter, obscuring first the stars and then the ring, rushing towards them, spots of red and green flickering within it as it came.

Darpo screamed beside him.

An explosion of incredible brightness, burning out

his eyes before the sensors failed. In his mind, there was only purple light, and a brief sensation of heat, and then there was nothing at all.

Ghaimish went up the stairs like a rush of wind, the cash bag bumping along behind him. Never in his life had he felt so exposed, and there was no place to hide, only the single catwalk of steel lattice stretching hundreds of meters. He hunkered down at the top of the stairs, their helical structure a shield from directly below, but all anyone by the shuttles had to do to see him was just look up.

He did not have to wait long to test the security of his position.

There was a screech of metal against metal that echoed from the walls, and a hatch opened in one of the two shuttles below him. A man in a blue jumpsuit stepped out onto the steel grill of the dock separating the shuttles, and descended a few stairs there, the hatch closing behind him. In an instant, there was a face at the thick window of one cockpit area, watching him walk away. *The crews are inside*, thought Ghaimish. *Six men*, he remembered.

Chest pressed to his knees, Ghaimish did not move even his head as the man walked beneath him and on towards the warehouse. When the footsteps had faded, he risked a peek at the shuttles, and saw that the face at a cockpit window was still there. He could not show his position, not now, for he might have to return to it. The shuttles were manned, but one crew member had left, walking calmly back towards the warehouse. Why? To surrender, of course. He'd heard nothing from the warehouse for minutes, now, no firing, no shouting. Silence. Had the crews taken a vote to surrender, or was it just one man giving himself up to Yesugen's troops?

Two shuttles, manned and fueled, meters away from him, and he had a bag full of cash in his hand. A sprint from dock, then out to the ring, and no cruiser could keep up with them. Hide awhile, then sneak back to Nan, or even the city, when things had cooled. Maybe. The risks were terrible, the chance he'd get away even worse, but what else did he have?

He had cash, and two crews grounded without pay for weeks. *I'll just have to see how hungry they really are*, he thought.

The face at the cockpit window disappeared, and Ghaimish scurried down the stairs, cursing at the loss of time. Nobody was coming from the warehouse, but he heard a faint sound from there, someone speaking loudly. He walked straight to the dock, making no effort to hide his rifle, and climbed the few stairs there, feet clanging on grill work. Faces appeared at cockpit windows on both sides of him, staring. He slung the rifle on his shoulder, held up the bag and pointed at it. "Payroll cash," he said. "Steward Jumdshan sent me to hide it in your ships before it's stolen from us."

Blank stares, even after he'd repeated himself three times. They couldn't hear him! He put the bag at his feet, rummaged in it, and came up with a fistful of wan notes, waved it at the nearest face, then stuffed the money in the bag again. "I want you to take this," he said, mouthing the words carefully.

There was a thud within the hull of one ship, and the hatch opened, a short, swarthy man in a blue jumpsuit standing there. "What is this?" asked the man. "You still have your rifle. We thought it was all over!"

"It is," said Ghaimish, "but not for us. I've got half our payroll here, and we're going to get out, if you're willing to risk it. Equal shares for all of us."

"You're nuts," said the man, but his eyes were on the bag of cash. "We've already surrendered, and we sent a guy down there to tell 'em that. They'll be back for us any second now."

"No time for discussion, then. Let's get going. Equal shares, mister. I'm serious, so fire it up."

The man laughed at him. "And do what? Fly through six feet of steel and concrete? The door is closed, and it'll stay closed."

"So blast your way out. You have the weapons for it. Make a jump over the horizon, and put Gutien between us and the cruisers. I'll show you where to go." Ghaimish let go of the cash bag, and put a hand on the sling of his rifle.

His move did not escape the man's notice. "Who are you?" he asked.

"Oghul Ghaimish. I worked with the Steward to set up our defenses here, but now he's dead, slaughtered like a pig, and the same thing will happen to us if we don't get going!"

The man scowled. "Yeah, I've heard of you. You stirred up a real mess for us, and now you want to get away. No dice, mister. We ain't goin' anywhere." Standing in the hatch, he looked over Ghaimish's head, and smiled.

"Tell you what. You put down that rifle, and bring the bag in here with you. We'll hide you under the floor after we split the cash. They'll only be looking for five people in here. When we're gone, you're on your own."

Ghaimish hesitated, his hand grasping the rifle sling. The man looked again towards the warehouse, and grabbed the edge of the hatch cover, as if preparing to close it.

"How do I know you won't turn me in?" Ghaimish growled.

"You don't, and you've got seconds to decide. They're comin' for us now, and you'd better get rid of that rifle unless you want to die."

"I don't think so," said Ghaimish, and he whipped the rifle off his shoulder, but too slowly. The man lunged from the hatch and tackled him. They went down struggling for control of the rifle. The bag at his feet was kicked open, and suddenly wan notes were fluttering around his head. He heard the bang of the hatch closing again, and got an arm around the man's neck and throat, pulling back and up under his chin, then jerked him to his feet and snapped his neck with a single twist.

The man slumped in his grip, but Ghaimish held him up as a shield, for a crowd had suddenly appeared on the floor below the dock: troopers in environmental suits, rifles raised, and behind them a cluster of men surrounding a tall woman with gaunt face and tusks who could only be one person.

"Going somewhere, Mister Kuril?" said the woman.

His rifle was at his feet. Ghaimish released his human shield, and grabbed up the rifle as the dead man fell, then crouched, firing rapid bursts at the woman and cackling insanely as she screamed and fell to the floor.

The bursts of twenty laser rifles struck him simultaneously.

CHAPTER SEVENTEEN
CONSEQUENCES

So, what are you two up to now? Huomeng said without words to his daughter.

He studied the console displays before him, but his mind wasn't aware of what he saw there. His Moshuguang co-pilot, Dahlmai, could do the watching, and then there was Mengjai, who seemed able to function in two worlds at the same time.

His son sat on the other side of Dahlmai from him, his fingers moving over a keyboard, eyes fixed on a screen showing their course, yet a part of him was with Yesui where she now spoke to them from the gong-shijie. Dahlmai was oblivious to their conversation.

As usual, Yesui was direct. *I want to move your ship,* she said.

Have you already practiced so much? asked Mengjai, continuing his work without a blink even though he and his father had long awaited this moment.

Enough. I've moved things much larger than you

and found them intact again. The range of the wave goes as the brightness of the light I bring from the threads. I have a fair idea of the relationship between them now, but a big jump is easier than a short one.

What's big? asked Huomeng.

Oh, a light year, or so, about the diameter of the cometary cloud.

Shanji is a half-hour away by light, Yesui. I don't want us ending up at the outer edge of our system. Don't we have to worry about collisions during a jump?

I did think about that, Father, she said petulantly. *It doesn't seem to be important. I've moved ice-balls through the whole cloud, and they remain intact. It's like local space moves aside when the wave comes past, and then settles back as it was.*

Space-time inertia, said Mengjai, smiling to himself.

Whatever. There are no collisions, Father. I'm certain.

Your mother would shriek at me if she knew I was even considering this, thought Huomeng.

I've told her I want to move your ship, but she just smiled and didn't take me seriously.

I didn't either, until now, said Huomeng, but teasing her, for he and Mengjai had anticipated this event ever since Yesui's discovery of her space-time wave.

But now you do.

Yes.

You'll try it with me?

A small one, as small as you can make it, and then back again. I don't have a lot of fuel to play with, Yesui. In fact, the more I think about this, the crazier it sounds.

Do it fast, Yesui, said Mengjai, *before he thinks too much. If I set a course at thirty-two degrees twenty hours forty minutes, Father, it'll take us past Shanji along a trajectory where there's only dust. If Yesui overshoots us by less than a light-hour, we'll still have the same travel distance to Shanji, but from the other side. See?*

So that was what he'd been doing at the keyboard. Huomeng stood up, went to Mengjai and looked over his shoulder at the screen.

This way, she won't have to jump us back and compound any errors, said Mengjai.

We'll lose antenna lock. Your mother will have fits when they lose contact with us.

We'll lose it temporarily with any jump we make off course. Look, Father, we'll end up somewhere along this trajectory. Make a call and tell them to search these areas if they lose contact with us. Mengjai's finger moved over the screen. *Tell them we're conducting an experiment on the way back.*

All this fuss, Yesui chimed in. *You don't think I can do this accurately. Well, you're* wrong!

You're not the one being moved, Yesui. We're just being cautious.

Details, she said. *Are we going to DO it? I have to get back to Lan-Sui!*

If we can wait an hour, you can wait a nanosecond! Make the call, son, said Huomeng.

Dahlmai watched them curiously, but silently, suspecting something was being plotted, and for the next hour they endured Yesui's mental mumblings about the pickiness of the scientific mind. The signal finally arrived, however, to verify without question a compliance with their request.

All right. We're ready, said Huomeng. Mengjai's hands were flying over the keyboard, putting in the positions of key stars in the direction of their intended trajectory.

You're sure? No other details to take care of?

Get on with it, Yesui, before Father changes his mind, said Mengjai.

Very well, and she was gone.

"What now?" asked Huomeng, suddenly apprehensive.

"Sit down, relax, and enjoy the ride," said Mengjai, smiling. He gave the keyboard a final tap, and leaned back in his chair, closing his eyes.

Huomeng sat down again as Dahlmai said, "What's up, sir?"

"We're doing an experiment, Dahlmai. Buckle up. We might experience some acceleration."

Dahlmai obeyed, but looked concerned. Huomeng looked at the observing screen and saw five stars there. One of those stars, bluish, was in fact Shanji, only a point of light at this distance.

Huomeng buckled up, leaned back and gripped the armrests hard with a sudden sense of doom. *This is insane*, he thought, and took a deep breath.

Before he could let it out, he suddenly felt heavy, and it was as if blood had been drained from his head, his vision blurring, a roaring in his ears.

He blinked once, then again, felt his heart pounding, then a brief nausea he suppressed by swallowing hard. His eyes were unfocused, everything a blur, but when he shook his head the nausea returned. He again swallowed hard, and just in time, for something burning like acid had surged upwards from his stomach.

Beside him, Dahlmai shook his head, hands like claws on his armrests. "What was *that*?" he gasped.

"Interesting," said Mengjai, opening his eyes and feeling everything within his father. "The brain uses visual cues to sense a temporal displacement. With your eyes closed, I think it would have been easier. Look, Father." He pointed to the observing screen.

An instant ago, there had been five stars there. Now, there were four.

Mengjai's fingers tapped on the keyboard. "Oh, my," he said, smiling.

Well? Is that close enough for you? It was Yesui, again.

"Just a moment," Mengjai said out-loud, and tapped on his keyboard again.

The stars showing on the observing screen moved left, and coming in from the lower right corner was a bright, blue ball the size of a small coin held at arm's length.

Huomeng gawked at the screen. "Shanji," he said softly.

"We're about twenty-two light seconds out," said Mengjai. *Yesui, you're incredible! That was a jump of half a light-hour!*

Thank you, she said smugly, then added, *It was easier to do because I had you there to target, Mengjai.*

My pleasure, said her brother.

Are you all right, Father? Yesui sounded concerned.

Some disorientation, a little nausea. Mengjai says I should have kept my eyes closed. I still can't believe my eyes. You did it!

Hmph, she said. *You're still surprised. That disappoints me, Father.*

No, no. You take everything you do as normal, and don't see how amazing it is to others. We can only imagine what you do!

I can do it again, if you want me to, she said.

Not just now, said Huomeng. *My brain and stomach are still in different time zones.* He laughed.

Hmmm. Maybe people should be sedated during a jump. We could—

Suddenly, she was gone. Mengjai raised a hand towards his father, and listened.

"Yesugen's calling her. There's trouble on Lan-Sui."

Huomeng couldn't hear them, but Yesui was back quickly.

Gotta go. More asteroids headed towards the city. I'll be right back!

Gone again.

"Can you tell me what's going on, sir?" asked Dahlmai. The man's face was ashen.

"Don't you feel well?" asked Huomeng.

"A little nausea, sir. What just happened? Is that really Shanji I see on the screen?"

Huomeng told him everything, and then called to check the rest of the crew aft. Two had experienced dizzyness, but no nausea. The other two had been in their bunks, and were still sleeping comfortably.

"No visual cues," said Mengjai, nodding sagely, then softly continued saying, "No ill-effects that can't be avoided, Father. We can go anywhere, now: Meng-shijie, the stars beyond, even our own galaxy. The whole universe is within our reach, as long as we have Yesui."

Back again, she chirped, *and I heard you, brother. I'll take it as a compliment.*

It was. Asteroids gone?

Flashed 'em to atoms. When we're finished here, I'm going back to remove the alpha ring from Lan-Sui. It's become a general nuisance.

Huomeng laughed.

Was that amusing, Father?

No, it's just that you're so matter-of-fact about removing an entire ring of debris from Lan-Sui. To this normal mortal, it's a miracle.

You're not so normal, she said, and he laughed again.

Okay, where do we go from here? asked Huomeng. *As close as we are to Shanji, I want to go home. I haven't seen your mother in over a year. For that matter, I haven't seen you, either.*

Nothing to see. I'm flopped on my bed.

And your room is probably a mess, said Mengjai.

You can clean it up for me. I have time to eat, and that's it. I have to watch Lan-Sui, Mengjai. The temperature hasn't changed lately, but the surface is all boiling. I think something big is about to happen.

When the compressional heat surfaces, you can expect a lot of evaporation until the new equilibrium temperature is reached, Yesui, and that could take years.

Yes, but there are huge plumes growing beneath the city right now. How high can they get? Will they reach the city?

Possibly, said Mengjai. *There could be some turbulence.*

SOME turbulence?

Well, a lot of it.

EXCUSE ME! interrupted Huomeng. *Getting back to my original question, when do we schedule more jump tests?*

Why? asked Yesui. *We don't need any.*

One jump, and you're an expert? We need more trials.

I don't think so, not as long as Mengjai is there for me to target. The rest is easy; targeting is the hardest part. When you're ready, why don't I jump you to Tengri-Nayon, and then you can bring Nokai back with you?

Oho! said Mengjai.

No comments, please.

Who's Nokai? asked Huomeng, confused again. *And Tengri-Nayon is over two light-years out, now.*

I told you long jumps are easier than short ones, Father. Nokai is a close friend of mine in Lan-Sui City, and we want to see each other in person.

Nokai is wonderful, said Mengjai.

Not funny, brother, but you still have my permission to clean up my room. I really have to go. Why don't you think about it, Father? Fill a freighter with cargo, and I can have it at Meng-shi-jie in a day. Very practical, don't you think?

Of course, said Huomeng, *but not right away. I've been gone too long as it is.* Suddenly, he was yearning for Kati again.

Hmmm. Yes, I see. Well, I'll be in touch, and Nokai is waiting for me. Remember that room, Mengjai!

Her presence was gone, as if a switch had been thrown.

Their little grunts, smiles and chuckles during the conversation had been noted by Dahlmai, who now looked uneasily at both of them.

"We were talking with my daughter," explained Huomeng, and then Dahlmai nodded with relief.

Huomeng looked over at Mengjai. "Who *is* this Nokai she mentioned?"

"Governor Wizera's son, an empath living in Lan-Sui City. Nice guy, but very deep and serious, and a little younger than Yesui." Mengjai raised an eyebrow. "Brace yourself, Father. Yesui is crazy in love with him."

"Aha!" said Huomeng.

There was light, and a humming sound. She was flat on her back, and her right side was numb, a dull

pain in her left. She opened her eyes, and was looking straight up at a light panel in a white ceiling. The
room had a sharp odor, like disinfectant. She tried
moving her arms, and her left one responded. She
raised a hand to her face, and found a polymer tube
taped to her mouth, two smaller ones crammed up
her nose.

Yesugen moaned, her left arm dropping back to her
side, exhausted by a simple effort. Her right shoulder
was a huge bulge of gauze and plastic, a tube connected
to it from a bag of clear liquid hanging over her head,
and there was no feeling in her right arm.

Her arm!

She scrabbled at the edge of covers pulled up to
her neck, and jerked them down, straining for a look,
then sighing in relief.

The right arm was there, but wrapped from wrist
up with bandages.

She heard his feet scuffing the floor before the
physician arrived to look down at her, a man her
husband's age, with a kindly face. He put his hand
on her forehead, and smiled.

"Awake at last," he said. "How do you feel?"

"Terrible," she said. "Groggy, and numb—over
here." She nodded towards her right shoulder as the
physician pulled her left arm down to her side and
tucked the covers up under her chin again. "It's hard
to talk with these things in my mouth and nose," she
complained, feeling as if she'd been gagged.

"Now that you're awake, we can have you
unplugged within a day, except for the shoulder,
of course. You need the saline and medication flows
for a few days yet," said the physician. "It was quite
a mess when you came in. Do you remember what
happened?"

"Yes." She saw that grinning, malevolent face, the flashes of blue as the man crouched there, aiming at her.

"Your husband and a guard were also hit as they shielded you. I've seen to both of them."

"Kabul?" she asked fearfully.

"Waiting outside, Madam. I'm sorry to say he's lost two fingers from his left hand, but he's been up and about for two days. I'll send him in shortly. He hasn't left your door for two days and a night."

"How long have I been here? And where am I?"

"Your flagship, Madam. You've been here nearly three days and nights, and I'm *keeping* you here another four. No arguments, please." He smiled again, and patted her left shoulder.

"Is it so bad?" she asked softly.

"Considerable muscle loss, as well as the lymph nodes. The scar is correctible, but much of the nerve damage is not. Within a year, you should have some feeling in the arm, and with physical therapy you should regain—"

"My *child*!" she gurgled loudly. How could she have forgotten it? She tried to sit up, but instantly fell back again. "I don't *feel* it!"

"Hush, hush," he said, and pressed gently on her left shoulder. "Your baby is fine, now, but she was certainly agitated when you were brought in to me. She didn't *like* her mother being shot."

"She? How do you know?" asked Yesugen.

"We did a scan, of course. Didn't *you* know?"

"No!" she said, but inside she was thrilled.

"When did you last see your physician, Madam?"

"It—it's over three months, I think."

The doctor scowled at her and shook his head. "You're my Empress, Madam, but I will not be patient with self-neglect. The health of you and your child must come before anything else in your life." He took her left hand, and patted it. "Would you like to see your husband, now?"

"Oh, yes," she gurgled past the tube in her mouth.

And a moment later, Kabul was gazing down at her, his left hand a ball of gauze and tape. "Yesugen," he said, and smiled.

"Oh, darling, your poor hand. I heard." She reached out an arm.

Kabul leaned over, embraced her tenderly, kissed her nose, forehead, cheeks, and nuzzled her throat as her arm went around his neck.

"I was so afraid," he whispered. "Your lips were blue when we were brought here, and I thought—"

"Shhh." She stroked his hair, pressed her cheek to his, and a little moan escaped her.

Kabul pulled back, looked down at her with narrowed eyes. "If it's any consolation, Kuril's remains were picked up with one scoop of a shovel and placed in a small bag," he said.

"Good," she said, then, "What's happened? I've been out for three *days*!"

"Gutien is occupied and the workers are back on the job. They've elected a new Steward, and now they're not so afraid of us. When we landed on Nan the workers met us with empty hands. They hadn't even armed themselves."

"So the moons are stable?" she asked.

"Yes, for the moment. Wizera has called several times to see how you are. He says he has a long-range plan for the moons that should keep peace here."

"Finally," she said. "And it appears Yesui removed the asteroid threat to the city."

"One bright flash of purple and blue. A couple of our pilots saw the thing. There's concern on the moons that some of the debris control ships might have been caught up in it. Nine of them are missing."

"I still remember Kati using the purple light against us. Now her daughter uses that same light as our ally."

"And much more, Yesugen. She came back this morning. We were scanning Lan-Sui's surface at the time, and watched everything she did. The alpha ring is gone. She destroyed every piece of it."

"I wish I could have seen that," said Yesugen.

"You will. We made a cube of everything we saw. I want you to rest, now. I'll come back in a few hours."

He touched her injured shoulder with his bandaged hand. "Two old warriors, and look at us, all shot up. I think we'd be wise to stay home in the future, and let younger people do the fighting."

"I'd like that," she said, and then, quite suddenly, the baby moved inside her. "Ohh," she gasped. "I've been waiting for that. I was so afraid I'd lost her."

Kabul smiled, took her hand in his. "I saw the scan. Your heiress is on the way. I wish we were home, Yesugen, right now. Niki must be missing us terribly, but I'm afraid we'll have to remain here awhile." He now seemed worried, brows knitted.

"We promised that to Wizera, dear," she said.

"It's more than you think. When I show you the tape, you'll see what is happening to Lan-Sui. It's frightening, Yesugen. It makes me realize that Yesui's powers are beyond my imagination. But now you rest, and get those tubes out. I want to kiss your lips when I come back." He squeezed her hand, and smiled.

"Me, too," she said, but her eyelids were suddenly heavy again as he left the room.

She slept a long, dreamless sleep, awakened once when they came to remove the tubes from her mouth and nose, a second time when Kabul's lips were softly on hers. He didn't say a word, and was holding her hand as she drifted off again.

When she awoke again, a nurse bathed her with a warm cloth, made her sit up, and fed her a tea that burned its way down inside her. "Tomorrow you walk, and we'll get you some solid food," said the woman.

The prospect of walking didn't excite her, and she wasn't hungry. She dozed again, while Kabul went out to feed himself, and awoke feeling better, clearer-headed. Her right arm remained numb.

Within an hour, she was bored. When Kabul returned, she asked to see the videocube of Lan-Sui, and he went away to get it. She asked that any calls for her be routed to her room, and it was done. When the tele-module arrived at her bedside, she punched at it with a finger to shut off the visual portion of transmission, and was still waiting for Kabul to return when Governor Wizera called again.

"I'm so relieved to hear your voice," said Wizera, "but we have a connection problem. I can't see you."

"I look the way I feel, Governor. There's no need for you to see it." Yesugen felt irritation at the sound of the man's voice: soft, gentle, and caring. Deep inside her, she resented the personal price she'd paid for his softness. "I'm mending as well as can be expected," she said.

"I certainly wish for your complete recovery, Mandughai, and I have some news that should please you."

That would be nice, for a change, she thought. "Oh?"

"I've decided to take control of Bator Corporation by making it publicly owned. Fifty-two percent of the stock will be distributed in equal shares to all citizens of Lan-Sui City and the moons. The rest comes to my government, in return for guaranteed subsidies of the moon operations. Gutien and Nan will have their own elected governing councils to handle those subsidies, and everyone shares the profits. So far, the response to my proposal has been quite positive, even from the moons. What do you think of it?"

At the moment, she really didn't care. "Well, it sounds better than what you've had up to now. I hope it's successful for you, and as long as Meng-shi-jie gets the fuels it needs, it's a workable plan for us."

"Good," said Wizera. "I—ah—do have another concern that's—ah—rather urgent, I think. Perhaps we can talk about it when you're feeling stronger? In a few days?"

Oh, no! What now?

"I might as well hear it now, Governor. What new problem do you have?" Sarcasm dripped from her voice, but she made no effort to hide it.

"It's not new, Madam," said Wizera sharply, "and both of us have anticipated it."

Hmmm. A little more forceful, now. That's better. "Yes?"

"Lan-Sui itself is now a problem. I'm sure you've seen what's happening to it."

"Kabul has a recent videocube of the surface, but I haven't seen it yet," she said.

"The surface is suddenly quite violent, Madam, and

new convective plumes have formed along concentric rings within the vortex directly beneath the city.
They've been growing at a rate of twenty kilometers
per day, and now they're about to reach us. We're
already experiencing turbulence here, and there has
been minor damage. Now I fear we'll be engulfed by
these new plumes, and destroyed. We have to get out
of here, Madam, and as soon as possible. We cannot
stay here."

"You want an evacuation?" she asked.

"No. There aren't enough ships in our entire
system to move all the people living here. I've called
in our eleven remaining debris-control ships to begin
moving the city to a higher orbit. Given time, they
can do it, but I don't think we have much time. I'm
asking for the loan of as many ships as you can spare
to move the city to higher orbit and stabilize it there.
It's quite urgent, Madam. My room is shaking even
now, and it's going to be a lot worse within a day or
two. If the plumes engulf us, we'll be shaken to pieces
here."

Kabul had come back, and was listening with her.
He pursed his lips, and shrugged, as if to say he found
Wizera's request a reasonable thing. He loaded the
cube he'd brought back, and turned on the monitor
in her room. There was a slow scan across a planet
now roiling everywhere with activity, a pattern of giant,
convective cells north and south of the equator, and
then there was a zoom in to look at the storm below
the city. Towers of new clouds in blue and red reached
out like fingers from concentric rings of boiling gases
within the vortex.

"Are you still there, Mandughai?" asked Wizera.

"Yes. Kabul is playing me the cube. It looks bad,"
she said.

"Will you help us?"

Kabul spoke loud enough to be heard by the man. "Our troops will be on the ground for weeks at the minimum, Yesugen. We have three cruisers idling in orbit." He raised an eyebrow, his own decision made.

She decided he was correct. "Very well," she said. "I'll send three of our cruisers to you within the hour. That's all I can spare."

"*Thank* you, Mandughai," said Wizera. "It's more than adequate, in fact, unless, of course, there's a sudden surge in storm growth. We don't expect that, and my ships are already here, preparing to engage. When can we expect your help?"

"Around eight hours," said Kabul. "We need a frequency for contact with your ships."

Wizera gave it to them, thanked them again, and again, and was gone.

"One thing after another," said Yesugen, still staring at the violence on the video monitor, "but I suppose we're responsible. This is Yesui's doing, and we've supported it."

"Ah, Yesui," said Kabul. "We're coming to that."

A moment later, the camera view suddenly shifted left from Lan-Sui's surface to where the alpha ring curved beyond it. An intensely bright ball of purple light was there, intersecting the ring, but fixed in position, the millions of ring particles from grains to small mountains rushing in their orbits to meet it. Where they entered, there was the lovely ring in yellows, reds and blues.

At the exit point, there was nothing.

"Thirteen hours it took her," said Kabul, "and then the ring was gone." He smiled, and shook his head in awe.

"Call the pilots, and give them their new assignment," said Yesugen. "And while you're doing that, as lousy as I feel, I'm going to chase down Yesui and have a little chat with her about this new problem she's created for us."

Kabul left without a word, and Yesugen closed her eyes, returning for the first time in months to the gong-shi-jie, the place where she could most easily, and quickly, find the Mei-lai-gong.

CHAPTER EIGHTEEN
JUMP

Nokai hadn't said so, but he feared for his life, and that fear hadn't gone away, despite her assurances.

I won't let anything happen to you, Nokai, she'd said lovingly, but at the time his room was shaking again and it was hard for him to believe her.

Can you reverse what you've done to Lan-Sui? he'd asked.

I suppose, but then all my work would be for nothing. Are the ships engaged yet?

Yes. They've been pushing on us for hours, but not once have I felt anything from it. It's going to be a terribly slow process, Yesui.

I'm watching, love, and I can move the city much faster than those ships. Trust me.

I want to, he'd said, but fear overcame belief for the moment.

She couldn't dare to tell him what she'd seen in real space, before the ships had arrived. The city was now nearly engulfed by a swirling plume that looked like a swollen thumb, its top flattened, and white with the formation of ammonia ice, growing by the hour. The entire vortex beneath the city now bristled everywhere with such plumes, and the pattern of concentric rings was fading before her sight, as if the center of the great storm was being pushed upwards with terrible force.

In her heart, she knew that the compressional heat she'd long awaited was about to surface, a great blast of evaporation that would extend far beyond the city, much further than the ships could move it in time. In her heart, she knew that what she had done to Mengjai's ship she would have to do here.

Yesui felt fuzzy, and knew the sign. Her body hadn't eaten for a day, perhaps more. She'd forgotten real time again. She returned to the gong-shi-jie and then to herself, opening her eyes in a darkened room. It was hot and stuffy, with unpleasant odors coming from bed clothes and her own body. *Ugh*, she thought, and put her feet on the floor. When she stood, her legs shook and she sat down again, waited, tried again, wobbled a few paces and turned on the lights, leaning against a wall for support.

The room was even more terrible than she remembered: bed a rumpled tangle of sheets and covers, piles of clothes everywhere, two trays of congealed food long turned cold on a desk. The sight of herself in a mirror was even more ghastly: hair tumbling over a face white as snow, dark, puffy tissue beneath her eyes, the robe hanging on her like a sack. It frightened her. *How long?* she thought, and there was an immediate reply.

You're finally back! Ready for a visitor?

It was Mengjai.

I don't feel so good, she said. *I'm shaking all over.*

That figures. Tanchun says you haven't eaten for two days. I'll have her get you something hot. Can I come in?

I suppose. She didn't really care, wobbled over to her bed and sat on the edge of it. A few moments later there was a rap on the door, it opened, and Mengjai was there, immediately frowning at her and wrinkling his nose at the odors in the room.

She hadn't seen him in over a year, and he seemed much older, his face narrower, cheekbones now defined. He still wore his ship's uniform: blue, tight fitting, the column of gold buttons, and black boots on his feet. He balanced a tray of food on one hand. "Your servant has arrived to feed you, Madam," he said, then grinned at her.

Yesui smiled weakly. "Food at last. I feel awful."

"No comment," said Mengjai. He put down the tray, came over and sat beside her, putting an arm around her and squeezing her shoulder.

"I feel bone—no meat," he said. "If I hug you, I might snap something."

Yesui leaned her head on his hard shoulder. "I forgot the time again. It's getting harder and harder to remember it. So much is happening at once, lately."

"You're more than a mind, sister. It won't exist without the body, and yours is turning into a skeleton. If Nokai saw you like this, he'd run away screaming. Now eat!"

"I can't move," she murmured.

"Your servant will help you," he whispered, and squeezed her gently.

Mengjai helped her to the desk, sat her down, even guided the first few bites of noodles into her mouth. "Now you do it," he ordered, and she did, but slowly.

Her stomach seemed cramped, hesistant to accept the food.

"You've really let yourself go, this time," said Mengjai. "Tanchun has been frantic, and Mother said she's going to come after you in the future. When you're gone, you're gone. They can't awaken you, but Mother can find you in a hurry."

"I'm glad she didn't come with you," said Yesui, taking another bite and feeling some warmth inside her.

Mengjai smiled. "Well, we only got back yesterday, and Shanji's business will be on hold for at least another day. Tanchun delivers meals to their room, and always comes out giggling to herself. Unlike you, our parents do not lack energy for physical pleasures, Yesui."

It made her smile, and she made a show of eating faster to tease him.

"*That's* the idea," he said. "Now, tell me what's new on Lan-Sui."

Yesui told him everything, including her intention to use the space-time wave to move the city.

"Hmmm. Tricky," he said. "You'll be working deep in a gravitational field where the threads are strongly curved."

"I have Nokai to target," she said, eating faster now, and the quivering of her muscles had subsided.

"Still tricky. When you make the jump, the city's instantaneous velocity will be critical, especially the radial component. Do you mind if I tag along when you're ready to do it?"

The food was gone, and Yesui was still hungry. "If you can get me more of this, *and* some honeycakes," she said.

"Done," said Mengjai, and he hurried out of the room.

While he was gone, Yesui tried to do something with her hair, but it fought back and she left it tousled. Her robe stank, and she changed into another one, the brief look at her naked self a shock, like looking at the body of an adolescent girl, not a woman. So when Mengjai arrived with another tray of food she ate greedily, polishing the meal off with five honey-cakes and rewarding her brother with a little burp that made him smile.

"So when do we go?" he asked brightly. "Better make it soon, while you-know-who are still occupied. Mother was serious. When you leave again, she's coming right after you."

"It has to be soon, anyway," she said, wiping traces of honey from her lips. "Better to move the city now, before the whole surface comes to a boil. What time *is* it, anyway?"

"Middle of the day. By dinnertime, Mother and Father might finally emerge from their den of lust. Are you feeling stronger, now?"

"Yes. All I needed was food. How about you?"

"Eager to go. I've missed going with you, Yesui. It's been a long time." Mengjai reached out, and held her hand.

Yesui squeezed his hand. "My baby brother," she said.

"And very talented in his own way," said Mengjai.

"What will they do when they see us flopped together here?" asked Yesui.

Mengjai laughed. "Mother will be after us in a nanosecond."

Yesui still held his hand, and lay down on her back. "So why are we waiting, brother?"

He lay down beside her, and grinned. "On board for Lan-Sui!" he said, then closed his eyes and rushed with her to the gong-shi-jie with its swirling, purple clouds of the light of creation, as seen by her mind.

Yesui moved with incredible speed, and everything was a blur to him. *Remember when I snuck along for a ride?* he asked. *You didn't move so fast, then.*

Yes, and it was nicer when I knew you were with me. Real space, now. Here we go!

A flash, and real space was there, a huge, boiling ball of gas filling their view. *Ohhh*, said Yesui. *I think we're getting here just in time, Mengjai. It's even worse than it was only hours ago!*

Mengjai was thrilled, a feeling he shared automatically with Yesui, enhancing her pleasure with the thing she'd done. *LOOK at that! I've seen computer models, but this is the real thing. Those big cells should spread out, distributing heat more uniformly, and then the color T should jump. It should be rising already!*

Mengjai, I can't see the storm below the city. It's GONE!

Are you sure we're on the right side to see it?

No, I'm not. I don't recognize anything. All the old surface features have disappeared! Nokai! Where are you? I'm looking for you!

No answer. Mengjai felt a surge of panic in his sister, and then there was the dizzying sensation of two transitions in rapid succession, and they were hovering only kilometers above roiling pillars of ammonia and hydrosulfide ices carried aloft with hydrogen, and helium not yet condensed into rain. *NOKAI!*

He felt the presence suddenly with her, an anxiety mixed with fear, and an image of his sister's face in a fan of green. At first, the presence was transient, there, then gone, a pause, then back again. Yesui shrieked, *I'M COMING, LOVE! I'M HERE!*

Yesui! Please. It's . . . tearing us . . . apart. I . . . can't move!

Mengjai actually felt Yesui lock onto her love, for one instant seeing inside him, feeling what he felt, lying on a hard surface beneath something heavy, everything shaking, rolling, a horrible roaring sound everywhere, holding in his mind the image of the woman he loved so dearly, a woman he yearned to see, to touch, but would not, for now he was going to die.

Nokai was gone, then back again, with two bright flashes of purple, and they were inside a boiling cloud of mist and shining flakes of ice, and the city was there, a round ball shuttered protectively by overlapping baffles of metal. The city was shaking and bouncing like a leaf in high wind, and for an instant Mengjai saw the glare of exhaust from ships under full thrust, tumbling with it.

They should shut down! shouted Mengjai. *We need velocity data, Yesui. We need the radial velocity!*

How? she asked. *I need to do this NOW!*

You can't make a jump without an estimate of radial velocity. The city could end up in interstellar space!

I don't have TIME! she screamed at him.

Call Yesugen. She must know something: total thrust, burn times, anything will help me make an estimate. Mengjai was already making wild estimates with imaginary scenarios and burn times of hours, and coming up with ridiculous radial velocities little better than a fast walk.

Yesui *did* try to call Yesugen, three times, while they watched the city tumble and Mengjai strained to see what ships, and how many, were pushing it. There was no answer.

And suddenly, there was a new presence with them.

*Hello again! I think you need some help here. Just
calm down, and we'll get this done quickly. Calm,
calm, that's it. Just bring the light from the threads,
and I'll give you a marker, a flash of purple. When
you see the marker, release the light. That's all you
have to do, Yesui, but do it NOW!*

Yesui? said Mengjai. It was as if she'd suddenly
assumed a new persona, or was talking to another part
of herself, for her panic was gone and she seemed
cut off from him.

Go to the threads.

They were there, a swarm of green tendrils curving
left and right beneath them in blackness, the roiling
cloud, the city, now gone, and now a new sight for
Mengjai. The threads drew near, not solid, but closely-
spaced spots of light. Nearer, and the spots were fuzzy.

*Go to Nokai. Think of only him. Go to the place
that calls you.*

This is crazy, shouted Mengjai. *You're making a
blind jump. You'll never find the city!*

Quiet, please. We're working.

Mengjai felt numb, as if a force had clamped coldly
on his mind, Yesui totally shut off from him, suddenly
controlled by something foreign, alien.

Not fuzzy, but many spots of light, like a ball of
individual stars, veering left as they homed in on one
of them. It was brightening, even as they approached.

*Don't wait. Bring the light forth, and watch for my
marker.*

Green light blazed forth in a horrible flash; he
barely saw the single strobe of purple at the instant
the light began to subside, and then there was only
the pinpoints of green, as before.

*There, it's done, and your timing was quite close.
The rest you can do by yourself.*

Thank you, Mind. It was Yesui, suddenly back with him, the old feeling of her presence familiar, yet Mengjai was still numbed into silence.

You're welcome. Sorry about your brother, but he was distracting us. He might be able to help you, now. Goodbye, Yesui, and good hunting. Find your man. That's very important to us.

Goodbye, Mind, said Yesui, and instantly Mengjai was released from his paralysis.

What did you do to me? shrieked Mengjai. *You cut yourself off from me! I couldn't even THINK!*

If you keep shouting, I'll do it again!

Flash. They were back in real space, the roiling cloud all around them.

The city, and the ships that had been pushing on it, were gone.

It worked! said Yesui.

Worked? For all I know, the city is at the center of the PLANET! Can we please contact Yesugen, and get some velocity data now? Mengjai tried hard to be calm, for fear that his sister might numb him again.

Of course. Mind said you might help me, now.

How nice of her, said Menjai. *How nice of YOU!* Something nagged at him when he said that, but then there was still another flash, and Lan-Sui was a ball again, like a dinner plate held at arm's length.

With all these transitions, I'm glad my body isn't here. I'd be throwing up all over the place, complained Mengjai.

Yesui ignored him. *Yesugen! I need some information.* Mengjai saw the great flagship of Meng-shi-jie hovering near them. *We need velocities!* he shouted.

Yesui, is that you? You sound different. Are you doing something near the city? We lost contact with our ships over two hours ago.

Oh, great! mumbled Mengjai.

Yesui?

Yes, it's me, Yesugen. The storms had engulfed the city and your ships, and I just finished moving them to a safer place, I hope.

You WHAT?

I moved them, and I'll explain how I did it later, but now I have to find them again. Can you tell me how fast the city was moving away from Lan-Sui when you lost contact?

No, we didn't get that, but it was slower than we hoped for. One cruiser ran out of fuel.

Total thrust, burn times, ANYTHING! shouted Mengjai. *And if her ships call in, she can locate them, and pinpoint the city for us.*

Yesui, is someone with you? asked Yesugen.

Just my brother.

MENGJAI?

I'll have to explain that later, too, but you heard what he wants. Do you have it?

I'll have to see—

Still hovering in real space, they waited as phantom presences long, agonizing moments until Yesugen got back to them.

Here it is: thrusts, and approximate burn times. The initial radial acceleration was one hundredth of a meter per square second. Burn times are seven hours, maybe more.

That's enough. I can figure it out, now, said Mengjai confidently, but Yesugen gave them the rest of the numbers anyway.

Yesui's anxiety was building again, and that meant action sometimes nearing blind flight when she was badly disturbed. Mengjai made no effort to calm her, the calculations totally occupying his mind. Yesui had abruptly left Yesugen, and was popping in and out of real space in a sort of random search pattern, each time calling, *Nokai!* and getting no response.

Two hundred meters per second max, he said, *and the horizontal component should be twenty-four kilometers per second from the old orbit. Hmmm. Ratio of ninety-five. Now tell me how long the jump was.*

What? Another flash. *Nokai!*

I need to know the approximate range of your space-time wave. It goes as the brightness of the light you draw from the threads, remember?

Yes—I mean, no, I don't know. It happened so fast.

Don't give me that. I saw your purple marker. You had it timed exactly.

Mind did that, I didn't. I don't KNOW! yelled Yesui, her anxiety nearing panic. Another series of two flashes, close together. *NOKAI!*

Mind? I think you've been alone too much in the gong-shi-jie, Yesui. You're scaring me, or teasing me, and I'm not in a mood for it. You had some kind of insight before you made that jump, and you know the range of that wave. Now tell me! How does it compare with the jump you made for my ship? Maybe that'll help.

Flash, and they were surrounded by shimmering purple. Yesui paused there, and said, *Shorter, but not by much.*

How much, then? Thirty light minutes? Twenty?

Maybe ten, she said, but he could see she was only guessing.

Okay, let's work with that. Ten light minute range, ratio of ninety-five—that's about a million kilometers radial.

A MILLION?

Yeah, about nine times Lan-Sui's radius. Pretty far out, well beyond the moons.

Oh, Mengjai! Flash again. This time, Yesui homed in on the vortex of Tengri-Nayon, the tiny dimple there that was Lan-Sui, using the number he'd just given her.

Empty space was there, a black void. *NOKAI!* she called, and inside she was aching with dispair. All that space, and somewhere was a ball only kilometers in diameter, undoubtedly damaged. Perhaps there was no power in the city, no heat, the atmosphere growing stagnant, people injured or dying from the buffeting of the storm. Nokai had been there the moment of the jump, but now . . .

How can I find him in all of this? she asked mournfully. Mengjai felt the ache in her, felt her wavering, her emotions so distraught that any second now she might return to herself from loss of concentration.

Keep trying, he said. *If Yesugen's ships are still alive, they'll call in. Try a little more, and we'll check back with her. Don't despair, Yesui. You got them out of the storm, and that was the first thing you had to do. You're tired. I can feel it. Your body is rebelling against your mind.*

I know. I can't think straight. If I lose Nokai, I've lost everything. Oh, Mengjai, I've killed him!

Stop it! Keep trying, one quadrant at a time, just once around Lan-Sui at this distance, and then we'll check in with Yesugen. Get busy, Yesui!

She did it, but slowly, transition after transition, a call in real space, a short pause in the gong-shi-jie, then back again, over and over. Mengjai wondered how long a pause in the place of creation was in real time. A minute? An hour? There were many pauses, and then they had completed a search at only one distance from Lan-Sui without results. How many more would be necessary? And how much time did the people in the city have? If the ships called in, there was hope, for they had been more exposed, more vulnerable to the storm. All power was likely out in the city. Fires? That would be bad, with an atmosphere already dying—

Mengjai, I hear everything you think. Please don't do that, said Yesui.

Sorry. Let's go back to Yesugen, now.

Okay, she said forlornly. It was worse than despair, now. She'd given up, lost hope. In her mind were words said to her by Nokai, private words, and the things she'd felt when he'd touched his face and body for her. Mengjai felt he was somehow violating his sister by hearing such private things.

Still a chance, Yesui. Let's go.

Flash, but they entered real space too far out, and she had to do it again. Her concentration was nearly gone, both from exhaustion and a growing sense of loss.

So when Mengjai saw the flagship gleaming in Tengri-Nayon's reflected light, he made the call to Yesugen himself.

Yesugen, it's Mengjai. We've searched a lot of space, and found nothing. Have you heard anything?

Where did you go off to? said Yesugen angrily. *You left me right in the middle of a sentence! And yes, we've heard from our ships, only a few minutes after you left.*

WHAT? shouted Yesui.

Their signal faded out after a few minutes, but we did get a fix as they passed behind Lan-Sui's edge. They're about twenty-eight thousand kilometers above the atmospheric edge, and they should be coming around again in a few hours.

Twenty-eight THOUSAND? said Mengjai, and immediately he was calculating again.

Are your people all right? asked Yesui. *Is the city with them?* Hope surged again within her.

Yes, the city's there, and the ships are communicating with it. There's considerable damage, but it's structurally intact. The captain I talked to seemed terribly confused by what happened, Yesui. He couldn't even describe it. What did you do?

I moved the space they occupied, and they went with it. I'll explain later, Yesugen. I have to see Nokai!

Nokai? Wizera's son? said Yesugen. *NOW WAIT A MINUTE!*

Flash.

Flash.

The surface of Lan-Sui roiled beneath them, but there were no vortices or bands of clouds to see, and the plumes had all come together, the surface now a mess of floccules pressed tightly together. It was like looking at a star close up, seeing the tiny, convective cells bringing energy to the surface, cooling, submerging again.

Mengjai had finished his calculations. *Twenty-eight thousand kilometers radial means a jump of nineteen light seconds! It can't be, but it must be! Tangential— ratio ninety-five—they would have gone around Lan-Sui two point nine times. Oh my, they were nearly directly above us when they came back.*

We're staying right here, said Yesui. *We're not moving, this time. NOKAI!*

Real time crawled by, Yesui repeating her call over and over, while Mengjai went over his calculations, a part of him refusing to believe the answers. *Nineteen light seconds? No, no. There's something I'm not understanding here. How could she—*

All thought was blown away by the rush of Yesui's euphoria when a sudden feeling brushed over them like a cool breeze, gentle and soothing, the signature of a presence even Mengjai remembered from a previous time with his sister.

NOKAI! DARLING, I'M HERE!

Yesui? Very faint, then *YESUI!*

You're ALIVE! she screamed.

Yes, I guess I am.

Two blinding transitions, a flash of purple as they zipped in and out of the gong-shi-jie. Yesui had targeted Nokai, and would not wait a single moment for the city to reach their position.

It floated serenely before them, a kilometer distant, a giant, metallic ball of baffled shutters still closed tightly without apparent damage. Two military cruisers and several smaller ships had engaged a thick ring around the city's circumference and their thrusters burned like coals as they pushed to deaccelerate it, bringing it to a lower, stable velocity in a new, higher orbit.

Oh, Nokai, darling, I thought I'd lost you. I've been searching and searching—

What happened? One second, everything was falling down around me, and then it was absolutely still. I think I blacked out for an instant. What did you do?

I moved you to a higher orbit, well above the storms. You should be safe here.

The whole city? How—

Not now, my love. Oh, how I want to be in your arms, but you can hold me in your mind, feel what's inside me. Mmmm. Mmmm.

What Mengjai felt was frankly erotic. He wanted to run away, but could not, and Yesui was so caught up in her passion she'd forgotten he was with her, her mask a shambles.

Oh, Yesui. Ohhh! said Nokai. *I love you. I LOVE YOU! I thought I'd never see you again. I thought I was dead.*

It went on, and on. Nokai was touching himself, his face, lips, arms, and places that shocked Mengjai, for he felt all of it, and Yesui was somehow doing the same thing to herself. It was all too much for him, too private, and he could stand it no longer.

Ahem, he said. *I really shouldn't be here, but I don't have any choice. Can you two please save what you're doing for another time?*

MENGJAI! said Nokai.

Sorry, mumbled Mengjai. *This is all very sweet, but we really need to get both of you together physically at the same place. I shouldn't be peeking at you like this, and I'd be a liar if I said I haven't enjoyed it.*

They were embarassed, both of them. Mengjai waited for an explosion of anger from Yesui, but it didn't come. Her mask went up, cutting off some wonderful feelings and sensations from him, but she seemed amused. *I forgot about you,* she said.

It has been a long time, Mengjai, said Nokai, trying to hide his own embarassment and failing, but at least now he wasn't touching himself.

How are things in the city? said Mengjai quickly.

Anything breakable is broken. My window is gone, and the streets are filled with rubble. My door is stuck closed; some men are coming soon to cut it out of the wall. My room is a shambles, and right now it's eerily quiet here.

No fires? No buildings down? Did you lose gravity?

No. Well—I see some fires—flashes. Parts of the city are dark. There must be casualties, Yesui. I don't see anyone in the streets. We shook like crazy for over an hour, and then it just stopped, like I said.

The storms had just reached you when we arrived,
said Yesui, *so I moved you right away.*

With incredible precision, I might add, said
Mengjai. *Unbelievable precision.*

How she had done it came back to haunt him:
talking to herself as if another being called "Mind"
were suddenly with them, the purple marker, a jump
far shorter than anything she'd attempted, then the
force that had paralyzed him. For one instant, he'd
sensed a hostility in the presence Yesui called "Mind,"
had felt threatened by it. The presence worked only
with Yesui, guiding her, yet he'd felt totally cut off
from his sister. It disturbed him deeply, for now he
felt the new presence had not been a part of Yesui,
but something else.

Thank you, Mengjai, said Yesui. *By the way, I am
glad you were with me, even though you had me
chasing around in deep space for awhile.*

*I did the best I could with the data I had. Look, you
two really need to be alone, and I'm stuck here. A quick
flash back, Yesui, and you can leave me on Shanji.*

Oh, I don't want to leave! she said.

I can wait, my love, said Nokai. *I've become
accustomed to waiting for you, and it's always
worth it. But I want to be with you. I want to be
with you always.*

Oh, Nokai, my sweet, said Yesui.

Let's not get started again, said Mengjai. *She'll be
right back, Nokai, and I really do want to see you
two in person together. I mean it.*

We're going to talk about that, Yesui murmured.

Thank you, Mengjai, said Nokai, and the feelings
coming from him really *were* wonderful, Mengjai
decided. It was no wonder Yesui was so crazy about
him.

Hurry back, darling, said Nokai. *I love you.*

Me too. Bye!

Flash. Yesui was giddy with love and excitement, while Mengjai only wanted to be back on Shanji.

They came out into the gong-shi-jie above the vortex of Tengri-Nayon to find a brilliant apparition in green waiting impatiently for them, arms folded across her chest, face stern.

We really must have a talk, dear, said the apparition.

MOTHER! cried Yesui. *Oh, Mother, not NOW!*

Not so quick. I'm not here to scold you. I just talked to Yesugen, and she told me everything that has happened. What you've done is truly wonderful, but really, my dears, that woman is flat on her back with terrible wounds, and you two have been darting in and out of her life without considering her condition.

We had to, Mother. There was no other choice, said Mengjai, *and it's over, now. I think Yesui has finished her work with Lan-Sui.*

You read me well, son. Mother's manifestation drifted away, and beckoned them to follow her. *Now, let's go home, and talk face to face about the things that are bothering me.*

But I have to go right back to Lan-Sui! Yesui protested.

What? The eyes of Mother's manifestation were now slits.

Mengjai jumped to Yesui's defense, if only because she'd left Nokai at his request. *It's Nokai, Mother. We barely had time to see he's alive and safe. Yesui promised to get right back to him after she's rid of her brother. Come on, Mother, your daughter's in love! We didn't bother you and Father when you were—*

All right, all right! Enough! But make it quick!

Mengjai, I want to see you in my rooms as soon as you can walk to them. Yesugen has made a request we need to discuss with your father, and Yesui should also be there for it. For the first time in nearly two years, I want us to have a meal together!

Mother hurried ahead, and they followed closely like pets, Yesui silent, a little angry, even as they made the transition to themselves.

Mengjai opened his eyes, felt Yesui briefly there, then gone, yet he was still holding her hand tightly. He released her hand, and sat up blinking in the light. Yesui stirred, her hand moving across her stomach and up over a breast to her neck and face, caressing herself. Already, she was back with Nokai. Her lips parted, and she sighed.

MENGJAI!

It was Mother, and so Mengjai fled from the room.

Nokai remained at the table with his father for a second cup of tea, after Mother had left the room. He smiled, and said, "At last there is peace in your heart, Father."

"Indeed there is, but it has taken years to achieve it, and there will certainly be new problems."

"The people have confidence in you," said Nokai. "They now see the wisdom of the difficult decisions you had to make."

"We would have been lost without Yesugen and Yesui," said Father. "I owe everything to them. What they've done for us shows me we can no longer afford to be isolated from other worlds."

Nokai was already inside the man, cautiously pushing at the network of his mind.

"I hear that Meng-shi-jie will establish an embassy on Shanji. Shouldn't we be joining them? We are, after all, part of the Tengri-Nayon system." Nokai's voice was soft and soothing, and his father's eyes glazed over for only an instant.

"I don't think Yesugen would have any objections to that, and it makes political sense to have formal ties with both worlds," murmured Father. "The only problem is that we have no trained diplomats."

Forgive me for this, Father, thought Nokai, *but my heart is Yesui's, and I cannot wait any longer to be with her in person.*

"Let's talk about that," said Nokai.

CHAPTER NINETEEN
COMPOMISE AND MYSTERY

For the first time in years, they were all together for a family meal.

To Kati, it seemed a kind of reunion, husband and son back from space, her daughter only flitting away to the place of creation when it was time for sleep. Mengmoshu and Weimeng were also there, the family elders sitting shoulder to shoulder across from Kati and Huomeng, talking softly to each other about little things.

Over the years, they had become close friends, often taking long walks with each other or sharing lunches by the pool in the hanging gardens below the palace when Mengmoshu's busy schedule allowed it. The affection they shared was that of dear friends, companions living each day as a gift to each other, and Kati was happy for both of them. Weimeng was still Mother to her, Mengmoshu her true father, a secret still kept, or so Kati thought. Kati had filled a void in the lives of both of them, and they had filled hers. To the children, they were *Gong Gong* and *Po Po*, and even Weimeng accepted it as blood truth.

Mengjai sat to his father's right, Yesui at Kati's left hand as Tanchun and her assistants served the meal of seven courses: a soup of broth and noodles like fine hair, selections of vegetables and seed pods, delicate strips of beef and shellfish from the western sea, tiny fish cooked whole with hot spices, and mounds of flat, starchy noodles, all eaten slowly with sticks in the traditional way. Between each course, there were toasts with ayrog: Yesui, for her work with Lan-Sui, Kati, of course, as Empress, then beloved wife. (This was Huomeng's doing.) Each family member was toasted in some way, but it was the toasts offered by Mengjai and Yesui that caused some emotion.

After the fish course, Mengjai cleared his throat and raised a cup high. "I have a toast for a good and gentle man, now far away, who has deep feelings for a certain woman, and I hope we will soon be his hosts on Shanji. To Nokai Wizera, Empath of Lan-Sui!"

They all raised their cups and drank, and Yesui leaned forward to smile beautifully at her brother, the feelings inside her washing over all of them, including Weimeng.

And later, after Tanchun had brought in a colorful arrangement of fruits and honeycakes to end their meal, it was Yesui who raised her cup and said somberly, "There is someone we have left out in our toasts, a woman who has been important in all our lives, but who is no longer with us, and I still miss her with all my heart."

All raised their cups as Yesui briefly closed her green eyes, blinking back tears, and Kati felt tears welling up in her own eyes.

"To my Tumatsin ancestors, she was Mandughai, but to the Moshuguang she was First Mother," said Yesui. "I knew her as a woman, my teacher and advisor, and I loved her. To Abagai, Empress of Meng-shi-jie, wherever she is!"

They drank. Tears wet Kati's cheeks; she grasped Yesui's arm, and squeezed gently. "I miss her, too," she said, and sniffled.

The somber mood stayed with them during dessert, but then Tanchun brought moist towels for them and it was time for serious talk. Kati began with a positive thing by saying, "It seems that Yesui's work with Lan-Sui has been successfully completed. The surface has stabilized, and is now radiating nicely at eight hundred degrees absolute."

"And rising," said Mengjai. "It should reach a thousand within a generation or so, and we might consider bringing the city into a slightly lower orbit even now."

"There are ships that can accomplish that," said Kati, "and Yesui's participation in the restoration of Lan-Sui seems finished. Yesugen has worked well with Governor Wizera in restoring political order on the moons, so that threat seems past. Our remaining involvement seems to be the supply of building materials for the repair of Lan-Sui City, and the need is immediate."

"So Yesui will jump a loaded freighter to Lan-Sui within a week," said Huomeng. "That will bring the total transit time down to less than a month."

"One or two jumps, Father," said Yesui quickly, then looked at Kati. "Each one will only take a few hours real time."

Both Weimeng and Mengmoshu looked soberly across the table, suddenly sensing the entire conversation was being directed at them.

Kati smiled. "Even less, as you gain more experience. Suddenly, Yesui has become a necessary part of our transportation system in jumping our ships back and forth between here and Tengri-Nayon."

"And anywhere else," interjected Mengjai. "With Yesui, the entire galaxy is open to us, and we can even think of going beyond it!" There was passion in his voice when he said it, but Yesui stared stonily ahead, saying nothing.

"This is true," Huomeng said softly, looking straight at Mengmoshu.

Kati breathed deeply to hold her patience and temper. Mengmoshu had steepled his hands before his face, a gesture she found foreboding, and Weimeng was looking confused.

"These are wonderful possibilities," continued Kati, "and are indeed things I dreamed of as a young girl in the gong-shi-jie. There are billions of worlds to be seen, but really, how many can be visited in one lifetime? The interaction with Meng-shi-jie and Lan-Sui is certainly valuable to us, and so I support Yesui's work in jumping our ships to their system, but anything beyond that is a problem for me."

"Even though you've dreamed of it," said Huomeng.

Kati put a hand softly on his arm. "Yes, dear. We had many dreams when we were young, and some have been accomplished only because we had focus. We did not try to do too many things, and we set priorities for our lives."

Huomeng scowled. "Yes, we have our priorities, but they are not necessarily the same as those of our children."

Mengmoshu raised an eyebrow, then, as Kati's face flushed red. "Get to the point, Kati," he growled. "I'm hearing the rumblings of disagreement among the four of you, and I hope to eventually hear what it's about."

Weimeng looked distraught. "You've been arguing over something?" she said.

"Ah, well, I guess I *have* been talking around things, Mengmoshu," Kati said, and she masked herself fiercely, for she'd nearly called him Father. "That's something I learned from you. All right, I'll get to the point. I have a serious disagreement with my family about what Yesui intends to do with the rest of her life, and we have agreed to put the issue before the two of you for your opinions."

There was an awkward silence, and all masks were up, making it even more horrible. "Well?" asked Mengmoshu.

"I think Yesui should tell you," said Kati, and her daughter stiffened beside her. "Go on, dear. Tell them."

Yesui took a deep breath, and said boldly, "It's just that I've decided I do not want to be Empress of Shanji."

Weimeng looked shocked. "Yesui, dear, it's your birthright! You are the first born."

Yesui shook her head, lips pressed tightly together. "I still don't want it. Let Mengjai be Emperor."

"But I don't want it either!" said Mengjai, raising his hands as if to fend off an attacker. "Being Emperor is the *last* thing I'd want to do."

Kati looked at her father. "You see?" *And Huomeng has taken their side in this.*

Everyone except Weimeng heard her.

"So what do you want to do in life, Yesui?" asked Mengmoshu.

"What I've been doing all along, *Gong Gong.* So many new things are happening all the time, and it's exciting. I'm doing useful things, and nobody can deny it. I'm doing things that *none* of you can do! How can you expect me to give that up so I can spend my time learning about duties I don't want or care about?"

"There *is* more to it than that," said Huomeng. "You've been endangering your health lately, and you don't seem to care about that either."

Thank you, dear.

"I've done something about that!" said Yesui. "I don't have to be gone so much, now, and I do it at night when I'd be asleep anyway. What is the *problem*?"

"The problem is attitude," said Kati. "The gong-shi-jie, the threads, everything has become a kind of addiction for you, and like it or not you are heiress to the throne of Shanji. You are nearly twenty-four, and not one minute have you spent learning about the affairs of your own planet! Not one minute have you spent learning about your own people. It's my fault, really, for giving you so much freedom, but both Abagai and I wanted you to develop your talents to their fullest. I think that has been accomplished, now, and it's time for you to prepare for your obligations *here*!"

"Obligations defined by *you*!" snarled Yesui, then lowered her eyes when Mengmoshu frowned at her.

"Yes! Who else do I have to take my place? Who else can bring forth the light, or travel in the gong-shi-jie to see Yesugen and whoever comes after her? You are The One, the Mei-lai-gong, and you must be Empress of Shanji!"

"How in Mother's name did all this get started?" asked Mengmoshu. "All this talk of succession to the throne seems premature to me. I presume you're in good health, Kati. Have you become weary of your position?"

"Of course not, Fa—, er, Mengmoshu," she said, her face flushing red again with the near-slip of her tongue.

To her surprise, everyone chuckled, even Weimeng.

"We all know about *Gong Gong*," said Mengjai. "We've all known it for years, Mother, so why don't you quit trying to hide it."

Mengmoshu smiled, and Weimeng put a hand on his arm. "Yes, even I know why my Mengnu was returned to me with the mind of a Searcher," she said.

I knew it first, said Yesui.

Kati was shocked, yet somehow relieved. Still, she felt some anger. "What other bits of knowledge do you hide from me?" she said testily.

"Oh, Mother," said Mengjai.

Huomeng took her hand in his, and beneath the table his knee pressed against her thigh. "We're all family, here," he said.

"All right, Father, I'm not weary of my duties, and I intend to continue them to the end of my days!"

"Oh, she said it, Mengmoshu," murmured Weimeng, and patted his arm when he smiled.

"That's just the *point*!" said Yesui. "I could spend my life learning things I won't use until I'm sixty, or seventy, and they're not related to what I want to do. I want to jump ships wherever people want to go. I want to see our galaxy, and galaxies beyond us. I want to use the violet light to create new *worlds*!"

Everyone was stunned. "Now *that* is a new idea," said Mengjai.

"It's what I want to do," Yesui said sullenly, now looking down at her hands.

Mengmoshu cleared his throat, and everyone looked at him. "Is anyone in this family familiar with the word 'compromise'?" he said.

They nodded silently.

"Good, because that's what's needed here. You've all made valid points, but they are not compatible in this real world we live in. Kati, when you first came to me you left a life in the mountains. For years, I dictated your new life, but made compromises to give you freedom to ride and learn the art of the sword and bow. I considered your needs."

"Yes, you did," said Kati, "but all of it was preparation for what I was destined to do."

"Destiny is a dangerous word," he said. "We prepared you to be Empress, and you were ready for it when the time came. It was our agenda, but you accepted it. You chose to be Empress. I did not twist your arm, and neither did Abagai."

"I remember feeling it had been decided for me, Father," said Kati.

"But you accepted it."

"Yes. I felt I could help my people, and that's what I wanted. I still want it. I don't want it to end with me."

"You wish Yesui to continue the good things you've done here."

"I do. She has the powers for it."

"But Yesui has made her own choice, and you would deny that? A parent does not choose a life for a grown child, Kati. That is not love. Yesui must make her own choices, now."

Kati was stunned into silence. Yesui was looking quite pleased with what she'd heard so far, but then Mengmoshu looked at her and said, "You must also compromise, Yesui. Your mother is correct in saying you are the only person who can replace her in the future. You are the Mei-lai-gong. The people hold you in as much reverence as they do your mother, yet you've never met them, never seen how or where they live, never given a thought to them. If your mother were to die next week, like it or not, you *would* be Empress, and I wonder what kind of Empress you'd be. Negligent? Uncaring? This is what we had before your mother was on the throne, and we will *not* have it again."

"I *do* care about Shanji *and* the people, and I've met the Tumatsin—once. I just haven't had time to—"

"You *make* the time for such things. I suspect what you *really* object to is learning business and politics you think you'll never use."

"Yes!" said Yesui, looking at Kati.

"There are those who can help you with these things when it's necessary." Mengmoshu snapped a glance at Kati as he said it. "That can come later, when you're ready, either by interest or necessity. But now you must meet the people you might someday rule; they must see you and know who you are. Everywhere your mother and I traveled, they asked about you. They were disappointed you weren't with us. You are Mei-lai-gong to them. You're revered, Yesui."

Yesui frowned. "What are you asking me to do, *Gong Gong*?"

"Spend less of your time in the gong-shi-jie, and more on Shanji. Travel with your mother, meet the people, see how she works with them, nothing more than that. It would also be an incentive for your mother to get out more, too. Both of you have isolated yourselves a great deal in recent years."

"We've all been guilty of it," said Huomeng suddenly, and he squeezed Kati's hand. "My own dreams have kept me away far too much lately."

"That won't be true anymore, as long as Yesui will jump our ships," said Mengjai, sensing a lessening of tension around him. "We can thank *her* for that!"

Yesui smiled faintly, but was deep in thought.

Kati sighed. "Perhaps Yesui *would* learn something about Shanji's affairs just by traveling with me. At least the people would see us together. Are you willing, dear?"

Yesui nodded. "Yes, as long as I have time for the gong-shi-jie. I can't give that up, Mother."

"Then that will be our compromise," said Kati.

Weimeng smiled, and said, "You'll also need time to be with Nokai. Will he be staying long?"

"It's just a visit," said Yesui, but her feelings betrayed her, and all but Weimeng could directly see she wanted it to be more than that.

"Yesugen is sending a delegation to us," said Kati. "We've decided to formalize our relations, and Meng-shi-jie will have a suite of offices for their Embassy in the Hall of Ministers. Nokai comes with them to visit Yesui, of course, but I think his father also expects him to look us over and recommend whether or not Lan-Sui should have representatives in the Embassy. They all boarded a freighter two days ago, and should be in position for Yesui's jump within a week."

"So the people of Tengri-Nayon and Tengri-Khan are coming together," said Mengmoshu. "Do you remember, Kati?"

"Yes, Father," she said with a new ache of remembrance, for the coming together of their people had been one of Abagai's dearest hopes. "I only wish she were here to see it happening. Would you help me choose our own delegation? The Moshuguang should be represented, also the Tumatsin, the Nobles, the people in the eastern cities. I want to send them out by return freighter after Yesugen's delegation arrives."

"Of course," said Mengmoshu.

Weimeng suddenly lifted her cup. "I've not yet

proposed *my* toast, and it's for all of us. Let us drink to the coming together of First Mother's people, in peace—and in love."

They all raised their cups, and drank to it.

Kati knocked softly on the door. *Yesui?*

"Come in, Mother," came the reply.

Yesui stood before a mirror, braiding her hair, and wearing the simple, black robe of the Moshuguang. Kati stepped up behind her, put hands on her daughter's shoulders and said, "There is color in your cheeks, now. You've been getting outside, I see."

"Yes," said Yesui, and she twisted away at a long braid draped over a shoulder. Her mask was down, mind open to her mother.

"Nokai will see how beautiful you really are," said Kati.

Yesui continued her braiding, but leaned back against her mother. "He'll think I'm skinny. If I had more time, I could fatten myself up to please him, but he'll just have to accept me the way I am."

Kati laughed. "He fell in love with what's inside you. He will certainly love the rest of it."

Their eyes met in the mirror, emerald green. "Do you really think so, Mother? I've been a mental image to him, but now he'll see the real me, without my embellishments."

Kati put her arms around Yesui's soft, lithe figure. "You're apprehensive."

"Yes." Yesui stopped her braiding, and sighed.

For a moment, they stood together silently in their embrace, and then Kati kissed her neck, murmuring, "I've been unfair with you, dear. I put my own ambitions before yours."

"I understand," said Yesui. "You think of Shanji's

welfare, and I have not. I'll try to change, Mother. You have."

"Changed? What do you mean?" Kati rested a chin on Yesui's shoulder, and they gazed at each other in the mirror.

"I've watched you change, especially since the time Abagai became ill. All those years when the three of us were together in the gong-shi-jie, and then suddenly I was alone. Abagai was too sick to make a transition, and you just weren't there, as if it was too painful for you to be there without her. I've been lonely in the place of creation, Mother. Lately, I've begun talking to myself with the loneliness, and when Mengjai heard me doing it once he even made an insinuation about my mental health. I think he was a little frightened for me."

Yesui touched her mother's hands. "I miss our times together in the gong-shi-jie, and you used to love it so much. Can we spend some time there? You haven't even seen the new Lan-Sui, have you?"

"No, I only talked to Yesugen," said Kati, but at that instant a sudden thought had popped out of nowhere into her mind, and Yesui saw it immediately.

"Oh, Mother, that would be *wonderful*! When can we do it?"

"How about tonight, when we're supposed to be asleep?" said Kati. She smiled, excited by her own idea. "It's far, Yesui, but we should be back before morning."

"*Yes!*" said Yesui. She turned, and hugged her mother hard.

Kati and Huomeng had gone to bed early and made love again, and now Huomeng was sound asleep, still cuddling her. Kati basked in the warm afterglow of their love-making and snuggled against him, her head on his breast. She closed her eyes, sighed, and called her daughter.

Yesui. Are you ready to leave?

I've stayed awake thinking about it. Oh, you've been having a good time, I see.

Now, now. I'll meet you at our usual place.

Bye, said Yesui, and she was already gone to the place of creation.

The matrix of purple stars was there, then gone, and the colorful vortices of stars stretched out in spirals within purple and blue clouds of creative light in every direction. Yesui was waiting for her, the manifestation a column of green showing her face and figure, eyes bright. It was the vision she showed to her beloved Nokai, and now she shared it with her mother.

How lovely, said Kati. *I can remember when all we could see of you was a little fan of green.*

That was before I wanted to be seen, said Yesui. *Will we leave from Abagai's favorite place?*

Yes, dear. You know the way.

It had been a long time since they'd traveled together, and so they moved leisurely, drifting towards the vortex of Tengri-Nayon and past another vortex that had once been red beyond red, but was now orange. *Remember that?* asked Kati. *I nearly lost you there.*

Yes, but it taught me the connection between mass and the violet light, Mother. A lot of my learning has been forced on me that way, and I still don't understand how we do what we do. Mengjai says it's as if our brains tap into some cosmic mind that governs the universe and lets us have our way with things.

An interesting idea, said Kati.

At Tengri-Nayon, they dipped into real space for a look at Lan-Sui. The surface was mottled with thousands of convective cells, the old vortices of storms and great bands of clouds all gone, at least for now. *I can feel him, but he's asleep*, said Yesui. *They're still moving towards the jump point, but it seems he's always with me, now.*

Only a little while, and you'll be together, said Kati.

Away from Tengri-Nayon, they followed a spiral of vortices to the edge of the galaxy where Abagai had been taken from them, and now there was only the quiescent, violet glow there. Far beyond, their destination sparkled like a cut gem of many colors, the galaxy Kati and Abagai had seen together during their visit to a nursery of baby stars. They headed towards it without pause at the galactic edge.

It was close in, that thing that took Abagai, right about here, said Yesui when they'd gone beyond the galactic edge. *Now there's only peaceful, violet light.*

Just before Abagai died, you said you felt a new presence, Yesui. Have you felt it since she left us?

No. For a while, I imagined Abagai talking to me, but it was only because I missed her so, and it passed.

I still think she's alive, you know, though not in the way we think of life, said Kati. *I think she was changed into something new.*

Their galaxy was a huge wheel behind them, and ahead was another, still small, but large enough for its accompanying halo of star clusters to be seen. *I know you think that, Mother. I want to believe it, too*, said Yesui.

Where we go was very special to her. She felt drawn to it.

Maybe she'll know we're there, said Yesui, but not believing it.

Both of them were saddened by such thoughts, and they were silent for awhile as Abagai's favorite whirl of dust and stars drew nearer, and nearer, and then it filled their view.

We go first to the innermost whirl of vortices, near the center. Watch closely, now, said Kati.

Interesting, said Yesui. *Along our way, I've only seen a faint glimmer of violet light, but now it's bright again, a halo of it pressing in around this galaxy, just like our own. Look, Mother! The purple and blue clouds of creation are back again, within the wheel, but not out here.*

Where the gong-shi-jie is, there is creation, dear.

So it seems, said Yesui, fascinated.

They drew close. *There! See the three vortices, straight ahead, where there are blue swirls in the purple?*

Yes, said Yesui.

They form a triangle. We make our transition right at its center.

Kati was overcome with excitement, and rushed ahead, Yesui right behind her. The flash of transition was brilliant, and then they were there in Abagai's favorite place where new stars were being born.

Ohhh, said Yesui.

All was as Kati remembered: the roiling wall of dust and gas, the protuberances ending in stalks tipped with stars newly born or about to be born, some glowing dimly, others already hot and spewing forth little jets of glowing gas in red to blue. It was the most beautiful sight she'd ever seen, and Kati felt happy about Yesui's reaction to it. For the moment, at least, her daughter seemed mesmerized, her presence flickering out and back again for a tiny instant.

The threads are all twisted and very dense beyond that wall of dust and gas, Mother. Something strange is going on here, said Yesui.

Not so strange, dear. This is a birthplace for new stars, a place of true creation in real space. Can you see why Abagai loved it so?

Oh, yes.

I think she meditated on her death when she was here. She spoke of a presence, something calling to her in this place. She said there were others in the universe who shared our powers. I think she believed they were calling to her when she was here. At the time it frightened me, because it seemed she was thinking only about her own death.

I feel no strange presence here, but the threads are unusual, said Yesui. *That wall of dust and gas obscures everything beyond it, and I'd like to see what's there.*

More dust and gas, I suppose, said Kati, still marveling at the sight.

There was a moment of quiet, but Kati felt curiosity turn to compulsion within her daughter.

Well? May we penetrate all that dust, and see what's there?

Kati suddenly felt a bit apprehensive. *You have the curiosity of your father and brother, Yesui. It seems I'm the cautious one in the family. To me, going into that wall of dust and gas is like jumping into water without knowing what's lurking beneath the surface. I like to know where I'm going.*

Yes, but the threads seem to be coming together behind that wall. I think we'd only have to penetrate a short distance to see what's causing that. Yesui was now excited by her compulsion, and drifted away from Kati, heading towards the wall.

I can't see the threads, dear. Can't we just enjoy the view?

Yesui still drifted away from her, looked over her shoulder with a playful smile. *Just a little way, Mother. Explore a new mystery with me. Please?*

Kati drifted forward, but slowly. *I don't like this, Yesui. I don't like it at all*, she said.

Yesui only smiled, and drifted closer to the wall of dust and gas that fed new stars. Closer, and closer, and now Kati was hurrying to catch up. Close to the wall there was structure to be seen, and movement, great bubbles in brown and green oozing to the surface and slowly streaming to feed the protuberances whose tips were new stars. Deep within the wall, light flickered, and its color was violet. Kati reached Yesui at the very surface of the wall, her daughter's manifestation just beginning to meld with it.

The wall of dust and gas began to roil as if heated from within, and violet light burst forth in a wave that pushed them back violently to where they had been, a sudden, new voice in their minds.

DO NOT COME CLOSER! IT'S NOT SAFE FOR YOU HERE!

They were shocked dumb, and could only stare as the wall boiled before them, a shimmering, violet curtain now close to its surface like a protective sheath. Kati had never felt such power in a presence, yet now it seemed to be gone again after issuing a stern warning to them and then throwing them back from the wall.

But Yesui was quickly angry, and bold again. *That was very rude!* she said. *We meant no harm. I only wanted to see what's behind all this dust and gas that makes the threads come together, and you had no reason to push us back like that! Who are you?*

Who I am does not matter, and if you come in here, you will never leave again. It's safe where you are, and you may watch the work if you wish.

Your work? asked Kati. *You mean all these new stars are your doing?*

Hardly. I'm only one of many. The young one with you sees deeply. She must be Yesui.

You KNOW me? said Yesui.

We've watched your work with the interface, and had some part in it. You're quite advanced for second form.

I don't understand, said Kati.

Of course not. You are first form, as was the one who proceeded you. You will have to begin more slowly here when your time comes. I, myself, have now reached fourth level. Excuse me. . . .

Gone, in a blink, and they seemed alone again, but the violet curtain still shimmered from the wall of dust and gas.

Someone wishes to speak with you, and I have duties. . . .

Gone again, the brief return of the presence startling them. Kati saw Yesui's manifestation darken, then disappear for only an instant before brightening again, and as Yesui returned there was suddenly a new presence with them, something that reminded Kati of what she felt from her own daughter.

You're peeking again, Yesui. It really isn't safe for you in here. You'll just have to wait until you're ready for it.

I know you! shouted Yesui, with great surprise and delight that only confused Kati.

Well, I hope so. I think we've done very well together. Why are you here?

This was the favorite place of a friend we lost in

death. My mother brought me here to see it, said Yesui. *Right now, I'm wondering if I'm really talking to myself.*

Whatever spoke to them was amused. *No, no, Yesui, but you've been assigned to me since you first reached the structure of the interface. Have I helped you?*

Oh, yes! said Yesui.

And this is your mother, said the presence.

Kati had been listening silently, like an ignorant child. *Yes, I am Kati,* she said.

Your line is unusual, though I've heard of such things. A first level giving birth to a second is actually quite rare. I've had a long apprenticeship at third level, but Yesui's abilities are not far behind my own. You must be proud of her.

I'm proud of both my children, said Kati.

You remember my brother, Mind. You had to make him be quiet, said Yesui, suddenly amused and carrying on as if nothing unusual were happening.

Kati's mind boiled with confusion and scattered thoughts: two supernatural presences at this birthplace of stars, Yesui taking it all matter-of-factly, Abagai drawn here before her death, then the bright ellipsoid of light she'd become before being swallowed up by a boiling manifestation of some terrible energy field.

Who are you? Kati asked.

We have no names here, but Yesui calls me "Mind," and you may do so if you wish. We are what you will become, but that's in the future, and I can tell you no more than that. You have important things to do first in your present lives. You too, Yesui; you're born second level, and your children will be of great interest to us.

Kati, there is a terrible grief in you that's unfounded. Your friend is with us, but what we do here is not

*the work of second levels. She's too far away for me
to call her here. I'm sorry. Perhaps another time.*

Abagai is ALIVE?

Again, that feeling of amusement. *Well, I suppose
I could say I'm alive, but not in a way you're ready
to understand. She exists, Kati, and she's happy where
she is. You will know her when your time comes. Ah,
that made both of you feel better!*

We've missed her, said Yesui, then, *Will you come
back to see me sometime, Mind?*

*Oh yes. As I said, you're one of my assignments.
But now I'm working on another one. If I remove the
barrier, will you stay where you are? We only put it
up to protect you.*

I promise, said Yesui.

Yes, said Kati.

*You may watch if you like. Yesui, don't worry about
finding me in the future. I'll find you. Bye!*

The presence was gone, and with it the violet
shimmering of the dust and gas cloud before them.
They watched it awhile, drifting in silence, watched
sparkles of violet within a protuberance, then a bright
flare at its tip as a new star spewed off dust and gas
in a long streamer to announce its birth.

By the time they left the place where Mind did her
work, five new stars had been born.

Kati and Yesui drifted slowly together towards the
great wheel of stars that was their home, at least for
now. Both felt awe and humility from what they'd seen
and heard, yet they were happy.

Abagai said there were others like us, said Kati.

Yesui was giddy with excitement. *Oh, we'll be more,
Mother. Much more!*

They went their separate ways at the signature of
Tengri-Nayon, Kati returning to the vortex leading to

herself, Yesui popping out of sight as she went to the place of the threads that Kati could not see.

By the time Kati was back at her desk, Yesui had jumped Nokai's ship a distance of two light years to bring him home to Shanji for what she hoped would be more than just a visit.

Nokai lay awake in his cubicle, awaiting Yesui's arrival and wondering how he would mask the things he'd seen and heard that had jerked him so violently from deep sleep. Surely The Mother Herself had taken him on the journey with Yesui; it was Her voice he'd heard, and the roiling mist with spots of light was a thing She had shown him before.

If he showed it to Yesui, she might think it came from her own memory, and was simply reflected by him. If he projected it strongly enough, she might not see his little secret regarding his role in the mission to Shanji.

He relaxed, coming close to sleep before her wonderful presence washed over him, her call gentle, so as not to disturb him.

Nokai? Are you still asleep? If so, you won't even feel this jump.

He showed her his vision of roiling mist and new stars, and a galaxy rushing away in the distance.

We are together, even in sleep, darling. And now I will bring us together more quickly.

A fuzzy, transient sensation, as if he'd fallen asleep for an instant, and that was all of it.

Soon, my love. Soon, she said, and then she was gone.

CHAPTER TWENTY
TOGETHER

Yesui had spent hours getting dressed in her rooms, but when she finally appeared it was in the plain, black robe of the Moshuguang. A trace of rouge was on her cheekbones, a hint of green around her emerald eyes, a colorless gloss enhancing the normal redness of her lips, and she'd pulled her hair away from her face to hang as a single tail reaching nearly to her waist. Kati looked her up and down, a bit surprised.

"I thought you might wear something more colorful," she said.

"This is what I am," said Yesui, and that was the end of that.

Kati herself was dressed in formal gold and her hair

was in buns for the occasion, but when her father arrived he was dressed like his grandaughter.

"Lovely," he said, looking them over, then offering an arm to each of them. "Our guests will be impressed by the sight of my ladies."

Mengmoshu led them to the elevator and down to the ground floor of the palace where Huomeng and Mengjai awaited them with an honor guard of six troopers in sparkling armor. They paraded to the monorail station by the Hall of Ministers where a crowd watched them board a car that took them up to the flyer port above the palace, and there they crowded into two flyers, the royal family in one, troopers in the other. Two other flyers would leave with them to bring back the delegation from Meng-shi-jie.

Mengjai was her pilot, but Kati still clutched at her knees as they lifted off.

Relax, Mother. I know what I'm doing.

Of course, dear. Yesui reached over to pat her hand in assurance as Kati swallowed hard to numb her usual liftoff nerves.

They lifted straight up, a panel in the dome opening for them, the four flyers forming into single file and heading north to the shuttle field on a butte above the valley where an invading army had once been evacuated from Shanji. On that day, the valley had been blackened by Kati's purple light, but now it was green with unripened barley used in central stores for the sick and elderly.

The freighter from Meng-shi-jie would come down later in the day to land at the large field east of Wanchou and begin loading for its return. With Yesui there to jump the ship, there was now sufficient fuel for a liftoff and the old days of shuttling materials to an orbiting freighter were over.

The shuttle bearing Meng-shi-jie's delegation was already gliding at high altitude as Mengjai brought them in to land with a gentle thump on a pad of concrete near the small terminal building. As they came in, Yesui's eyes had closed briefly, and she'd smiled.

"Does he know you're here?" asked Kati, for Yesui had masked herself for that brief moment.

"Yes," said Yesui, and twisted the fingers of her hands tightly together. "Oh, Mother, I am *so* nervous."

They barely had time to reach the proper shuttle pad before they saw it coming, high up, a shape like some great bird gliding lazily towards them. The honor guard formed a line, the royal family in a line opposite them, both some fifty meters from the landing pad as the craft came in on magnetic lifters, hovering, then dropping the last meter with an impact that sent a shuddering wave beneath their feet. Workers scurried to position a ramp of stairs for descent from the exit hatch.

Yesui's anxiety was now awful. Mengjai put an arm around her and squeezed, but it didn't help. And when the hatch finally opened, they were all in agony from the waves of apprehension and fear coming from the Mei-lai-gong. She stood firm, but her eyes were wide, her breaths short and rapid.

Four men emerged from the hatch and descended the stairs, then walked towards them in single file. As they came closer, Yesui's agony was suddenly joy, and Kati felt something pass through her like a warm breeze, soothing, but transient. The honor guard snapped to attention at port arms as Kati smiled and held out her hand in greeting.

The first man was the oldest of the delegates, perhaps sixty; he bowed deeply when Kati extended her hand, then shook it warmly and smiled.

"I am Wang Mengnu-Shan-shi-jie," Kati said softly. "Welcome to Shanji."

"I am Mongke-Temur, Madam. Mandughai has chosen me as her ambassador, and I'm honored to serve her world and yours. She sends her regrets that her husband Kabul is not here to meet you in her stead, but with the imminent birth of their second child he simply refused to leave her side."

"He's where he should be," said Kati. "There will be many opportunities for us to meet in the future. This is my husband, Huomeng, my son, Mengjai, and Yesui, my daughter."

Mongke-Temur shook hands with the men, then bowed deeply to Yesui. "We are in your debt, Mei-lai-gong," he said simply.

Yesui smiled faintly and nodded, but she was looking past him towards the others, all dressed like Mongke-Temur in tailored, single-piece suits, powder blue, with wide, black belts and short boots.

"These are my assistants Toktamish and Kharloin," said Mongke-Temur. Both men were in their thirties; they shook hands and bowed silently. Behind them, last in line, was a tall young man with a long, chiseled face and eyes that seemed green until he came close, and then Kati could see the eyes were light brown with green flecks in them. He was lovely, almost delicate in appearance, but it was his presence that struck her, a quiet serenity about him that made her feel comfortable, and then he looked past her, towards Yesui. His eyes seemed to glow, lips parting in a beautiful smile, and the feeling of love was so intense that Kati reached instinctively for Huomeng's hand.

"With your permission, Madam, we are not delegates of Meng-shi-jie alone," said Mongke-Temur, "but of the entire Tengri-Nayon system. Antun Wizera, Governor of Lan-Sui, has requested representation and sends his own son as ambassador. This is Nokai Wizera, who will represent Lan-Sui and its moons if that is acceptable to you."

"It certainly is," said Kati, extending her hand as Nokai bowed to her. "Welcome, Nokai. We've looked forward to meeting you for a long time."

Nokai's grip was warm and light, yet firm. "It's my honor to serve The Mother, and her worlds," he said, looking straight into Kati's eyes.

So this is the face that has captured my daughter's heart, thought Kati.

My heart is also a captive, came a soft reply in her mind.

"This is my husband Huomeng," said Kati, and the men shook hands.

Mengjai grinned as Nokai turned to him and said, "I believe we've met before, Mengjai, but not like this."

Their hands clapped together. "Good to see you at last, Nokai," said Mengjai, and turned the man left to face Yesui.

Kati would never forget that long moment of beginning, when there were unmasked feelings that made all hearts ache in such a wonderful way, and yet few words were spoken. Nokai stepped up to Yesui, and it seemed to Kati that Yesui's face had never been more beautiful.

"Hello, Nokai. Here I am," said Yesui softly.

"Yesui," said Nokai. *My darling. My love. I'm here for as long as you'll have me.*

That will be forever, said Yesui, her mask down, but then it was quickly up again.

The moment was missed by the other delegates, for Mengmoshu had stepped forward to greet them and was leading them back towards the flyers. Mengjai followed, then Huomeng, but Kati held back for a moment as Nokai and Yesui came close together without touching, Yesui's head at the level of his shoulder. They looked at her expectantly, and Kati smiled.

Together at last, and we know how you feel about each other. It is all right to show it.

Kati turned away from them. She did not see the kiss, but felt Yesui's pleasure from it. And when she risked a glance over her shoulder, she saw them walking behind her, shoulders touching, hands at their sides, fingers intwined. For one instant after her glance, their masks were down.

How did you manage to do it, Mister Ambassador? asked Yesui.

Oh, I have my methods, said her Love.

It was near dawn of the day following Nokai's arrival when Yesugen called to Kati in sleep.

Kati, it's Yesugen! Can you join me in the gong-shi-jie? I have something special to show you.

The call drew her from deep sleep to a state of dreams, but it was guilt that brought her awake. The presence of Yesugen reminded Kati that she'd said nothing to the woman about what had happened to Abagai. Such wonderful news, kept to herself, distracted by Yesui and Nokai finally being together on Shanji.

Kati yawned, but kept her eyes closed, Huomeng's body warm at her back. *I'm coming, Yesugen*, she answered. *You caught me asleep.*

The purple matrix flickered once, then the flash of transition, still so quick for her, and she floated in the shimmering clouds of creative light. There was a column of green coming towards her from the direction of

Tengri-Nayon's vortex and Kati moved quickly towards it. It was Yesugen, her manifestation smiling serenely, then gesturing to a little fan of green that followed it.

The sight brought back memories of a time when Kati had called Abagai to come and watch Yesui take her first steps in the gong-shi-jie. *Yesugen!* she shouted. *You have a* daughter!

They came close together, Yesugen smiling broadly now. *I wanted you to witness her first time here,* she said.

When Yesui had first seen Abagai, she'd been shy, her little manifestation melding with Kati's, but such was not the case with Yesugen's child. The little green fan had brightened at Kati's approach, turning into a wavering flame, but standing fast.

This is Tirgee, said Yesugen.

I feel her, said Kati. *She's very bold, like her mother. She's not frightened by me, only curious. Hello, Tirgee. I am Kati.*

The little flame wavered, still bright, but didn't move.

She's only six weeks old, said Yesugen. *I would have brought her here sooner, but the birth exhausted me, and my wounds made it even harder. I will bear no more children, Kati. My physicians have seen to that.*

We're both blessed with two children, said Kati. *It's more than enough, with the duties we have.* Kati sensed a sadness in Yesugen, and a tired feeling. *This past year has been difficult for you.*

Yes it has, but now I can get back to the building of my own world. Has our delegation arrived?

It has, and Nokai with them. Yesui is helplessly in love with him. I wish you could have seen them together. Did you know that Nokai is to be Lan-Sui's ambassador on Shanji?

Tirgee's little flame-like manifestation suddenly moved, and began circling the two of them.

Yes. I approved it only after I met Nokai face to face. He seems to have more common sense than his father, and he's certainly more than an Empath. I felt a deep probe while I talked to him, Kati. There is power beneath that passive countenance he shows to people.

Yesui sees everything, and loves him. That's enough for me, said Kati.

His belief in what he calls The Mother is extreme, added Yesugen. *Tirgee! Stay close to me!*

Tirgee had tired of circling them, and was boldly wandering back towards the vortex of Tengri-Nayon. She stopped, wavered, drifted slowly towards them again.

Exploring, said Kati, then, *Yesugen, there's something I must tell you, something that happened to Yesui and me a few days ago. I should have told you sooner, but I was distracted. It concerns your mother, Yesugen, and it's wonderful!*

Yesugen frowned at her. *Mother?*

Let's take Tirgee on an exploration, and I'll tell you along the way. Kati began to drift in the direction of Abagai's observing place for her special galaxy, and Yesugen followed her. When Yesugen turned to call Tirgee, the little green flame was already hurrying to catch up with them.

They drifted slowly, and Kati told Yesugen everything she'd seen and felt with Yesui in that distant birthplace of new stars, the place that Abagai had taken her to before her death or conversion. She told her about the conversation with the creators, the fact that Abagai was now one of them, but far away, that someday they might talk to her.

The news was cause for joy, but it also stirred hurt and envy within Yesugen. *Even up to her death, there were things she showed you, but not me,* she said.

I'm sure she didn't mean to hurt you, said Kati. *She loved you, Yesugen. In the end, she trusted you with the care of Meng-shi-jie.*

Tirgee had darted ahead of them, and the rim of the galaxy was visible, vortices ending, only shimmering violet beyond it. They picked up their pace to stay close to the child.

Will you take me there? asked Yesugen. *I don't know the way.*

I'll show you the way, and soon. I promise, Yesugen, and someday you can take Tirgee there to meet her grandmother.

If she doesn't run away before then. Tirgee, stay with us!

Tirgee had reached the galactic rim, and stopped at Yesugen's call. As they approached the child, Kati pointed out towards the violet shimmering, and beyond it to something sparkling with many colors. *That is the place, and it's not as far as it seems.*

They stopped to gaze at it. Tirgee was still exploring, back and forth along the edge of dust and gas ringing their galaxy. Her mother was distracted, but Kati saw what the child did, and knew what it meant, for she'd seen the same thing done by her own daughter several times.

At several places along the rim, Tirgee's little flame flickered, dimmed, then disappeared for only an instant before returning brightly again.

They watched Abagai's galaxy, and talked, and then it was time to leave.

Tirgee reluctantly followed them home.